His broad shoulders strained the limits of his flannel shirt.

And his loose jeans outlined his muscular thighs as he donned protective gloves and hunkered down in front of the cage.

Everything about him was big, including his hands, and yet Emily knew he performed surgery. Strong yet precise, firm yet tender... There was no telling what those capable hands would feel like on her bare skin. A shiver of desire passed through her.

She gave herself a mental eye roll and bawled herself out. Now? She was lusting over Seth when the German shepherd was suffering from who knew what? The animals here depended on her to keep them healthy and safe and to find them new homes. They came first. Always.

Seth Pettit was a gorgeous man. He'd also given up his night's rest to help this dog. She'd best get her mind on the matters at hand.

A Cure for the Vet

Ann Roth & Julie Benson

Previously published as *Montana Vet*
and *The Rancher and the Vet*

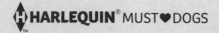

ISBN-13: 978-1-335-04180-7

A Cure for the Vet

Copyright © 2019 by Harlequin Books S.A.

First published as Montana Vet
by Harlequin Books in 2015 and
The Rancher and the Vet by Harlequin Books in 2013.

The publisher acknowledges the copyright holders
of the individual works as follows:

Montana Vet
Copyright © 2015 by Ann Schuessler

The Rancher and the Vet
Copyright © 2013 by Julie Benson

Recycling programs
for this product may
not exist in your area.

Printed in U.S.A.

CONTENTS

Ann Roth lives in the greater Seattle area with her husband. After earning an MBA, she worked as a banker and corporate trainer. She gave up the corporate life to write, and if they awarded PhDs in writing happily-ever-after stories, she'd surely have one.

Ann loves to hear from readers. You can email her at ann@annroth.net.

MONTANA VET

Ann Roth

To animal lovers everywhere

Chapter 1

So far, this had been a day of surprises—and not the good kind. Sitting at the front office desk, Emily Miles massaged her temples and thought back to eight o'clock, on what she'd assumed would be a normal Tuesday. She'd assumed wrong.

First Rich Addison, the seventy-something veterinarian who had volunteered at The Wagging Tail since Emily had opened the shelter four years ago, had shared the unwelcome news that he was retiring.

Retiring! The poor man's wife had given him an ultimatum—either leave his career behind and start traveling with her, or live out the rest of his days as a divorced man. His last day was Friday. Emily had no idea where she'd find his replacement, and Rich hadn't come up with any names, either.

On this warm, sunny day in the second week of September—normal weather for Prosperity, Montana—

she'd opened all the windows. She easily heard the collective howls and barks coming from the dog runs in the backyard, where the six abandoned and/or abused animals she was sheltering until she found them good homes were enjoying the day as best as they could. At least they had been. The unhappy sounds made her wonder if they somehow understood this dire news and what it meant.

Because without an on-call veterinarian to come in when necessary, she would have no way of knowing if the animals she took in suffered from a contagious disease, or how to treat those in need of medical attention. She would be forced to close down.

Then where would these abandoned, innocent creatures go? To the pound, where they would probably be euthanized. Emily couldn't bear the thought.

An annual fund-raiser brought in enough to keep The Wagging Tail afloat, and Emily counted every penny. As yet, the only two people on the payroll were herself, and she took only enough to cover the rent and supplies, and Mrs. Oakes, the part-time office manager.

As busy as Emily was with the shelter, she also ran a website design and management business from home. The work took up considerable time, but was interesting and covered her personal bills, and sometimes subsidized shortages that fund-raising didn't cover.

But neither her earnings nor the shelter's budget was enough to pay a veterinarian. Someday. For now, she needed a volunteer, preferably long-term. The trouble was, most of the animal doctors in town worked full-time and then some, devoting any spare time to other, larger facilities. Finding someone willing to come to her little shelter without compensation was difficult.

If that wasn't enough, Emily needed him or her by the end of the week—just three days from now.

Could the day get any worse?

It could and had. While she was still reeling from Rich's stunning news, Mrs. Oakes, who worked Tuesday through Friday, had called in sick with a case of stomach flu. Edgar, the senior citizen volunteer who answered the phones on Mondays, had been busy with other commitments, leaving Emily to man the front desk. Then the Tates, the couple scheduled to foster and, fingers crossed, adopt the high-strung red setter that had been at the shelter for nearly a week, had postponed until Friday. With the kennel filled to capacity, Emily had counted on freeing up the dog's cage for another animal in need.

Instead she'd had to turn away two dogs. She'd spent several hours calling everyone she knew, pleading for someone to take in one or both animals. With a lot of begging, she'd finally found them temporary homes. They needed to be seen by a vet, and someone needed to pay for those services.

Her head was pounding now, and her empty stomach was demanding food. With a sigh, she stood and carried her half-empty mug of tepid coffee through the archway off the front office, which had once been a living room. A short walk down the hall led to her small office, formerly a den. There she retrieved her purse from under the desk and dug through it for aspirin. She downed the pills with a healthy slug of the coffee—a combination guaranteed to give her stomach fits if she didn't eat posthaste.

Until now, she hadn't had the time. "I need lunch," she said.

Susannah, the three-legged whippet Emily had taken

in and adopted when she'd first opened the shelter, had been napping on the doggy bed in the corner. Now she trotted over—if you could call her odd, limping gait a trot.

Although Emily lived in the apartment upstairs, every morning she stowed a sack lunch in the kitchen on the main floor. Susannah accompanied her there, licking her chops and wagging her tail.

"You already had your meal," Emily said, but the dog knew she was a soft touch.

Moments later, she returned to Mrs. Oakes's desk with the sack lunch and a fresh cup of coffee. Susannah was excited now, yipping and grinning as only she could. "Oh, all right," Emily said. "But first, sit!"

She quickly obeyed. Emily always marveled over that. After all, Susannah had only one front leg. When she'd arrived at the shelter at the age of about one year, she hadn't even been house-trained.

"Good girl," Emily cooed. Reaching into the lunch bag, she pulled out the dog treat Susannah had known was there. Seconds later, content, the dog settled down on the braided rug nearby.

Emily was munching on her sandwich when the two-way radio buzzed. Caroline, one of the regular volunteers, was out back with the dogs.

"I have to leave soon," she said. "Do you want me to put everyone back in the kennel?"

"They've been out for a while now, and I cleaned their cages and filled their food and water dishes, so yes. Thanks, Caroline—you're the best." Emily meant that. The volunteers who gave so much of their time and effort kept the shelter going.

She finished her lunch, sipping her coffee and culling through applications from the high school kids who wanted to volunteer this semester. Doing so would earn them community-service credit, an annual requirement for students at all four of Prosperity's high schools.

Suddenly Susannah woofed, moved awkwardly to her feet and loped toward the door with her tail wagging. It had taken almost two years of patience and TLC, but she'd finally learned to trust people. The bell over the door jingled.

"Come here." Emily snapped her fingers. The dog obeyed, but wasn't happy about it.

An instant later, a girl entered the office. She looked to be fourteen or so, and was tall and gangly, just as Emily had been at that age. Her shoulder-length, light brown hair had bright red streaks in it, and bangs that same red all but obscured her large eyes. She moved hesitantly toward Emily, her obvious self-consciousness at odds with the sullen look on her face.

It was that contrast that reminded Emily of her own painful adolescent years, as a lonely teen whose mother worked long hours to put a roof over their heads, after Emily's father had left.

"Hi." She smiled. "I'm Emily Miles, the founder of The Wagging Tail."

"Hi." Not even a semblance of a smile.

Susannah jumped up and raced forward with her tail waving. Smiling now, which did wonders for her face, the girl petted the happy canine. "Cool dog. What happened to his leg?"

"Actually, she's female. Her name is Susannah. When she arrived at the shelter, she had a bad infection in her foreleg. We had to amputate."

The girl looked horrified. As if knowing they were talking about her, Susannah woofed softly and retreated to the rug.

"Some of the dogs we take in are in pretty bad shape," Emily said. "But with love, patience and a good home, miracles can happen. I'll bet you're here because you want to do a semester of community service at The Wagging Tail."

The girl's eyes widened in surprise. "How did you know?"

"It's that time of year. I didn't catch your name."

"Taylor."

"Nice to meet you. Which school do you attend?"

"Trenton High."

The school was less than a mile from the shelter. Emily nodded. "Are you a freshman?"

"Sophomore."

"Okay. Do you have any experience with dogs?"

Taylor looked at her as if she were crazy. "I like them."

"Have you ever owned or taken care of one?"

The girl shook her head and crossed her arms. "Why are you asking so many questions? I said I liked them." As in, *Isn't that enough?*

Not exactly the warm and friendly personality Emily wanted at the shelter. Although Taylor had been both with Susannah. As a teen, Emily had never been this sullen, certainly not when she wanted a job.

"I've had a lot of interest from high school kids this semester, and I may be full," she said. Most of them had left any attitude behind and put on their best faces. "But if you'd like to fill out an application, I'll look it over and get back to you."

"You don't want me."

For one telling moment, Taylor's shoulders slumped. Then the surly look reappeared and she raised her head.

Emily guessed that she'd been rejected by someone,

somewhere. Having been there herself, when her father had walked out of her life, she sympathized. "I didn't say that," she replied with a smile. "School started in late August, and here we are a few weeks later. Most of the kids who want to work here applied last week." She patted the stack of applications on the desk. "I'm in the process of selecting volunteers now."

"We only moved here a few days before school started. I would've come in sooner, but I just found out about this place."

While it seemed a plausible excuse, Emily wondered if Taylor's attitude had cost her opportunities at other organizations. Wanting to help the girl, she opened a desk drawer and pulled out a blank application. "There's still time to apply." She handed the form over. "Why don't you fill this out?"

"Whatever." The girl stuffed the paper into her backpack. "Where are the other dogs?"

"They spent most of the afternoon out back. Now they're in the kennel—that building over there." Emily pointed at what had once been a large, detached garage. "Would you like to meet them?"

"Uh, yeah." Taylor's snarky tone indicated that this was obvious.

Shaking her head at the girl's hostility, Emily leashed Susannah, then led Taylor down the concrete walkway. The afternoon sun had barely begun its descent toward the horizon, but already the air was noticeably cooler and felt like autumn. In central Montana, the weather was known to change quickly, and in a matter of hours, the temperature could vary by as much as twenty degrees.

Leaving Susannah tethered outside the kennel, Emily opened the door and gestured for Taylor to enter. Harvey, the architect Emily had met when he'd adopted a mixed-breed female from the shelter, and who she'd started dating soon after, had reconfigured the garage into a perfect space to house the dogs. Six large cages were spread across the clean cement floor, each equipped with a dog bed, and food and water bowls. A sink and tub for bathing the animals filled one corner, and a stainless steel exam table took up another, along with shelves and cabinets laden with towels and supplies. One large, airy window flooded the space with light, and good insulation and a heating and cooling system kept the temperature comfortable no matter what the weather.

"As you can see, we're currently filled up," Emily said.

Taylor looked puzzled. "But there are only six dogs here."

"Unfortunately, right now, this is all I have room for. We also have two quarantine huts for when new dogs come in."

Another of Harvey's contributions to the shelter. Emily could actually think about him now without a twinge of the heartbreak she'd suffered when he'd left some fifteen months earlier.

Taylor angled her head and frowned. "Why do you quarantine new dogs?"

"Because they might carry infectious diseases, and we don't want to expose the other animals."

A brown-and-white spaniel-terrier mix whined, and Taylor headed forward.

"Wait," Emily cautioned in a low voice. "He's been abused and could bite you out of fear. To keep him from feeling threatened, lower your eyes and put your knuckles close to the bars so that he can smell you."

Taylor looked taken aback, but complied. After much sniffing and studying her, the dog at last licked her hand through the bars.

"He likes me." She looked pleased. "What's his name?"

"We don't usually name them," Emily explained. "We let the families who adopt them do that."

She checked her watch. The front office had been empty for some minutes now. "I need to get back to the office, in case the phone rings or someone else comes in."

Taylor nodded, and they headed back. As they sauntered down the walkway, the girl's cell phone trilled out bars from some rock song. "If you wanna stick around you gotta cut me some slack," a male voice twanged.

She glanced at the screen and frowned before answering. "Hey, Seth," she said in a bored voice. She listened a moment. "No, I ditched the bus. I'm at The Wagging Tail. The. Wagging. Tail," she repeated, with exaggerated impatience. "It's a dog shelter?" Another silence. "It's for community service. I'm supposed to volunteer, remember? Can you pick me up here?" She listened again. "Yeah, I know I was supposed to call." The irritated breath she blew was loud enough for the person on the other end to hear. "I forgot, okay? Bye." She disconnected.

Talk about unfriendly. She'd been okay with the dogs, but Emily couldn't picture her working at the shelter. Not when Emily had the pick of kids she assumed would be easier to work with. Still, it was only fair to look at her application—provided she turned one in.

"Seth will be here in a little while," Taylor muttered.

"Is he your boyfriend?" If so, the poor boy was a glutton for punishment.

"Boyfriend? Eww." The girl pantomimed sticking her finger down her throat. "Seth is an adult—he's why we moved here."

Ah, so he was Taylor's father. Emily couldn't believe she called him by his first name. This girl was a handful, and Emily felt for the parents. She imagined that if she'd ever called her dad by his first name, she'd have been in major trouble. That is, if he'd stuck around until she hit her teenage years. Since he'd taken off when she was nine, she could only guess.

"Where are you from?" she asked as they entered the front office.

"San Diego."

"That's a big city. Even at the height of tourist season, we only have about seventy thousand residents in Prosperity." Most of the locals were either ranchers or made their living from the tourists, who flocked to the area in late spring and summer for hiking and fishing. And also to visit Prosperity Falls, which was famous for its beauty and a popular place for marriage proposals and weddings. "When the tourists leave, we drop down to sixty thousand," she added. "Is Seth a rancher? Is that why you decided to move here?"

"You ask a lot of questions," Taylor said. "I didn't get a say in whether I moved or not. Otherwise, I would've stayed in San Diego. Seth isn't a rancher, but he used to live here. His brother has a ranch on the other side of town."

Interesting. "What's his profession?"

"He's a veterinarian."

"Is he?" Emily didn't hide her interest. "And his specialty?"

"Large animals."

"You mean livestock?"

Taylor nodded.

"Does he ever treat dogs?"

"Sometimes. When he was at a ranch the other day, he treated a border collie with worms." Taylor shrugged. "While I'm waiting for him, I may as well fill out the application."

Emily handed her a pen. The girl sat down on the old couch that had belonged to Emily's mother before she'd married Bill, around the time Emily had opened The Wagging Tail.

Taylor pulled earbuds and an iPod from a pocket in her backpack and listened to music while she worked on the application.

While Emily sat at the desk, her thoughts whirled. The girl's father was a veterinarian. Maybe he'd be interested in volunteering at The Wagging Tail. Of course, if he did agree to help out, Emily would have to let Taylor do her community service here.

She wasn't thrilled about that, but to bring in a new veterinarian, she could definitely put up with a little attitude.

Some fifteen minutes after Seth Pettit ended the irritating phone call with Taylor, he parked his pickup in the driveway of The Wagging Tail. She tried his patience in every way, but he was determined to bring her around.

The building, a small two-story structure that looked more like a home than an animal shelter, had a big fenced yard and a couple large dog runs.

Seth didn't remember a shelter on this side of town. But then, he hadn't been in Prosperity since just before his eighteenth birthday, some seventeen years ago, when the town had been smaller and less developed.

Back then, he'd been a kid with a huge chip on his shoulder and a penchant for getting into trouble. He'd resented Sly, his big brother, for trying to rein him in, and had all but ignored Dani, their baby sister. One semester short of graduating high school, he'd dropped out instead. Vowing to never return, he'd left Sly and Dani in his dust.

Funny how things changed. Karma was a bitch with sharp claws.

In the almost three weeks since Sly and Taylor had moved here, he'd seen Dani twice and Sly once. The first time the three of them had met after all these years, Seth had dragged Taylor along, Dani had come with her husband, and Sly had brought his wife and two kids. It had been an uncomfortable reunion. Especially with Sly. Dani had quickly forgiven him for staying out of touch all those years. But Sly? Not so much.

Seth's fault, and he meant to fix the rift he'd caused. With barely enough money to tide him and Taylor over for a few months, he also needed to get his business up and running pretty quick. Otherwise they'd have to move out of the two-story house he rented. He wasn't about to let that happen. Taylor had been through a lot and had moved enough, and Seth meant to put down roots right here. The house, a run-down three-bedroom, wasn't exactly top of the line, but it had the potential. Come spring, the landlord planned to sell it. He'd offered Seth first option to purchase, and Seth wanted badly to take him up on it. For Taylor and him, but also to prove to Sly that his screw-up kid brother hadn't turned out so bad, and could be responsible for someone else. He had about six months to save up the down payment.

Last but not least, he had to figure out how to get

Taylor to stop hating him. Piece of cake—and the moon was made of sterling silver.

He headed up the cement walkway to the front door, past a black-and-white The Wagging Tail sign decorated with paw prints. The porch, nothing more than a concrete slab, held a welcome mat, and a hand-lettered sign tacked to the door invited him to come inside.

Seth wiped his feet and did just that.

Taylor was sitting on a sagging couch, with a pen in her hand and her head bent over some papers. Surely not homework. Getting her to do that was harder than pulling a decayed tooth from a bad-tempered bull's mouth.

She looked up at him and frowned. "I'm not ready to go yet. I need to fill out this application."

"Hello to you, too," he said. "You're too young to apply for a job."

A look of pure resentment darkened her face. "I *told* you—it's for community service."

There was no point in reminding her that she'd already visited a food bank and a used-clothing collection center and had turned up her nose at both.

But then, she turned up her nose at everything. For some reason, apparently this place was different.

The woman sitting behind the front desk was studying him curiously. She was a real knockout—big eyes, an intriguing mouth and wavy, collar-length blond hair that was tucked behind her ears.

"Hi." She smiled and stood, tall and long-limbed, and rounded the desk. A hot-pink, feminine blouse framed smallish breasts and hips, and faded jeans showcased long, slender legs. She could've been a model.

A three-legged whippet joined her, tail wagging.

"I'm Emily Miles, founder of The Wagging Tail. And this is Susannah." The woman extended her arm.

"Seth Pettit."

They shook hands. Except for a few cursory hugs from Dani, it had been a while since Seth had touched a woman, even in this casual way. Emily had delicate bones and soft, warm skin, and he held on a moment longer than necessary. Blushing, she extracted her hand.

He turned his attention to the dog, letting her sniff his knuckles in greeting. "Hey, there, Susannah."

"Why don't you come into my office and we'll talk while Taylor completes her application," Emily said. "It's right down the hall."

Wondering at that, he shrugged. "Okay. I'll be back shortly," he told Taylor.

She didn't bother to look up from the application. "Whatever." The word seemed to be her mantra.

He followed Emily down a hall, a short distance, but enough for him to check out her fine backside.

She led him to a windowed room just big enough for a desk, two kitchen-style chairs, a bookcase and filing cabinet and a doggy bed. Papers cluttered the desk, along with the usual computer, printer and phone, and a framed photo of an older woman with the same flirty mouth, smiling up at a man with a thick beard and silvery hair, who looked vaguely familiar. Although Seth had no idea why. Emily's parents, he guessed. A clock and a dog calendar adorned one wall, and dark red curtains framed the window. That was about it.

She gestured at the chairs, which were both across from the desk. "Please, sit down."

They took seats, Emily nudging a pile of folders to one side, to make room for a lined yellow pad.

"Taylor tells me that you're a veterinarian and that you're new in town," she said.

"That's right. I'm looking to build my business. If

you know of a rancher looking for a vet who makes house calls, I'm your man."

"If you make house calls, then in no time, you'll have more business than you can handle," she said. "How long have you been practicing?"

"Four years now."

Twin lines marred the smooth space between her eyebrows as she moved the pad to her lap and jotted something down. Seth couldn't see what.

"And you specialize in large animals?" she asked.

"Mostly cattle and horses."

"Taylor mentioned dogs."

"Now and then, but I don't have a clinic or an office." At the moment, he couldn't afford either. But someday…

More scribbling.

"What happens if you need a clinic?" she asked.

"I have an agreement with Prosperity Animal Hospital, on the north side of town."

"I know that place." She jotted that down, too.

Weird. It almost felt as if she was interviewing him.

"How does your wife like Prosperity?"

"I'm not married." A couple times he'd come close, but nothing had worked out.

"Oh." Emily brought her hand to her hair and fiddled with it. "I assumed— Never mind. I didn't realize there were any ranches in San Diego."

The comment puzzled him. "I'm sure there are, but I wouldn't know. I've only been there once or twice, and not for long."

Her turn to look confused. "I'm pretty sure Taylor said she was from San Diego."

He nodded. "She is."

"I don't understand. Aren't you her father?"

No one ever understood until he explained. Dani, Sly and their families knew the facts, as did the teachers and counselors at Taylor's school. Now Emily would, too.

"It's complicated," he began, giving her an out if she didn't want to know. She nodded, and he went on. "Taylor's mother and I were involved. We moved in together when Taylor was about five. Four years later, Annabelle broke things off and kicked me out."

She'd stuck with him while he finished college, assuming that eventually they'd marry. Then immediately after earning his undergrad degree, he'd started vet school. Annabelle had continually pushed him to propose, but between school and a part-time job, he'd been too busy to think about much else. That was his excuse, anyway. The truth was he hadn't been ready for marriage. Hell, he'd never even told her he loved her. He'd liked her fine, but hadn't been capable of taking the next step. Tired of waiting for that ring on her finger, Annabelle had ended the relationship.

Story of his life.

"I see." Emily frowned. "If you don't mind my asking, why is Taylor living with you now?"

"I'm getting to that. In the years we lived under the same roof, she and I grew close. Annabelle never knew who Taylor's father was. Although it wasn't me, Taylor considered me to be her father, and I loved her like a daughter.

"At the time, we lived in Sacramento," he went on. "I moved out, and a few days after the breakup, Annabelle packed up and left. She didn't tell me about that or say where she was going, just cut me out of Taylor's life." Not all that different from what Seth had done with Dani and Sly, he'd come to realize a few years later.

Standing on the other side of the fence had sucked, big time. "I tried to find them, but never did," he finished.

He'd missed the girl terribly and knew she was likely missing him, too. "Fast-forward six years. I was still in Sacramento, with my own veterinary practice." A few months earlier, his mentor from his undergrad days, Professor Greenfield, had died of cancer. Like Seth, the professor had been estranged from his family. Filled with regret, he'd begged Seth to make up with Sly and Dani before it was too late.

Seth had been mulling that over, assuring himself that he had plenty of time to make amends with his siblings, when the bomb that had radically altered his life had dropped. "Annabelle's attorney contacted me with the news that she'd been in an accident and had passed away," he said. "There was no other family, and in her will, she'd named me to assume guardianship of Taylor."

Annabelle's passing at the young age of thirty-five, the same age Seth was, had added a sense of urgency to make up with Sly and Dani sooner, rather than later. You never knew when your time was up.

"What a shock that must have been for both you and Taylor," Emily said. "Poor girl. It must be hard to lose your mother at such an early age."

Seth knew way too much about that. He'd lost his own mother when he was ten. Less than a year later, his father had followed her. "I think her death knocked us both to our knees," he said.

As bad as he'd felt for Taylor, at first he'd balked at the idea of assuming responsibility for the girl he hadn't seen in six years. But if he didn't step up, she would go into foster care. Seth couldn't let that happen, couldn't let her go through that.

After both his parents died, Dani had been shuffled

into foster care. She'd lucked out, though, when Big Mama, her foster mom, had adopted her. Meanwhile, Seth and Sly had been shipped off to Iowa to live with an uncle who never tired of reminding them that he hated kids. No child deserved to live with a man like that.

"No wonder," Emily murmured.

"Pardon me?"

"Taylor seems to have a bit of an attitude."

And then some. Seth nodded. "The adjustment has been rough on her. On both of us."

He was at his wits' end. In the weeks since they'd moved here, no matter what he did, Taylor had shown nothing but contempt and loathing for both him and Prosperity. She hadn't made a single friend or become involved in any school activities.

This dog shelter was the first thing she'd expressed an interest in. Seth needed Emily to give her a chance. "Be honest with me," he said. "Are you going to let Taylor work here?"

Emily caught her full lower lip between her teeth. "Before we talk about that, I'd like to show you around. It'll only take a few minutes. We'll go out through the front door, so you can let Taylor know. She can stay here and keep Susannah company."

Curious to see the place that had finally piqued Taylor's interest, Seth readily agreed. "Let's go."

Chapter 2

"Tell me about the dogs," Seth said, as Emily led him toward the kennel.

At five feet ten in her bare feet and even taller in boots, she didn't have to look up at people all that often. But Seth was several inches taller, and she had to do just that to meet his eyes. They were an unusual shade of silvery blue, and looked especially striking against the afternoon sky.

"I take in animals that have been abandoned and sometimes abused," she said. "My job is to find them permanent homes with loving families."

He absorbed her words with a somber expression. "You haven't chosen easy work."

"No, but it can be so rewarding."

Seth listened thoughtfully. "Is that how you got Susannah?"

Emily nodded. "She was one of the first dogs to

come here when I opened my doors." The whippet, with her injured leg, malnourished body and trembling fear, had quickly wormed her way into Emily's heart.

"How did you get into this work?" Seth asked.

"My very first job was with a woman who groomed and boarded dogs while their owners were out of town," Emily said. She'd taken the job so that she could help her struggling mother make ends meet. "She had a soft place in her heart for abused dogs, and fostered and adopted a few while I worked for her. Like all living creatures, they need love and affection, along with a strong dose of patience. Give them those things, and they're loyal friends for life." Unlike people, who could walk away at any time and break your heart. "I've been in love with dogs ever since."

"Running this place can't be cheap. How do you fund it?"

"Through private donations, most of which I raise at an annual fund-raiser the first Saturday in November," she said. "But I couldn't do it without my volunteers." Mentally, she crossed her fingers that she could persuade Seth to sign on as one of them. "The dog groomer I just told you about? She comes in a couple times a month to bathe and groom the dogs. The rest of the time, I get to do the job." Emily wrinkled her nose.

"I'll bet that gets messy."

He flashed a smile she felt clear to her toes. It had been over a year since she'd even noticed a man, and Seth Pettit was a seriously attractive male, tall and solid, with a broad forehead and a strong jaw. She smiled back. "Even when I wear protective clothing, I usually end up a dripping mess. You don't want to see me when I finish that job."

He chuckled at that, and so did she.

"You do this full-time?" he asked.

She shook her head. "There isn't enough money for that, so I double as a web designer—I create and maintain websites. I enjoy the work, plus I get to set my own hours."

"I've been told I should put up a website, but I'm not sure I need one."

"Can't hurt," Emily said. Wanting Seth to know more about the shelter, she gestured around. "Isn't this a nice space? It used to be part of a ranch that was subdivided and sold off. I rent it from a couple who love animals. They even adopted one of our dogs. They didn't mind when I turned the garage into a kennel. As long as I pay the rent on time, they're happy."

At the kennel, she opened the door and led Seth inside. He moved slowly and deliberately toward the cages, letting the dogs take him in.

"Hey, there," he greeted them.

Each one took note of his low, soothing voice, and a few wagged their tails.

It was obvious that Seth Pettit had a way with animals. Probably with women, too, Emily guessed, with another flutter of interest.

But she wasn't about to see him as anything but a potential volunteer veterinarian at the shelter. Her life was very full and a lot simpler without a man in it, and she liked it that way.

After a moment, they headed outside again. "I'm impressed with what you're doing here, Emily." He held the door open for her. "Now I understand why Taylor wants to work here."

"About that," Emily started, ready to work a deal. It was chilly now, and wishing she'd put on a sweater, she chafed her arms. "Our dogs need friendly, warm volunteers. And Taylor—"

"Hear me out." Seth held his hand palm up, silencing her. "She's not a bad kid. She just needs a little time to get used to all the changes in her life. I'm no therapist, but I know in my gut that doing her community service here would be really good for her. What can I do to convince you to let that happen?"

His eyes pleaded for understanding. He didn't know that he'd provided the perfect segue to the subject Emily wanted to broach. "Funny you should ask," she said. "The vet who has volunteered here since I opened the shelter just retired unexpectedly. I need a replacement."

Seth eyed her. "You're asking me to volunteer at The Wagging Tail."

Crossing her fingers at her sides, she nodded. Only a few yards from the front office now, they stopped to finish the conversation before stepping inside.

"I have an awful lot on my plate right now," he said.

"You're building a practice and settling in. I understand. I'm not asking you for forty hours a week, or even twenty. I just need someone to perform routine health checkups on any new animals we take in, get them vaccinated, and whatever else they need. And of course, to give them the medical attention they might need if they get injured or sick while they're here."

"How much time are we talking?"

"You saw for yourself that I only have room for six animals. There are also two quarantine huts where new arrivals stay until they're cleared to join the others. Probably one to two hours per week, barring unexpected emergencies."

"So one day a week for two hours?" Seth asked.

"Or more, depending on when we take in a new animal and if someone gets sick. I'll try not to bother you at night or on weekends."

"You'll give Taylor a job if I agree to this?"

Emily nodded.

"Throw in a free website consultation and design and I'll do it. For one semester, while Taylor's here. But understand that if you need me at the same time as someone in my practice, they come first."

A semester was better than nothing. Who knew, maybe she'd convince him to stay on permanently. At the very least, she had a few months to search for someone else.

Relieved, she smiled. "Fair enough. Thank you, Dr. Pettit."

"I go by Seth."

"Okay, Seth. Please call me Emily. Community service begins on Monday."

"Great. Do me a favor, and don't tell Taylor about our arrangement. Let her think she got the job because you want her for herself."

"I can do that," Emily said. "I'll call her tomorrow and let her know."

He nodded. "We have a deal."

They shook on that. Seth's big hand almost engulfed hers. His grip was firm and strong and warm, and for some reason, Emily wanted to hold on for a while.

Way too attracted to this man, she quickly let go, pivoted away and hurried toward the front door.

"I don't see why you need to volunteer at The Wagging Tail while I volunteer there," Taylor said as Seth drove home. "That is, if Emily chooses me."

Taylor didn't want him involved in anything she did. In her life at all, for that matter. He stifled a weary sigh.

"The vet who was helping Emily retired, and she asked me to help out. I'm only going to do it until January, and my own business comes first. Trust me, I won't get in your way."

Taylor snickered. "You're *always* in my way."

Seth missed the days when she'd been little and carefree, and had simply taken him at his word. But those times were long gone, and a lot of baggage had filled the gap in between. "I'll only come to The Wagging Tail when Emily calls, and if she hires you, to pick you up—that's it," he said, striving to sound patient. At Taylor's stony look he added, "If she doesn't have a vet to handle her dogs' medical issues, she'll be forced to shut down."

Taylor's eyes widened. "I guess it's okay, then."

One hurdle successfully crossed. Relieved, Seth rolled the truck up the cracked blacktop driveway of their house. He pulled into the carport. Before he even killed the engine, Taylor slipped out the passenger door. Without a thanks-for-the-ride or a backward glance, she pulled a house key from her jeans pocket and headed for the house.

Seth followed. As a kid, he'd always been ravenous when he got home from school. He was pretty sure she must be, too. But she went straight through the kitchen and toward the stairs.

Wafer thin, she was way too skinny. He couldn't let her disappear into her room without something to eat. "Hold on," he called out. "Want a snack?"

"No, thanks," she said over her shoulder.

"It's okay to eat in your room or anyplace in the house. It's yours, too. You don't have to hide upstairs."

"I'm not hiding and I'm not hungry."

She spent way too many hours texting and fooling

around on FaceTime with her friends in San Diego. Time she should be spending making new friends and getting involved at Trenton High.

But as she continually reminded him, her home was in San Diego and there was nothing for her here. And he reminded her that she lived in Prosperity now. She didn't like that at all.

At least she had her community service work lined up—a first step toward settling in. Seth hoped.

She was almost up the stairs now. "Do your homework before you talk with your friends," he called out.

Muttering, she took the last few steps quickly. Seconds later her bedroom door closed. Loudly.

Seth muttered, too. For his own benefit, he'd talked with a couple specialists about the situation. He wanted Taylor to meet with the school counselor or see a social worker or therapist, but she refused. He knew that he couldn't force her to get help.

He was in his "office," for now a corner of the living room, tackling paperwork and thinking about ways to drum up business, when his cell phone rang.

"This is Zeke Jones," a gravelly voice said. "I got your name from Barton Michaels." Michaels owned a ranch where Seth had treated a sick heifer the previous week, and had gotten Seth's name from an ad he'd placed in the *Prosperity Daily News*. "Got a cow with a bad case of pinkeye," Zeke went on. "It's in both eyes, and I'm worried about it spreading through the herd. She's starting to lose weight, too."

This was not good for Zeke, but Seth was pleased for the referral from Michaels. "Where are you?" he asked. He jotted down the address. Although it was nearly dinnertime, he said, "I'll be over shortly."

After disconnecting, he headed upstairs to tell Taylor. Maybe she'd come with him. Through the door he heard loud music from The Wanted, a band she listened to constantly. He knocked a couple times before she heard him.

"What do you want?" she asked through the closed door.

"Open up."

Seconds later, the door opened a fraction, just enough for her to poke her head through.

"I have to go out and help a rancher with a cow who has pinkeye," he said, raising his voice above the music.

"Whatever." She started to close the door.

"Why don't you come along?" he asked. "It's bound to be interesting." And might help them bond.

She looked as if she'd rather eat worms. "What's interesting about pinkeye?"

"In a cow, it can be dangerous. It hurts a lot more than it does in humans. An infected animal often keeps her eyes closed because of the pain. She avoids sunlight, too, and stops foraging for food and water. If she doesn't get well quickly, she could die."

"That's not interesting at all."

The door shut rudely in his face. Patience fraying, he bit back a frustrated oath. When he was in vet school, she'd loved watching him work with sick or injured animals. Not anymore. Since he'd taken Taylor in and they'd moved here, he'd made sure to invite her along on any call he made when she wasn't in school. So far, she'd always turned him down.

"I should be back in an hour or so, but I'll phone when I know for sure," he said through the door. No reply. "If you want dinner while I'm gone, there's leftover lasagna in the fridge," he added.

Nothing but hostile silence.

His fraying patience snapped. This time he opened the door without knocking. "Did you hear what I said?"

"I didn't say you could come in here." Arms crossed, Taylor shot daggers out of her eyes.

"Tough. Did you hear me or not?"

"I heard."

Seth nodded. "See you later. Get that homework done before you start texting or using FaceTime."

"Yes, sir." Sarcasm dripped from her words.

When he was through the door, she slammed it.

Irritated at himself for losing his cool, he scrubbed his hand over his face and headed back down the stairs. Living in the same house with an angry teenage girl was a lot tougher than he'd ever imagined.

Would she ever give him a break?

After locking the shelter doors late Thursday afternoon, Emily drove toward Prosperity Park. Her mother and Bill lived on the edge of the park, and were lucky enough to have an impressive view of Prosperity Falls from their living room window. A view that had cost a bundle, but Bill was a partner in a large insurance company and could afford it.

He gave Emily's mother whatever she wanted, and she wanted to travel. In two days, they would leave for six whole weeks, touring Spain, Portugal and France.

Emily was jealous, but in a good way. If she didn't have the time or money to travel, at least they did. Tonight they'd invited her over for dinner and to say goodbye.

The sun was about to set and vivid pink streaks colored the paling sky. The usual rush-hour traffic filled the highway, but Emily didn't mind. With beauty all around her and dinner plans, she couldn't help but be happy.

Too happy for a ho-hum night with her mom and Bill. She really needed to get out more.

She parked in the driveway of the house, which was a stunning mixture of cream-colored brick, river stone and tempered glass. The landscaped yard was nothing like the trampled grass around the shelter grounds. Carrying a bottle of Spanish wine she'd picked up, she followed the flagstone walkway to the raised brick stoop, then opened the front door and let herself in.

The place was quiet. Leaving her jacket and purse in the entry, Emily headed for the living room, on the opposite side of the house. The huge space was only marginally smaller than her entire apartment, and decorated with beautiful, expensive furnishings.

Where were her mother and Bill? After stopping to admire the falls from the picture window, Emily checked the state-of-the-art kitchen. No one there, either. She peered out the sliding glass door that opened onto the back yard and patio. The grill was out and ready for action, but she didn't see her mother or stepfather.

She set the wine she'd brought on the granite counter and returned to the living room. "Hello?" she called. "Mom? Bill? I'm here!"

"We'll be right out!" Her mother's muffled reply came from the direction of the master bedroom.

A long few minutes later, the couple appeared, with their arms around each other's waists. Her mother looked slightly disheveled and radiant, and Bill wore a big grin. Emily didn't want to think of what had put the glow in their faces. Some things were too gross to contemplate. Four years of marriage and they still acted like newlyweds.

They were insanely happy, which was wonderful. After Emily's father had walked out and left her mom struggling to pay the bills and keep a roof over their heads, she deserved a loving man. She liked to say that Bill's wealth was the icing on her happiness cake.

Emily didn't care about Bill's money. He was a good guy who really cared about her mother. She wanted a man like Bill. She'd thought she'd found him in Harvey. They'd discussed marriage and children multiple times, and she'd assumed that they would be together forever.

Then a well-known architecture firm on the East Coast had offered him a plum job. Emily hadn't wanted to give up her beloved shelter, but she'd been ready to find her replacement so that she could go with him. Things hadn't worked out the way she'd imagined, however. Harvey had taken his dog with him, but not Emily. She'd been single ever since.

Her mother came over to exchange cheek kisses with her. Bill gave her a hug.

"How's the packing coming along?" she asked.

"We were just working on that, only then we got a little distracted." Her mother and Bill exchanged meaningful glances.

He chuckled. "We sure did."

TMI—too much information, Emily thought. She cleared her throat. "I noticed you uncovered the grill out back."

"We're having steak tonight." Bill licked his lips and patted his slight paunch. "Are you hungry, Em?"

"Starving."

"Me, too. As soon as I fix the drinks, I'll fix the steaks."

In the kitchen, Emily's mother and Bill kissed as if they were about to part for days before he stepped through the sliding glass door to the patio.

Her mother watched him go with a dreamy sigh. Emily shook her head. Sometimes the lovey-dovey stuff got old. "What can I do to help?" she asked.

"Set the table and open that bottle of wine so it can breathe. I'll heat the rolls and empty the salad into a bowl."

While they worked, they caught up on each other's lives, just as they had when they'd lived in the one-bedroom apartment where Emily had grown up—on the rare occasions when her mother had been home in time to help with the evening meal. Usually, Emily had prepared it alone.

Before long, Bill returned with the sizzling steaks. They sat at the kitchen table and loaded their plates.

"Are you excited about your trip?" Emily asked as they ate.

"Just a little." Bill's lips twitched.

He and Emily's suddenly gleeful mother exchanged brilliant grins, and then launched into a detailed itinerary of where they were going and when. Emily had already heard most of before, but didn't mind hearing it again. In their excitement, the two finished each other's sentences and occasionally interrupted one another. They were so involved in the back and forth that they seemed to forget she was there.

Emily felt like a third wheel. Melancholy crept in, and no longer hungry, she picked at her food. At times like this, she wished she was part of a couple.

But that would mean dating again, which she hadn't done since Harvey. Emily's wayward thoughts homed in on a certain sexy veterinarian. She quickly dismissed that idea. She'd had to resort to arm twisting to get Seth to take the volunteer job in the first place, and she wasn't about to jeopardize that by going out with the man. If he was even interested. Because if they were to go out and then things between them soured… At any time, he could walk away from the shelter. Besides, between it and her website business, she was way too busy to date.

Which wasn't exactly the full truth. The thing was, even though it had been more than fifteen months since Harvey had left, and even though Emily was totally over him, she wasn't over what he'd done. Bad enough, breaking her heart. He wasn't the first. But leaving her behind without a backward glance, the same as her father had? She wasn't about to put herself in that position ever again, and she for sure wasn't ready to start dating. Besides, the dogs at the shelter depended on her, and that was where her focus needed to be—on providing them with a temporary place to stay and finding them good homes.

Refusing to be ignored for one more minute, she changed the subject. "I had an unpleasant surprise this week." That got her mother and Bill's attention. "You remember Rich Addison, the veterinarian who's volunteered at the shelter since I opened our doors? He decided to retire."

Knowing what that meant, her mother frowned. "What are you going to do?"

"I think I've found a replacement."

"Already? That's great!" Bill looked pensive. "I've sold insurance policies to most of the animal docs in town. Who is it?"

"Actually, he's new here, having recently moved back

from California. His name is Seth Pettit and he works mostly with livestock."

"I know Seth." Bill nodded. "He phoned shortly after he arrived, and I set him up with the insurance he needs."

Her mother frowned. "If Dr. Pettit works with livestock, why is he volunteering at the shelter?"

"He likes to be called by his first name," Emily said. "His…" She paused. How to explain Taylor? "He's guardian to a teenage girl who will be doing her community service at The Wagging Tail."

"They're volunteering together." Bill gave a nod of approval. "I used to do that with Kara." His daughter from his first marriage, now in her early forties. "It's a good bonding experience."

"They won't exactly be doing their volunteer work at the same time," Emily said.

"Still, it's nice that they'll both become familiar with the shelter. They'll have something to talk about."

She hadn't thought of it that way, but Bill was right.

They were finishing their dessert when her "dog emergency" pager buzzed. The number of one of the volunteers who rescued abused animals showed on the screen. "I need to check this," Emily said. "Excuse me."

She stepped into the hallway and returned the call. Moments later, she reentered the kitchen. "Sorry to eat and run, but a new dog is coming in tonight, and I have to make some calls."

First, to the couple who'd said they wanted the red setter, to make sure they picked him up in the morning, which would free up a slot for the new animal. Then, to Seth Pettit. Tonight she would quarantine the new arrival. Depending on what Seth found when he examined the dog, the animal would either move in with the others or stay in quarantine.

Chewing a bakery cupcake, her mother nodded.

"That's okay, Em," Bill said. "Between packing and other things, your mother and I have plenty to keep us busy."

Once again, they exchanged a private, loving look. *Brother.*

Emily kissed and hugged them both. "I'll miss you two," she said. "Call and email when you can—and send pictures."

"We will," her mother said. "Good luck with the new vet. And the new dog."

Before Emily even reached her car, she'd pulled out her phone.

Chapter 3

"Can I come with you to The Wagging Tail today?" Taylor asked Seth over breakfast Friday morning. They were sitting in the nook off the kitchen.

Since they'd moved here, this was a first. She'd never asked to go on a call, and for a moment, Seth wondered if she was finally accepting him and settling into her new life. Then his natural cynicism kicked in. Did she really want to watch him examine the shelter's newest dog, or was this a ploy to get out of going to school? Likely the latter.

"If it wasn't a school day, you could," he said, "but I don't want you missing any classes."

His own words took him aback. Damned if he didn't sound just like Sly had all those years ago, whenever Seth had tried to weasel his way out of going to school.

Would wonders never cease.

Taylor's dirty look told him he'd guessed right. "I hate you and I hate Prosperity!"

Seth winced, but he'd heard it before, more times than he could count. You'd think he'd be used to that, but every time she used the *H* word, it stung. He'd be damned if he'd let on how badly. "Look," he said. "You'll probably see the dog Monday, when you go to the shelter for orientation."

One skinny shoulder lifted, then dropped. She turned away from him and stared out the window that faced the raggedy backyard—who had time for yard work?—and the house behind them. The leaves on the trees scattered around the yard were starting to turn. Seth hadn't lived through an autumn in Montana for a long time, but he remembered the intense reds and yellows that dressed up the landscape. He also remembered how quickly the weather could turn. Almost as quickly as Taylor's moods.

In the tense silence he'd grown used to, he scraped the last of his Wheaties from his bowl and finished his coffee. After he and Taylor had been reunited, he'd tried hard to ease the transition by talking about his own life and asking questions about hers. When that had failed, he'd offered to take her to a movie or a concert of her choice here in Prosperity, or to drive her and any friends she made.

No luck with that, either. She'd turned him down and tuned him out. Out of sheer desperation, he'd asked her what *did* she want. She had a ready answer for that. She wanted him to take her back to San Diego, drop her off and let her live her life without him in it. Ouch.

If only she'd make friends at school. Even one would help. As far as Seth knew, it hadn't happened. Taylor went to school downcast, and came home with the same dark cloud over her head. They'd been in Prosperity almost a month now, and he still had no idea how to help her adjust. Since she wouldn't talk to a professional, he could only wait for her to settle in and accept that this was her new life.

The way things stood right now, he wondered if she ever would.

"It's almost time for you to catch the bus," he said. "I'm not sure when I'll be home. After I leave The Wagging Tail, I have appointments at two ranches on opposite sides of town. One with a sick bull, and the other with a horse that won't eat. Call me when you get home this afternoon."

Taylor barely nodded.

Shortly after she trudged to the school bus and boarded—would she ever walk like a carefree teenage girl?—he grabbed his doctor bag, hopped into the pickup and headed for Emily's.

The sun was already bright, with the Cascade Mountains in sharp relief against the clear blue sky. Today would be warm, more like summer than fall. That and a couple of paying appointments on the schedule boosted his spirits. Whistling softly, he cracked the window and slipped on his sunglasses.

He looked forward to seeing Emily this morning. He wouldn't mind getting to know her...

As if he had time for that. Building his business, making amends with his brother and dealing with Taylor took up every minute—and then some.

She probably had a boyfriend, anyway. A beautiful woman like her would.

But if she didn't?

Seth didn't exactly have a good track record with women. With relationships, period. He wasn't about to wreck Taylor's community-service experience by getting involved with the woman who'd hired her. Because if he and Emily did get involved, it wouldn't last. It never did.

He was almost at The Wagging Tail. Pushing his wayward thoughts aside, he signaled, slowed and turned into the driveway.

Standing at her kitchen window Friday morning, which was directly above the shelter and faced the front door, Emily peered anxiously through the curtains. The dog that had arrived last night was skin and bones, with what looked like a bad case of mange, and she was anxious for Seth to check her out and put her on the road to a clean bill of health. He was due at eight, a few minutes from now.

Emily didn't usually start the coffee downstairs until closer to nine, but today she went down and started it early, in case Seth wanted a cup. Then she returned to her apartment to make her lunch.

She was sliding her sandwich into a plastic bag when she heard a truck trundle up the driveway. Right on time. When she peered out the window, Seth's dark green pickup was braking to a stop. He didn't glance up, giving her the opportunity to study him openly. In loose, slightly faded jeans, cowboy boots and a long-sleeved blue twill shirt that emphasized his broad shoulders, he looked good. Really good.

Her heart lifted, and not just because she needed his veterinary skills. He pulled a medical bag and a lab coat from the truck.

For the second time in thirty minutes, she hurried down the stairs, answering the door before he knocked.

Seth looked surprised, his startling, silvery-blue eyes widening. "Am I late?"

Emily's cheeks warmed. She wasn't sure why she was blushing. Maybe it was the intensity of his expression. "You're right on time," she said. "It's just... I'm anxious about this dog. Thanks for making us your first appointment of the day."

"This time fits easiest with my schedule."

"Would you like some coffee?"

"No, thanks. Let's take a look at the new arrival."

Leaving the door unlocked for Mrs. Oakes, Emily headed with Seth for the quarantine hut.

"Tell me about her," he said on the way.

"She's a mixed breed, about the size of a retriever, with thick fur. She has mange."

He nodded. "Where did she come from? Did you check for a microchip?"

"Two of my volunteers found her wandering along Ames River. She's pretty scared and full of fight, but working together, they were able to get her into their truck and bring her here. We didn't find a tag or microchip, but just in case, we're posting Lost Dog signs all over the area." Emily didn't expect a response. "I'm pretty sure she's been abandoned, and by the looks of her, she's been on her own for a while."

"Has she had any water or eaten anything since you took her in?" Seth asked.

"Water and a little food last night, and again about an hour ago." Emily had slipped a long-handled spatula through the food gate to deliver this morning's nourishment. "Her belly is distended, and I know that feeding her too much, too quickly, could cause her intestines to twist."

"Right." Seth looked impressed. "Is your friend who bathes the dogs coming in this week?"

Emily shook her head. "I'll be doing the job myself, after you check her over."

In the small quarantine hut, Seth looked even bigger. He donned the lab coat, probably to protect his clothing. As they approached the animal, she scrambled to the back corner of the cage, growling and baring her teeth. Emily hated that the dog was afraid. No, she wasn't just afraid, she was terrified. Her thick coat was matted, with an ugly bald patch on one side. It hurt to look at her.

"Stay back here," Seth ordered under his breath.

Emily nodded and he slowly neared the cage, with his eyes lowered and his body turned sideways to minimize any perceived threat to the animal.

"Hey, there, girl," he murmured in a deep, friendly voice that flowed over Emily and took all her worries away. The man could make a fortune using that voice as a relaxation specialist.

When the dog continued to growl and bare her teeth, Seth froze, but continued to speak softly and without any trace of fear. Long minutes later, the growling stopped and the dog dropped her threatening stance. Seth carefully extended his arm so that his hand almost touched the cage, with his knuckles facing the canine. All the while, he continued to talk to her. After a long time, she inched closer and sniffed him through the wire.

When that seemed to go well, Seth calmly extracted a dog biscuit from his lab coat pocket and dropped it through the bars. The hungry female snatched the treat and inhaled it.

"Good girl," he crooned.

Oh, that voice. As seductive and rich as dark chocolate, it washed over Emily. The dog wasn't nearly as enamored, but she did seem less wary.

"You're really good with her," Emily said in a low voice that wouldn't upset the animal. "Do you want to muzzle her during the exam?"

"I think I'd better."

Emily pulled the device from a shelf against the wall and handed it to Seth. After donning protective gloves, he unlatched the cage door. Before the canine knew what he was up to, he'd slipped the muzzle over her mouth and fastened the straps. She didn't like that at all, but Seth continued to speak in a reassuring voice. When she calmed a little, he brought her out.

Emily was impressed. She slipped into the smock she kept on a hook, and pulled on rubber gloves. While Seth examined the dog and administered the needed vaccines, she cleaned the cage, replaced the dirty bedding and filled the bowl with fresh water.

Then she joined Seth at the exam table.

"She's malnourished, but seems to be in reasonably good health, considering. It's obvious that she's had pups, but I'm not sure if she's been spayed. Can you hold her while I shave her belly and check for a scar?"

Emily nodded. She held tightly to the dog while Seth did what he needed to. The poor thing was shivering with fear.

All the while, Seth spoke reassuringly. "You've been spayed and that's real good. Emily, keep hold of her while I can check her teeth and gums."

While Emily continued to restrain the animal, Seth removed the muzzle. "We won't get the test results until Monday or Tuesday," he said as he worked. "Meanwhile, I want you to give her an antiparasitic medication for the mange. I have enough for two doses with me, and a sample vial of a flea shampoo that will help with her secondary skin infection. You'll need more of both. When we finish here, tell me which pharmacy you use and I'll phone in the prescriptions."

"How long should I keep her in quarantine?" Emily asked.

"Mange can be contagious, so keep her away from the others until it clears up. That could take a while. Hold tight to her a little longer."

He rifled through his medical bag until he found what he was looking for. "Hide this pill in some wet dog food, and it should go down easy. Let's get her bathed."

"That's not part of your job description," Emily said. "Besides, I'm a pro. I've been bathing dogs for ages."

"I don't doubt that, but this one has a lot of fur and she's frightened. I'll give you a hand, just this once."

Grateful for the help, Emily accepted the offer. "Are you sure you have time?"

Seth checked his watch. "I do if we get the job done in under twenty minutes. Where do you want to do this?"

"It's nice today. How about outside."

Seth nodded and glanced around the little hut. "Is that a dog tub in the corner?"

"It is."

After adding shampoo, a sponge and several towels to the heavy tub, Emily dragged it toward the door. Seth refastened the muzzle on the dog, slipped a leash around her neck and followed.

This morning, autumn seemed months away. Birds chirped happily and the air was warm. Squinting against the light, Emily zipped up her smock.

The dog fought her bath with everything she had, and

despite the protective smock, Emily was soon soaked through. Ten minutes later, the animal was shampooed and rinsed, toweled dry and back in her clean cage.

Emily removed the useless smock. Even her head was wet. Seth's, too. His short, dark brown hair looked almost black, and drops of water glistened like crystals. When he removed his sodden lab coat, she saw that he was every bit as wet as she was.

"We both look like drowned rats," she said, laughing.

Shaking his head and chuckling, he grabbed two towels from the dwindling stack on the shelf and tossed one to her.

Watching him towel off, even fully clothed, was mesmerizing. His wet shirt clung to his flat belly, and the muscles in his arms flexed while he rubbed the water from his hair. He caught her gaping at him. His eyes warmed and a smile hovered around his mouth.

Her face hot, Emily put the bath supplies away. Seth hunkered down in front of the dog's cage, where the newcomer was devouring half a bowl of food with the pill embedded.

"Feeling better, huh, girl?" he asked, when she finished the meal.

The dog angled her head at Seth, then, to Emily's amazement, licked his hand.

After spending less than an hour with him, some of it in a bath, no less, she'd decided to trust him.

Emily was impressed, and if she were honest with herself, just as smitten. Clearly, Seth understood and liked dogs, which elevated him ten notches on her admiration scale. She could so develop a crush on this man—if she was in the market. Which she wasn't.

"What kind of dog do you have, Seth?" she asked.

"None right now. A couple months before I moved back here, Rollie, my black lab, died of old age."

"Why don't you get another one?" she asked, stuffing her smock and the wet towels into a plastic bag to be laundered. "Would you like me to wash your lab coat?"

"No, thanks. I'll get a new dog when life settles down and I have time." He put the muzzle away. "At the moment, my hands are full—both with getting the business going and with Taylor." A pained expression crossed his face.

"Is everything okay?" Emily asked.

"I wouldn't know." He balled up his wet lab coat. "She only speaks to me when she has to, and then it's one or two words. This morning, she almost bit my head off. She wanted to come with me, but I made her go to school instead. Now I'm regretting that. This would've been just as educational."

"You can bring her with you another time. I'm sorry she's so difficult."

"Hey, it's not your problem."

No, but Emily wished she could help. "When you and Taylor are ready for a new dog, don't forget The Wagging Tail," she said.

"I won't." He checked his watch. "I should go."

She nodded and they left the quarantine hut.

As Emily sauntered beside Seth toward his pickup, he tried hard to keep his eyes off her chest and on her face. Trouble was, her off-white blouse was wet and almost transparent. He could see the pink lace on her bra, and her rosy, perky nipples.

A certain part of him woke up and stirred. He willed his body to behave.

As his renegade eyes darted to her breasts again, she

glanced down at herself. Blushing, she hugged the bag of wet towels to her chest.

They were a few yards from the truck when a silver Ford sedan pulled up. A plump, fifty-something woman exited the car.

"That's Mrs. Oakes," Emily said. "She manages the office."

"Good morning, Emily," the woman said with a curious look. "Who's this?"

"Mrs. Oakes, meet Dr. Seth Pettit, our new vet."

Seth flashed a smile. "Nice to meet you."

"And you, as well." She fluttered lashes thick with mascara. "Welcome to our little corner of making the world a better place. By the look of you both, I can see that we've taken in a new dog who didn't care for his bath."

Seth glanced down at his wet shirt and realized he looked like he'd been hit with a water balloon. He was just as soaked as Emily, but on her, wet looked seriously good.

Emily nodded. "She has mange and God knows what else. For now, she'll be staying in quarantine. Oh, and the Tatse should be here this morning to take the red setter."

"It's about time. I'll keep an eye out for them." Mrs. Oakes gave Seth a warm smile before aiming a sly look at Emily. "Emily could toss that shirt in the dryer for you, and give you a cup of coffee while you wait for it."

Both sounded good, but he'd already been there longer than planned. "I appreciate the offer, but I need to go. Nice meeting you, Mrs. Oakes."

"You, as well. I look forward to your next visit, and I'm sure Emily does, too." With a flirty toss of her short brown hair, she sashayed toward the building and disappeared inside.

"Was she flirting with me, or trying to push you and me together?" he asked, shaking his head.

"Both. Her husband left her last year, and she's hungry to meet a new one."

Seth chuckled. "Besides the fact that I'm about twenty years too young for her, I have too much on my plate to date right now. Why would she want to push us together?"

"Because she thinks I should get married." Emily rolled her eyes.

"You're single, then?"

"Yes, and I like it that way."

Seth absorbed this with interest. He wondered why she preferred to be alone. Not that her love life was any of his business. "I can't believe a woman like you isn't with someone," he said.

"A woman like me?" She looked puzzled.

"You're beautiful, smart and passionate about your work. Any man would be lucky to be with you."

Another telltale blush colored her face. "I am dedicated," she agreed, brushing off the compliments.

Making him wonder again. Did she not realize how extraordinary she was? He barely knew her, but he knew enough to appreciate her commitment and passion for the animals she cared for.

"So you're not dating anyone?" he asked, because he wanted to know.

"Between running the shelter and managing my web business, I don't have time."

Her eyes were a pretty light blue, the same color as the early morning sky. A man could get lost in them. "Lack of time—something we have in common," he said, and to his own ears his voice sounded a shade huskier than normal.

She hugged the bag of wet towels closer. "Tell Taylor that I look forward to seeing her on Monday."

"Will do. I hope she behaves herself. By then, I should have the results of the dog's blood work. Before I forget, I need your pharmacy information."

Pulling her phone from her hip pocket, Emily found the number and gave it to him. "Thanks again for making this your first stop of the day," she said.

"No problem." With her helping, he'd actually enjoyed examining and bathing the squirmy, scrawny mutt. "I'll phone in those prescriptions right away. You have your work cut out for you with that dog."

"I'm used to it. Bye for now." She extended her arm, all businesslike.

Touching her was every bit as electric as the other times they'd shaken hands. By the flush in her cheeks and the darkening of her pupils, Seth knew that she felt the same powerful awareness.

He glanced at her mouth again. The cleft in the center of her top lip begged him to taste it, and that plump lower lip... Suddenly he wanted to kiss her. Badly.

The responding desire in her eyes was irresistible.

He reached for her, but she shot a nervous glance at the big window of the front office. "Mrs. Oakes is probably watching us. She's a big gossip."

"Noted." He pulled Emily around the side of the house, out of view. "Now we're safe," he murmured, caressing her soft, soft cheek.

She didn't answer, but her eyelids lowered a fraction. When he leaned in for the kiss, she stopped him.

"No," she said, stepping back out of reach. "Don't."

Despite the *kiss me* signals from her, she'd changed

her mind. Feeling both disappointed and relieved, he gave a terse nod. "I'll, uh, see you Monday."

Seth climbed into his truck and drove away.

Chapter 4

By two o'clock Monday, Emily was ready to begin the orientation for the eight fifteen-and sixteen-year-old community-service volunteers.

They began to trickle in to the shelter. First a girl from Jupiter High, a school on the south side of town. Then a boy and girl from Merrybrook, the high school in the wealthiest part of Prosperity. The rest, a girl and three boys, hailed from Trenton, the school Taylor attended.

Except for Taylor, the Trenton kids entered the building together. Minutes later, she wandered in alone. She barely acknowledged the others from her school, and vice versa. Were they excluding her because they were juniors and she was a sophomore, or for some other reason?

Emily remembered her own teen years, wanting so badly to fit in and be liked. She hadn't exactly been popular, but she'd known she could count on the few friends she'd had. She hoped Taylor would be as lucky.

She passed around the name tags she'd made. "Welcome to The Wagging Tail orientation," she said. "Let's start by introducing ourselves."

After the introductions, Matt from Merrybrook posed a question. "This is a small shelter. How are you going to find enough for all of us to do?"

"Good question. To answer that, let's take a tour of the place. You've all seen the kennel, and we'll visit it again today, but there's a lot more. While I show you around, I'll explain what you'll be doing."

She led them through the main floor of the house, pointing out her office, the supply closets and the kitchen. Outside, they visited the dog runs, and finally, the quarantine hut that housed the dog Seth had examined. The other hut stood empty.

"What's wrong with him?" asked Cat, the only student from Jupiter High.

"She's a female," Emily corrected. "She has mange and worms, but our veterinarian, Dr. Pettit—oops, he prefers to be addressed as Seth—assures me that she'll be okay. Speaking of Seth, Taylor, would you mind if I mentioned your connection to him?"

The girl glanced down. "We don't have a connection," she muttered. "Except that I'm stuck living at his house."

"This dog arrived Thursday night," Emily went on. "After Seth examined her Friday morning, he sent her blood and stool samples to the lab."

She hadn't stopped thinking about his gentle ways with the dog, or the fact that she'd almost kissed him. Her strong desire and feelings for him had startled her. Why him, and why now?

Maybe it was time.

But did she really want a distraction she didn't need in her life right now? No, she told herself. She didn't.

"Earlier, Seth called with some good news," Emily said. "Other than mange and worms, this dog is healthy. Considering that she was starving when she was picked up, and had probably been living on the streets for a while, that's great news."

"If she's healthy, why does she have to stay here by herself?" Cat asked.

"Because both mange and worms are contagious. She's on medicine, and I'm bathing her with a special shampoo. The worms will be gone quickly, but curing the mange will take longer. She's still available for adoption, but until her skin is cleared up, I can't move her into the kennel."

"You mean these dogs get *adopted*?" Cat asked. "I'm adopted."

"That's interesting, Cat. I'm just as careful finding a stable home for our dogs as a human adoption agency is finding a good home for children. Anyone interested in adopting one of our dogs must fill in a detailed application and meet with me, both here at the shelter and in their home."

All the teens seemed impressed.

The tour ended in the kitchen, which was the best place to gather a group. The teens crowded around the kitchen table. Emily stood in front of them. "There are a couple more things to discuss," she said. "First, keeping this shelter open costs money. Besides rent, dog food and supplies, I pay a part-time office manager. You'll meet her next time."

"Don't forget Seth," commented Birch, one of the boys from Taylor's school.

"Actually, we're fortunate that he's volunteering his services. People always want to know where I get the funds to keep this place running. The money comes mostly from private donations. Every year, in early November, I host a fund-raiser. This year, you and your families are all invited. You're also going to play a big part in the event. Which brings me to the brainstorming party I'm hosting for our fund-raiser, two weeks from Friday, in my apartment, which is upstairs in this building." Emily gestured in the direction of the staircase.

"I'd like you all to come, so please write down the date or put it in your phone. We'll have pizza from Harper's Pizza, and I'll be asking for your ideas."

They gave her blank looks, so she explained. "For example, last year, we hosted a dinner and raffle at the Bitter & Sweet downtown. People bought raffle tickets for a chance to win various prizes. They also donated money. That night, we took in enough to stay open one more year."

"Cool," Cat said.

"It's very cool," Emily agreed. "So be thinking about ideas for that."

"What if we have to work or there's a football game?" Shayna from Merrybrook asked. "I'm on the cheer squad and I can't miss the game. Same with Matt—he's on the football team."

"Come for an hour, then, but if you can't, you can't," Emily said. "Now it's time to figure out who you want to do your community service with, and which day you would like to volunteer. Since there are eight of you, and community service days are Monday through Thursday, you'll work in teams of two."

Matt exchanged confused looks with Shayna. "You aren't going to assign us?"

Emily shook her head. "I'm leaving that up to you. Keep in mind that it's always good to make a new friend from a different school. Feel free to get up and walk around and get to know each other. I'll give you a few minutes."

Standing out of the way, she watched the teens pair up. Most of them stuck with kids from their own school. But there were five from Trenton, and Taylor ended up the odd person out. Cat was also alone.

From across the kitchen, the two girls eyed each other. Appearance-wise, they were polar opposites. Cat was petite and curvy. About five feet two, she wore dark eye makeup and her dyed-black hair was boyishly short. A crop top hugged her torso, and under a flouncy, tie-dyed skirt she wore blue tights and black ankle boosts. Taylor was about Emily's height, and willowy, her long red bangs all but hiding eyes with far less makeup. She was dressed in a sleeveless, hooded knit tank top that covered her boyish hips, tight jeans and TOMS flats.

Cat moved first, heading toward her. "It looks like we're the only two left," she said. "Do you want to work together?"

Her expression impassive, Taylor shrugged. "Guess so."

Emily moved to the white board attached to the wall and clapped her hands for attention. "Now that everyone has a partner, let's figure out who comes on what days. Then you can go home, and those who choose Tuesday, Wednesday or Thursday can come back later this week."

What should have been a simple process took almost thirty minutes, but at last everyone was satisfied.

Taylor and Cat had chosen Thursdays. They parted without saying much to each other. Emily hoped they would become friends. She didn't know about Cat, but Taylor could use one.

* * *

When Seth parked in front of The Wagging Tail after orientation, Taylor was outside, waiting for him. He didn't see Emily or any of the other kids.

"Hey," he said, sliding out to greet her.

Wearing her trademark earbuds, her head moving to the beat of whatever song she was listening to, she barely glanced up from her phone to acknowledge him. She moved toward the truck.

"Where's everyone else?" he asked.

She didn't seem to hear him, so he pulled the buds out of her ears.

"I'm trying to listen to a song," she said, shooting him a dirty look.

"How about listening to me instead. Where are the other kids?" he repeated.

"Already gone."

"What about Emily?"

"She's inside, I guess."

"I need her to let me into quarantine to check on that new dog," he said. "You want to come with?"

"I already saw her. She's skinny and gross looking." Taylor bit her lip. "How long before her fur grows back?"

"First we have to get rid of the mange. Once she's healthy, she should have all her hair back in about two months. By then, she'll have put on a lot of weight, too."

"Emily can't keep her that long. She might need the space for another dog."

"Then let's hope she finds a good home for this one and the others."

Taylor nodded. "I'll wait in the truck."

"If that's what you want. There's a granola bar and a can of the pop you like on the passenger seat for you."

A look of pure scorn darkened her face. "I'm not a little kid, Seth."

No, but sometimes she sure acted like one. "You're welcome," he said. "Everybody gets hungry after school."

She didn't reply. The earbuds were back in place, and she was texting away.

"Be right back," he said, not expecting a reply.

A heavyset, gray-haired man who looked to be in his seventies sat at Mrs. Oakes's desk. Seth nodded. "I'm Seth Pettit, the shelter's vet this semester."

The older man's face lit up. "Nice to meet you. I'm Edgar Bell. I volunteer here on Mondays." They shook hands. "Too bad you're here for such a short time—we could use a long-term vet. We appreciate your service, though."

"Thanks. Is Emily around?"

"Check her office."

Although her door was open, Seth knocked before entering.

Emily was sorting through papers, and looked pleasantly surprised to see him. "Hi," she said.

Every time he saw that smile, he liked it more. She sure was pretty, especially in the silky blouse that fluttered when she moved. "I like that blue top."

The flush he'd come to anticipate colored her cheeks. "I dressed up a little today for orientation. Where's Taylor?"

"Waiting in the pickup. How'd she do this afternoon?"

"Pretty well. This year, I have eight kids, five from Taylor's school. I asked them to pair up and choose which day of the week to come. Taylor picked Thursdays. She'll be working with Cat, a girl from Jupiter High."

Not one of the Trenton kids. That was disappointing—she could use a friend at her school. Still, she'd found someone to work with, which was good news. He grinned. "So she finally she made a friend."

"I wouldn't exactly call them friends just yet, but they definitely could be."

Seth hoped. "Since I'm here, I may as well check on the quarantined dog."

"Of course. Would you mind going alone? I need to return phone calls from a couple of prospective adopters. The door to the quarantine hut is unlocked."

Seth left. The female mutt appeared perkier than she had a few days earlier, and her eyes were brighter. "Lookin' good," Seth told her before he returned to the pickup.

When he climbed in, he noted that the snack he'd brought Taylor were gone and the can of soda was empty. He wisely refrained from mentioning it. "How was orientation?" he asked as the pickup rolled down the driveway.

"Fine." She gave him a pained look. "I know Emily needs a veterinarian to volunteer at The Wagging Tail, but why does it have to be you?"

"We've already discussed this," he said. "What's going on?"

"Everyone knows that I live at your house."

Her unhappy expression made no secret of how she felt about that. "It's your house, too," he reminded her.

No comment. Seth shook his head. "If my volunteering here bothers you that much, I could tell Emily I changed my mind and quit," he said. "But I'd rather not leave her in the lurch."

Taylor mumbled something that sounded like, "You'll probably just leave, anyway," but Seth wasn't sure. He wondered what that was about.

She made a face. "Just don't show up when I'm there."

Just before eleven o'clock that night, Emily called Seth.

"Hello?" He sounded groggy.

She hated that she'd awakened him, hated bothering him in the evening, period. "It's Emily," she said, stepping outside to escape the awful barking in the kennel. "There's a German shepherd mix who's been here for almost a week, and I think he just had a seizure." She shivered in the brisk night air. "Now he's acting weird, and the other dogs are freaking out. Dr. Addison, the veterinarian before you, didn't uncover anything wrong with him, but obviously, something is very wrong."

She hoped that whatever it was could be fixed. Otherwise, no one would ever want to adopt him. "I need to get him out of the kennel and take him to the animal hospital, where they have a twenty-four-hour emergency clinic, only I…" Admitting this next part was unnerving. "I'm a little scared of him. I don't think I can get him into the car without help."

There were other volunteers she could call, but she wanted Seth's calm manner to soothe both the dog and herself. Because right now, she was a nervous wreck.

"From your place, that's a twenty-minute–plus drive," Seth said. "Let me scribble a note for Taylor and throw on some clothes, and I'll be there."

Thank goodness. Emily let out the breath she hadn't realized she'd been holding. "I'll be in the kennel," she said.

As wide-awake as she was, and right now she was

crazy and wide-eyed, she was also weary. Having put in a long day that continued for hours after orientation, and had included setting up appointments with prospective dog adopters as well as several hours of work on the websites she maintained, she longed to climb into bed and sleep. Tonight that didn't seem likely.

But she was used to that. Over the last four years, she often spent a night or two a month dealing with some animal crisis or another.

Now that Seth was coming over, she thought about dashing upstairs to her apartment, trading the ratty sweats she'd changed into hours ago for jeans and a top, and pulling a comb through her hair. But she refused to leave the German shepherd for that long.

Seth would just have to take her as she was, sweats and all.

After what seemed like forever, but was actually no more than ten minutes, he was knocking at the door of the kennel.

At last. Emily let him in.

Chapter 5

Seth looked sleepy and needed a shave. But he was there. Emily wanted to hug him. Instead, she nodded toward the German shepherd's cage. "As you can hear, he's growling and barking and has all the other dogs upset," she said over the loud noise. "He's been at it nonstop. Plus he keeps bumping into the bars of his cage. I think he's gone crazy."

"Dogs often go temporarily blind after a seizure," Seth said, rolling up his sleeves. "Some bark and growl, too. Let me take a look at him. Then we'll get him out of the kennel, so that the other dogs will calm down. I'll need a muzzle."

He donned a pair of protective gloves and hunkered down in front of the cage, his broad shoulders straining his flannel shirt. Loose jeans outlined his muscular thighs.

Everything about him was big, including his hands,

and yet Emily knew he performed surgery. Strong, yet precise, firm, yet tender… There was no telling what those capable hands would feel like on her bare skin. A shiver passed through her.

She gave herself a mental eye roll and bawled herself out. Now? She was lusting over Seth when the German shepherd was suffering from who knew what? The animals depended on her to keep them healthy and safe, and find them new homes. They came first. Always.

What was the matter with her? She'd certainly never lusted over Dr. Addison. But then, he was short and round and in his seventies.

Seth Pettit was a gorgeous man. He'd also given up his night's rest to help this dog. She'd best get her mind on the matters at hand.

Careful to stay out of his way, she stood ready in case he needed her. Speaking in a low voice, he opened the door of the cage, slipped on the muzzle and gently guided the dog out. Although the barking increased to earsplitting levels, Seth continued to speak in the same low, calm voice.

Moments later, he straightened. "Let's figure out where to put him."

"Are we taking him to the hospital?" she asked.

"Not tonight. Right now he needs to be in a safe place. If I'm right, and the blindness and barking are after-effects of the seizure, eventually they'll fade away. In the morning, you'll want to take him to any local vet who sees dogs, and get tests to determine what caused the seizure."

Emily nodded. "One of the quarantine huts is empty."

"This could take hours," Seth said. "I'd rather put him someplace where you can be comfortable and accessible if he needs you."

Emily had to think about that. "I don't want him upsetting Susannah, so he can't stay in my apartment. But I could put him in the front office and sleep on the couch."

"That doesn't seem like a very comfortable place for you to bunk."

"I'll manage."

"All right. Let's go."

Seth hefted the animal, grunting with the effort.

As soon as they stepped into the darkness and closed the door to the kennel, the noise level inside dropped considerably.

"The other dogs are calmer already," Emily said.

Busy with his heavy load, Seth nodded, but didn't speak.

As they approached the office, the motion-detector lights flashed on. It was almost cold enough for Emily to see her breath.

She'd left a light on in the office. After quickly opening the door, she stood back while Seth brought the dog inside and gently deposited him on the rug.

"If you'll wait here with him, I'll go back to the kennel and get his bed, so he'll have a familiar place to sleep," she said.

"I'll get it." Seth left.

The dog was still barking and growling. "If you stop making those noises, I'll remove that muzzle," Emily promised, to no avail.

She was relieved when Seth returned with the bedding. "Where do you want this?" he asked over the noise.

"How about right here, next to the couch."

He set up the animal's bed.

"Um, should we leave the muzzle on?" she asked. "So he doesn't bite?"

"Until he stops barking. What are you going to use for a pillow and blanket?"

"My apartment is upstairs," Emily explained. "I'll grab what I need from there."

"You live up there? Will Susannah be okay if you're down here?"

"She'll have to be."

"Want a hand with your stuff?" he asked.

For some reason, the thought of Seth alone upstairs with her at almost midnight was unnerving. "Why don't you stay with the dog, instead," she suggested.

She took a pillow and blanket downstairs, then went up again to say good-night to Susannah. The whippet was upset, probably because she could hear the German shepherd. Emily returned to the office, ready to say good-night to Seth.

"I should be okay now," she said over the barking. "Thanks for coming over tonight."

"I'll keep you company until he quiets down." Seth spoke equally loud.

"But you have to get up in a few hours."

"And you don't?"

Emily bit her lip. "I'll never be able to pay you back."

"You already are, by being nice to Taylor and building me a website."

"Taylor's not so bad." She hadn't started on his website yet. "I'm a little behind on things, but I'll be able to work on your site in a week or so. In the meantime, I'll email you a questionnaire. Fill it in and send it back, and we'll go from there."

Seth nodded. "I'll watch for it."

Her throat a little sore from keeping her voice raised,

Emily set the pillows and blanket on the desk and sat on the couch.

She'd turned off all the office lights, and the only illumination came from the hallway, making the space feel cozy despite the shepherd's continuous barking. Seth joined her on the couch.

"You sure you want to bunk in here?" Seth asked. "You could probably sleep upstairs—as long as you're close enough to reach him if he needs you."

Emily shook her head. "I don't want to leave him alone. If my being here helps him in any way, I'm happy to do it."

"That's above and beyond."

She saw respect and admiration in his eyes, and it made her feel good. "It's all part of my job," she said.

The German shepherd was still going at it, but with less volume. Seth figured he'd quiet down soon. Then he would go home and get some sleep.

"Why did you decide to be a vet, Seth?" Emily asked beside him, her voice a welcome contrast to the dog's harsh barks.

Talking would help keep him alert, and he grabbed on to the question. "I like animals. They don't put on airs—they are who they are."

"They also love us unconditionally." The corners of her mouth lifted, as if the thought made her happy.

There was that, too.

"You mentioned family here," she said. "Taylor says your brother is a rancher."

"That's right, and my sister owns a restaurant. They're both married."

"Two siblings." Emily sighed. "You're so lucky. I don't have brothers or sisters."

"I'm not as lucky as you'd think."

"Oh?"

Not about to tell her that he'd pretty much ruined both relationships, he said, "Let's just say it's been a rocky road with those two, with most of the bumps caused by me." A road he was determined to smooth over. "What about your family?"

"Well, right now my mom and her husband, Bill, are on a six-week tour of Spain, Portugal and France. And by the way, Bill sold you your insurance policy."

"Bill Habegger is married to your mom? No kidding. Sometimes this town feels a lot smaller than it is." Seth was amazed. "I saw the photo on your desk and *knew* I recognized the man in it. Bill doesn't have that beard anymore."

"He shaved it right after that picture was taken."

"He mentioned that trip. He's a nice guy."

"He's great. Anyway, he and Mom live across town, not far from Prosperity Falls. Why did you leave Prosperity?"

"Both my parents died. I was eleven, and my older brother, Sly, and I went to live with an uncle we'd never met, in Iowa. He didn't want any girls, so Dani, that's my kid sister, stayed here and went into foster care."

Why was he telling Emily his story? She was probably bored. Only with her lower lip caught between her teeth, and her eyes wide, she didn't look bored.

"I'm sorry, Seth. That can't have been easy."

She had no idea. "No, but it helps me understand what Taylor's going through. Anyway, Dani got the best end of the deal. Her foster mother adopted her." Seth and Sly hadn't fared as well.

"The uncle who took you in didn't adopt you?"

"He didn't exactly like kids," Seth said. "Another

thing about Dani—she married her best friend. Nick."
Seth had met Nick when he and Sly had returned to
Prosperity, before Seth had left for what he'd thought
was for good. He'd never imagined that Dani would fall
in love with the guy. Some people were lucky that way.

"What about you? Have you lived here all your life?"
he asked.

"My mom and I have, but not my father. He left when
I was in grade school."

Seth shook his head. "You, Taylor and me—we've
all been through rough times."

"You and I survived to tell the tale, and Taylor will,
too. Have you ever been married?"

"No, but I came close once. You?" he asked.

"I was engaged once."

"Really." Seth was surprised. Not that she'd been engaged, but that whoever she'd been with had somehow
lost her. "What happened?"

"Are you sure you want to hear the story?"

"Why not?" He nodded at the dog, which was still
barking. "We have time."

"I'll give you the five-minute version. I met Harvey when I interviewed him about adopting one of the
dogs."

"Interviewed?" Seth asked.

She nodded. "The animals at the shelter have been
abandoned and some have been abused. They need
plenty of TLC, and I'm not about to let just anyone
walk out of here with one of them."

"That makes sense. About your ex…"

"He's an architect. After he adopted a dog, he offered
to help me turn the garage here into the kennel area.
Later he built the two quarantine huts. Somewhere during those two projects, we started dating. Fast-forward

almost a year. We got engaged and rented an apartment together. Six months later, he got a job offer from a company on the East Coast."

"And you didn't want to leave Prosperity," Seth guessed.

"No, I was willing to go with him. I figured I could find someone to run The Wagging Tail and that I'd start a shelter in our new city." She splayed her fingers and glanced at her hands. "But Harvey didn't want me there. That's when I moved in upstairs."

Seth couldn't believe it. "Harvey was a damn fool."

"Thanks," she said. "I agree, but it took me a while to realize it."

"Did you love him?" he asked. Not that it was any of his business.

"I wish I could say no, but I did. I thought he loved me, too." She sighed. "I was wrong."

Seth wanted to deck the bastard for hurting her. Hardly aware of his actions, he put his arm around her and pulled her close to his side.

"It's been almost a year and a half since he left, and I'm over him now," she said.

"I loved Taylor's mom, too," he admitted. "I just didn't realize it until she and Taylor split."

"Have you been in a relationship since?"

"A couple, but nothing long-lasting." He seemed doomed that way. "What about you?"

Emily shook her head. "I've been too busy with the shelter and my web business."

They were both quiet then. The barking continued, but at a slower pace. Seth yawned and stretched, and so did Emily.

"In the spring, my landlord is putting the house where Taylor and I live on the market," he said. "It has good bones, and with upgrades and a couple coats of paint, I think I can make it into a real nice place."

"You're going to buy it?"

"If I can save up the money for the down payment."

Emily bit her lip. "I wish I could pay you something."

"I didn't tell you to make you feel bad. I just thought you should know." He couldn't have said why.

She nodded. After a long pause, she asked, "Do you have any nieces or nephews?"

"Two nieces, both my brother's."

"That's great. I hope to have kids someday."

"You should," he said. "You'll make a great mom."

She angled her head. "What makes you say that?"

"The way you mother the dogs here."

"Aww, that's so sweet." A smile lit her face. "Thanks for staying with me. You're a pretty cool guy, Dr. Seth Pettit."

"Ditto. Hear that?" He cupped his hand to his ear.

"Hear what?" Emily asked.

"Exactly. The dog finally stopped barking." Seth stood and went to his patient.

The shepherd was sitting on his haunches near the desk. Speaking in a low voice so as not to startle him, Seth approached and shone a penlight into his eyes. A moment later, he switched it off and shook his head. "He's still blind, but I think it's safe to remove his muzzle. You might want to get out of here until I gauge whether he's going to bite."

Emily shook her head and joined him. "I'm not afraid of him anymore."

The dog seemed relieved to be rid of the muzzle. Seth didn't blame him. He could probably leave now, but was oddly reluctant to go.

For the first time since he'd arrived, he finally looked

Emily over. She was wearing baggy sweats, with her hair pulled into a loose ponytail. She glanced down at herself and laughed. "You're one lucky man, Seth. I don't think any other guy has ever seen me looking like this."

Seth had never met a woman like her, able to laugh at herself at her own expense. His mouth quirked. "The joys of animal care. You look cute."

"No, I don't."

"To me, you do."

Her laughter died but not her smile. In the dim light, her eyes seemed to sparkle. He couldn't look away.

Then a yawn escaped. Emily followed suit, then nudged him with her elbow. "Go home, Seth, and get some sleep."

It was time. At the door, it seemed natural to kiss her. He leaned in, cupped her face in his hands and slid his lips lightly across hers. Just a little taste. A casual good-night.

It wasn't enough for him. By the yearning expression on her face, not her, either.

Her arms stole around his neck and her soft lips opened, inviting him to explore. The long, deep kiss heated his blood and hardened his body.

He wanted more. A lot more.

But this wasn't the time or the place—or the woman. If and when he found the time, she would be someone who wanted what he did—release without complications. It was obvious to him that Emily wasn't like that. No doubt she'd expect loving words and feelings, when experience had proved time and again that Seth was lousy at both. As badly as he wanted to get nice and intimate with her, that path would lead straight to trouble. And he already had enough of that in his life.

Reluctantly, he pulled back.

Emily's eyes fluttered open. She looked thoroughly kissed, slightly dazed and extremely sexy.

To hell with smart. He knew he'd be back for more.

He cleared his throat and forced himself to open the door. "Good night, Emily."

"Good night, Seth."

As he walked out, the sound of his name on her lips lingered sweetly with him.

Chapter 6

On Thursday afternoon Emily was in the front office, filling Mrs. Oakes in on Taylor and Cat, when Taylor traipsed in, hauling a bulging backpack that had to weigh a ton.

It was a cold, cloudy day and the wind buffeted the old windows. For the first time this year, Emily had cranked up the baseboard heaters, and both she and Mrs. Oakes wore thick cardigans.

Apparently Taylor hadn't gotten the message that summer was over. She wore a zip-up, short-sleeved, cotton hoodie. The mere sight of those bare arms gave Emily goose bumps.

She greeted the girl with a smile. "Welcome back, Taylor. It's good to see you. Aren't you cold?"

"A little, but I'm okay."

Emily introduced her to Mrs. Oakes and said, "As soon as Cat arrives, I'll put you both to work."

Taylor bit her lip. "Do you think she'll come?"

"I haven't heard otherwise," Emily replied.

Moments later, she arrived. Cat, too, had dressed for warm weather, in a tank top that barely covered her stomach, and a lightweight shrug. Mentally shaking her head at both girls, Emily greeted her and, again introduced Mrs. Oakes.

The two girls exchanged perfunctory smiles and studied each other warily. Determined to put them at ease, Emily brought them into her office and directed them to sit down in front of her desk.

"A new dog came in yesterday," she said. "She's in quarantine right now and awaiting the results of her lab tests."

Seth had stopped by late yesterday afternoon to examine and vaccinate the animal. Still reeling from their kisses and not ready to face him, Emily had made sure she was out, interviewing a prospective adopter.

This morning, she'd finally pulled herself together. She needed Seth for his veterinary skills, but she wasn't ready for anything else. Even if she had enjoyed his company the other night. Make that *thoroughly* enjoyed.

Since meeting Seth—since those steamy good-night kisses—her body had awakened from a long sleep. Her mind might tell her she wasn't ready for intimacy, but the rest of her wanted it.

Not that anything was going to happen. She couldn't risk jeopardizing the professional relationship she had with Seth. He seemed to enjoy working with the dogs, and she couldn't help but cross her fingers that he just might decide to stay on after Taylor's semester of community service ended. Okay, maybe Emily also wanted to protect herself from becoming involved with him and then getting hurt. And right now, she wasn't going to think about Seth Pettit and his kisses.

"Let's go over what I want you to do while you're here," she said. "We walk our dogs at least once a day, and I'd like you to do that. You'll start with one dog each, and when you bring them back, you'll walk another."

"Are we supposed to go together?" Cat asked, glancing at Taylor.

Emily nodded. "We keep the leashes in the kennel room."

"How is the dog who had the seizure?" Taylor asked. "Is he okay?"

Emily figured she knew about that. "Seth told you about him?" she asked.

The girl nodded.

Emily bet he hadn't mentioned the good-night kisses. Oh, could he kiss… *Hey,* she reminded herself, *I'm not going to think about him or that anymore.* She wasn't.

Cat was giving her a blank look. "You have no idea what we're talking about," Emily said. "Why don't you explain, Taylor?"

The teen jumped in eagerly. "Remember the German shepherd in the kennel? We saw him during orientation? He had a seizure."

Cat looked stricken. "What's wrong with him?"

"Seth diagnosed him with epilepsy," Emily said. "That was confirmed later, when I took him to the animal hospital for tests."

"I told you he knew about dogs." Taylor almost sounded proud of her guardian.

Cat gave a sage nod. "A boy in my class has epilepsy. Once, he had a seizure in the lunchroom. It was scary.

After, they took him to the nurse's office. Now he takes something to control the seizures."

"Seth said the German shepherd was blind and barking like crazy," Taylor said.

Emily bit her lip. "I was worried, and awfully relieved when Seth came. He said that blindness and constant barking sometimes follow a seizure, and that eventually they fade. He was right about that, too—a few hours after the seizure, the shepherd was back to his normal self."

Not so with Emily. She'd been keyed up for hours, and not just because of the animal's unnerving epsiode. Seth's potent kisses had been pretty stimulating.

"Since we're talking about the German shepherd, why don't you walk him and the little short-haired mix first?" she said. "Those two get along pretty well."

"I don't know…" Taylor gnawed on her baby fingernail. "What if he has another seizure?"

"Just like that boy in Cat's class, he's taking medicine now to prevent that," Emily assured her. "He should be okay."

"But what if he isn't?"

"Then contact me immediately on my cell or my pager."

"Where do you want us to take them?" Cat asked.

"This is a rural area, so anyplace around the shelter is good. A fifteen to twenty minute walk is ideal. They're going to want to run free, but please don't let them off their leashes. We don't want them to turn back into strays. It's chilly this afternoon. Would either of you like a sweater or jacket? I have extras."

Both girls accepted the offer. Five minutes later, they leashed the two dogs and left.

Mrs. Oakes shook her head. "What is it with teenagers and skimpy clothes?"

"I have no idea," Emily said. "At least they were smart enough to borrow sweaters. Cat and Taylor will be working together the whole semester. Do you think they'll make friends?"

"Of course. If walking those dogs together doesn't do it, I don't know what will."

Taylor and Cat headed down a path that crossed a wide field. Taylor was in charge of the German shepherd. Emily was right—he was eager to run. Straining at his leash, he pulled her along at a rapid clip. "He wants off his leash," she said.

"So does my dog," Cat replied. "You heard Emily—we can't."

"I'm having trouble keeping up. Slow down," Taylor ordered, but the shepherd didn't listen. She was almost running now, and starting to sweat despite the cold. She wanted to pull off the sweater she'd borrowed from Emily, but didn't dare let go of the leash.

Finally, tired of racing along, she dug in her heels. "Stop!"

To her surprise, the command worked. The German shepherd obeyed, coming to an abrupt stop.

Cat tried the same thing with her dog, with the same result. They went on at a slower pace.

"What's your favorite class?" Cat asked, still huffing a little.

Taylor felt more comfortable around her now. "At my other school, it was band. I don't like any of the classes at Trenton." The only reason she was doing community service was because if she didn't, she'd get in a lot of trouble.

"Trenton has a band," Cat said. "I heard them when our school played yours in basketball last year."

"Yeah, but I don't want to join," Taylor said.

She wasn't planning to stay in Prosperity that long, and was doing everything she could think of to go home to San Diego. All she needed was a place to stay.

Seth wouldn't mind if she left. He'd be happy. He didn't want her around—he'd proved that before, when he'd walked away from her and her mom. He was taking care of her now only because he had to.

"What's your instrument?" Cat asked.

"I don't have one anymore, but I used to play the trumpet. Do you play anything?"

"I took piano for a few years, but I'm into art now. I'm going to be an artist someday."

Taylor thought that was cool. She gestured at Cat's boots, an awesome lime green, with blue stars on the toes. "Did you paint those yourself?"

Cat nodded.

"They're super cute. I don't know what I'm going to be."

"Maybe a musician."

Taylor wasn't into playing music now. "I don't think so."

"If you could do anything you wanted in the whole world, what would you pick?" Cat asked. She had this funny way of angling her head when she asked a question.

Taylor knew what she *didn't* want to be—a secretary. Her mom had been one, and had hated it. Taylor had no idea what she wanted to do when she was out on her own, but she definitely wanted enough money to go on vacations and buy clothes anytime she wanted, and not have to worry about paying bills. "I haven't decided yet," she said. "We should turn around now."

"I love dogs," Cat said as they steered the animals toward the shelter.

"Me, too. If I didn't, I wouldn't be doing my community service here."

Cat looked wistful. "I wish I could have one, but my mom is allergic. We have a tropical fish tank instead." She made a face. "I like fish, but they can't take a walk with you or cuddle up. What do you think of Emily?"

"She's okay." Taylor wasn't happy that Seth was volunteering at the shelter, but it wasn't Emily's fault that she'd needed a vet exactly when she'd met him. Anyway, for all his faults, he definitely knew animals.

Cat's head angled sideways. "How come you call your dad Seth?"

Since Taylor had moved to Prosperity, no one had asked. She didn't mind explaining. "He's not my dad," she said. "He's my guardian."

"Why aren't you living with your parents?"

Taylor was aware that Seth had explained the situation to the teachers and his family, but none of the kids in her school knew.

"Because I don't have a dad, and my mom died in a car accident," she explained, with barely a quaver in her voice.

Cat's eyes widened. "Bummer."

"Yeah."

It wasn't just the secretary job that her mom had disliked. She hadn't liked Taylor much, either. Lately they'd been fighting a lot, their last battle at breakfast on the very day of the accident.

Taylor felt sick when she thought about the way she'd acted and the things she'd said that morning. Her parting words to her mom had been mean and hateful. She pushed the painful memory from her mind and concentrated on the dog, which was sniffing something on the ground in front of them.

"Did your dad pass away, too?" Cat asked.

"I don't know." Taylor shrugged. "I never met him. My Mom wasn't sure who he was."

"Oh. I know the names of my birth mom and dad, and that they were sixteen when she got pregnant with me. They gave me up for adoption."

"Wow," Taylor said. She couldn't imagine how that must feel. "Do you ever see them?"

"Nope. I don't even want to. Is Seth a longtime family friend or something?"

Taylor shook her head. She hated talking about this, but Cat had asked. "When I was little, he lived with my mom and me. Then one day, he just picked up and left. My mom was so upset that she moved us to another town."

"That sucks."

It had. Taylor was never, ever going to trust Seth again.

"Then how come you live with him now?"

"Because my mom had something in her will about him being my guardian." Wanting to change the subject, she said, "We're almost back."

"I'm ready for a break. Unless Emily wants us to walk the other two dogs right away."

Taylor sighed. "She probably does."

Over a sandwich on Thursday, Seth studied his sorry bank account statement and stressed about the week's less-than-full schedule of appointments. At this rate, he'd never pull together the money he needed to buy the house. And he wanted that almost as badly as he wanted his relationship with Taylor to improve.

Things had to change, and fast. He needed to sharpen his focus on building the business, and not let other stuff distract him. Namely Emily and The Wagging Tail. He wasn't sorry he'd kissed her the other night, but it shouldn't have happened. Because since then, he spent way too much time thinking about her and wanting more.

As for the shelter, he wished he hadn't agreed to volunteer there. Sure, caring for those poor animals felt good. But so far, the little amount of time he was supposed to spend with them each week had turned into a bigger commitment than he'd expected.

Briefly he considered quitting. But no, he wasn't about to go back on his promise. Want to or not, he would stick it out until Taylor finished her community service at the end of the semester. On the positive side, Emily had agreed to get his website up and running, and that would probably help his business. Which reminded him that he needed to fill in the questionnaire she'd sent, and return it to her ASAP.

Suddenly his cell phone rang, the screen indicating a call from his brother. Pleasantly surprised, Seth picked up. "Hey, Sly."

"Got a laboring heifer in trouble," Sly said by way of a hello.

"What's the problem?"

"She's been laboring for hours now, but the calf isn't coming. I tried to grab hold of it and so did Ace." Sly's foreman. "No luck. We need your help."

Words Seth had never thought to hear from his brother. "I'll be right there," he said, already on his way to the pickup.

Fifteen minutes later he pulled up the long driveway of Pettit Ranch. His brother had done well for himself. Everything about the ranch sang of his prosperity— freshly painted buildings, hills dotted with livestock, men hard at work, and a house anyone would be proud to live in.

In the not too distant future, Seth's house—it *would* be his—would look just as fine.

Sly was waiting for him near the barn.

"Hey," Seth said.

His brother nodded and tipped the brim of his hat. He stood a hair over six feet tall, a half-inch shorter than Seth, with the same silvery-blue eyes. Dani had the Pettit eyes, too.

Sly's hands were low on his hips and he wore a guarded look, as if he expected trouble from Seth. This was a good opportunity to prove that any trouble between them was long past.

"The heifer's in the calving pen," Sly said. "This way."

He led Seth around the barn and past two outbuildings. The cow was inside a room set aside for problem births, lying on her side. Her breathing was labored, and she made pained noises. Ace stood nearby, watching closely.

"Have you tried chains or a calf puller?" Seth asked.

"Twice in the last hour," his brother replied.

Seth examined the bovine and made a quick decision. "She's carrying twins. She needs a Cesarean—now. I could use your help—both of you."

They nodded. After rolling up his sleeves and donning his lab coat, Seth shaved the area where he would make the incision. He administered the anesthetic, and while waiting for it to work, disinfected the cow's side. When he was sure she was numb, he got busy.

He didn't speak again until he'd opened her up. "Look at that—one of the calves is blocking the birth canal. No wonder she couldn't deliver."

He pulled out the calves, putting one in Sly's care and the other in Ace's. While they saw to the newborns, Seth cleaned the dam's—the mother's—abdominal cavity. Then he sutured her up. He didn't draw an easy breath until he'd tied off the threads.

"As soon as she recovers from the anesthetic, put her in with her calves," he said. "Meanwhile, I suggest you tube feed them at least once, to make sure they get the nourishment they need to grow stronger."

"You set it up," Sly said. "Ace and I will make sure it happens."

Seth put the tubes in place and stuck around through the first feeding. "Those calves look better already," he noted. "Dams don't always know how to take care of two at the same time, so keep an eye on them."

"I'll stay with them tonight," Ace volunteered. He was a good man who knew his cattle.

Seth shook hands with him, and left him with the animals. Then it was just him and Sly, heading out of the building.

"Thanks, brother," Sly said.

Seth nodded and removed his lab coat, folding it with the soiled area inside. "Where do I wash up?"

"In the barn.

When Seth finished, he dried his hands and rolled down his sleeves.

For a few moments he and Sly stood facing each other. Now that the excitement was over, familiar uneasiness filled the air. Seth shifted his weight and picked up his medical bag. "All right then," he said.

He was turning to leave when Sly spoke. "If I don't offer you a cup of coffee, Lana will have a fit."

The man had a good five inches and seventy pounds on his wife, but she had him wrapped around her baby finger.

Seth checked his watch. "I've got a little while before I pick up Taylor, and I could use some coffee. Is Lana still at work?"

She owned two successful day-care facilities, and took her kids, ages four and eighteen months, to work with her.

Sly nodded. "She should be home around four. Johanna and Mark will be surprised to see twin calves."

Seth thought it was sweet that they'd named their son and daughter after his and Sly's parents.

He liked his brother's big, cozy kitchen, which was warm and colorful. There was evidence of his children everywhere, from the bright finger-paintings attached to the fridge with magnets, to the overflowing box of toys in the corner.

Sly had the family that he, Seth and Dani had all wanted, and Seth envied him. But he wasn't the kind of man to keep a relationship going for long—he didn't know how.

Sly pulled out a container of oatmeal raisin cookies his part-time housekeeper had made, and Seth helped himself. "These are great," he said, chewing with relish.

"I'll let Mrs. Rutland know you like them."

They nursed their coffees in silence. In the mounting tension, Seth began to wish he'd turned down his brother's invitation.

After a while, Sly cleared his throat. "How does Taylor like Trenton High?"

"According to her, everything about it sucks. She hates me, too." Seth wondered how she was doing on her first working afternoon at The Wagging Tail. He hoped she liked the work enough to stick around the whole semester and get her community service credit.

The corners of his brother's mouth lifted in a semblance of a smile. "Sounds just like someone I used to know."

"Come on," Seth said. "I was never as bad as Taylor."

Sly sat back and eyed him. "Does she get into fistfights with other kids?"

"Not that I know of."

"Has she ever tossed a brick through a store window and been picked up by the police?"

Seth shook his head and let out a self-deprecating laugh. "I was a little butthead, wasn't I?"

"And then some."

"You were no picnic, either, Sly."

"Hey, I did the best I could."

It was the closest either of them had come to apologizing for the past. They hadn't had an easy time, with their uncle randomly screaming at them for some offense, and occasionally using his fists or his belt to make a point. When he wasn't ignoring them and letting them fend for themselves.

Seth and his brother left a lot unsaid, things that needed airing. But the moment passed.

No surprise there. They'd never been forthcoming with their feelings. Not to each other.

Seth checked his watch. "It's getting late, and we both have things to do."

"Right." Sly stood and, without fanfare, ushered him

to the door. "Thanks for your help today. How much do I owe you, and where do I send the check?"

As badly as Seth needed the money, he wasn't about to take a penny from his brother. "I'm not going to charge my own brother."

"Free appointments don't pay the bills."

That was Sly, the practical one. Since Seth had left Prosperity at the age of seventeen, he'd learned to be practical, too. Otherwise he would never have earned his GED or attended college and vet school.

"I'm doing okay," he lied. Soon enough, he would be—God willing. "If you want to pay me, tell your rancher friends about me. Word of mouth is the best way to build my practice."

He and his brother shook hands. Sly didn't invite him to come back, but at least he'd sought him out for his veterinary skills. That counted for something.

As Seth headed for the pickup, a call came in from a rancher whose cow had gone lame.

When he disconnected, he was frowning. He needed to check on the animal, but that would make him late to pick up Taylor. She'd have to wait around at the shelter. He didn't envy Emily that.

Chapter 7

Taylor didn't look happy as she disconnected from her cell phone. "Seth is going to be late."

Cat had already been gone a good half hour and Mrs. Oakes had just left. It was getting dark, and Emily guessed that the girl wanted to go home. "I need to go out and run a few errands. I'm happy to drop you off on the way," she offered.

The teen brightened. "You'd do that?"

Emily nodded. "You'd better call Seth back and make sure it's okay."

Five minutes later, the girl was seated in the passenger seat of Emily's hatchback. Furious rain pelted the car. "It's really coming down," Emily said.

"It doesn't rain like this in San Diego."

"Montana is a lot different than where you're from. Soon it's going to be much colder here."

"Then it'll snow." Taylor actually looked excited. "I've never seen snow, except in pictures or on TV."

Emily laughed. "Trust me, you're going to see tons of the stuff."

Wondering how Taylor and Cat had gotten along, but not wanting to ask point-blank, she skirted the subject. "How did you like your first day of community service?"

"I wasn't sure what to expect, but walking the dogs was kind of fun."

"Did Cat enjoy it, too?"

"I guess. I mean, she didn't say she hated it."

"Do you and she have anything in common?"

"We both like dogs."

That was a start. "Anything else?"

"I don't know," Taylor said. "Cat is an artist. I'm not. She painted her boots."

"I wondered about that." The light ahead turned red, and Emily braked to a stop. "What about you, Taylor. What do you like to do?"

"Nothing much," she said with a shrug.

"What do you do when you're not in school and not studying?"

Taylor fiddled with the zipper of her hoodie. "I talk on FaceTime with my friends in San Diego."

"I'll bet you miss them."

"A lot."

"Do you think you'll see them again?"

"Definitely."

"When is Seth taking you back for a visit?"

"I don't know." She compressed her lips. "It doesn't really matter, because I'm going to live there again."

"You mean when you graduate from high school."

"Way before then."

Did Seth know about this? With Taylor so unhappy, he probably did. Adjusting to their situation couldn't be easy for either of them, and Emily's heart went out to them both. If only she could do something to help. "But Seth plans to buy the house he's renting, for you two to live in permanently," she said.

Taylor didn't respond, just stared out the passenger window so that Emily couldn't see her face. Who knew what she was thinking?

The rain had slowed enough that Emily was able to relax and take in the surroundings. In the growing darkness, she noted that they were in a modest area of neatly maintained yards and houses. "This is a nice neighborhood," she said.

"I guess. The next street is ours."

Emily turned onto a narrow street of one-and two-story homes. Cheery light shone through the windows. Families were inside, catching up on each others' days and cooking dinner. Although it had been decades since Emily's father had walked out, suddenly her heart ached for what she'd never had. A house and two loving parents.

"It's the one with the dark green trim," Taylor said, pointing ahead.

Emily pulled into the driveway and studied the non-descript two-story. It wasn't the Ritz, but it looked good to her. Taylor didn't know how lucky she was. "This is nice," she said.

Another shrug conveyed that she wasn't impressed.

"I always dreamed of living in a place like this," Emily admitted.

"Why didn't you?"

"Because my parents split up and my mom could only afford a one-bedroom apartment."

"My mom and I lived in apartments, too. Our last complex had a pool. Sometimes my friends came over to swim."

"That sounds fun."

"I liked it." Taylor lifted her hips and extracted a house key from her jeans pocket. "Thanks for the ride."

"You're welcome. I'll see you next Thursday. Don't forget to ask Seth about the fund-raising party. I really need you there."

"I'll ask him tonight."

Emily waited in the driveway until the girl dashed up the walk, unlocked the door and disappeared inside. Just as she started to back out, Seth drove up. Her heart actually lifted in her chest, as if she was a teenage girl Taylor's age. She gave a mental eye roll. That had to stop.

Seth recognized Emily's light blue hatchback. He hadn't expected to see her, and wasn't sure he liked the hitch in his gut.

Wanting to thank her and find out how Taylor had behaved on her first day at The Wagging Tail, he pulled up next to her, set the brake and exited the pickup. By the time he walked to the driver's side of her car, she'd put her window down.

"Looks like you've been busy," she said.

Seth glanced down at himself. Not anticipating a second call this afternoon, he'd brought only one lab coat with him. It had been too filthy to use twice. Smears of mud and God knew what else stained the front of his shirt. "This can be a pretty gross job," he said, his mouth quirking.

"You know I understand." She smiled and it was like the sun came out.

He leaned down, resting his arms on the open window. "It's been quite a day," he said, wanting to tell her about it. "I did a C-section on one of the cows at my brother's ranch and delivered twin calves. Then I stopped at another ranch and took care of a lame cow with a nasty abscess. I washed the goo off my hands and arms, but didn't have a spare shirt with me. Thanks for giving Taylor a ride home."

"No problem. I needed to go out, anyway, and pick up dog food."

Seth nodded. Although Taylor was likely in her room, wearing her earbuds and bent over her cell phone, he lowered his voice. "How'd she do today?"

"Not bad. I think she enjoyed it."

"Did she and the girl she's doing community service with get along all right?"

"You mean Cat. As far as I could tell, they did fine together."

Seth was relieved. "She sure could use a friend in town."

"On the drive here, she mentioned moving back to San Diego before she graduates high school."

"Did she now?" Given how much she disliked Prosperity, Seth wasn't surprised. "That's not happening," he said. "This is her home now."

"You might want to make sure she understands that."

"Trust me, I tell her all the time. Not that she hears me."

"Maybe if you share your thoughts about fixing up the house after you buy it, or ask her for her input, she'll change her mind. When I was her age, I would've been thrilled to live in a house like this."

"You told her about that?" he asked, frowning.

"You haven't." She looked surprised. "Was it supposed to be a secret?"

"No, I just… I wasn't planning on telling her until I have the money for the down payment."

"In case your plans fall through, you don't want to disappoint her." Emily bit her lip. "Sorry I said anything."

"Don't worry about it. I'll get there. Hell, I probably *should* say something. Wouldn't make much difference, though—she isn't interested in hearing about any plans for a future with me in it." He was about at the end of his rope. "The girl could use some counseling."

"That sounds like a good idea. Have you talked with the school?"

He nodded. "They gave me a couple names, but Taylor won't have anything to do with therapists. She thinks she's fine."

"Gosh, that sounds challenging."

For some reason, knowing Emily sympathized helped. It was good to be able to talk to her about this. "Hardest thing I've ever had to deal with."

They shared a long look, and just like that, electricity charged the air between them. Seth wanted to kiss her as he had the other night, his desire so strong he barely restrained himself.

Even in the dark, he could see Emily's expressive eyes responding with the same heat. She *wanted* him to kiss her.

He almost groaned. With very little effort he could lean in a fraction and do just that.

But Taylor could look through the window at any time, and his shirt was filthy. He straightened. "I'll let you go now."

"Right." Emily shook her head as if to clear it. "Before I leave, you should know that I invited the community-service kids to a pizza brainstorming party for my annual fund-raiser. It will be a week from tomorrow, after school, upstairs in my apartment. I'm not sure exactly what time we'll finish, but not too late."

Seth nodded. "Are parents and guardians invited?"

"The more, the merrier, so if you'd like to come…"

Oh, he wanted to be there, all right. Just him and Emily, with the curtains pulled. That wasn't going to happen, but a guy could fantasize.

"Taylor will be there—that is, if I can convince her to come," he said. "Of course, if I try to do that, she probably *won't* come."

They shared a smile at that.

"She acted as if she wanted to be there," Emily said. "She said she was going to ask you about it."

"That's a good sign. Before she met you, she didn't show interest in anything in Prosperity. All that mattered were her friends in San Diego. Now she's involved with the shelter and might even have a local friend." Seth shook his head in admiration. "You're a miracle worker." A beautiful one, to boot.

Emily laughed self-consciously. "Credit the shelter dogs for any changes you see in Taylor," she said. "Spending time with them… No matter what we do or how many mistakes we make, they love us. With all that trust and love, we can't help but be our best selves."

Seth couldn't have said it better himself, and agreed wholeheartedly. Emily amazed him with her insights.

The more he got to know her, the better he liked her.

"Taylor really likes dogs, Seth," she went on. "I know you want to wait until things settle down, but maybe you should get one now."

"I'll think about it."

Overhead, thunder boomed and a shard of lightning split the sky.

Emily glanced upward, into the blackness. "It's going to pour again." She nodded toward the pickup. "You'd better put your truck away and hurry inside."

"Right." Forgetting that he shouldn't touch her, Seth reached through the window and ran his finger across her cheek. Her responding shiver only ratcheted up his desire for her. He dropped his hand and stepped back. "I'll see you soon. Have a good weekend."

"You, too."

He climbed into the pickup and put up the window, just in time. Furious rain pelted the ground and pounded on the roof of the truck. Instead of pulling into the carport, he turned in his seat and watched Emily back down the driveway.

He didn't look away until her taillights disappeared down the street.

When Emily heard the sound of a honking horn Saturday night, she grabbed her jacket. "I'm going out with Monica and Bridget, and I'll be back in a few hours," she told Susannah. "Behave."

She headed outside, where her two best friends were waiting for her in Bridget's Mini Cooper. They hadn't seen each other in weeks, and on the twenty-minute drive across town, they caught up on each other's lives.

"Have you heard from your parents?" Monica asked as soon as Emily settled into the back seat.

"Since they landed in Madrid, I've had two emails from them," Emily said. "Now that they've recovered from a bad case of jet lag, they're having a great time."

"Bowling on a Saturday night isn't as cool as touring

Europe, but this should be fun," Monica said. "If we're lucky, we just might meet some cute guys."

Petite, perfectly proportioned and outgoing, she had no trouble attracting men.

"You'll probably meet several," Bridget lamented in an envious tone. "You always do, and I hate you for it."

At five feet eight and a half, the strawberry blonde was bigger-boned than Emily, with a pretty face. Although she had a ready laugh and dropped wisecracks like a pro around Emily and Monica, she tended to be more reserved in mixed company, which made meeting men difficult.

"Just because I make friends easily with the opposite sex doesn't mean I've had any luck finding my Mr. Right," Monica lamented. At thirty, she'd already been married and divorced.

None of them had had very good luck with that.

After a glum silence, Bridget straightened her shoulders. "We're not here to moan and groan about our sorry love lives. Tonight is about having a great time. First on the agenda, bowling-alley dinner."

"I've been thinking about the hot dogs and greasy fries all day." Emily licked her lips.

"Don't forget root beer," Monica said. "The high-cal kind. Why not? We'll bowl off the excess calories."

They all laughed.

"So, Emily, how's the new volunteer veterinarian working out?" Monica asked.

Over the phone, Emily had mentioned Seth and Taylor, and how the teen had come to live with him. He kissed like a dream, but she wasn't going to mention that. It wouldn't happen again, so why get them all excited?

"Seth is really good at his job," she said. "I'm going

to build a website for him." She would start that as soon as he returned the questionnaire she'd emailed.

Bridget glanced at her in the rearview mirror. "He's going to pay you?"

Emily shook her head. "This is my way of paying *him* for volunteering at the shelter."

"What about the poor, motherless teenage girl who lives with him?" Monica asked.

"Taylor. Community service only started this past week, and Thursday was her first real day to volunteer. She wasn't exactly Miss Happy Face, but she did okay. Let's hope things work out."

Monica caught them up on her job as an interior designer for commercial businesses, and Bridget shared a story about a customer at the consignment women's clothing store she owned. After that, they lapsed into a comfortable silence. It was a crisp fall night, with a full moon.

"A moon like that puts me in a romantic mood." Bridget sounded wistful. "Too bad there isn't anyone to get romantic with."

"You'll meet someone," Monica said. "And so will I. You, too, Emily." She snorted. "If you're ever ready."

"I will be, but not just yet."

"I wish you'd get over Harvey. He doesn't deserve for you to waste your time pining over him."

"As I keep reminding you, I *am* over him. You know how busy I am. Between the shelter and my web business, it's a wonder I ever get out and have fun."

"Don't use your passion for those dogs or your website business as excuses," Bridget warned. "Otherwise, you just might end up like my aunt Arlene."

The fifty-five-year-old woman, victim of a nasty divorce some fifteen years earlier, had never recovered, and was lonely and unhappy.

Emily wasn't about to let that happen. "I promise," she said. "If I'm still single five years from now, you both have my permission to smack me upside the head."

Bridget turned into the parking lot of the bowling alley. "Look at all these cars," she said. "It's busy tonight."

The bowling alley was crowded and noisy with families, couples and singles like them. There were no available lanes, so they left Emily's name with the woman in charge. While they waited for a lane to open up, they rented shoes. Emily's were scuffed and ill-fitting, but that was part of the bowling experience. Next, they bought dinner, and sat down at a small table to eat.

"What'd I tell you—there are tons of cute guys here without dates," Monica commented as she licked ketchup from a fry.

"So I see." Bridget nodded at a male about their age who was headed for one of the bowling lanes. "Look at the man in the faded jeans and flannel shirt."

"I'm looking," Monica murmured. "What do you think, Em? Is he hot or what?"

He *was* good-looking, but he couldn't compare with a certain volunteer veterinarian. Emily pushed the thought away. "He's not bad."

"Not bad?" Monica gaped at her. "Maybe you need glasses."

No, she just needed to stop fantasizing about Seth Pettit.

"Emily, party of three, lane six is ready for you," a female voice announced over the PA.

After quickly disposing their trash, Emily and her friends headed there.

"You drove tonight, Bridget," Emily said when they'd settled their things on the bench seating. "You're up first."

Bridget's ball rimmed the gutter before glancing against two pins. She made a face. "Pathetic." As soon as the machine returned her ball, she bowled again. When only one pin toppled over, she shrugged good-naturedly. "At least I tried."

Monica went next. She did an odd little twist and released the ball, sending it speeding toward the pins. At the last second, it veered left and cut a neat swath through the left third of them.

"Darn!" She compressed her lips. The second roll toppled three more pins. "Six," she said. "Whoop tee doo."

"Way to swivel your hips, though," Emily said.

They were all laughing when Bridget glanced to the left. Sobering, she leaned in a little and lowered her voice—as if anyone could hear over all the noise. "Don't look now, but that guy in the next lane is checking you out, Monica."

Monica turned her head, catching the man in the act. After a brief hesitation, he waved and gave a slow, confident grin. As soon as she smiled back, he sauntered over.

Bridget elbowed Emily. "What'd I tell you."

"Hello, ladies," the man said. "I'm Bart." He looked at Monica. "And you are?"

"Monica. These are my friends, Bridget and Emily."

Bart nodded, then returned his attention to Monica. "I like the way you bowl. That hip thing is something else."

Monica blushed. "I don't know where I learned that. It's just what I do."

"It's cute, but it cuts down on the effectiveness of the ball. I could teach you how to fix that."

"I'm up," Emily announced, but Monica and Bart were too busy making eyes at each other to pay her any attention.

Emily bowled a spare. Bridget clapped and whooped. "Way to go, Em!"

"When you're hot, you're hot." Laughing, Emily blew on her fingers and rubbed them against her upper chest.

That caught Monica's attention. "I should get back to my friends," she said.

Bart nodded. "Nice meeting you ladies." He pointed at Monica. "I'll talk to you later." He ambled off.

"Just look at him," she murmured. "I love ranchers—all muscle, no fat. He asked for my number." She looked pleased with herself.

"And you obviously gave it to him. I would've, too." Bridget let out a sigh. "I so envy you, and I'm darned tired of being single. You're up again, Monica."

Emily wasn't envious. Liking a guy, wanting him to like her, waiting for him to call, then getting disappointed or hurt... Who needed that?

For a while, she and her friends bowled and laughed and forgot all about men. They were on the last frame and talking about calling it an early night, when Bridget whistled softly. "There goes my idea of the perfect man. Too bad he has a date, because for him, I'd be willing to flirt like Monica."

Emily followed her friend's gaze. To her surprise, she saw Seth Pettit. What was he doing here?

His arm was around an attractive woman who looked vaguely familiar. His head was bent toward her while she animatedly talked. Taylor and another gorgeous man about Seth's age accompanied them. For all Seth's words the other night about having too much on his plate to date, it appeared that he had a girlfriend. That had happened fast—he hadn't lived here that long.

Yet he'd kissed Emily as if he meant business. Then a couple of days ago, when she'd driven Taylor home, he'd looked at her like he wanted to do it again.

Emily wasn't sure what bothered her most—the lie, the kiss, the *I'm interested* heat in his eyes or the fact that her pulse rate bumped up at the sight of him.

Suddenly Seth glanced her way, almost as if he felt her gaze. His eyes widened. He said something to his girlfriend, then flashed Emily a heart-stopping grin and steered the woman toward her.

Refusing to smile at the dirty bum, she crossed her arms over her chest.

Chapter 8

For reasons undetermined, Emily eyed Seth coolly and then dismissed him altogether. She sure wasn't happy to see him.

Puzzled, he took his arm from around his sister. "Hey, there. Didn't expect to run into you."

"Hello, Seth," she replied in a voice as aloof as her expression. "Hi, Taylor."

"Emily!" To Seth's astonishment, Taylor's lips curled into the closest thing to a smile he'd seen since he'd taken custody of her. "What are you doing here?"

"Bowling with a couple of girlfriends—or trying." Her laugh seemed force and excluded him. "None of us is very good. Seth and Taylor, meet Monica and Bridget."

At least her two friends smiled. The short one with the sassy black hair fluttered her eyelashes. He wasn't impressed. Wasn't interested in the tall redhead, either.

Emily was the one he wanted. She was the prettiest woman in the place. Her pale yellow sweater clung softly to her breasts, and dark jeans hugged her sweet behind. Seth wanted to grab hold and pull her close. Not that he would, even if they were alone.

Because right now, she looked as if she'd rather drop a bowling ball on her foot than be standing there, talking to him. He had no clue why she was giving him the cold shoulder.

"Since my brother seems to have forgotten I'm here, I'll introduce myself," his companion said. "I'm Dani, and this is my husband, Nick."

"Ah, you're Seth's sister." Some of the starch went out of Emily's spine. "I thought you were his date."

She'd been jealous. Well, well. Seth liked that a little too much. He fought to hide his grin, then gave himself a mental kick in the butt. As attracted as he was to Emily, he was not going to get involved with her.

"It's nice to meet you both." Emily smiled. "I'm Emily Miles."

"The woman who owns The Wagging Tail," Nick said.

Emily looked surprised. "You've heard of us?"

"On the drive over, Taylor only mentioned it and you half a dozen times."

Taylor blushed furiously and frowned, but Nick gave her a teasing smile that seemed to coax her into relaxing. Seth envied his brother-in-law. Taylor never let him off that easily.

"Have we met?" Dani asked Emily.

Emily frowned. "Not that I know of, but I think I've seen you around."

"Do you ever eat at Big Mama's Café?"

"I used to go a lot, but not since I started the shelter. Did we meet there?"

"You might have," Seth said. "Dani owns Big Mama's."

Clearly proud, she beamed. "Actually, I own it with my mom. She's retired now, but she started the business over forty years ago."

"Your mom is Big Mama?" Emily was impressed.

Dani laughed. "That's right. She used to be my foster mom, and then I got really lucky—she adopted me."

"Lucky is right," Emily said. "My mother's idea of cooking is to open a prepackaged meal and warm it up. Big Mama's a wonderful cook. Those cinnamon rolls…" Just thinking about them, Emily groaned.

Everyone in the group echoed her, which made Dani laugh again. These days, almost everything did. She was that happy.

"She doesn't make those anymore and neither do I, but we have a couple of great chefs."

In the silence that fell, Seth turned to Emily. "I didn't know you were into bowling."

"As you can see from my ratty, rented shoes, I'm not. I freely admit that I really suck at it." She didn't look at all upset about that.

"We're all terrible at bowling," the woman with the reddish hair agreed with a laugh.

Seth couldn't help but smile. "I'm not great, either, but I needed a night out."

He'd been about to bust out of his skin with restlessness, needing to do something on a Saturday night besides paperwork, dealing with Taylor and watching the tube. Having gone too long without sex didn't help, either.

If he'd been alone this evening, he would have

headed for a bar to have a beer and maybe meet a willing woman. Living with a surly teenage girl didn't allow for that. Especially when she had no friends and nothing on her agenda. Staying home had seemed the right thing to do.

"Dani and Nick called tonight and invited Taylor and me along. Taylor said okay, and I figured, why not?" Seth was pleased that she'd wanted to come.

"I had no idea she was a bowler until tonight," he went on. "I'm counting on you to give me some tips," he said to Taylor, and placed his hand on her shoulder.

"I don't bowl anymore," she muttered, moving quickly out of reach.

That stung. Would she never let him give her affection?

Emily's sympathetic gaze took in both him and Taylor. "What made you stop?" she asked.

Taylor hung her head. "It was something I used to do with my mom."

Everyone sobered up at that. Seth's chest hurt for her. "I didn't know," he said.

"Because you didn't ask."

Feeling even worse, he shifted his weight. "Would you rather we leave?"

"We're here now. We may as well stay."

"That's the spirit." Emily gave Taylor a thumbs-up. "I know that wherever your mom is, she's smiling at you right now."

A guilty expression flitted across Taylor's face. What was that about?

"While you're here, be sure to order some fries from the food counter," Emily said. "They're yummy."

"Oh, we will." Dani smacked her lips. "That's one of the reasons I dragged everyone here tonight."

"That's my Dani." Nick put his arm around her and kissed her lightly on the lips. They'd been married two years, and every time Seth saw them they still acted like honeymooners.

"Taylor, did you ask about the fund-raiser pizza party?" Emily asked.

Without so much as a glance Seth's way, she nodded. "I can come."

Emily's face lit in a smile. "That's terrific. Will you be joining us, too, Seth?"

"That depends on Taylor," he said carefully.

"I don't want you there."

"Ouch," he muttered, none too softly.

"But I do." Emily glanced at him. "You know animals so well, and I'm sure you have some great ideas on how to raise money for our shelter."

"I don't know…" Taylor bit her lip.

"Think it over."

Seth appreciated that Emily was letting the kid make up her own mind. If he'd had more of a chance to do that when he was growing up, life would have been easier for everyone.

The announcement came over the loudspeaker. "Pettit, party of four, lane twelve is ready for you."

"Have fun," Emily said.

He nodded. "I emailed that questionnaire back this afternoon. If you want to get together and talk about my website, I have time on Monday."

Her gaze met his, and then skittered away, as if staring into his eyes was dangerous. With so much heat between them, it was definitely dangerous.

"We don't actually need a face-to-face meeting," she said. "I'll look over your answers, and we'll go from there."

"Suit yourself. Good night, ladies."

Emily and her friends headed off.

"So that's the 'famous' Emily Miles," Dani commented as the three women left. "I see why you like her, Taylor. She's pretty cool. Hey, Nick, why don't you and Taylor get the fries. Seth and I will meet you at our lane."

His sister hooked arms with him and they headed off. "There's something between you and Emily," she said, with a canny look.

"Uh, yeah. I'm the volunteer vet at her shelter, and she's letting Taylor do her community service there."

"I mean something more."

"Like what?"

"There's a pretty obvious attraction between you two."

True, but that was none of his sister's business.

"But it's more than that," Dani went on. "You seem to really like each other."

She was enjoying her life, which was great. But she tended to see the world through rose-colored glasses.

"Just because you're happy and in love doesn't mean everyone else should be," Seth said. She opened her mouth, but he cut her off. "Let's bowl."

"When you told us about Seth, you forgot to mention that he's drop-dead gorgeous," Monica said as she, Emily and Bridget exited the bowling alley. "Is he seeing anyone?"

Bridget scrutinized Emily. "From the way he looked at you, I'd guess that he'd like to be seeing *you.* I'll bet if he asked you out, you'd get interested in dating real fast."

Emily *was* interested, and running into Seth tonight

had only confirmed that. Her feelings scared her. She wasn't about to risk getting involved with him. "He is attractive," she hedged. "But he's getting his practice off the ground and has his hands full with Taylor. You saw how she was with him. He doesn't have time for anything else, and neither do I."

Monica scoffed. "If that's what he told you, he's changed his mind. The way he looked at you… Whew." She fanned herself.

Emily knew she was blushing, and felt relieved that the scant light from the parking lot concealed the fact. "I'm riding shotgun," she called out.

"Back to what you said about not having time to date," Monica said, while Bridget eased out of the parking space. "No one can work all the time, not even you. Hanging out with us now and then isn't enough. You need to get a life."

"That's right," Bridget said. "Two words—Aunt Arlene."

Emily rolled her eyes. "FYI, I *do* have a life, and it's pretty full. And there's nothing wrong with spending an occasional evening with my BFFs. Bowling was a hoot, and don't forget our great greasy food fest. In my book, that's good livin'."

"It was fun," Monica agreed. "But I wouldn't mind getting some of my kicks with a sexy man." She blew out a breath. "I don't think it will be with Seth Pettit, though. He's all about you."

"For sure." Bridget glanced at her. "What are you afraid of, Em?"

"I'm not afraid," she insisted. Then sighed. "I guess I am a little wary of getting hurt again. The men I care about tend not to stick around."

"You can't judge all guys based on what Harvey

did," Monica said. "He's a stupid jerk. And anyway, we're talking dating here, not falling in love or getting engaged."

She had a point.

"If Seth asks you out, promise you'll go," she went on.

Bridget pulled up Emily's driveway. "Thanks for the ride," Emily said, reaching for the passenger door.

"Not so fast." Monica poked her. "What about Seth?"

Emily turned around in her seat so that she could see her friend. "He isn't going to ask me out. But if he does, I'll think about it. Okay? I'll talk to you soon."

Chapter 9

Monday morning, Emily sat in her office, nursing her coffee and reading through the questionnaire Seth had answered and emailed back. She'd printed it out, and as she reviewed his comments, it was obvious that he'd given his website some thought and knew what he wanted.

A decisive guy who liked animals and had made a commitment to finish raising a girl he wasn't related to made Seth Pettit a one-of-a-kind man. Who, according to Monica and Bridget, was interested in her. What was Emily supposed to do about that? She didn't want his interest—at least not the rational part of her.

Suddenly, the shelter doorbell rang. Susannah woofed and stood up. It wasn't even eight o'clock yet, and Emily wasn't expecting anyone. The shelter didn't open until nine, but from time to time, people showed up unannounced to discuss adopting a dog, or to drop one off.

Before answering the door, she shut her pet in the office. "I'm not taking any chances of exposing you to a contagious disease," she explained. "I'll be back as soon as I can to let you out."

Wondering what to expect, she opened the door.

To her surprise, Seth stood there.

"Hey," he said, holding up a white bakery box bearing the Big Mama's Café logo.

The unmistakable aroma of cinnamon rolls still warm from the oven made Emily's mouth water. "Cinnamon rolls. Wow." Her stomach gurgled in anticipation. "I've been wanting one of those since Saturday night. How did you know?"

"Because I have, too. We're lucky that even though the restaurant is closed on Mondays, they sell these. Got any coffee?"

"As a matter of fact, I do. Come in."

When Seth entered the room, Susannah woofed from Emily's office.

"I put her in there in case you were someone dropping off a stray," she said. "I'll go and let her out."

"I'll come with." Seth shrugged out of his parka. "We can eat these while we discuss my website."

"You didn't have to drive all the way over here, Seth. I told you the other night, we can easily do this by email or phone."

"If possible, I want to nail down the design today. As busy as we both are, now seems like the perfect time." His eyes sparkling with humor, he held up the bakery box.

She laughed. "Bribing me with cinnamon rolls will get you pretty much anything. It just so happens that I was looking over your answers when you showed up. Let's get our coffee, and then do this."

Emily opened her office door. Woofing happily, Su-sannah hurried to Seth's side and nosed his hand for a rub. He didn't disappoint. He set the box in the center of her desk, where the dog couldn't reach it, and then accompanied Emily to the kitchen. Within minutes, they returned to her office with plates, napkins and steaming mugs.

Seth sat across the desk from her. Emily bit into a cinnamon roll, closed her eyes and moaned in ecstasy.

When she opened them, he was studying her with a hooded look that went straight to her belly. Her nerves began to hum, and for a few moments she forgot all about the bakery treat. Hastily glancing away, she pushed the questionnaire across the desk and asked for clarification on one of his answers. Seth explained, and they moved on to other comments.

"Since you're here, let's check out some of the sites you listed that have features you want," she said.

Seth pulled his chair around next to hers so that they could both see the computer screen. Between his com-ments and her input, she managed to get a clear idea of his vision.

"I have everything I need now," she said when they'd finished. "Over the next few days, I'll put together a prototype and send you a link. You tell me what you like and don't like about it, and I'll make adjustments from there."

"Great."

Instead of moving his chair around the desk again, he left it beside hers, which was a little unnerving. She sat back, distancing herself a little. "Did Taylor enjoy bowling?"

"I couldn't tell." He glanced at her mouth and frowned.

"What?" she said.

"You have something right there." He touched his finger to his own mouth. "It looks like icing from the cinnamon roll."

Emily licked the spot with the tip of her tongue. "Did I get it?"

Seth cleared his throat. "Not quite."

He leaned in and rubbed the spot with his finger. "See?" He held it out to her.

He was so close, she could see the silvery flecks that made his blue eyes so interesting. Make that mesmerizing. She couldn't look away.

Without thinking, she licked his finger clean.

He let out a low, masculine growl. "I know you want more than I can give, and I keep telling myself to stay away from you. But I can't resist you."

What did he mean, she wanted more than he could give? Emily wondered. She would find out later. Right now, there were more important things on the agenda. She leaned in and met him halfway.

Emily tasted of cinnamon rolls, coffee and her own sweet self. Seth lost himself in a kiss that left him hungry for more. Needing to touch her, he ran his hands up her slender back. She was small-boned and delicate, yet also strong, with an eagerness that matched his.

Need hit him hard—emphasis on *hard*. He wanted her.

He skimmed his hands up her sides, to her breasts. She went still and inched back, silently granting him the access he wanted. Her breasts filled his palms, all warm and soft. She moaned right into his mouth.

His body on fire, Seth kissed her again, this time

more deeply. Her tongue tangled restlessly with his. He wanted her naked, wanted inside her.

He was easing her back against the desk when Susannah woofed and the latch to the front door clicked.

Emily jerked away and shot a startled glance at the clock. "It's nine o'clock. That's Mrs. Oakes."

She tugged down her sweater. Tucked her hair behind her ears. But nothing could erase the thoroughly kissed, pink plumpness of her mouth.

Seth swallowed hard. He didn't move. Couldn't. "I'd better not stand up right now," he said, with a wry look at his erection.

"Oh." Emily's eyes widened. "Just scoot your chair back around the desk and try to look busy."

He complied. All business, she stared at the computer screen in studied concentration.

"Morning," Mrs. Oakes called from the front room.

"Good morning," Emily replied.

"Hey, Mrs. Oakes," Seth said.

His voice brought her into the office. "Well, hello," she cooed, a warm smile following her curious expression. "I swear it feels like winter today. But it's nice and warm in here."

Emily blushed. "Seth and I are working on his website. He brought cinnamon rolls from Big Mama's. There's one for you, in the kitchen."

"For me?" Mrs. Oakes beamed. "You're a keeper, Seth Pettit."

He wasn't used to that kind of talk, and it made him uncomfortable. "I'm just a guy with a sweet tooth," he said.

Emily was sweet enough to satisfy his craving for sugar. As if she read his mind, her gaze connected with his and held. Seth wanted badly to kiss her again. With Mrs. Oakes hovering around, it wasn't going to happen.

He slid his chair back. "I'd better go. There's a horse with a rotten tooth waiting for me. But first, I'll check on the dog with mange. I'll let myself into the quarantine hut. Catch you later."

Over the next few days, Emily placed the German shepherd and a golden retriever mix in new homes. She barely had time to let out a breath of relief before a new dog arrived early Thursday morning. He was waiting in quarantine for Seth to examine him.

As soon as Mrs. Oakes returned from lunch, Emily left to pick up dog food and other supplies. Despite the sun, the temperature hovered just above freezing, and when she returned an hour later with her purchases, her hands stung from the cold.

After placing her purse and a case of dog biscuits on Mrs. Oakes's desk, she blew on her fists. "I should've worn gloves. While I bring in the rest of the supplies, would you mind opening this box and setting aside a package of treats for you know who?"

She didn't fool Susannah. Tongue out and tail wagging, she obviously knew exactly what was in the box.

"Will do," Mrs. Oakes said. "You just missed Seth. He seemed sorry that you weren't here."

Emily was both relieved and disappointed. Although she wanted to see him, she needed time to pull herself together. Not so easy, with the constant fantasies she was having. Fantasies that involved the two of them. She could almost feel his hungry mouth on hers again, and his hands on her breasts...

Just the thought made her nipples tighten.

It was bad enough that she wanted him. Worse still,

she liked him. *Really* liked him, way more than was wise.

Mrs. Oakes was giving her a curious look, and she busied herself opening the box she'd just asked the office manager to open. "What did he say about the new dog?"

"First, good news! He checked on the female with mange again. She's almost ready to move into the kennel. He phoned in a couple of prescriptions for the new dog, and left a note on your desk. You're supposed to call with any questions. I hope you'll come up with some. You need to contact that man."

Clearly, the woman wanted Emily and Seth the get together, but for so many reasons, it just wasn't a good idea. "If I have any, I'll ask when he picks up Taylor this afternoon. I'd better bring in the rest of the supplies."

"Need any help?"

"You're not supposed to lift heavy things," Emily reminded her. Mrs. Oakes had problems with her back, and the last thing either of them needed was for her to wind up home in bed while pulled muscles healed. "But feel free to give you know who a you know what."

Emily drove around to the rear of the building. While she shelved the food and stacked new bedding and other supplies, she went back to thinking about Seth, and why what they were doing was dangerous.

If the kisses and more that they'd started continued and escalated, the shelter could be jeopardized. Seth had agreed to stay through the semester, but he could always change his mind. Emily wanted him to stay on indefinitely. She certainly didn't want to push him the other way.

Even riskier, if her feelings for him continued to grow… Scared by the very idea, Emily firmly pushed the thought away. She wouldn't *let* them grow. She didn't have the time for a relationship, and neither did Seth.

Never mind that they both seemed to have the time and interest to fool around.

Remembering the feel of his hands on her breasts while they shared delicious kisses, she went all soft inside. But when he changed his mind and grew tired of her—what then? Because that was what men did, at least the men in Emily's life. One day they loved you, and the next, they were gone.

The smartest and safest thing to do was to stay focused on the reason Seth had come into her life in the first place—to care for the dogs. For the sake of them and the shelter, she wouldn't kiss or be alone with him again.

There was only one little problem. Now that her body was awake, she wanted more. So much more.

No, she told herself. Just *no.* Resolved, she put the last of the supplies away.

Emily was surprised when Taylor and Cat entered the shelter together. This time they'd both dressed for the weather in coats, jeans and boots.

No longer cautious or reticent, they chatted animatedly, and once or twice, Taylor even laughed. Seth would be pleased.

"Lots of news," Emily told them. "The two dogs you girls walked last week have both found permanent homes. We took in a new male this morning, and Seth has already been here to check him out. He seems to be in reasonably good shape. And the dog with mange is almost ready to move into the kennel."

As soon as Taylor heard Seth's name, she grimaced. Why did she dislike him so much? Emily wanted to ask, but not in front of Cat or Mrs. Oakes. "Today I'd like you to walk two other dogs," she said. "Then Taylor, you'll input the data about the new arrival into our computer database, and Cat, you'll launder the new towels and blankets I bought today."

Several hours later, while the girls waited for their rides home, Emily reminded them about the fund-raiser party. "See you tomorrow night, right?" she asked.

Both girls nodded.

"Is everyone from community service going?" Cat asked.

"Matt and Shayna have that football game and can only come for a little while, but everyone else will be staying until the meeting ends. Seven adult volunteers will also be here."

"My parents are coming with me," Cat said. "Are you bringing Seth, Taylor? He sounds cool and I want to meet him."

What would Taylor say? Emily didn't move a muscle.

"He's coming, but only because Emily invited him," the girl said.

Cat grinned. "Epic." Current slang for *really cool*. "Taylor, have you seen the dog getting a bath on Vine?"

"No. Show it to me."

Cat fiddled with her phone, then beckoned Emily over. "You should see this, too—it's hilarious."

Watching two teenage boys wrestle with a reluctant animal and get drenched, Emily laughed as heartily as the girls.

Cat was putting her phone away when a car horn beeped. She peered out the window. "There's my mom. See you tomorrow night. I'll text you, Taylor."

"It's great that you and Cat are getting along so well," Emily said as the door closed behind her.

"We have to work together, so we may as well." Taylor shrugged, as if making a friend was no big deal. "Seth just pulled up. Bye."

As she exited the building, her whole demeanor changed. Her shoulders slumped and her footsteps got heavier.

Emily had the feeling the downcast manner was for Seth's benefit. Could it be that she wanted him to think she was more unhappy than she actually was?

Chapter 10

"You don't have to come tonight," Taylor said, as Seth pulled the truck into the small parking area of The Wagging Tail. Not counting Emily's car, there were close to a dozen vehicles already there. "I mean, if you'd rather go out or something."

Seth shook his head. "I told Emily I'd be here. I'm looking forward to this."

Not the meeting—seeing Emily. They'd exchanged emails about his website, but he hadn't talked to or laid eyes on her since Monday morning. It almost felt as if she was avoiding him. Nah. She was as busy as he was—that was all.

"Why are you *really* here?" Taylor asked, giving him her tough-girl look.

If they hadn't spent over a month under the same roof, he would have missed the vulnerability buried under her hard expression. "What are you getting at?" he said.

"You're spying on me, and I don't like it."

Now he was confused. Did she really think he was here to watch her every move? He snorted. "I have no reason to spy on you, Taylor, not tonight or ever. You're a good kid."

"If you think I believe you…"

He'd barely set the parking brake before she jumped out of the pickup, her coltish legs eating up the space between the truck and the front door.

Teenage girls. He'd never understand them.

When he entered the office, Mrs. Oakes was collecting her purse and shrugging into her coat. "Now that you're here, I can lock up and go home," she said.

"You waited for us?" Seth asked.

She nodded. "You're the last ones."

Taylor glared at him. "We're late because of you."

"Would you rather I left a calf with a barbwire gash on her back to fend for herself?"

"No, but… Forget it."

Mrs. Oakes gave Seth a sympathetic look. "Will the calf be all right?"

"Now that I cleaned her up and treated her, she will."

"That's good. The stairs to Emily's apartment are behind the kitchen. There's a big group up there. Have fun, and both of you have a good weekend."

"You, too, Mrs. Oakes." Taylor smiled at the woman before she headed for the stairs.

At least she was civil to other people.

She didn't utter another word to him. Emily's apartment door was open a fraction and voices filled the air.

As if Seth were invisible, Taylor walked in ahead of him.

The small living room was crowded with teens and a dozen or so adults, and smelled like fresh-baked pizza that made his mouth water. On one side of the room, several large pies filled a table.

Emily's hair was loose and wavy, and she was dressed in flowing, silky-looking pants and a matching top that was both feminine and sexy.

"You made it."

Her smile encompassed both of them and transformed her from pretty to beautiful. Seth didn't hide his appreciation. Flushing, she glanced away.

"Put your coats in the bedroom down the hall, then make yourself a name tag and help yourself to pizza and pop."

Before Seth had shrugged out of his jacket, Taylor tossed him hers and again separated from him.

He gave Emily a what-can-you-do look.

"We need to talk later," she said, in a voice for his ears only.

Wondering what she wanted to talk about, he headed for the bedroom. Her apartment was old and small, but she'd made it homey with colorful throw rugs and interesting dog photos on the hallway wall.

He added his and Taylor's coats to the pile on the bed. The room was barely big enough for the queen-size bed. Seth couldn't help but imagine the two of them, lying there together...

"Excuse me, everyone," Emily said over the noise.

He quickly rejoined the group, stopping to print his name on a name tag and slap it on his chest.

"Help yourselves to pizza and something to drink, and please introduce yourselves to each other. My student volunteers have all met, but the adults don't know you and some don't know each other. Let me quickly introduce my adult volunteers to all of you. Over there are Caroline, Janice, Patty and Lester, the angels who bring the dogs to the shelter, walk them in the morning and do whatever else is needed. Barb and Irene are great at stepping in whenever they can. Last but definitely not least, Seth Pettit, the tall man heading toward the pizza table, is our amazing volunteer veterinarian."

People looked at him and murmured in appreciation. Uncomfortable being singled out, Seth gave a modest nod.

Before he made it to the pizza, a teenage girl with heavily made-up eyes, a friendly smile and artsy-looking clothes, waylaid him, Taylor reluctantly following.

"I'm Cat, Taylor's friend," she said. "Thanks for taking care of the shelter dogs."

He smiled. "Any friend of Taylor's is a friend of mine. Nice to meet you."

With a mortified expression, Taylor pulled on her friend's arm. "Let's find a place to sit."

As they moved away, Seth took his place at the end of the line. As soon as he helped himself to pizza, he looked for a place to sit. Emily had set out folding chairs, but the kids had ignored them in favor of the floor.

Sitting cross-legged against the wall, Taylor and Cat were carrying on an animated conversation. He'd never seen Taylor without the sullen look. She chattered away, punctuating the conversation with smiles, just as the nine-year-old girl he remembered once had. She'd finally made a friend. Relieved, he grinned to himself. Maybe now she'd accept that Prosperity was her home.

He found a seat beside several parents, most of whom looked to be around his age.

He introduced himself all around and was pleased to learn that the couple beside him were Cat's parents.

"I met Cat earlier," he said. "She and Taylor have become friends. She seems warm and outgoing."

Her father laughed. "Unless she's in one of her moods."

Seth shook his head. "I know exactly what you mean."

"I understand you and Taylor are from San Diego," Cat's mother said.

Seth was surprised that she knew about that. Taylor must have told Cat. "Taylor is," he corrected. "I'm from Sacramento, but I was born here in Prosperity."

"You and Taylor are from different cities?" Cat's father looked confused.

This wasn't the time or place to get into that. "It's a long story I don't want to get into right now," Seth said.

Suddenly Susannah bounded into the room with her odd gait. Emily snapped her fingers, and the whippet moved to her side. A moment later she trotted over and greeted Seth with a wagging tail and a pleading look.

"Hey, girl," he said, patting her. "I didn't bring any dog biscuits with me tonight." Undaunted, the animal trotted off in search of a snack from someone else.

Emily moved to the front of the room, near an easel that had been set up. "That's Susannah, and she's looking for food," she said over the noise. "Don't give her any."

Matt and Shayna exchanged *uh-oh* looks. "Um, we just did," Shayna said.

Emily didn't seem too upset. "It's not your fault. When she looks at you with those big brown eyes, she's pretty hard to resist."

Low chuckles filled the room.

"Matt and Shayna have a football game tonight and will be leaving soon, so we should start our meeting," Emily said. "Every year I host a fund-raiser so that The Wagging Tail can continue operating. When I first started accepting high school kids for community service three years ago, I realized what a valuable resource you all are. During our brainstorming session tonight I'm calling on your creativity." She paused to smile.

"All right, let's get started. Who has ideas for this year's fund-raiser?" Several hands went up. "You don't have to raise your hands," she said. "Just call out your ideas."

"Sell candy," Jessie said.

Emily wrote it down. "What else?"

Kids and adults began to call out suggestions.

"Sell magazine subscriptions."

"Write a story about The Wagging Tail, put it in the school paper and ask for donations."

"Hold a silent auction."

"Have a car wash."

"Host a bake sale."

The ideas had petered out when Matt and Shayna stood to leave, along with Matt's mother. *"Sorry,"* the woman mouthed.

"No problem. I'm glad you made it." Emily smiled at the teens. "See you two next week. I'll let you know what we decided then."

Twenty minutes later, the group had pared down the list of ideas to a silent auction, stories in the high school paper from the schools represented—articles to be vetted by Emily before submission—and asking a reporter to write an article for the *Prosperity Daily News*.

"Now we need to find companies willing to donate

to the silent auction," Emily said. "Who wants to solicit our local businesses?"

Every kid volunteered for that job. They discussed where to go for donations, and divided up various business areas. Taylor and Cat asked for a section of downtown.

When the meeting ended, Seth was surprised that several hours had passed.

Wondering what Emily wanted to talk to him about, he hung around until only he and Taylor remained.

"Let's go," she said.

"First I need to talk to Emily."

"About what?"

He raised his eyebrows at Emily. "You heard the girl."

She fiddled with her hoop earring. "We don't have to talk tonight," she said. "It can wait."

Too curious for that, Seth shook his head. "Let's do it now."

Emily glanced at Taylor. "Do you mind waiting a little longer to leave?"

"Whatever." She pulled her phone from her pocket. "I'll be in the office."

As her footsteps echoed down the steps, Seth turned to Emily.

With everyone but Seth gone, Emily's living room should have felt bigger. But he somehow made it seem even smaller. For some reason, standing there in her apartment and explaining that the kissing had to stop seemed dangerous. Plus, after a long day and busy evening, she was tired.

"I enjoyed tonight," Seth said, his eyes warm. "You're a natural at conducting a meeting."

"Thanks, but what really matters is how much money the fund-raiser brings in."

"How much are you looking to raise?"

She gave him a number. "That's what we need to keep the clinic running for another year. And it would be nice to be able to pay you and some of our other volunteers something."

"You know I could use the money," Seth said. "But watching Taylor laugh and enjoy herself—that's the best payment of all. I hardly recognized her."

"Credit her friendship with Cat for that. They seem to really like each other."

"But without you, they wouldn't have met." He glanced at the overflowing wastebasket and cluttered table. "I'll give you a hand with this stuff."

If only he wouldn't look at her with those heated eyes... He made her want things she shouldn't, dangerous things that could put the shelter at risk and leave her with a broken heart.

"Emily?" Seth gave her a funny look. "I said, where do you want me to put the trash?"

"There's a bin behind the building. I'll take it out later. You already gave up a big chunk of your evening and you offered a free animal exam for the silent auction," she said. "That's enough. Besides, Taylor is waiting downstairs."

"She won't mind. She's probably texting or talking to someone on FaceTime. I'll take the trash down when I leave." He started flattening the folding chairs she'd set up. "Let me put these away. Then you can tell me what you wanted to talk about."

The man wouldn't quit. All right, then they would talk tonight. Emily collapsed two of the folding chairs and hefted them. "The utility closet is off the kitchen. This way."

She led him down the hall, past at least a dozen framed photos of dogs and their new human families.

"You have pictures like these in the other hallway, too," Seth said. "They're nice."

"Every one features a dog from the shelter. After they're adopted, I snap a photo so that I can remember them." Emily opened the accordion door hiding the washer and dryer. "In here."

When they returned to the living room, Seth eyed her expectantly. It was time for that talk. She gestured for him to sit on the couch, and plunked down on the coffee table across from him.

Their knees were almost touching, which was distracting. She slid the table back a little and, suddenly nervous, brushed an imaginary thread from her sleeve. "The other morning, you said something about me wanting more than you can give. What did you mean?"

"Is that what you wanted to talk about? I meant that you're not a casual relationship kind of woman, but I don't have time for anything else. I hardly even have time for that."

He was right—she wasn't into casual flings. On the other hand, assuming she might want something serious when she didn't... Determined to set him straight, Emily folded her arms. "I don't happen to want a serious relationship just now." She pushed an image of Bridget's aunt Arlene, with her pinched expression, from her mind. "Relationships take a lot of time and work, and there are too many other things to worry about."

"Exactly." Seth blew out a breath that sounded like relief. "Good to know we're on the same page."

"Along those lines, I don't think we should be kissing each other," Emily added.

"Probably not. But when I'm with you, I don't always think straight."

He glanced at her lips, sending a rush of longing through her. "I'm the same way," she admitted. "When I'm around you, I…" How to explain? She swallowed. "I've never experienced this…this *feeling* with any other man."

"It's called animal magnetism, and we sure have it." At the moment, his eyes were more silver than blue, and bright with desire. "It doesn't help that you have the sexiest mouth on the planet."

She did?

"When I see you, I want to touch those lips." He leaned forward and ran this thumb across her bottom one.

Her mouth automatically opened a fraction, and he made a pleased sound. "You're such a responsive woman. I want to taste you, claim you."

That intimate, low voice… Every nerve in her body shivered with longing.

Then footsteps sounded on the stairs.

"That's Taylor," Seth muttered, dropping his hand.

Emily's eyes opened—they'd drifted shut without her realizing it. She jumped up and smoothed her silk tunic. "This is why we shouldn't be alone together anymore."

"It's probably safer that way." Seth gave her one last hungry look then grabbed two bulging plastic trash bags.

Taylor entered the room, her eyes narrowing. Did she suspect that Emily had been about to go up in flames?

"What's taking so long?" she asked.

"We were cleaning up and talking about the fund-raiser," Seth replied, as if nothing was amiss. "How about giving me a hand with these?"

Downstairs, Emily waited for them to dispose of the trash and leave so that she could lock up. "Good night, and thank you both for coming and for helping me clean up," she said.

She didn't relax until she turned the dead bolt and heard Seth's truck purr down the driveway.

Chapter 11

Late afternoon on the first Sunday in October, Seth headed with Taylor to Sly and Lana's. Normally, his brother and sister-in-law had Sunday dinner at Lana's parents' house, but not tonight. As usual, Taylor had her earbuds in, leaving Seth to his own thoughts.

At the moment, they centered on his brother. They hadn't seen each other or spoken since Seth had delivered the twin calves a couple weeks earlier. But Seth thought about him often, wondering how to close the huge cavern that separated them, or if that was even possible.

Take tonight's invitation, which had come from Lana, not Sly. At first, Seth had been reluctant to accept. Who needed another uncomfortable evening? But Dani and Nick were also coming, with big news of some kind. Whatever it was, Dani wanted Seth to hear it from her. He'd missed so much family stuff, he figured he'd better show up.

Over the last few hours, the temperature had dropped to below freezing, and clouds had gathered in the darkening sky.

Taylor hugged herself and pulled her long legs under her. Despite her winter parka, she looked cold. And yet she didn't so much as touch the truck's heat controls. When she wasn't giving him dirty, sullen looks, she seemed overly timid, almost as if she was afraid that she might somehow disappoint him.

The huge contrast confused and really bothered him. It was weird, too. His only disappointment was her continued dislike of him and everything he did and said. Although, since the meeting at Emily's last Friday, she'd become somewhat more talkative.

Seth wondered what she'd think if she knew that he lusted over Emily. Since their talk, they'd made a point of never being in the same place without someone else present, but that didn't curb his desire for her. Not being able to touch or kiss her only made his hunger stronger, to the point that he fantasized about her all the time. He needed a woman and soon, or he just might explode.

"Feel free to crank up the heat," he said, raising his voice so that she'd hear him over whatever she was listening to.

She pulled off the earbuds, fussed with the temperature and directed the heat vents on the passenger side toward her feet. "It's cold."

"Trust me, soon it'll be a lot colder," he said.

"That's what Emily said. When Cat and I were texting earlier, she said it could snow tonight. I didn't think that happened until November."

"In central Montana, you never know. Once, when I was a kid, we got a foot of the stuff in September."

"Epic."

"You aren't kidding." He made a mental note to pick up a sled.

Taylor pulled off her earbuds. "Can I go to Cat's for an overnight?"

Pleased that the girl had invited her over, Seth readily agreed. "If you want to. When are you thinking?"

"Friday night."

"Sure. I'll drive you over."

The ranch was just ahead. He signaled and slowed, then turned at the Pettit Ranch sign. The pickup trundled up the long gravel driveway to the house. He didn't see Dani and Nick's truck, or Sly's, for that matter.

By the time he parked and climbed out, Taylor was on her way to the front door.

Lana opened it. Johanna, who was almost four, ran to greet her. Mark, age fourteen months, toddled forward. Taylor gave them both hugs. She was good with them.

"Hi, you two," Lana said. She kissed Seth's cheek and then hugged Taylor.

"Hey, Lana." Taylor accepted the hug and returned it.

Seth wished he could hug her like that. At least she was nicer to him than she had been.

She went off to play with Johanna, Mark squealing and toddling after them.

Seth handed Lana the flowers he'd picked up at the grocery store. "These are for you."

"Aww, thanks. Come into the kitchen while I find a vase. Dani called," Lana said as he accompanied her down a wide hall to their big, homey kitchen. "She and Nick are running late. Sly's out picking up dessert, so it's just us. How about a beer?"

"Thanks." Seth slid onto a chair at the breakfast bar. "Need any help with dinner?"

She shook her head. "There's nothing left to do but toss the salad. Taylor seems a lot more comfortable than she did the last time she was here."

"She's doing better. Community service at the dog shelter has helped. She made a friend there. She'll be staying at her house Friday night."

A night to himself. Seth hadn't fully digested that yet. He figured he'd go to a bar and look around for a woman, someone to take his mind off Emily. *Yeah, buddy. Good luck with that.*

Before long, Dani, Nick and Sly arrived.

"Look who we ran into as we pulled up the drive," Dani said. She kissed Lana's cheek and gave Seth a sisterly hug and kiss. "Our big brother bought *two* apple pies and a gallon of ice cream for tonight."

Her eyes seemed to sparkle with excitement, making Seth wonder about her and Nick's news.

Seth and Nick warmly clapped each other's shoulders. But Sly merely nodded at Seth, as if they were acquaintances instead of brothers.

That stung, but what had he expected? Not about to let on, Seth acted as if all was well. "How are those twin calves doing?" he asked.

"So far, so good."

The conversation ended there. To Seth's relief, Lana called the kids and summoned Taylor and the adults to bring the food to the table.

Everyone sat, but before they could dish up, Dani gestured for them to wait. "Nick and I have an announcement to make." Smiling at each other, the couple clasped hands before she went on. "We're expecting."

"No kidding! That's fabulous!" Lana said.

Sly whooped. "About time."

Happy for his little sister and her husband, and pleased to be in on the family's good news, Seth grinned. "Congratulations."

Even Taylor smiled. "Is it a boy or a girl?" she asked.

"It's too early to tell," Nick said.

"Why are you all so happy?" Johanna asked.

"Because you're going to have a new baby cousin," Dani said.

The little girl seemed pleased. "I want to meet my cousin right now!"

"You can't until— When is your due date?" Lana asked.

"Early March." Dani beamed.

"In the spring," Lana told her daughter.

"Now that I'm pregnant, I'm always hungry." Dani looked at the food and rubbed her hands together.

Seth and Sly both chuckled.

Dinner was a noisy, happy affair. Seth found himself enjoying the chaos. He liked being here, and questioned why he'd left home all those years ago.

Because he'd been hotheaded and angry with Sly for trying to run his life. Trying to act like their dad when they both knew that he was dead.

What if Taylor felt the same way about him? *Hell.* The insight stunned him, but didn't change the fact that she needed his supervision. At the very least until she turned eighteen. Three whole years away. If things kept going the way they were now, by then he'd probably have aged fifty years.

"I hear you're doing your community service at The Wagging Tail," Lana said to Taylor. "Do you like it?"

"It's a pretty cool place. Emily takes in dogs that

have been abandoned. Some have been abused, too. She finds homes for them."

"You volunteer there as the vet, right?" Lana asked Seth.

"That's right, and I agree with Taylor—it's a great place." Thanks to Emily.

"On the first Saturday in November, we're doing a fund-raiser to raise money for the shelter," Taylor went on.

Seth noted the "we," which made it sound as if she were a real part of The Wagging Tail. Emily's doing again. She was something else, and he was beyond grateful to her.

"Sly and I will contribute to that," Lana said.

Sly nodded. "Just tell us where to send the check."

"You can do that," Seth said. "You can also contribute to the silent auction. Do you have anything to donate?"

"I do," Dani said. "One dozen Big Mama cinnamon rolls."

The last time Seth had enjoyed a cinnamon roll had been with Emily, followed by a red-hot kiss. Damn, he wished he'd stop thinking about that.

"I'll donate one week of free day care," Lana offered.

"What can I do?" Nick said. "I don't picture people bidding on touring Kelly Ranch."

Lana and Dani exchanged looks. "That's not a bad idea," Lana said. "I'll bet plenty of people in town would like to experience a day in the life of a rancher."

Dani nodded. "A mini dude ranch experience. Nick, you and Sly could both offer that."

The two men glanced at each other and shrugged. "Why not?" Nick said.

Taylor smiled. "Epic. Emily's going to like all those things."

"Seth mentioned a girl you've made friends with at the shelter," Lana said. "Tell us about her."

After shooting Seth a *how dare you talk about me behind my back* frown, Taylor answered. "Her name is Cat. She's adopted, and she goes to Jupiter High. I'm going to her house Friday night for a sleepover."

She said it as if it were no big deal, but Seth knew how important that night was to her.

"What happens if Emily can't find a home for one of her dogs?" Nick asked.

Taylor frowned. "I don't know. That hasn't happened since I've been there."

"If it happens, it's rare," Seth said. "She's pretty good at placing the animals."

Sly and Lana glanced at each other, and he gave a subtle nod. "Lately we've been talking about getting a dog," she said.

"Can we, Mommy? Really, Daddy?" The little girl began to bounce in her seat and clap her hands. Squealing, Mark joined in.

"You should call Emily right away," Taylor said. "She'll have to come over and check you out, but I'm sure she'll like you. I'll put in a good word for you when I see her on Thursday."

"Sly, aren't you and Nick looking for a fourth to round out your poker table on Friday night?" Lana said. "I'll bet Seth plays."

Sly glanced at Seth, his face unreadable. "You interested?"

So much for heading to a bar Friday night. Seth nodded. "Sure am."

"The game is at Tim Carpenter's ranch, which is adjacent to ours. You can pick me up."

"Tim is my cousin," Lana said. "He and Sly have been playing poker since before we got married."

Sly nodded. "We play for money. Bring a wad of it."

"Will do," Seth said, knowing his brother was too careful with his money to squander much in a poker game. Seth couldn't afford to gamble more than a few dollars, and probably shouldn't even risk that, but he was damned if he'd miss a chance to hang out with his big brother. "I'll bring an empty bag, too, to haul my winnings home."

When Seth and Taylor left an hour later, he was in a great mood. His sister was expecting and the meal together had been less tense than he'd figured.

All in all, it had been a pretty good evening.

Emily stood at the picture window in the front office, watching fat snowflakes fall to the ground. "Look at that snow come down."

Taylor and Cat crowded in beside her. It had been a rare slow Thursday, so quiet that Mrs. Oakes had left early, and Emily had caught up on a pile of shelter paperwork and finished Seth's website. The girls had walked the dogs and worked on the fund-raiser, finishing with time to spare. Now they were waiting for their rides home.

"As fast and furious as it's falling, I can't believe the forecast is for only an inch or so," Emily said. "It's supposed to melt quickly, too. When the flakes are big like that, it means the temperature is mild."

Taylor's face was pressed to the window, like a young child's. "It was supposed to snow last Sunday, only it didn't. I've never seen actual snow before. It's beautiful."

"Yeah," Cat agreed. "But after awhile, we get pretty tired of it. Just wait. Hey, if it doesn't melt, maybe we can go sledding or ice skating when you come over tomorrow."

Taylor looked wistful. "I only know how to roller skate. Plus, I don't have any ice skates."

"No worries—I'll teach you," Cat said. "You can borrow my mom's skates. She won't mind."

"So you two are hanging out tomorrow?" Emily commented, pleased that Taylor and Cat's friendship had expanded beyond the shelter or shelter-related activities.

Taylor nodded. "We're having a sleepover."

"We're going to eat pizza and watch movies and stuff," Cat said.

"Great. If you know how to roller skate, Taylor, you should pick up ice skating fairly easily. It's a lot of fun, and so is playing in the snow."

Wanting to take advantage of Taylor's uncharacteristic excitement, Emily hatched an idea. "We still have ten minutes before your rides will be here. Let's go outside and show Taylor what snow is all about. You can come, too, Susannah."

She reached for the dog's sweater and leash, both of which she kept on a hook near the door. With a joyous *woof*, the whippet limp-raced toward her.

After snapping on Susannah's sweater, Emily donned a coat and gloves and her wool hat. The girls did the same, and they headed out.

For a while, Taylor, Cat and Susannah raced around the yard. The dog barked and the girls stuck out their tongues, tasting the snow and laughing. Emily had never heard Taylor laugh before. It was a nice sound. Before long, Cat's mother arrived to pick her up.

"Bye, Emily," Cat called out. "See you tomorrow, Taylor. I'll text you later."

"Okay." Taylor waved.

The snowfall began to taper off. "Do you want to stay out for a while longer?" Emily asked.

"Yeah. This is fun."

"Playing in the snow never gets old. I'm sure I've been doing it since I was a toddler, but my very first memory goes back to when I must've been about three or four. My dad and I built a snowman. I remember that it seemed to take forever to roll the snowballs for the body and head. When we finished, the thing looked huge to me." The good memory of her father was one of a handful she cherished.

"Were you afraid of it?"

Emily laughed. "I don't think so. My dad held me up and helped me press in the rocks I picked for her eyes. Yes, our snowman was actually a snow girl."

Taylor kicked the ground, sending up a cloud of powdery snow. "I never knew my dad."

"Mine left when I was nine. That's almost worse than never knowing who he was."

"I was the same age when Seth walked out on my mom and me."

According to what Seth had told Emily, he hadn't walked out on Taylor. He'd wanted to maintain contact. She barely suppressed her surprise. "Are you sure about that?" she asked.

The girl rolled her eyes. "I was *there*. One morning I went to school. When I came home, he was gone. My mom was so upset that we moved away. He had her cell number, but he never called to say he missed me or that he was sorry, not even once."

"I don't understand," Emily asked. "Why did he leave?"

"Because he didn't want a kid."

Emily frowned. "Did your mom tell you that?"

"She didn't have to."

"You should talk to Seth and see what he has to say about it."

"What for? He'll only lie."

"He doesn't lie." Of that, Emily was sure. "Why would you think that, Taylor?"

"I don't want to talk about him anymore," the girl replied with a stony look. "Hey, is it true that no two snowflakes are alike?"

If she wasn't interested in sharing her thoughts, so be it. But Seth should know about this. Emily doubted Taylor would fill him in, so she would. Taylor wouldn't like it, but the poor man was tearing his hair out, trying to help her adjust to her new life. He needed all the insights he could get.

"That's what I've always heard," she said. "So many snowflakes, each of them unique. It boggles the mind."

Taylor squinted at the flakes gathering on her jacket sleeve. "So far, none of them look the same."

Emily checked her own coat sleeve. "Not a one. They're so pretty and lacy."

"Yeah." Taylor gaped in shock at something on her forearm. Suddenly her face crumpled, as if she was in pain.

Alarmed, Emily hurried to her side. "What's wrong?"

The girl pointed at a snowflake. "This is exactly like the design of the necklace I gave my mom for Christmas last year."

"It's beautiful," Emily said. "She must have loved it."

"She wore it a lot. I gave it to the undertaker and he put it on her in her casket." Taylor bit her lip. "What do you think it means?"

For a moment, Emily considered the question. "I'll bet it's a message from her. She's telling you she's okay and that she loves you."

Taylor's eyes filled, and Emily's heart ached for her. "You miss her, huh?" she said softly.

The girl bit her lip and nodded. Then she wiped her eyes. "I'm cold. I want to go in now."

Inside, Emily removed her outerwear, and hung it up. "You look like you could use a hug."

Looking as if she was barely holding herself together, Taylor held up her hands, keeping Emily at bay. She was still grieving terribly for her mother. Emily mentally added that to the things to share with Seth.

She wanted to talk more, but the phone rang. "I'd better answer that," she said with an apologetic smile.

Taylor barely nodded. Still wearing her coat and hat, she faced the window and stared out into the dusk.

Ten minutes later, Emily disconnected and joined her at the window. "That was Lana. She said that after hearing your rave reviews about The Wagging Tail, she and Sly are interested in adopting a dog."

Taylor brightened a little. "She said she was going to call. She and Sly are nice. So are their kids, Johanna and Mark."

"I guessed that from talking with her. I'm going to their ranch early next week, to meet them and review what's involved in adopting a dog from our shelter. Thanks for telling them about us."

"Sure."

Seth's truck pulled to a stop out front, the headlights shining through the window.

"There's Seth," Taylor said.

She looked sad again. Emily wanted to hug her, but the girl didn't want that. "Remember—your mom is always with you," she said.

Without meeting her eyes, Taylor nodded, then turned and slipped out the door.

The girl's grief stayed with Emily, and throughout the next day, she thought about her often. She didn't get a chance to call Seth until late Friday afternoon. When he didn't answer, she left a message. "It's Emily. I'm calling about Taylor. When you have a minute, give me a buzz."

In a break during the poker game Friday night, Seth checked his cell phone for messages. Taylor might call, or some rancher with an emergency. To his relief, there was only one message—from Emily. Either a new dog had come in or one of the others was sick.

"Excuse me," he said, stepping into the hallway.

Frowning, he listened to the message. Why did she need to talk about Taylor? She'd seemed fine when he'd dropped her off at Cat's a few hours ago. It must not be too important or she'd have contacted him before now. And yet something was important enough that she'd called. Deep in thought, he returned to Tim Carpenter's living room.

"Everything okay?" Nick asked as Seth took his place at the card table.

"Emily left a message. She needs to talk to me about Taylor."

"You worried?" Sly asked.

"A little, but Taylor's at Cat's tonight." Seth pushed

his concerns away. "I'll touch base with Emily tomorrow. I'm here to win back the money I've lost, and then take you three for more. Whose turn is it to deal?"

"Mine," Carpenter said. Roughly a decade older than Seth, he had a gruff manner, but seemed like a decent enough guy.

"Speaking of Emily," Sly said, while Carpenter shuffled the deck. "She's coming over next week to meet us and talk about a dog. The process seems almost as complicated as adopting a kid."

Sly ought to know—he and Lana had adopted their son.

"Emily doesn't let just anyone adopt a shelter dog. She makes sure she places them in good homes." Seth picked up his card. Pleased to see a pair of kings, he pushed two blue chips to the center of the table.

Carpenter tossed in two more. "I'll raise you."

"I wouldn't if I were you," Sly said.

The two men seemed tight. Seth envied Carpenter for that. He wished he knew how to get tight with his brother again.

For now at least, the tension between them had faded, overrun by the competitive nature of the game.

Around nine, the game broke up, as the other three poker players were ranchers and needed to be up early.

Seth had enjoyed himself as he hadn't in a long time. Joking and bluffing had taken his mind off Taylor, the slower than anticipated growth of his business, his shrinking savings and Emily. He'd eaten a ton of nuts, jerky and chips with dip, had smoked a cigar and drunk a couple beers. Best of all, he'd come out even, winning as much money as he'd lost.

He wasn't supposed to pick up Taylor until late tomorrow morning. Barring emergencies, he planned to sleep in, a luxury he rarely had time for.

He walked out with Nick and Sly, and then drove Sly back to Pettit Ranch. In the darkness, the thin coating of snow covering the fields glinted under his headlights. The highway was clear but slippery, and he drove with care.

"Any time you need a fourth, I'm available," he told Sly.

"I'll keep that in mind."

"Tim Carpenter's an interesting character."

"A bit rough around the edges, but not a bad guy." Sly yawned.

"Tired?" Seth asked as he pulled up Sly and Lana's driveway.

"Dead on my feet."

Seth pulled to a stop near the front porch. Sly opened his door and then glanced over his shoulder at him. "Good night, little brother."

He hadn't called Seth "little brother" since before Seth had left town. Hearing it felt good, and he grinned. "Night, Sly."

Traffic on the highway was light. It was still relatively early—plenty of time to head for a nearby bar and check out the women. But he wasn't in the mood. Besides, it had been a long week and he was tired. Ready to call it a night, he turned toward home.

Seconds later, he snorted. "Thirty-five years old, and too old for a wild night out—that's pitiful."

Surprising himself a few minutes later, he changed his mind about going home, and headed for Emily's instead.

Chapter 12

The lights were on in Emily's apartment, and Seth thought he heard Susannah barking up there. It took her a while to answer the front door.

"Seth." Twin lines formed between her brows. "What are you doing here?"

Why *was* he here? Seth rubbed the back of his neck. "I was passing by and figured this was a good time to talk about Taylor—if you let me in."

After hesitating, she opened the door wider and stepped back. Once inside, he noted her loose, faded sweatshirt, raggedy jeans and fuzzy slippers. Her hair was pulled into a knot on top of her head with a plastic clip, and loose strands floated around her face. She looked sexy—go figure.

"Uh, were you in bed?" he asked, imagining her there, naked under him.

"In these clothes?" She laughed. "I was cleaning my apartment."

"On a Friday night?"

"I know, I'm pathetic." The fine lines returned and deepened, and she crossed her arms. "I thought we made an agreement not to be alone together."

"Right, but you wanted to tell me about Taylor, and since I was out, I figured I may as well hear it in person." Her closed body language and slightly compressed lips let him know what she thought of that idea. He shouldn't have come. He reached for the door. "Never mind—I'll call you tomorrow instead."

"You drove all the way over here, and you're obviously concerned about Taylor. You may as well stay. But I won't invite you upstairs, and let's keep our distance from each other."

"Agreed."

She sat down at Mrs. Oakes's desk. Seth took the couch across the room. "This far enough away?" he teased.

Her lips didn't so much as twitch.

"Where's Susannah?" he asked, crossing his foot over his knee.

"In the apartment." Emily pulled the clip from her hair and twisted it into a new knot. Not about to be corralled, the loose strands quickly fluttered free.

"I've never seen you with your hair up like that," he said.

"It's not exactly flattering."

"I think it's cute. You could almost pass for a high school kid."

"Which is exactly why I only wear it up when I'm cleaning house. I'm thirty years old, and I don't want to look like a teen."

No one could mistake her for that. She didn't have a lot of curves, but she was all woman.

She sniffed the air and wrinkled her nose. "You reek of cigar smoke and beer."

"You can smell me all the way over there?" Seth figured he must stink pretty bad. "I played poker with my brother tonight, but I only had one cigar and two beers over three hours. I'm totally sober. Do you have any breath mints?"

Emily rooted through Mrs. Oakes's desk, then tossed him a packet of Tic Tacs. "Speaking of your brother, his wife, Lana, contacted me the other day. They heard about The Wagging Tail from Taylor. I'm going out to their ranch next week, to talk with them about adopting a dog."

"Sly mentioned that earlier tonight. Nick played poker, too, and another guy, a cousin of Sly's wife who owns the ranch adjacent to theirs. Did you know that Dani's pregnant?" He wasn't sure why he needed to share all that with Emily—wasn't sure she cared.

"I hadn't heard about Dani. Please tell her congratulations from me. So you played poker tonight. Did you win anything?"

"Yeah, but I lost some, too. In the end I came out even."

"Better than losing your shirt." Emily checked her watch. "It's barely nine-thirty. If the game broke up this early, it must've been a bore."

"Not at all." Seth shrugged. "You know how ranchers are—up at the crack of dawn. I actually enjoyed myself."

"You sound surprised about that."

"I was. Sly and I used to be close, but now things are a little tense," he admitted, wondering why he was also telling her about this. He didn't talk about his issues with his brother, not even with Dani. But now that he was here, he couldn't seem to keep his mouth shut.

Emily nodded. "The night when the shepherd had his epileptic fit, you mentioned something about a 'rocky road' with your family, but you never said what happened."

"Here's the nutshell version—I acted like a class-A jackass."

"We've all done things we're sorry about." She hugged her waist. "Like me, expecting Harvey to take me with him when he moved across the country."

"I'm thinking he's also a jackass."

"True." She flirted with a smile. "I realize now how lucky I was that I didn't go with him. Prosperity is my home, and leaving it and The Wagging Tail would have broken my heart. What makes you a 'class-A jackass'?"

She looked genuinely interested, and tonight Seth didn't need much coaxing.

"I told you that Sly and I lived with an uncle after our parents died, and that Uncle George didn't like kids," he said. "He pretty much left us alone—except when we irritated him. We did that way too often. Then, let's just say, things got ugly." Seth wasn't about to get into the nasty details of verbal smack downs and physical abuse. "We learned to steer clear of him. I was mad at the world. I got into fights, earned bad grades, skipped school, had a few scrapes with the law—stuff like that."

Remembering, he winced. "Someone needed to take me in hand, and my big brother got stuck with the job. Just before Sly finished high school, our uncle died. As soon as Sly graduated and I finished eighth grade, we packed up and moved back to Prosperity. He had this idea that we'd reunite with Dani and be a family again."

"And it happened," Emily said.

"Not exactly. We were gone four years. By the time we returned, Big Mama had become Dani's family. Sure, we saw a lot of her, but we never lived under the same roof again. Sly rented an apartment for him and me, and enrolled me in high school. He tried to parent me and tell me what to do. That worked real well." Seth snickered. "I got tired of being stuck under his thumb and tired of battling him all the time, so I quit school and hopped a bus out of town. I left a note for Sly and Dani so they wouldn't worry, and when I decided to settle in California a few months later, I sent a postcard. I didn't give them any contact information, just said I was okay."

Emily didn't comment, but she was easy to read. She thought that leaving Sly and Dani in the dark all those years had been mean and thoughtless. She was right.

Seth had also missed huge landmarks—his brother's wedding and the birth of his and Lana's daughter, as well as Dani's wedding and so much more. Now he felt like an outsider, just punishment for his sins. He managed a sardonic smile. "Told you I was a jackass."

"You were young and impulsive, and hurting," she said with sympathetic look. "At least you let them know you were okay. Believe me, that's a big deal. When my father took off, he never contacted us again."

Emily had suffered through her own piece of hell, Seth realized. "That had to hurt. How old were you?"

"Nine."

The same age Taylor had been when Annabelle had asked Seth to move out, and probably one reason she and Emily got along so well.

"It's good that you decided to move back here when you took custody of Taylor," Emily said.

Seth agreed. "A dying friend who was also estranged from his family told me I'd best come home and make up with mine while I still could. Then when I found out about Taylor... I figured that now was the right time." He wanted badly to make amends. "I won't lie—I also wanted to show them that even though I'd dropped out of high school way back when, I managed to earn my GED, and graduate college and grad school. That I made something of myself."

His success was the one thing he felt good about and proud of.

"A week or so before the move, I contacted Sly and Dani and let them know I was coming home, and explained about Taylor. That's when I found out just how pissed off at me they were." He was still shaking his head at himself and what a thoughtless jerk he'd been. "Turns out that the whole seventeen years I was gone, they'd been trying to find me. If that doesn't make me a class-A jackass, I don't know what does."

Emily looked pensive. "Well, it's all behind you now. Still, I understand where they're coming from. You don't have a big family to begin with. It's the same with my mom, stepdad and me. We don't always see eye to eye. Heck, a lot of the time, they drive me crazy." She smiled at that. "But we're still family. You, Sly and Dani are *family*, and I'm sure they're happy that you're here now."

Maybe Dani was, but not Sly. Sure, he was probably relieved that Seth was alive and well, but that was as far as it went.

Seth stifled a frustrated groan. Sometimes he wished he could go back and redo the parts of his life that he'd botched up, but that was impossible. "Have you had any contact with your father?" he asked.

Emily looked sad. "About six years ago I hired a private investigator to track him down. It turned out he'd developed a drug problem and had lived on the streets for years. He died when I was in high school."

"That's terrible," Seth said.

"Yeah." She sighed. "At least my mom and I know what happened to him. Back to Dani. That time at the bowling alley, she didn't seem at all angry with you."

"She's a lot more forgiving than Sly. It's not so easy to get back into his good graces."

"Have you tried apologizing?"

"Not in so many words, but he knows I have regrets."

"Are you sure? He can't read your mind. You really should apologize."

"We're guys. We don't talk about those kinds of things."

Until now, Seth had never shared his personal stuff with anyone. He didn't know why he'd chosen Emily. Now that he'd aired his story, he was tired of talking about his sorry self. "I came here to find out about Taylor. I thought she was doing okay. Then your call came in. What's she done?" he asked warily.

"She's been doing well, but the other day, when we were outside enjoying her first snow, she made a few comments I think you should hear about."

Emily's sober expression worried him. Not at all sure he was ready, he mentally braced himself. "Such as?"

"This is between us, okay? She didn't swear me to secrecy or anything, but she probably wouldn't want me telling you."

"It stays between us—you have my word."

Emily looked relieved. "We were talking about how no two snowflakes are alike, and she was testing the theory by studying what landed on her coat sleeve. One in particular reminded her of a necklace she'd given her mother. She had the undertaker place it around her neck so that she was buried with it.

"She actually cried, Seth, but I could tell she didn't want me to see." Emily's eyes welled up, no doubt in sympathy. "She acts tough, but she really misses her mom."

He could identify. His own mother had died when he was just a kid, his father following her a year later. "I don't doubt that," he said, wishing he could ease the pain. "This whole adjustment has been really tough on her. Thanks for sharing this."

"There's more." Emily squared her shoulders, as if fortifying herself to reveal a weighty truth. "She claims that you walked out on her and her mother."

Seth couldn't have been more stunned if she'd slugged him in the chest. "What?"

"Apparently that's what her mother told her."

He did a slow burn and muttered a few choice four-letter words. "Is there anything else?"

"I'm afraid so." Emily bit her lip. "Taylor believes you left because you didn't want her in your life."

"That's a total lie," he said through gritted teeth.

He scrubbed his hand over his face. Then, too rattled to sit, he stood and began to pace the room. "Annabelle left me without a thought for Taylor. If she was still alive, I swear, I'd wring her neck. She took Taylor away, where I couldn't find her."

"Hold on there—you're jumping to conclusions," Emily said. "Annabelle may have told Taylor that *you* left *them*, but I asked Taylor if her mother had actually said you didn't want her. She answered no, but said that it was obvious."

"Because I didn't get in touch with her. Believe me,

I tried, but I couldn't find her." Remembering that help-less anger, he paced to the wall, turned and paced back. The feeling had been similar to when his parents had died and the courts had separated him and Sly from Dani, and sent them to Iowa.

Pace, pace, turn. With sudden insight he realized that his anguish over losing contact with Taylor wasn't unlike the pain Dani and Sly had suffered over his dis-appearance.

He was worse than a class-A jackass. *Pace, pace, turn.* He was a stupid bastard. And shaken to the core.

A couple times as a kid, when he'd displayed the slightest vulnerability toward anything, whether a girl or an animal, good old Uncle George had punched him one to make him stronger.

Those punches had only made him angry, and he'd learned to wall off his feelings. Which pretty much ex-plained his inability to open up and love anyone. To-night, though, emotions flooded out of him like water through a broken dam. "What the hell am I supposed to do now?" he muttered.

"First, stop pacing—you're making me jumpy," Emily said. "Second, explain what happened to Tay-lor. Tell her the truth."

Nowhere near ready to sit again, Seth glared at Emily and kept moving. "According to you, talking cures ev-erything."

His tone was as harsh as his expression, but she didn't so much as flinch. "Because it's the best way I can think of to work out a problem," she told him calmly. "At least, most of the time. Okay, it didn't work so well with my ex, mainly because he'd fallen out of love with me. If he ever loved me in the first place."

She let out a self-conscious laugh. "In hindsight, I

have my doubts. I know that no one can talk another person into loving them. But with you... I'm pretty sure Taylor has deep feelings for you, and you certainly care about her. If I were standing in your shoes, I'd talk things through with her. It can't hurt."

"Now I know why she hates me—she thinks I don't want her."

Seth felt sick to his stomach. And scared, too. He returned to the couch and sank down heavily. How was he supposed to fix this? Hell, he couldn't even fix the mess he'd caused between him and Sly.

He thought back to the countless relationships he'd ruined in his life. God, he was a screwed-up mess.

"You're upset," Emily said softly.

His laugh sounded more like a howl of pain. "Damn straight I am."

Unable to meet her eyes, he rested his forehead in his hands. But he heard her stand and walk around the desk.

With his head in his hands and his massive shoulders hunched, Seth looked defeated. Tension and hurt radiated from him in waves so thick that Emily could almost see them.

Her heart ached for him, and she forgot about keeping her distance. Wanting, needing to ease his pain, she sat down beside him on the couch. He didn't acknowledge her.

She nudged him with her elbow. "You're way too keyed up. Turn your back to me."

Now he looked at her, a dark frown on his face. "What for?"

"So that I can work some of that tension out of you."

He gazed at her with bleak eyes. "Why would you do that?"

"Because you're a good man."

Muttering something that sounded like, "The hell I am," he turned away from her and bowed his head to bare his neck.

Kneeling to reach him more easily, Emily started with his shoulders. His muscles were knotted and rock hard. His neck was just as bad.

While she kneaded out the kinks, her mind whirled. He'd been through so much, and so had his siblings. And poor Taylor, thinking he didn't want anything to do with her, when he'd been every bit as torn up as her by their separation.

Seth let out a satisfied moan. "God, that feels good."

"I'm glad it's working. Your shoulders and neck are much looser now. If you lean forward, I'll do lower."

He bent at the waist, exposing his long, broad back. His shirt rode up a fraction, revealing a small wedge of male skin. Not an ounce of extra fat on him anywhere— just muscle. Under her ministrations, the tension in his corded biceps slackened and eased.

Not long ago, these powerful arms had held her. Tonight she hungered to feel them around her again. She hungered for more than that, for things she shouldn't want.

It wasn't too late to move away and ask him to leave. That would be the smart thing to do, but at the moment, Emily didn't care about smart.

A low sound of desire filled the air. From her own lips, she realized.

Seth sat up, his head snapping her way. His silvery, hot eyes speared her. "Emily," he said, his voice hoarse. "You're killing me."

She swallowed. "I am?"

"Uh-huh." His warm hands cupped her face. "For

the love of all the animals on the planet, if I don't kiss you, there's no telling what will happen."

Her breath hitched and her breasts began to tingle. "I feel the same way. But my dogs and I need you here at The Wagging Tail, and I don't want to do anything that might cause you to leave before the end of the semester." She needed the time to find a replacement. Unless... "Um, but if you decide to stay on longer... we could really use your services."

He didn't even pause to think that over, just shook his head. "I gave you my word that I'll stay until Taylor's community service ends. That's all the time I can spare. Until then, I'm not going anywhere."

He swept his thumb across her bottom lip, his eyes silvery with heat. "You do understand that I have too much on my plate to get seriously involved."

"You know I feel the same way." She meant that. She did. At least she thought so. At the moment, it was hard to think *what* she wanted.

As long as Seth volunteered at the shelter at least until the end of the semester, and she kept her heart safe, which she definitely would, everything would be fine.

He tilted her chin up but didn't make a move, which was teasing but intoxicating. Humming with need, she puckered her lips in a silent plea.

He captured her mouth with so much need and passion that she forgot to think. His kisses quickly grew deeper and hungrier, making her long for more.

Then somehow she was on her back on the lumpy couch, with Seth bracing his weight above her. His eyes were closed. He had thick eyelashes, the kind she'd always wished she had. She ran her fingers over the planes of his face and felt the stubble of his beard.

His eyes opened, slits of molten silver. "What are you doing?"

"Exploring your face."

"I'd rather explore your body." He cupped her breast and groaned. "You're not wearing a bra."

Emily was so immersed in sensations and pleasure that she could barely form a reply. "I... I never wear one when I clean house."

His low chuckle rumbled through her. "From now on, whenever you get the urge to clean, call me. I'll come right over and help."

He pushed her sweatshirt all the way up and silently studied her.

Two of the things she disliked about her body were her boyish hips and her small breasts. But Seth's groan of pure male satisfaction made her feel voluptuous and sexy. Her nipples tightened and she grew damp between her legs.

His expression was intent and sensuous as he skimmed one finger lightly across her nipples. Emily moaned and gave herself over to him.

Then, yes! His mouth replaced his finger. Later, when she was squirming with need, he unbuttoned her jeans, pulled the zipper down and slid his hand inside her panties. Between her legs, right where she wanted him.

Dear God in heaven.

She wished they were both naked, but Seth soon made her forget everything but the pleasure.

He knew just what to do, slipping his fingers inside her and moving his thumb across her most sensitive part. Delicious tension coiled low in her belly. Moments later, with a shudder, she climaxed.

He kissed her again, another deep, long kiss. After

tugging her zipper closed, he sat up, pulling her with him, and straightened her sweatshirt.

"I'm leaving now, while I still can. Otherwise, I just might take you upstairs to bed and finish this."

As much as Emily wanted him, she shook her head. "I'm not ready for that."

"Didn't think so."

Filled with doubt, she walked him to the door. "You're sure that what just happened won't cause problems?"

He glanced at his erection and gave a wry smile. "Oh, there's a problem, all right, but nothing I haven't dealt with a million times before. Even so, I feel better than I did earlier."

"What are you going to do about Taylor?"

"I'm not sure, but when I figure it out, I'll let you know. Good night, Emily." He kissed her again, with a tenderness that left her aching for more.

Through a slit in the blinds, she watched him drive away.

Chapter 13

"Did you and Cat enjoy yourselves?" Seth asked as Taylor buckled herself into the truck. On the drive to pick her up, he'd made up his mind to take Emily's suggestion and talk to her—after he gauged her mood.

"It was okay," Taylor said in the understated way he'd come to expect.

She wasn't wearing her usual tough-girl expression, and she didn't reach for her earbuds. Yep, she was in a decent enough mood for a talk.

"What'd you do?" he asked.

"Ate pizza, watched movies and stuff." She shrugged.

"What about Cat's parents?"

"After the pizza came, they left us alone." She yawned. "Her mom made waffles this morning."

"Sounds good."

Taylor yawned again.

"You're tired." He wasn't surprised. Sleepovers had nothing to do with sleep. "This is a good day for a nap."

"Yeah."

"How about some music," he said, gesturing at the radio. "You pick the station."

He didn't have to ask twice. She fiddled with the buttons until she found a Nirvana song. Not the country-and-western music Seth preferred, but he could live with it.

They lapsed into silence, and he decided to wait a little longer to talk to her.

It was a cold, gray, October afternoon, made for sitting in front of the fire and watching football. Or burrowing under the covers with a willing woman.

With Emily.

As responsive as she'd been last night, he could imagine what sex with her would be like. His body began to stir. He willed it to behave.

It was a relief that she didn't want to get serious any more than he did. He wasn't going to think about the other part of the evening. Baring his soul to her when he would have been better off keeping his big mouth shut.

Now she'd seen him at his worst, his weakness exposed.

Since those bad years with Uncle George, Seth never let anyone see him as Emily had last night. But the things she'd shared about Taylor had hit him where it hurt, and he'd been too stunned to play tough.

He'd half expected her to mock him for revealing his pain. Instead, she'd worked the kinks out of his tense muscles. Her warmth and concern had turned him on even more than before.

Seth wasn't sure what that meant, and didn't want to know.

He was almost home now. Time for that talk while Taylor was a captive audience.

"I had a good time at the poker game," he said, wading in cautiously.

She gave him a sideways look. "Did you win any money?"

"You sound just like Emily." He chuckled. "I came out even, which is better than losing."

"You talked to Emily last night?" Taylor looked curious.

"I saw her."

Her eyes narrowed a fraction. "Are you dating her?"

What the hell had given her that idea? "Nah—we're friends." Although technically, after last night they were a lot more than that. "She called during the poker game, and after I dropped off Sly, I stopped by. She's going over to his and Lana's next week to interview them about adopting a dog, and is real happy you recommended The Wagging Tail."

Taylor looked pleased before her expression turned apathetic. "They know that you and I both volunteer at the shelter."

"Yeah, but I never thought to suggest they adopt a dog from there. You did." Curious, he turned the conversation back to Emily. "Emily and I aren't dating, but if wc were, I get the feeling you wouldn't like it."

"What difference would that make? You'll just do what you want. My mom always did."

Interesting. "How so?"

A shrug. "Most of the guys she dated were total losers. I tried to tell her, but she didn't listen."

She hadn't had an easy time, and Seth imagined that Annabelle hadn't, either. "Some people are hard learners," he said. "They only learn through experience. In that way, your mom and I were alike. But I promise that the one thing I will always do is listen to you."

And it was time to get down to the nitty-gritty. He weighed his words carefully. After braking for a red light, he met her eyes. "I hope you don't put me in the same loser category as some of your mom's exes."

Taylor was silent, her expression blank. She could have been thinking anything.

"Look, I know these past few months haven't been easy for you," he said as the light turned green and he drove on. "You've had huge changes to adapt to—losing your mom unexpectedly, coming to live with me, leaving San Diego and moving to Prosperity. None of that is easy, and there aren't many people who could adjust. But you're handling it like a trouper, and I'm real proud of you. And, Taylor…" He had to stop and clear his throat. "I'm sorry your mom is gone, but I'm awful glad you're back in my life."

She blinked in surprise, and he caught a glimpse of the vulnerable girl she was, before her expression hardened. He barely had time to wonder at that before she spoke.

"You never told me about the house."

It took him a minute to figure out that she meant their rental. Weeks had passed since Emily had mentioned his plan to Taylor, and the subject had never come up. "That's right," he said. "I want to buy it and fix it up for the two of us. I didn't think you were interested in hearing about that."

"I'm not." She rummaged through her tiny purse. Moments later she slid out her iPod and earbuds, put them on and turned her face toward the passenger window. Shutting him out once again.

That had gone real well. Seth winced.

He wasn't sure what kind of reaction he'd expected, but not this. He swore softly. Emily was wrong—talking with Taylor had been a bust.

He wished he had a plan B to fall back on, but for the life of him, he couldn't think what it should be.

In the kennel, Emily stood across the exam table from Seth and held firmly on to one of the shelter's newer arrivals, a medium-size male who looked to be part retriever, part Welsh corgi. Seth had cleared him from quarantine days ago, but the poor pooch had something in his paw. Scared and in pain, he shook and whimpered.

It was a relief that her Wednesday morning volunteers had taken the other dogs out. They'd probably be upset by this.

"That hurts, huh?" Seth murmured to the animal, in the steady, calming tone Emily had come to expect.

Although his big, capable hands dwarfed the tweezers, he wielded them with practiced skill. Since their passionate make-out session Saturday night Seth and his hands had filled almost her every waking thought. And his mouth… Emily stifled a dreamy sigh.

Oh, she wanted him.

But what really melted her was that he'd opened up and shared his past and his fears about Taylor. That couldn't have been easy for him. She so liked this man, and every time she was with him, no matter how hard she fought herself, her feelings grew. If she wasn't careful, she'd wind up with a broken heart.

No, thank you.

She wasn't going to let that happen, wouldn't let herself fall in love. Not now, and not with Seth. He didn't want love, and neither did she.

Got that, heart?

She really should keep her distance from him, but this morning, he needed her help while he worked. Although if she were honest, she'd admit that he could probably handle the dog by himself. Yet here she was.

He extracted a long thorn from the dog's right front paw and held it up for her to see. "Look at the size of this thing."

Emily was appalled. "No wonder he's been limping and crying. I wonder where he picked that up."

"Beats me, but the paw's infected. He needs antibiotics. I'll phone in a prescription. Meanwhile, I happen to have some ointment with me that will ease the pain and soothe the inflammation."

After applying the salve, he gently wrapped the injured paw. "Leave this bandage on for as long as you can."

Emily nodded.

"Good boy," he told the dog, gently ruffling the fur between his ears. Seth set him back in his cage, then washed up. Emily shrugged into her parka and walked out with him.

From out of nowhere, an icy wind blew through the yard. Despite her heavy jacket, she shivered. By the calendar, they weren't quite a month into autumn, yet it felt like winter.

"I was really impressed with your brother and his wife when I visited Pettit Ranch on Monday," she said as they headed toward Seth's pickup. "They're coming here today, and should arrive soon."

"They have a nice spread. Which dog do you think they'll want?"

Emily thought about that. In the six weeks since Seth had first volunteered, all the dozen and a half or so animals he'd treated had been adopted. Now, counting the male he'd just seen, there were six more available, some more suitable than others for a family with young children.

"The bulldog-poodle and spaniel-terrier mixes are the gentlest," she said. "I don't think either of them has been abused, so they should be able to tolerate kids."

Seth nodded. He hadn't mentioned Taylor since the other night. Curious, Emily broached the subject. "Have you and Taylor had a chance to talk?"

A pained look crossed his face. "I tried."

"Things didn't go well?"

"Nope. I didn't get very far before she shut me out. That was Saturday, and she's barely said two words to me since." He scrubbed his hand over his face. "Told you I suck at talking about personal stuff."

Emily felt for him. "Maybe it'll go better next time."

He gave her an *are you crazy?* frown and stopped in his tracks. "Suffer through this crap again? I'll pass."

He couldn't just leave things the way they were. It wasn't good for either him or Taylor. "I know it's hard, Seth, but you can't give up," Emily said. "You two *have* to talk, and sooner is better than later."

"Easy for you to say. You don't have to live with her."

"But I—" The sudden set of his jaw and his slightly narrowed eyes silenced her.

"You're not a therapist, and Taylor isn't your problem. So butt out."

Apparently she'd hit a sore spot. And here she'd thought Seth had trusted her enough to discuss the situation. Emily was taken aback and a little intimidated. But she'd never been one to hold in her opinion, especially when she was fighting for something that mattered. And Seth's relationship with Taylor mattered a great deal.

"You two are both hardheaded," she said. "You need help. *Someone* has to get involved, and it may as well be me."

Emily faced Seth with her hands on her hips and her chin up. He'd just told her to butt out, and had fixed her with the stern look that shut most people up.

But not her.

He wasn't used to that and wasn't sure what to make of her. Yet, he knew one thing for certain—the way she'd stood up to him was sexy. But then, everything about her turned him on.

The cold wind ruffled her hair. She pushed it back, out of her eyes. His unwitting gaze flitted over her. He'd never seen a hot-pink parka before. Pink wasn't his thing, but it sure looked good on her. He also liked the snug-fitting jeans and her long legs.

He liked Emily, period. And despite her unwanted advice, he wanted her more than ever. But dammit, she teed him off. "You don't quit, do you?" he muttered.

"Not when—"

Tired of her unwanted advice, Seth kissed her.

A long, thorough kiss that had her melting against him. His mind blanked. He was unzipping her parka when the sound of a car penetrated his clouded mind.

Sly and Lana's burgundy minivan rolled up the driveway. Damn. Seth stepped back.

Looking dazed, Emily tugged her parka down and smoothed her hair.

By the smiles on his brother and sister-in-law's faces, they'd seen everything.

Seth swore under his breath. Should've kept his

hands to himself. But around Emily, that was impossible.

"What are you doing here?" Sly's mouth quirked. "Besides making out with Emily."

Seth scowled at him. "I was treating a sick dog."

"Is that what you call it?"

Seth had had enough. "I have an appointment—gotta go." That was true. For the first time since he'd hung out his shingle in Prosperity, he had three appointments scheduled in one afternoon. If business kept picking up, he'd soon be able to add to his savings and build up what he needed to buy the house. "Good luck choosing a dog."

Out of her car seat, Johanna raced toward him. "Hi, Unca Seth! Hi, Emily!"

Squealing, Mark toddled behind her.

Seth greeted his niece and nephew and bid his goodbyes. Then he tossed his medical bag into the pickup, climbed in and took off.

Chapter 14

"That's two businesses we signed up so far!" Taylor exclaimed after she and Cat exited a hardware store.

They were spending today's community-service hours in downtown Prosperity, soliciting donations for The Wagging Tail's silent auction. She'd never imagined that signing people up would be this easy.

She and Cat high-fived. When they hung out together, Taylor didn't think about her mom, and forgot that Seth had taken her in only because he was forced to. She didn't miss San Diego so much, either. Even if it was cold here.

Her feet were freezing, and despite her gloves, so were her hands. "We deserve a break, someplace where we can get warm," she said.

Cat didn't reply. She was too busy watching a boy and girl across the street share a kiss, right there on the sidewalk. A moment later, they broke apart and smiled at each other. Holding hands, they turned the corner.

Cat sighed. "That's how I'd like to get warm. I wish I had a boyfriend."

Taylor wouldn't have minded, either. Although boys didn't seem interested in her. Anyway, Seth probably wouldn't let her date. He thought she was a baby, which was even worse than her mom. She'd set Taylor's curfew at eleven o'clock—one of the many things they'd fought about. Seth was even worse. He expected her to call when she got home from school, as if she was a little kid. "Where to next?" she said.

"How about—" Cat cut herself off and nodded at a lanky boy striding up the next block. "He's cute."

"*Really* cute," Taylor agreed. "Is he going into Java Jim's? We can warm up there *and* ask the manager to donate to the fund-raiser."

"What are we waiting for?" Cat asked.

A few minutes later, giggling and smoothing their hair, they pushed the heavy glass door open and entered Java Jim's.

The boy already had a drink and was taking it to a booth. As they passed him on their way to the order counter, he smiled.

"Up close, he's even cuter," Cat murmured under her breath.

The manager wasn't in, so they left their phone numbers with the girl who took their coffee orders. They bought cookies, too. In no time, they were carrying mugs and treats to a booth across from the boy's.

He was doing something on his phone, but as soon as they sat down, he set it aside and grinned. "Hey."

Cat smiled back. "Hey."

"Hi." Taylor flashed her own smile, but his attention was on Cat.

"I haven't seen you in here before," he said.

"This is our first time."

They talked back and forth, Taylor, too, exchanging their names. Isaac was sixteen and attended Denton High. He had an after-school job at Java Jim's. This was his day off, but he liked hanging out here. He was doing his community service at the local YMCA. Taylor and Cat told him about The Wagging Tail and the silent auction.

"I'll put in a good word with Derek, the manager," Isaac promised.

"That'd be great," Taylor said.

"Hey, do you want to sit with us?" Cat asked.

"Yeah." Isaac slid in beside her, across from Taylor.

At first, he conversed with them both, but before long he was talking only to Cat. Taylor finished her coffee and cookie. She pulled out her phone and texted Hanna and Kayla, her two best friends in San Diego. She'd been out of touch with them for days. Both texted back, but they were busy and had to go.

Cat and Isaac were talking about music now, neither of them even glancing at Taylor. Sitting there with nothing to do was boring and uncomfortable. "Excuse me," Taylor said, scooting out of the booth to use the bathroom.

Neither seemed to notice. Feeling invisible, just as she had when her mom had had a boyfriend, she followed the sign for the restrooms. During those times, her mom had tended to forget Taylor existed. Seth had been the one boyfriend of her mom's who'd paid attention to Taylor and treated her like she mattered.

But it turned out that he hadn't really cared, either.

As she headed back to the booth, she wished she was at home—no, Seth's house wasn't home, she reminded herself. She was only there temporarily. Still, she wished she was at the house now, in her room, listening to music and doing whatever. At least then she wouldn't feel like she'd been forgotten.

Instead of sitting down, she checked the time. "It's getting late," she said. "We need to catch a bus back to the shelter."

"I guess I have to go." Cat tore her gaze away from Isaac.

"Can I have your phone number?" he asked.

"If you give me yours."

They traded phones and input the information.

As Cat stood, Isaac followed suit. "Are you busy tomorrow night?"

She gave him a big smile. "As a matter of fact, I'm not."

On the way to the bus stop, she made a *squee* sound and pirouetted. "I have a date with Isaac!"

As the bus headed toward the shelter, she talked nonstop about how much she liked him. She didn't say one word about leaving Taylor out of the conversation.

Taylor was happy for her friend, but also a little jealous.

Did Cat even care if she was around?

Saturday afternoon, Emily headed for Pettit Ranch to gauge how the Pettit family and the spaniel-terrier female they'd adopted were adjusting to each other. A phone call would probably suffice, but she preferred to see for herself. After the visit, she'd go home and tackle a few of the must-finish items on her fund-raiser to-do list. Not exactly a thrilling way to spend a Saturday evening, but with the event just three weeks away, getting things done was a priority.

Lana let her into the beautiful Pettit home with a smile on her face and a wiggly toddler in her arms. "Hi, Emily. Come in."

"Thanks. Hi, Mark."

"Hi," the little boy managed to say before his mother put him down.

"Be gentle and don't scare the doggie, okay?" Lana told him. He moved silently into the great room.

"She gets skittish when there's too much noise," Lana explained as she hung up Emily's coat.

It had been only three days. "Give her time and she'll adjust."

In the great room, dog and kid toys lay scattered across the carpet. Sly was sprawled on the floor, Mark now in his lap. Beside them, Johanna "read" a book. The picture of domestic tranquility.

Emily envied the family. Sly and Lana had what she eventually wanted—a great marriage and cute kids. *Someday,* she told herself. When she was ready and met the right man.

The spaniel-terrier's sleeping cage sat against the wall. The door was open and the dog inside, where she probably felt safer. Although her ears pricked forward in clear interest and curiosity, she stayed put.

"Hey, Emily," Sly called softly. "The pooch is doing okay. I'll see if I can coax her out."

He offered her a dog biscuit, his gentleness reminding Emily of Seth. The Pettit brothers were both big, handsome men, with the same silver-blue eyes, but Seth was the one who made her go weak.

The offer of a treat was too good to resist, and the

dog ventured out. Already she'd put on some weight, a good sign.

As soon as she gobbled down her biscuit, Johanna and Mark clapped—noise that sent her dashing back into the cage.

Johanna looked stricken. "We scareded her."

"Scared," Lana corrected, ruffling her daughter's hair. "She's a little shy, just like your brother is around strangers."

"That's right." Emily nodded. "She'll get used to you."

"She'd better," Sly muttered. He didn't look happy.

"Are you having second thoughts about keeping her?" Emily asked, hoping that he wasn't. The dog deserved the chance at a normal life with these wonderful people.

Lana gaped at her. "No way. She's a member of our family now."

Emily let out a relieved breath.

"Tell Emily what you named her," Lana said to her daughter.

"Brown Cow, 'cause she's brown and white, just like a root-beer float." Johanna licked her lips. "My favoritest drink in the whole world."

Emily laughed. "That's a perfect name for her."

Lana smiled. "We shortened it to Brownie."

"Bohnie," Mark crowed.

Having seen all that she needed in order to reassure herself, Emily thanked the family and turned to leave.

"It's almost dinnertime," Lana said. "Why don't you stay? We have plenty of food—if you don't mind meat loaf."

Despite the pile of work waiting at home, Emily was strongly tempted. She didn't have to stay late, and it *would* be nice to eat with the Pettit family. "I love meat loaf, and I'd like to join you," she said. "But only if you let me help with the meal."

"Of course." Lana checked her watch. "We should probably get started—Seth and Taylor should be here any minute."

"They're coming to dinner?" Emily asked, trying to appear nonchalant.

Lana nodded. "Is that a problem?"

Only because Emily liked Seth so much. "Of course not—if you don't think they'll mind that I'm here."

"The way Taylor sings your praises whenever we see her?" Lana shook her head. "She'll be thrilled."

"I know Seth won't mind, either." Sly's lips quirked.

No doubt he was thinking about the kiss he'd caught them sharing. Telltale warmth climbed Emily's face, and she knew she was blushing.

Lana hooked arms with her. "We'll be in the kitchen. Johanna and Mark, you and Daddy keep Brownie company."

After Emily washed up, Lana handed her a knife and an apron, directed her to slice potatoes, and began to gather ingredients for the meat loaf.

"Don't say anything about that kiss, okay?" Emily cautioned. "Taylor has no idea."

"Your secret is safe with Sly and me. I don't think the kids saw anything."

Emily barely released a relieved breath before Lana hit her with a question.

"What exactly is going on between you two?"

Wasn't that the billion-dollar puzzler. "I know what it looks like," Emily said. "But it's nothing—not really."

If you didn't count the hunger and passion that seemed to grow each time they were together.

Lana glanced up from the giant bowl where her hands were buried. "Do you want there to be?"

In her heart, Emily did, but her logical mind kept reminding her that getting serious was too risky. "My ex-fiancé and I broke up a year and a half ago," she explained. "I'm not ready for a new relationship."

"You're not over him yet."

"Oh, I definitely am. It's just… I'm a little wary of getting involved again."

"That makes sense. But maybe it's time to take a chance and see what happens."

Every time Emily talked to Bridget and Monica, which was at least once a week, they said the same thing. "I don't know." She glanced at the pile of sliced potatoes. "This isn't a good time for either Seth or me. Between the shelter and my web business, I'm super busy. He's just as busy juggling the building of his practice with the demands of a teenage girl."

"In other words, you're perfect for each other." Lana's smile was pure Cheshire cat.

Emily frowned. "How so?"

"You both love animals with a passion, you both care about Taylor and you kissed each other the other day like you meant it. In my book, that's a winning combination."

"Look, that's Emily's car," Taylor said as Seth pulled up at his brother's house just before dinnertime on Saturday. She sounded more animated than she had all day. "I wonder what she's doing here?"

So did Seth. "Sly and Lana took that dog home Wednesday, and Emily likes to follow up a few days later. She's probably checking to see how they're doing."

"Cool." Taylor was already out of the pickup.

By the time Seth reached the front door with a bouquet of flowers for the hostess, Taylor had disappeared inside.

He found her sitting on the floor in the great room, along with Emily, Sly and the kids. Nearby, the sleep cage of the dog they'd chosen from the shelter yawned open, with the dog inside sticking her nose out. Johanna was sitting close beside Taylor, and Mark had climbed onto her lap. Taylor was talking animatedly with Emily.

Her arms around her knees, Emily looked right at home. Suddenly, she laughed at something.

With her head back and laughter on her face, she was beautiful. Seth wanted her more than ever. As if she felt him watching her, she glanced up. Their gazes held, and his body jumped to life. Seth willed it to behave.

"You're here to check on the dog," he guessed.

She nodded. "She's doing great. Sly and Lana invited me to stay for dinner."

"Sweet," Taylor said.

Seth suspected the invitation had something to do with the kiss his brother and sister-in-law had witnessed the other day.

"Look at the gorgeous flowers Seth brought," Lana said, holding up the bouquet. "Wasn't that sweet?"

Seth's face got all hot, and his brother gave him a searching look. "I need a beer and you need a vase. Join me?"

In the kitchen, Sly rooted through a cabinet. He found a vase and handed it to Seth. "Make yourself useful. Want a beer?"

"Sure."

"That kiss I saw looked pretty hot," Sly commented as he pulled two cold ones from the fridge. "What's with you and Emily?"

His brother always had been blunt. Seth narrowed his eyes. "If you're trying to play matchmaker, quit. I like her, but we're not dating."

Although they sure were fooling around together.

"Why the hell not?" Sly asked.

"I'll give you two big reasons—Taylor and my practice."

Sly snorted. "You can't work all the time. As for Taylor, she worships the ground Emily walks on. She'd probably be happy if you and Emily started going out."

"I doubt that," Seth said. "She doesn't like me much. I wouldn't want any of that hostility to rub off on Emily."

"I don't see that happening. Give Taylor time and she'll come around—just like we're doing with Brownie."

If only it was that simple. "Brownie, huh?"

"Johanna picked out the name." Sly dug a bottle opener from a drawer and handed it to Seth.

They opened their beers. Instead of heading back to the great room, they settled on chairs at the breakfast bar.

Sly raised his bottle. "To adjusting to change."

They clinked bottles and drank. Since the poker game, the tension between them had lessened, and tonight Seth was more relaxed around his brother than he'd been in a long while.

It felt like the right time to apologize. Seth set down his beer. "Sly, I—" His throat clogged up, and he had to stop and swallow. "I shouldn't have stayed out of touch all those years. It was a crappy thing to do."

Sly didn't argue. "Damn straight. Put yourself in my place. Bad enough that you quit school and scribbled a one-sentence note when you took off. Months later we get one puny postcard, with zero contact information on it?" He gave a meaningful frown, took a sip of beer and went on.

"All those years, Dani and I wondered if you were dead or alive. Which sucked, and pretty much turned me off of having a family." He shook his head. "If Lana hadn't accidentally gotten pregnant, I don't know that I'd ever have married or had kids."

Seth knew about the unplanned pregnancy, but he'd had no idea about the rest. "From what I've seen, you're a great dad," he said.

"I try. But I screwed up so bad with you that I couldn't see doing the same thing to another kid."

Sly thought he was responsible for Seth's behavior? Seth squinted at him. "You didn't screw up, Sly. You're only three years older than me. Hell, you did the best you could. And I didn't exactly make life easy. I screwed myself up."

"Losing our parents and going to live with Uncle George didn't help." Sly's face darkened. "Those were bad times for both of us."

They both stared straight ahead, each taking long pulls on their beer.

Seth darted a glance at his brother. "Making things right with you—that's one reason I moved back here. I'd like to put the past behind us."

Sly was quiet for so long, Seth wasn't sure he'd heard.

Finally, he cocked his head. "I can do that." Once again he raised his beer. "To moving on."

"Moving on," Seth repeated.

When they set their empty bottles on the bar, Sly clapped a warm hand on Seth's shoulder. "It's good to have you back in the family."

"It's great to be here."

They returned to the great room. Emily wore a questioning look—almost as if she guessed that something important had happened between him and Sly. Seth gave a slight nod toward his brother and grinned. Emily's brilliant smile lit him up inside. Man, he felt good.

"Um, Seth?" Wearing a curious frown, Taylor glanced from him to Emily.

He hoped she didn't ask about them. He wouldn't know what to say. For sure not the truth—that he spent way too much time fantasizing about getting naked with Emily. "Yeah?" he said, wary.

"Cat just texted and invited me to another sleepover at her house tonight. Can I go?"

"You mean right now?"

She shook her head. "After dinner."

"It's her turn to come over to our house."

"I want to go over there. Please."

"As long as no one minds if we eat and run," he said, but his eyes were on Emily.

"Don't look at me," she said. "I'm an impromptu guest here."

"Not a problem with us," Lana said.

Seth nodded at Taylor. "Then okay, you can go. But next time, Cat stays at our house."

A rare smile bloomed on Taylor's face, and for a minute, she looked as if she wanted to throw her arms around him. Naturally, she didn't, but it felt like a giant step in the right direction. Tonight, life seemed bright with promise.

That got him thinking.

Talking with Sly had turned out well. Hell, if he could iron out the mess with his brother, maybe he ought to try again to talk with Taylor. Couldn't hurt.

He would do it while she was in her good mood and a captive audience—tonight, on the drive to Cat's.

Chapter 15

By the time Taylor packed an overnight bag and Seth steered toward Cat's house, night had fallen. Traffic was light, and from what he could tell, Taylor's good mood was holding. He was searching his mind for the right way to talk about the things he needed to say, when she started fishing through her purse. No doubt searching for her earbuds and iPod.

Forget choosing the perfect words. If he didn't start the conversation now, it wouldn't happen. "Can you hold off on the music?" he asked. "I want to talk to you."

She all but winced, as if she expected harsh things to come out of his mouth. *Damn.* "Relax—I'm not going to yell at you," he said. "I, uh… This is important."

He had her attention now. Scant light from the dash cast her face in shadow, making it harder to read her expression. But the inquisitive flash in her eyes was plain enough.

Here goes. He cleared his throat. "Those years when you were out of my life—I really missed you."

He felt her surprise, which was followed by a skeptical snort. "If that's true, why didn't you get in touch?"

Surely she knew the answer. Then again, why would she? Hadn't Annabelle told her that he'd walked away? "Because I had no idea where you were," he replied. "When your mom and I split up, I had every intention of keeping in contact with you, and I told her so. She never mentioned leaving town. I found out when I stopped by with a Hard Rock Café Barbie a few days later. You'd been asking for it for weeks."

"Why would you buy me that? You didn't have the money, and it wasn't my birthday."

"No, but I knew you'd be upset that I'd moved out. I wanted you to know that no matter what happened between your mom and me, I still cared about you. But when I got to the house, it was empty. I had no idea where you and your mom had gone."

Taylor gave him a sideways look. "You left first. My mom was so upset we *had* to go someplace new."

"That's what she said?" Seth started to utter a four-letter word, but stopped himself. He wasn't about to go off like that in front of Taylor. Besides, getting mad wouldn't solve anything. Gripping the wheel, he reined in his anger. "Your mom broke up with me because she wanted to get married and I didn't. I wasn't ready."

"No, *you* broke up with *us*. She said you never wanted to see us again. You sure never called. Why are you lying, Seth?"

"Everything I'm telling you is God's honest truth," Seth said evenly. "I did try to call. I loved you like you were my own flesh and blood. Losing you hurt like h— really bad. That first week after you left, I must have called your mom a dozen times. She wouldn't pick up. Then she got a new number, unlisted."

He remembered that awful time—the hollow feeling in his chest, wondering what Taylor was thinking, and knowing she was hurting as much as he was. "I spent years trying to find you. My whole life was divided between going to school, working and looking for you."

He'd given up hanging out with his buddies, hadn't dated. There'd been no time for those things.

For all his honesty, he got a curled lip from Taylor.

"I don't believe you." Although the heat in the truck was cranked up and she wore her winter jacket, she wrapped her arms around her waist as if she was cold. "My mom wouldn't lie."

And yet, she had. Seth halted at a four-way stop and looked hard at Taylor before he drove on. "If your mom really believed that I never wanted to see you again, why did she name me as your guardian?"

"Because she was out of her mind? I don't know. But she wouldn't lie."

Realizing that he wasn't going to change the teen's mind, he blew out a frustrated breath. "Believe what you want." A moment later, calmer, he went on. "If I could go back in time, I'd make sure your mom and I worked out a way for me to keep in touch with you. But you and I both know that we can't go back and change the past. We only have now. Your mother is gone, and you and I are both here together. That's not going to change."

Taylor maintained a stony silence. She wasn't softening at all. As usual, his attempt at a heart-to-heart had failed—his cue to give up and cut out. This time, he didn't have that option, wouldn't take it if he did. Taylor was too important to him.

They were almost at Cat's house. Not much time

left for talking. There was only one thing to do—go for broke.

Sucking in a breath, Seth headed into unfamiliar territory. "I care about you, Taylor. Your being here… It means a lot to me. I want us to be a family," he finished, his voice breaking with feeling.

Hating that he was losing control, he clamped his jaw.

Spilling his guts got him nowhere. No reaction at all. Damn, that stung. His spirits plummeting, he signaled and pulled into Cat's driveway.

Taylor grabbed her stuff. As she reached for the door handle, she turned back to him. "I'll think about it."

Before he could react, she slid out of her seat and shut the door behind her.

A lump lodged in Seth's throat. He watched her stride to the front door and disappear inside the brightly lit home, this willowy, awkward teenage girl who'd turned his life upside down. Mulling over what had just happened, he backed out.

She hadn't exactly gushed out the "I want us to be a family, too, Seth" response he'd wanted, but at least she hadn't shut him out.

It was a start, and he felt outrageously good.

His thoughts flashed to Emily and the dinner at Sly's tonight. She got along great with the family, and her relationship with Taylor kept growing stronger.

Opening up and talking *had* helped. Emily had been right all along. Her insight and smarts had paid off, big time. She'd want to know about this.

Seth found a place to pull off the road.

She answered right away. "Hi." She sounded surprised. "That was a nice dinner tonight."

"Yeah."

"You and Sly cleared the air, huh? That's so great."

"Sure is. Listen, I just dropped Taylor off at Cat's. I talked to her tonight, too. Can I come over and tell you about it?"

She hesitated a moment, and his elation slipped a notch. He figured he could tell her right now, over the phone, but he preferred to do it in person. He wasn't about to question why being with her now was so important. It just was. "You have plans," he guessed.

"Big ones—working on the fund-raiser."

Seth scoffed. "On a Saturday night?"

"The big event is only three weeks away."

"Why are you so stressed about it? I thought you and your volunteers had lined up all the silent auction donors you need."

"There's still quite a bit to do."

"Can't you ask Taylor and the other high school kids to help you out? I'll bet the adult volunteers I met at the brainstorming thing would be happy to lend a hand, too."

"Believe me, next week they'll all be pitching in."

"Then it's settled—no work tonight. I sure don't want to sit around at home. Let's go out." On a whim, he decided where. "Ever played pool?"

"Once. I'm about as bad at it as I am at bowling."

"I'll give you some pointers. See you in a few."

He disconnected. Whistling, he pulled back onto the road and sped toward Emily's.

Emily barely had time to brush her teeth before Seth knocked at the front door.

"He's here," she told Susannah, slightly breathless. Whether from running around getting ready, or simply because Seth had arrived, she wasn't sure. She gave the dog a quick back scratch. "See you later."

Downstairs, she checked her hair before she let him in. As soon as Seth strode through the door, she could see that something was different, even since dinner tonight. He seemed lighter, almost carefree. Without the usual solemnity and worry etching his face, he looked years younger. And breath-catchingly handsome.

Oh, she liked this man.

Lana's words came back to her. *Maybe it's time to take a chance and see what happens.* As scary as the thought was, Emily had to admit that it appealed to her. She just wished she knew where Seth stood.

He helped her into her coat, and she had to know. "Is this a date?"

When he paused, she knew the question had thrown him off.

"You sound like Taylor," he said. "A couple of weeks ago, she asked if we were seeing each other. She didn't like the idea."

"Really." Emily frowned, wondering where the girl's question had come from. She'd seen the two of them together only a few times. "What did you tell her?"

"That we aren't."

"So this isn't a date." *Oops.* She felt foolish for even letting her thoughts go there. "Taylor will be pleased about that."

"Hold on there." Seth's eyebrows notched toward each other. "The thing with Taylor was weeks ago. That was then and this is now. Yeah, this is a date."

Emily's mind spun with the possibilities. Once again, doubts consumed her. Given her growing feelings for Seth, and the risks to her heart, should she even go out with him tonight? Probably not.

"Look, I know you don't have time to date right now," he said, clearly misinterpreting her hesitation. "Neither do I, but it's Saturday night, and Taylor's gone until tomorrow. I don't think she'd be all that upset anymore, and I sure as hell don't want to sit at home, catching up on paperwork or watching the boob tube. We both deserve a night out. Why shouldn't we spend it together?"

At least she knew where things stood—that her feelings for Seth went deeper than his for her. "You make some good points," she said.

Reminding herself to keep her heart safe, she headed with him into the brisk night air. "I'm really curious about your conversation with Taylor."

Seth seemed eager to share it. "It happened on the drive to Cat's."

He opened the passenger door of his pickup and Emily climbed up. "What did you talk about?" she asked, when they were both seated and buckled in.

"The past, now…a lot of stuff. Things didn't go so well at first." Seth started the truck and drove toward the road. "Especially when I explained that it was never my intention to leave her, and that her mom took her away without a word to me. She didn't believe me, but she still listened."

"That's a positive sign," Emily said.

"Definitely." He rolled his shoulders and then cleared his throat. "I told her that I care about her and that I want us to be a family."

What it would feel like to hear those words directed at *her*, Emily couldn't even imagine. And why should she? Seth didn't have those kinds of feelings for her, and neither did she toward him. Or so she told herself.

"Pouring out your heart like that can't have been easy for you, Seth."

"It was worth the effort. She said she'd think about the family thing." Despite the darkness, the grin on his face was easy to see.

No wonder he was in such good spirits. "Sounds as if you two hit a milestone."

"To quote Taylor, it feels epic."

His giddiness was infectious and Emily laughed. "First you straighten things out with Sly, then you make headway with Taylor. You're on a roll tonight."

"Taylor and I still have a long road to travel, but things are definitely moving in the right direction. Thanks to you."

"Me?" Emily had no idea what he meant.

"You pushed me to talk to Sly, and you pushed me to try again with Taylor."

"Yes, and you about bit my head off."

"There is that." He didn't look at all contrite. "But hey, I took your advice, and it worked. I'm in a good place right now, and I want to celebrate with you."

In other words, keep it light tonight. She could do that. "Then let's. I assume we're going to Clancy's?"

"You know the place?"

"Only because in high school, a date took me there once."

"So that was your one time playing pool. Was he your boyfriend?"

Emily shook her head. "It was our first and last date."

"Was it him or the game?"

"Actually, it was me. He asked me out again, but I wasn't interested."

"I'll bet he was sorry about that. I'm guessing a lot of guys wanted to date you."

"Not really." Even back then, she'd been wary of getting too close to any boy. In hindsight, she realized her reluctance had been fallout from her father's leaving as he had. "You, on the other hand, probably had dozens of girls after you."

"Not that many, but a few. Back then, I was a bad boy. Some girls go for that."

Seth gave a sexy, cocky grin, and Emily pictured him as a teenage heartthrob, with girls vying for his attention.

"Did you play pool with any of your dates?" she asked.

"There was one girlfriend with a table at her house. I used to go over there and play with her and her dad. When she and I split up, I found a pool table at the YMCA and kept at it."

"So you play regularly?"

"Not anymore. Before I left Prosperity all those years ago, Sly, Dani and I played at Clancy's a few times. Then when I was in college, I competed in minor tournaments. I needed the money."

"At last, the truth comes out," she teased. "You must be really good."

"I'm not bad," he said with a modest shrug.

"And to think that I'm out with a pool shark."

Seth chuckled, and Emily knew that keeping things light was going to be easy.

A few minutes later the neon Clancy's sign came into view. The parking lot was full, so Seth found a spot on a side road.

The main hall was packed and noisy, but they found a pool table in an adjoining room in the back. Here, there was room for only two tables. The other was taken by an older couple in matching "I heart Clancy's" T-shirts. They nodded a greeting and then returned to their game.

To the accompaniment of country-and-western music pounding from the old-time jukebox, Seth helped Emily choose a cue, and selected one for himself.

"You want to go first?" he said in a loud voice after racking the balls.

She shook her head. "You go ahead."

Seth chalked his cue and began. He made the game look easy, gracefully shooting balls straight into various pockets. At the rate he was clearing the table, Emily doubted she'd get a turn this game. Not that she minded. She was content to watch him.

The way his big body canted at the waist. The play of his arm and chest muscles, stretching his flannel shirt taut across his broad shoulders. His faded jeans and long legs, splayed and braced when he took a shot. And his very fine masculine butt. Everything about him was sexy, even his slightly scuffed boots.

He was also smart and warm. And great at kissing—and other things. Emily sighed. She could fall for him so easily.

That spooked her a little. Okay, a lot. Suddenly, she wanted to go home, where it was safe. She was about to tell Seth that when he set down his cue and eyed her.

"You're bored."

If he only knew how unbored she was. How badly she wanted him. "Not at all," she said. "I'm just worried about everything I need to do before the fund-raiser."

"Uh-uh." He wagged his finger at her. "There'll be no more thinking about that tonight." He grabbed her cue from its place against the wall and handed it to her. "Your turn."

"But you haven't missed yet."

"That's okay. Go ahead and chalk up, and I'll teach you some pool tricks."

Moments later, he stood behind her. Reaching around, he covered her hands with his. She could feel the heat from his solid frame and the warmth of his breath against her ear. Her body went soft inside and her heart just about thudded out of her chest.

"Bend down a little, so you're almost at eye level with the table," he said, guiding her into position.

Now his groin was flush with her rear end. Emily could feel his arousal. Barely able to form a coherent thought, she stammered, "N-now what?"

"Keep your eye on the ball, and aim for where you want it to go."

His lips grazed her ear when he spoke, and a delicious shiver ran up her spine.

"Which ball first?" he asked, his voice gruff.

"R-red."

"Line it up. Aim. Go for it."

He stepped back, taking his warmth with him.

Emily missed. "Shoot," she said.

But Seth wasn't looking at the wayward red ball or the table. His hot eyes roved over her, heating her everywhere they touched. After pausing for a smoldering look at her mouth, he met her gaze with unconcealed need. She could no more look away than fly.

"Game's over," he said.

"You don't want to finish it?"

His eyes grew hooded and he shook his head. "Let's get out of here."

Emily was silent as she and Seth made their way to the street where he'd parked. He kept his arm around her. The breath chuffed from his lips in clouds that mingled with her own.

In her mind, she waged a silent battle. *Yes, be with him tonight. No, protect yourself and hug a pillow instead.*

As soon they reached the pickup, he braced her against the passenger side, plowed his fingers up under the back of her hair and kissed her. Gently at first, then deeper and with more urgency.

When her legs could barely support her, he broke the kiss. "I want you," he growled.

Although Emily felt the same about him, she was also conflicted. She bit her lip. "I've never had sex outside of a relationship."

"I thought… Seems like you… Oh, hell, I misread things. I'll take you home."

He unlocked her door and she climbed in. While he walked around the driver's side, she thought about what she really wanted. Her mind assured her that going home was the safe thing to do, but her heart and body didn't want that.

It was all so confusing.

The engine purred to life. Seth adjusted the heat. He was reaching to release the parking brake when she placed her hand on his forearm. Eyeing her, he sat back.

"I don't want to leave like this, Seth. I want to be with you, but I'm nervous."

His eyes seemed to glow with heat. "One of the things I like most about you and me is that we're straight with each other. Okay."

Their relationship, if Emily could call it that, was so different from what she'd shared with Harvey. He'd lied about loving her and about always being there for her. But with Seth, she knew up front that he wasn't interested in love. He respected her enough to be frank, and that meant a great deal to her.

Cupping her shoulders, he turned her in her seat to face him. "As bad as I want to make love with you tonight, I think we should wait until you're sure about this."

"But now is the perfect time," she argued, because she wanted him so much. "Taylor's gone all night, and you don't have to worry about her. We won't get this chance again."

"Yeah, we will. There'll be other overnights."

She laughed self-consciously. "Are you trying to talk us out of being together tonight?"

Somber and intent, he tipped up her chin. "Make no mistake, Emily—I burn to be buried deep inside of you. But not if you have doubts. I want this to be good for both of us. And when it finally happens, it'll be dynamite."

His patience and understanding awed her. She'd never met a man like him, had never felt such hunger for anyone.

But what about the risks to her heart?

In the end, her desire drowned out the fear of falling for him. "Your house or mine?" she asked.

"Don't mess with me."

"I wouldn't tease about this."

He gave her a long, searching look. Apparently what he saw in her eyes satisfied him, for he nodded. "My place is closer."

On the drive to his house, he turned on the radio. A woman with an amazing voice was singing about her broken heart. Emily wasn't about to let her heart get broken. Tonight was about slaking the hunger that wouldn't go away, nothing more.

It seemed like no time before Seth pulled into the carport and opened her door.

The drapes in the house had been pulled against the night, and lamplight blazed inside. He unlocked the side door off the carport and stepped back, letting her precede him. They stepped into a small entryway. Emily barely had time to glance at the couch and matching armchairs in the living room before he ripped off his coat and removed hers. Right there in the entryway, he kissed her.

"You smell so sweet," he said, when they came up for air. "Like honeysuckle. A breath of summer in the cold of winter."

Dazed with desire, she could barely speak. "I'm trying a new shampoo."

"Keep using it."

He went back to kissing her, and for some time she lost herself in his warmth and the scent and taste that were uniquely his.

When they pulled back again, they were both breathing hard.

"Before we go any further…" Seth brushed strands of hair out of her face. "Are you sure about this? If not, tell me now, and I'll take you home."

Emily was positive. As long as she kept her heart safe…

He tucked her hair behind her ears, skimmed his thumbs across her cheeks, leaving a trail of heat everywhere he touched her.

"I'm sure." She wrapped her arms around his neck. "Make love with me, Seth."

Chapter 16

Eager to get Emily into bed, Seth tugged her toward the stairs. They didn't make it far before he stopped to taste her and nuzzle the sensitive place where her neck curved into her shoulder. She shivered in his arms.

She was incredibly responsive and eager, and he'd never wanted a woman so much. He kissed her again. She responded with a passion that went straight to his groin, and he almost lost control right there on the steps. But she deserved better.

By the time they reached the second floor, they'd lost their shoes and their shirts. In the bedroom, he switched on the bedside table lamp, then tore off the bedspread and tossed it aside.

Locking her eyes on him, Emily unfastened her bra. It slid from her shoulders and dropped to the floor. The nipples of her small, perfect breasts were already swollen and rigid.

Recapturing the mouth he couldn't get enough of, he eased her onto the bed. Some time later, he left her lips for her breasts, licking and tasting until she was gasping and restless. Wanting her naked, he unfastened the button on her jeans and pulled the zipper. "Let's get rid of these."

"Yours, too," she said.

They made short work of disposing of their remaining clothing. Seth looked his fill at the beautiful, willing woman waiting for him. Flushed skin, kiss-swollen lips, eyes bright with hunger.

His.

He explored her rib cage with his mouth and his hands. Her navel. As he slowly moved lower, she swallowed audibly and shifted restlessly. He slid his palms up her petal-soft inner thighs, which opened readily. Even before he parted her slick folds, she was lifting her hips. "Please, Seth."

"Is this what you want?" He touched her most sensitive part with his tongue.

"Oh, sweet heaven."

He'd barely begun before she pushed him away. "Too soft, too hard?" he asked.

"Not enough. I need you inside me."

She didn't have to ask twice. "Give me a sec." He moved away, opened a foil packet and put on the condom. When he returned to Emily, she held out her arms.

Seth covered her with his body, and in one slick move, slid into her warmth. *Home.*

"This—you—feel so good," he said. He wanted to go slowly and make their first time together last, but she was frantic and active, gripping his hips with her thighs and squeezing him with her inner muscles.

"Easy," he warned through gritted teeth. "Or this will be over way too soon."

"I *want* soon. I want now."

With that, he lost control, pushing deeper and faster until the world blurred and nothing mattered but completing the act with Emily. She cried out and they soared together, in a long, shuddering climax that shook him to the core.

Blown away by the intensity of the pleasure they'd just shared, he rolled to his side and brought her with him.

When he came back to earth, he kissed her lightly on the lips. "Told you we'd be dynamite in bed."

Rosy-skinned and looking thoroughly loved, she let out a satisfied sigh. "That was…wow. There really are no words."

"Any regrets?"

"None." She smiled drowsily.

They understood each other perfectly—best feeling in the world. Grinning, he pulled her against his side.

They both went quiet, and Seth thought she might fall asleep. Keeping his arm around her, he switched off the lamp with his free hand. He stared into the darkness. He liked having Emily beside him in his bed. A lot.

He cupped her smooth hip, and she snuggled closer, all warm and willing and sweet. Yep, he could definitely get used to this. Emily in his bed, every night…

Seth quickly squelched that thought, for several reasons. With his track record, he was sure to mess things up, and she'd been hurt enough. Then there was Taylor. Now that their relationship had finally turned the corner, he needed to make sure they continued to move forward. Add in his practice, which was finally expanding, and there wasn't time for a serious relationship.

It was a relief that Emily didn't want that, either.

They would see each other when they could, and leave it at that. His eyes drifted shut and he dozed off.

Seth's breathing was slow and even, signaling that he was asleep. Sated and relaxed, Emily was ready for sleep, too. Thoughts drifted through her mind. Love-making had never been like this. Seth had made her feel desired, beautiful and cherished—complete.

His hand tightened on her hip, sweetly and posses-sively. Feelings flooded her—warmth and joy and a feeling dangerously close to…love.

No, not love!

Emily started to panic. If Seth had given any indi-cation that his feelings had deepened, she might be, shock of shocks, willing to take the risk and give him her heart. But he'd made it clear that he didn't have the time or interest for love.

She needed to go home. Now.

She untangled her limbs from Seth's and woke him. "I should get back. Susannah's probably pacing the apartment, and what if one of the other dogs needs me?"

"Okay." Seth flipped on the lamp.

By the time they collected scattered clothing and dressed, it was almost midnight. Emily was sitting in a chair, pulling on her boots, and Seth was scooping their coats from the floor where they'd dropped them in their haste to make love, when the front door clicked.

"What the hell?" he muttered.

Emily scrambled to her feet—just as Taylor walked in.

At the sight of them, the girl stopped in her tracks, eyes wide with surprise.

"Hey," Seth said.

He'd pulled on a T-shirt but had left his flannel shirt unbuttoned. Certain that she looked equally rumpled, Emily smoothed her hair.

Taylor turned an accusing glare at her guardian. "I tried to call you to pick me up, but you didn't answer. Cat's dad had to drive me home."

"I, uh, didn't hear the phone. I thought tonight was a sleepover."

"It was supposed to be, but Cat… We had a fight."

"Oh, no," Emily said. "What happened?"

"I don't want to talk about it." Taylor shoved her bangs out of her face and scowled at Seth. "You said you weren't dating Emily. Why can't you ever tell me the truth?"

He blew out a loud breath. "We did go out tonight, but it wasn't planned. Otherwise, I would have told you. This was a spur of the moment thing."

"That's exactly what you said the last time." Taylor looked pretty unhappy.

"Are you upset that Seth and I went out?" Emily asked.

"No. I just… Why doesn't anyone ever tell me anything?" The girl's eyes filled with tears, which she hastily brushed away.

"I tell you stuff all the time," Seth said. "And I don't lie to you. Ever."

Emily nodded. "I'll vouch for that. If you ever want to talk about anything, I'm here for you."

Taylor hung her head, and Emily realized she needed more, some kind of explanation about tonight. "You want to know what happened?" she said. *I think I'm falling for Seth.* "Suddenly you had plans, but Seth didn't. Neither did I. We had this crazy idea to go out and play pool." Hoping to make the girl smile, Emily added, "He's good and I stink, so you know how that ended."

Unfortunately, Taylor seemed to find nothing funny in that.

"When the game ended, I wasn't ready to go home yet," Emily went on. "So we came back here for a while." She gestured at their coats. "Seth was about to drive me to my house."

He nodded. "It's late, and Emily needs to get home. You and I will finish this conversation when I get back."

"I'm tired. I'll be asleep." Taylor turned away and started for the stairs.

"Hold it right there. Say good-night to Emily."

Taylor stopped and stiffened her spine before she pivoted to face them. "Good night, Emily."

Emily ignored the exaggerated politeness. "Night, Taylor. I'll see you next Thursday."

With a terse nod, the girl spun around and hurried up the stairs.

"That went well," Seth muttered as he backed out of the carport. He hadn't seen Taylor this upset in weeks. "I thought she'd be okay now if you and I went out. Wrong."

"You should probably talk to her again about that," Emily said. "But I'm pretty sure she's more rattled by what happened with Cat. They'll make up."

"They'd better. Taylor needs all the friends she can get. What do you think happened?"

Emily shook her head. "With teenagers, it could be anything. It must have been a pretty bad fight, or Taylor wouldn't have come home. She was already angry. Then she walks into the house and finds you and me alone. I can't imagine what she must be thinking."

"For starters, that I lied to her about dating you."
That stung. "I wish to God that she trusted me."

"I'm sure that in time, she will. It's a good thing we
straightened up the bed."

"And that we weren't still *in* it."

Emily turned on the radio, and for the rest of the
drive, they listened in silence to oldies. In Seth's mind,
he replayed the evening. He and Emily, talking and
laughing at the pool hall. Taking her to his bed and
loving her.

Then the thing with Taylor. As soon as he got back
home, he would find out what had happened tonight,
and make her understand about him and Emily. For now,
as much as he hated seeing her mad, it was a relief that
for once, Cat shared the hot seat.

He pulled up in front of the shelter and let the engine
idle. "I enjoyed tonight—all except the very last part."

"So did I."

Her hair was messy, her lips still a little swollen from
their loving. Such a passionate, beautiful woman. He
wanted her even more than before. "I want to see you
again," he said. "Soon."

Soft light warmed her eyes. "Oh, Seth, I…" Cutting herself off, she caught her bottom lip between her
teeth in a telltale sign of uncertainty. "But what about
Taylor? Don't you want to focus on her and building
your practice?"

"Of course, and I intend to make sure she understands that. But I need more than that in my life. You
and I laugh together. We get along great and neither of
us is looking for anything deep. Why shouldn't we see
each other?"

She blinked and the warmth vanished. "With the
fund-raiser coming up and so much to do… I can't."

The surprising reply caught him off guard. Before he could react, she opened the passenger door.

"Good night, Seth." Without a backward glance, she slipped out of the truck.

Confused, he shook his head. What had just happened?

Chapter 17

Lots of tasks needed Emily's attention Monday afternoon, but a bad case of stress made focusing difficult. Unable to sit still, she stood and stared out her office window. Attuned to her mood, Susannah stuck close by, studying her with worried eyes.

"I'm fine," she soothed, but the dog wasn't buying it.

The reason for her anxiety? Later this afternoon, a new dog was coming in, and she needed to contact Seth.

They hadn't spoken since Saturday night, which was both a relief and a disappointment.

He had asked to see her again. His intent gaze had almost convinced her that he'd changed his mind and wanted a deeper relationship. Fool that she was, she'd been ready to hand over her heart. Then he'd made it nice and clear that he wasn't interested in serious.

He assumed she felt the same way—after all, only

hours earlier, she'd assured him of that. The trouble was she no longer did.

If only she'd stayed home and worked Saturday night. Emily scoffed. As if that would have made a difference. The truth was, even if she'd hidden away upstairs, she would still be in a world of trouble.

Susannah licked her hand in canine sympathy. "I know you like him, too," Emily said.

All the dogs did. As wonderful as he was at doctoring them, right now she wished he wasn't the shelter vet. Because if she didn't have to see or talk to him, forgetting him would be easier.

She no longer wanted him to stay on as the vet here, and he certainly didn't want to. Time to pull her head out of the sand. "As soon as this fund-raiser is over, I'll concentrate on finding a replacement veterinarian," she added.

Which was all well and good, but didn't change the fact that she needed to let Seth know about the new dog. With a heavy sigh, she picked up the phone.

He didn't answer, and she left a message. She was organizing the list of donations various businesscs had offered, when she heard the bell over the front door.

"Taylor," Mrs. Oakes said, her voice carrying into Emily's office. "This is a surprise. We don't usually see you except on Thursdays."

"I need to speak with Emily."

Wondering if she was here to get angry about her and Seth, or talk about Cat, or something else entirely, Emily stood. Then Taylor entered her office.

"Hi." Emily didn't bother with a forced smile, just gazed at the girl with what she hoped was an open expression.

"Hi." Avoiding eye contact, Taylor bent to the task of greeting Susannah.

"I heard you tell Mrs. Oakes you wanted to talk?"

Taylor nodded, shut the door and took a chair across the desk.

"If this is about the other night…" Unsure what to say, Emily let the words trail off.

Taylor looked surprised. "How did you know?"

"I thought Seth explained again after he took me home."

"Huh?" Understanding dawned on her face. "Oh, you mean you and him. We didn't talk about that, or anything else. I can't talk to him."

"You most certainly can."

"Maybe I don't want to. Since you brought it up, are you and Seth together now?"

"No." Emily shook her head. "We're both really busy. I've got this fund-raiser and the shelter and my website business. And Seth…" He didn't want love.

Before she could go on, Taylor gave a satisfied nod. "Good."

"You don't like us to see each other outside the shelter," Emily said, just to clarify.

"Not really."

Then her decision was for best. Still, she needed to find out more. "May I ask why?"

"Because… I didn't come here to talk about that." Taylor gave her a surly look.

"Still, I'd like to know."

"Because then…"

The girl's lips clamped shut, and for a long moment Emily didn't think she'd answer. Just in case, she remained silent.

After a moment, Taylor glanced down at her hands.

"Because then you'll both forget that I exist," she said, in a voice so soft Emily barely heard the words.

Emily's heart ached for her. She also wondered why Taylor would think such a thing. "Oh, honey, neither of us could ever do that. You're too special for me to forget, and I happen to know that you are Seth's main focus."

Taylor made a sound of disbelief.

"He really cares about you," Emily explained.

The girl's eyes narrowed suspiciously. "He said that?"

"All the time. You should hear the way he talks about you. You mean the world to him. He wants you to be happy."

Doubt colored Taylor's expression, before her face went blank. "If that's true, why won't he take me back to San Diego?"

"Because you live in Prosperity."

"I hate it here!"

The forceful tone shocked Emily. "I don't know what to say, Taylor, other than this is your home now."

"I *knew* you'd side with him. Forget it." She stood to leave.

Feeling completely out of her element, Emily sighed. "Please don't leave like this, Taylor."

To her relief, the girl plopped back down. But she didn't speak.

Emily guessed she needed to get the ball rolling. "What happened at Cat's the other night?"

"I do *not* want to talk about that or her," Taylor stated flatly.

Ah. "You're still in a fight."

"No duh. That's why I'm here. Can I start coming on Tuesdays instead of Thursdays?"

Emily didn't even have to pause to think about that.

"That's when Matt and Shayna volunteer. I need you on Thursdays."

Taylor tugged on her jacket sleeve. "But I don't want to work with Cat anymore."

"You've been such good friends. Don't you think you should talk and make up?"

"What for? She doesn't care about me. She only cares about *Isaac*." Taylor sneered the name as if it were something distasteful.

"Who's Isaac?"

"A boy we met when we were getting businesses to donate for the silent auction. He and Cat had a date Friday night. Now they're going out. All they do is text and talk on FaceTime."

She sounded jealous. Emily gave her a sideways look. "Does Isaac have anything to do with what happened Saturday night?"

With that question, Taylor dropped the *I don't want to talk about that* pose and poured out her heart. "I don't even know why she invited me over. She sure didn't want to hang out with me. At least not after Isaac contacted her. All she wanted to do was talk to him."

"That doesn't sound like much fun for you."

Taylor glanced at the floor, as if meeting Emily's gaze might cause her to fall apart. "She took her phone into the bathroom and locked the door. I waited in her bedroom. Where else would I go—downstairs with her parents?" Taylor rolled her eyes.

"Is that when you tried to call Seth?" Emily asked.

"No. For a while, I talked to a friend in San Diego, but she had to go. I knocked on the bathroom door, and told Cat that if she didn't want me around, I'd leave. She said to go ahead."

Despite Taylor's *who cares* shrug, pain clouded her

eyes. Emily wanted to comfort her with a touch or a hug, but sensed that she simply wanted a friendly ear.

"I know how you feel," Emily said. "Something similar happened to me once, when I was a little older than you. I didn't date much in high school, and neither did my best friend, Andrea. Then she met Gene, a boy from a different school. He asked her out, and before long, they were spending all their spare time together. Andrea didn't have room in her life for me anymore."

One more person Emily cared about had deserted her—at least at the time, that's how she'd interpreted what had happened. She remembered feeling mad and jealous, but most of all, alone.

She had Taylor's full attention. "What did you do?"

"I'd lost my best friend, and I was miserable. Even worse, we were in a lot of the same classes. We'd always sat together, and the teachers had made up their seating charts that way. Which meant we were stuck in our usual seats. Things were pretty tense. We didn't look at or speak to each other, and boy, was that uncomfortable."

Talking about it brought back some of the pain and helped Emily understand what Taylor was going through. "A few weeks later Andrea and Gene broke up. She was really sad, and she called me. I went over to her house and we hugged and cried and talked. We decided that no boy would ever come between us again, and promised to always make time for each other."

"And did you?"

"Pretty much. During those last two years of high school, Andrea must have had five or six boyfriends. I dated a few guys and had an after-school job. But we still talked almost every day, and we managed to get together once or twice a week. When it was time for us to go to college, Andrea moved to Missoula. I stayed here and commuted to the local community college. Her junior year, she started dating a guy from Missoula. When she graduated, she stayed there to be with him. They're married now, with three kids. But she and I are still friends. So take heart—things will work out between you and Cat."

"I don't think Cat wants to be friends anymore." Taylor hung her head.

"I'll bet she does. Why don't you give it a few more days and then talk to her?"

"You mean on Thursday afternoon," Taylor said with a shrewd look. "You're just trying to get me to come back on my usual day."

Smart girl. "Partly," Emily admitted. "I need your help getting ready for the fund-raiser, and I also want you and Cat to make up. You're too good of friends to let some boy get in the way." The office phone rang. "I should probably answer this," she said. "It could be about the new dog that's coming in this afternoon. But don't go yet."

She answered the phone and heard the masculine voice she knew so well. "Hey, it's Seth."

Her traitorous heart lifted. "Hi, Seth," she said, for Taylor's benefit.

The girl signaled Emily not to let on that she was there. Emily nodded.

"When do you expect the new dog?" he asked.

"He'll probably be here sometime in the next one to two hours. Then I'll need time to admit him and get him settled."

"Perfect—I'm booked up until around five," Seth said.

"Feel free to come after that, or even tomorrow morning."

"Later today works better for me. I'm still thinking about the other night." His tone became low and intimate.

Emily's body responded instantly, going hot with longing. She pivoted her chair around so that her back was to Taylor and the girl couldn't see her expression. "Me, too," she admitted.

"I knew it. Look, I know you're busy—we both are. But using the fund-raiser as an excuse not to see me again? Come on, Em. We agreed to be honest with each other."

She wasn't about to discuss that now. "Why don't we talk when you get here."

"That's all I ask. See you in a couple of hours."

Emily disconnected and pivoted the chair around. She couldn't read Taylor's expression. "We're getting a new dog anytime now, and Seth will be over after his appointments to examine it," she said. "If you want to do your homework and wait for him—"

"No!" Taylor shook her head and jumped up. "I don't want him to know I was here. I need to go."

"But how will you get home?"

"There's a late bus for kids who stay for after-school activities. I'll catch that."

"Okay." Emily walked her to the door. "So I'll see you Thursday?"

"Sure," Taylor said, but she wouldn't make eye contact.

Vaguely uneasy, Emily returned to her office.

Jessie and Birch, two of the other community service volunteers from Trenton, were on the after-school bus. They greeted Taylor, but headed toward the rear without inviting her to join them. She was used to that. Anyway, she didn't feel much like making conversation.

The bus was less than half full, and she slid into an empty seat in front, where she stared out the window at the gray afternoon. She felt kind of gray, too.

She wasn't sure what Seth had said to Emily on the phone, but she could tell it was something about the two of them. No matter what Emily said, it was easy to see that they were into each other. She'd even turned her back on Taylor to talk to him.

Taylor knew what that meant. She'd been through it with her mom too many times. Having a boyfriend meant that she was forgotten. Hadn't it just happened with Cat?

That stuff Emily had told her about being special? Ha. And Andrea? Nice story, but it didn't apply to Taylor.

Guys were the same way. When they were into a girl, they didn't see Taylor anymore. Now that Seth liked Emily, he was bound to forget she existed, just like before.

Once again, she was alone. Unwanted. Her shoulders slumped. She thought about San Diego and the friends there who cared about her.

And came to a decision. She would run away and stay with them.

That'd show Seth, Emily and Cat. Taylor didn't need any of them.

She sat up straighter, until she thought about how she was going to get there. She didn't have the money for a plane or a bus ticket. Well, she wouldn't let that stop her. She would borrow from her friends and pay them back later.

During the last few minutes of the bus ride, she

pulled out her phone and texted Kayla and Hanna, letting them know what she needed.

As soon as they sent the money, she would leave for good.

Chapter 18

After stewing—should she tell Seth Taylor had been there and that she was worried, or keep her confidence?—Emily connected with Monica and Bridget on a three-way call for advice.

She updated them on Seth—on everything from what had happened Saturday night, to the talk he expected to have when he stopped by later. Then she filled them in about Taylor.

"What do I do?" she asked.

Monica, who was still seeing Bart, the man she'd met at the bowling alley, laughed. "For starters, knock some sense into your head. Seth is a honey. Tell him you changed your mind and that you want to see him, after all."

"I agree," Bridget said. "He likes you."

"That's just it—he *likes* me," Emily replied. "He

wants to keep our relationship casual. I told him that I do, too, but the trouble is I'm falling for him."

"It's about time," Bridget said. "I envy you."

"Well, don't. I'm not happy about this."

"Can't you two just relax and let it all unfold?" Monica asked. "That's what Bart and I are doing."

"I don't see that happening with Seth and me."

"Because you're scared."

Emily wasn't going to argue with that. How could she, when it was true?

"You know where fear will get you," Bridget said. "Two words—*Aunt Arlene*."

Emily glanced up and shook her head, but of course, her friends couldn't see her. "We all know I have issues with getting involved again, but let's move on," she said. "I'm not sure what to do about Taylor. Do I tell Seth that she stopped by today, and what she said?"

"If I was a teenage girl and I told an adult about a problem with a friend and then she blabbed about it to either of my parents, I'd be furious," Bridget said.

"I agree," Monica seconded. "Teenage girls are drama queens. By tomorrow, Taylor and her friend will probably be thick as thieves again."

"Maybe I'll hold off, then," Emily said. "Or maybe not. I think I'll play it by ear." Downstairs, the bell over the door jingled. "Oops, the new dog is here— gotta run."

"Keep us posted," Monica said.

By the time Seth showed up, Emily was pretty much a nervous wreck. First and foremost because of the talk he expected to have. When she'd explained that she was too busy to see him the other night, it had been dark, and as soon as she uttered the words, she'd hurried inside. Telling him again, face-to-face and in a lighted room, seemed a lot more daunting. Mainly because Seth Pettit was a hard man to resist. But her heart was at risk, and for her own good she needed to convince him that she meant it.

Then there was Taylor and what to do about her. A part of Emily agreed with Monica and Bridget that the whole drama would soon pass. Plus, she didn't want to risk alienating the girl. Yet at the same time, a nagging feeling she couldn't shake urged her to share her concerns with Seth.

"You seem tense," he said after she let him in. "I'm not trying to pressure you into seeing me if you don't want to, but I want to know what changed the other night between my place and yours."

"Well, I…"

The warm, intent gaze that made her long for the things Seth wasn't interested in giving searched her face. Not about to admit that she was afraid of her own feelings, she glanced down. "It's difficult to explain."

"This is about the sex." He massaged his forehead, as if he had a headache. "I knew we should have waited."

Emily hadn't wanted to. "I'm not at all sorry it happened, Seth."

"It—*we*—were phenomenal."

His hot look melted her, but she steeled herself against her feelings. "I really am busy," she said. "Volunteers can only do so much. This is my fund-raiser, and everything needs my okay. Plus there are details that I need to handle myself, like organizing the donations, and the countless little things that pop up. We're a small organization, with under two hundred people expected at the fund-raiser, but pulling it all together is still a huge job."

Seth opened his mouth, but Emily didn't want to hear whatever it was he would say. She hurried on. "Speaking of the fund-raiser, I really need to get some stuff done tonight. I got the new dog settled in about an hour ago, and he's waiting."

"Fine—change the subject and blow me off." Aggravation flared in Seth's eyes, and he waved his hand in a curt gesture. "Go on and get to work, then. I'll examine the dog and email my report."

Now she felt terrible. "I'm not blowing you off, Seth. I'll work after you leave. Let me grab my coat and come with you."

They headed for the quarantine hut. Snow swirled around them, large flakes that reminded her of Taylor's first experience with snow. Emily didn't want to ruin the relationship with her by betraying her trust, but...

"Emily? You're a million miles away. I said, tell me about the dog." His cool voice and body language were all business now, as if they'd never been anything but shelter owner and volunteer veterinarian.

Although this was exactly what she assured herself she wanted, she didn't like it. She was so mixed up. "He's young, maybe a few years old, with poodle and black lab in him," she said. "His eyes are blue, and I'm guessing he's also part collie or husky. He's pretty upset. It took me and two volunteers to get him into a cage. I'm worried about Taylor," she blurted out.

Instantly, Seth warmed to her again, and her heart lifted in relief.

"She's in a bad place, that's for sure. Sunday was dismal, and so was this morning. For a little while there, I felt sure we were making progress. Now it's almost as bad as when we first moved to Prosperity." He blew out a breath. "For every step she takes forward, she seems to take two back. But I don't think this is about you and me. I'm pretty sure it's about Cat. I wish I knew what happened."

He needed insights, and Taylor needed help. Emily had to step up—even if the girl would be angry. "Taylor doesn't want me to tell you this, and I hate breaking her confidence, but this is important. She stopped by after school today."

They entered the hut, which felt cozy and warm after the cold night air.

"Hold that thought until I examine this dog."

Like most of the other shelter animals, this one snarled and bared his teeth. Unlike the others, he wouldn't allow Seth to approach the cage, even with the offer of a doggy treat. Growling a fierce warning, the dog leaped at the bars, banging the cage hard in an attempt to get out.

"If I'm going to examine him tonight, I'll have to sedate him first," Seth said in a low voice. "You know the drill."

Emily mixed a sedative with a small amount of food, then, using a long-handled spatula, placed the bowl in the cage. The dog ignored it until Seth and Emily moved to the corner, which in the small hut was as far away from the cage as they could get.

It took nearly fifteen minutes before he gobbled down the food.

"Finally," Seth murmured. "While we wait for the drug to take effect, tell me why Taylor came by today."

"As I said earlier, she won't like that I told you, but I have to. She asked to switch her community-service day to Tuesday, so she can avoid Cat."

Seth whistled. "That's one doozy of a fight."

"It's more of a misunderstanding, and it revolves around a boy named Isaac."

"Taylor has a boyfriend?" Seth didn't look happy about that.

"Not Taylor—Cat. Apparently, she'd rather be on FaceTime with Isaac than be with Taylor. That's what happened Saturday night. Cat ended up telling Taylor to go home."

"No wonder she's been so upset." His eyes narrowed a fraction, as they often did when he was thinking. "Why the hell did Cat invite her over?"

"Maybe she hadn't planned to talk with Isaac that night."

"Teenagers." Seth shook his head. "It's a miracle anyone survives those years. Are you going to let her switch to Tuesdays?"

"No. Two other kids come in that day. I suggested she work things out with Cat."

"But you're worried she won't."

"Who knows? They're teenage girls. What makes me nervous is that Taylor seemed…removed. Nothing I can put my finger on, but I get the feeling that she won't show up on Thursday. Oh, and she also mentioned moving back to San Diego."

"Not that again. I'll talk to her, and I'll make sure she shows up when she's supposed to."

"She's going to be upset that I told you."

"I'll keep that in mind." Seth glanced toward the cage. "He seems to be more relaxed now."

But not by much. As they neared the cage, the dog growled and snarled and butted the bars hard. He wasn't going to cooperate. Emily was glad she'd accompanied Seth, because he needed two extra hands to help muzzle and hold him still during the exam.

"He seems in okay shape right now, but I see evidence of abuse," Seth said, pointing out old whip scars. "We'd better bathe him now, before the sedative wears off."

They both ended up wet and sustained a few scratches, but they managed the job. They dried the animal as best they could, removed the muzzle and returned him safely to his cage. After toweling themselves off, they donned their coats and headed back to the office. The snow was coming down harder now.

"The roads will be slick," Emily warned. "You'd better leave now, or you might not make it."

Seth nodded. "I'll get back to you with the lab test results. If you change your mind about us..."

He started to reach out and touch her face, but dropped his hand instead.

Then he was gone.

Before heading for home, Seth sat in the truck at the end of the shelter's driveway and phoned Harper's for a pizza to go. Dinner. On the way to the restaurant, the snow and patches of black ice coating the road took all his focus. Once he had the pizza, he headed carefully for home. He was tired, hungry and out of sorts. Mainly because Emily had stuck to her decision. She wasn't going to see him outside the shelter.

Dammit, he liked her. He didn't buy her *I'm too busy* excuse, but he couldn't force her to share the real reason she'd changed her mind. What choice did he have but to let her be?

From now on, he was the shelter's volunteer veterinarian, period. Being around her was bound to be awkward, but he'd given his word to stay until Taylor completed her community service. The day she finished, want to or not, he would go his separate way and probably not see Emily again.

Now he had to deal with Taylor.

As usual, she was upstairs. He knocked on her bedroom door. "I brought home an extra large pepperoni and chicken pizza with pineapple—your favorite."

"I don't want any."

He'd figured as much, but was in no mood for her shenanigans. No kid gloves tonight. He opened her door. "Then you can watch me eat. You're coming downstairs, and we're going to talk over dinner."

She gave him a look that could kill—eyes flashing, mouth in a thin line. But she came out.

In silence, they washed up. Taylor got herself a pop, and Seth opened a beer.

He set out the plates and napkins, and then pointed at her chair in the breakfast nook. They both sat down. Seth dug in.

After all of two seconds, she relented. "I guess I'll eat."

Getting tough seemed to have worked. He smiled to himself.

He waited until they'd both slowed down before he started. "You haven't said two words to me since Saturday night. If you still hate me, that's your choice. But I'm not taking you back to San Diego. You can't just run away from your problems."

She looked suspicious. "Have you been checking my texts?"

"I wouldn't do that. Why, should I be?"

"Don't you dare!" She eyed him. "Emily told you I came in today, didn't she?"

Not about to lie, he nodded.

"I asked her not to say anything!"

"And she feels bad about that. She only said something because she's worried about you."

Taylor's upper lip curled. "Yeah, right."

"What's that supposed to mean?"

"I was there when you called this afternoon. I know what's going on with you and her."

As of midnight Saturday night, nothing at all. He scowled. "And what exactly is that?"

"You like each other."

Emily *had* liked him, but not anymore. Seth snorted. "What's that got to do with her being worried about you?"

"I don't know how she could be. She doesn't have time for me, and neither do you. No one does!"

With her dramatic flair, Taylor could write for the soaps. "Of course I do," he said in a reasonable tone. "So does Emily. By the way, from now on, she and I won't be seeing each other outside of the shelter."

"That's what she said, but I don't believe her."

"You don't have to, but it's true. And FYI, just because two people are involved doesn't mean they forget someone as important as you."

"She said that, too." Taylor snickered and crossed her arms, but the vulnerability beneath that glare…

Seth figured this particular issue had nothing to do with Cat or with him and Emily. "I get the feeling this has happened to you before," he said.

One shoulder lifted and fell.

He'd bet the four new ranches he'd added to his practice that this was about Annabelle. He knew how she'd been with him at first, lost in the newness of his moving in, but he also knew that her feelings for Taylor had never diminished. "People get weird when they're in love," he said, "but that doesn't mean they stop loving everyone else."

Doubt crept into Taylor's eyes, before she put on her stubborn face. "They sure act that way."

"I know. But trust me, you matter. Got that?" He waited for her terse nod before continuing. "I expect you to go to community service on Thursday."

"But I don't want to see Cat!"

"You made a commitment, and you're going." He didn't like the defiant look on her face. "I can always pick you up at school and drop you off there." He knew she'd hate that.

"No way. I'll walk over, like I always do. But only because you're making me."

He responded to her dirty look with a benign nod. "Thank you."

"You told Seth I was here on Monday!" Taylor exploded when she marched through the shelter door Thursday afternoon. "You said you wouldn't!"

Mrs. Oakes glanced at Emily with a *teenage girls— what can you do?* expression.

But Emily felt terrible. "I apologize," she said. "I did it because Seth was worried about you, and so was I. Will you forgive me?"

Taylor's only response was a stony look.

Today wasn't going to be easy. "I'm so glad you're here," Emily soothed. "With the fund-raiser next week, I could really use your help."

"Like I had a choice."

The bell above the door jingled, and Cat strolled into the front office. The surly look she shot Taylor was enough to make Emily cringe, but Taylor studiously ignored her friend. The tension between them was so thick that Emily could almost reach out and touch it.

The girls were mad at each other, and Taylor was angry with her. Wonderful.

With this afternoon's full agenda, Emily couldn't afford to wait for them to make up on their own. Ignoring the animosity swirling through the room, she greeted Cat with a smile. "Now that you're both here, follow me."

She led them to the kitchen and gestured at the table. "This afternoon, you're going to decorate cards for each of the items donated to our silent auction."

"I can do that," Cat said, as if Taylor wasn't in the room. "What kinds of decorations are you thinking?"

"That's up to you. Each item has its own card and needs a design that will draw attention and, hopefully, bids.

"For example." Emily picked up a card from the stack. "This is one of the items from Dani Kelly and Big Mama. 'Free brunch for six from Big Mama's Café,'" she read. "Your job is to make the card look enticing. Art supplies are in the cupboard to the right of the sink."

"I'm on it." Cat headed for the cupboard.

"What about me?" Taylor asked, pointedly glancing away from the other girl.

"You and Cat will be working on this together."

Neither looked happy. With grudging nods, they pulled out supplies. Crossing her fingers that they'd finally make up, Emily left them alone.

Some two and a half hours later, Taylor handed the finished cards to Emily for review. Cat plunked herself onto the couch and checked her phone.

They still had roughly thirty minutes before their rides arrived. Not enough time to start a new chore, but they needed something to do. Suddenly, Emily had an idea.

"We got a new dog on Monday," she said. "The lab tests came back okay, but Seth and I believe he was abused. He could use some company."

"I'll go," Taylor said.

Cat frowned. "Hey, I wanted to do it."

"Why don't you both visit him?" Emily suggested. "Be aware, though, that he is hypersensitive. He needs positive, loving people around him. You'll have to put that anger aside."

"Whatever," Taylor muttered.

Cat shrugged.

The grudging agreement wasn't ideal, but better than their blatant hostility of before. "If you move too close, he gets upset, so just sit and be with him."

Without glancing at each other, the girls headed off.

By the time Seth arrived, both Mrs. Oakes and Cat had left.

Pretending not to care for him was just as difficult now as it had been Monday night. Emily managed a smile. "Hi."

He gave a terse nod. "Where's Taylor?"

"In the kennel, sitting with the new dog. She's pretty mad at me for telling you about her and Cat." Emily bit her lip. "I hate that. I tried to explain that I was concerned, but she didn't want to listen."

"She'll get over it. What about Cat?"

"She's upset, too, but not with me. She went home a few minutes ago. I made the girls work together on decorations for the silent auction. Then they both sat with the dog. I wouldn't let them visit him until they agreed to put aside their anger."

"And did they?" When Emily nodded, Seth shook his

head. "No kidding." For a moment he lost some of his stiffness and looked impressed. "You're saying they're friends again?"

"Judging by their behavior, I don't think so."

"Bummer, but I'll bet they will be. You're amaz— I appreciate the update," he said, distant again. "I'll get Taylor and we'll be off." He turned away and walked back outside.

Emily didn't like this new, aloof version of Seth, but it was best this way. Or so she tried to tell herself. Her heart didn't buy it.

And with Taylor mad at her… This had not been a good afternoon. Wishing she could make amends with the girl, and aching for the warm man she knew and cared for, she locked the door behind him.

Chapter 19

Seth was about to head to a Friday afternoon appointment with a new rancher client when his cell phone signaled a call from The Wagging Tail. Frowning, he picked up. "Hey, Emily. Listen, I'm booked up this afternoon, but if it's an emergency, I could come this evening. Or first thing tomorrow."

Thanks to the town's healthy grapevine, his reputation was growing. This past week his schedule had been full nearly every day. Even better, he already had appointments set for the following week. If business continued to pick up at the same pace, next month he just might be able to sock away a hefty portion of his earnings for that down payment. "Hey, that website you created for me is working. One of the ranchers asking for an appointment found me that way."

"I like hearing that. Thanks for letting me know."

She sounded as removed and businesslike as him. How had they gotten here?

"Is this about a new dog, or has one of the other animals taken sick?" he asked.

"Neither, so you don't need to come over. I wanted to tell you about Taylor."

Seth groaned. "What'd she do this time?"

"This is actually good news. She's not mad at me anymore, and guess why?" Emily didn't pause long enough for him to come up with anything. "Remember the new dog you stopped by to examine Monday night? Taylor is here now, visiting him. She asked to sit with him after school every afternoon. That's okay with me, but I told her I needed to check with you."

"I'm fine with it." He'd have to pick her up every day, which would be a pain. If business hadn't improved and things between him and Emily weren't so strained, he wouldn't mind so much, but now... "I probably won't be able to pick her up until around dinner time."

"She says she'll walk back to Trenton and catch the after-school-activities bus, so you'll only have to come get her on Thursdays."

"Now that I'm getting busy, that's a relief."

"I think she's ready for a dog."

"Good to know." Seth wasn't going to say anything else before he disconnected, but he wanted Emily's input on something. "Yesterday she asked if anything had come for her in the mail. She's never cared before."

"Is she expecting a package from one of her San Diego friends?"

"She wouldn't say, but I could tell she was hiding something. I get the feeling that whatever she's up to, she knows I won't approve."

"I have no idea what it could be."

"If you find out anything, let me know."

"I doubt she trusts me enough to confide in me again," Emily said.

"But if she does…"

"I can't promise. I don't want to let her down by running to you every time she talks to me. From now on, I'm going to tell her up front when I hear something I think you need to know. She may get mad but at least she'll know I'm being direct with her."

"That makes sense," Seth said, admiring Emily for her straightforwardness. A long pause ticked by, ended by him. "I should go."

"I hope you're still coming to the fund-raiser Saturday night," Emily said.

"I said I'd be there, and I will."

To his own ears he sounded testy. He felt like crap. He missed the easiness he and Emily had shared not that long ago. Until things changed between them, he hadn't realized how much he enjoyed talking with her, how she filled in the gaps in his life.

Tough noogies, buddy. She's moved on.

"I'll let Taylor know that you've okayed her to visit the dog any afternoon she likes," Emily said.

"Don't work too hard." That sounded lame, but was the best he could do.

Scowling at the world, he disconnected.

Today was Wednesday, the third day in a row that Taylor had visited Paint. Emily didn't allow anyone to name any of the dogs, but this one had a splash of black on his back, just above his tail, that reminded Taylor of a paint stain she'd once gotten on her favorite shirt. She couldn't call him Paint Stain, but Paint worked.

"It's our secret," she confided in a quiet voice.

As softly as she'd spoken, Paint and the five other dogs in the room all perked up their ears. Taylor liked spending time with them without other people around. They let her know right away if they liked her or not. No phony smiles or pretending they were friends until they got a boyfriend.

Not wanting to think about Cat, who she would never, ever be friends with again, Taylor turned her attention to the abused dog a few feet away.

He was still nervous and wouldn't let her come near without baring his teeth and growling. But if she did what Emily advised and stayed quiet, he let her inch a little closer.

Taylor wasn't mad at Emily anymore, especially now. She'd said Paint wouldn't let anyone else do that, and that he was starting to trust Taylor.

Knowing that made it easier for her to get through the lonely days and wait for the letter from Kayla and Hanna. They were trying to scrounge up the money she needed, and trying to figure out how she could stay with one or the other without telling their parents, who would contact Seth.

But now, Taylor didn't want to leave Paint. Maybe she'd take him with her. Did they allow dogs on Greyhound buses? She'd have to find out.

The problem was, he wasn't ready to go anywhere, and Taylor planned to leave on Monday. The fund-raiser was Saturday night, and she didn't want to miss that. She couldn't leave Sunday without Seth knowing. But Monday, while he was working, she would skip school, head for the bus station and go.

Things between her and Seth were better now, and he was bound to be upset. Taylor felt bad about that, so bad that she wondered if she should stay in Prosperity, after all.

But, no. He'd left her when she was nine. Now he'd find out how rotten that felt. Because believing that her mom had lied, had done what Seth said and taken her away from him when he'd wanted to stay in her life, was too painful to imagine.

She just wished Kayla and Hanna would hurry up and send the money.

Thursday afternoon Mrs. Oakes was out, running an errand for the upcoming fund-raiser. Emily was sitting at the front desk when Taylor arrived. "Can I sit with Pa—the new dog—for community service today?" she asked.

"You can certainly do that later—if there's time," Emily said. "Today I need you and Cat to work on a few last-minute things for the big event."

Taylor gave her a murderous look. "But I hate working with her!"

Out of sorts thanks to sleep deprivation—the final push to get everything ready for the fund-raiser was exhausting—but also because she missed Seth, Emily frowned. "This thing with you and Cat has gone on long enough. It's time to make up."

"Like that'll ever happen."

"It will if you apologize to her."

Taylor's lips thinned. "Why should I? She's the one in the wrong."

Not about to take sides, Emily nodded. "I understand, but someone has to make the first move."

"It won't be Cat. She doesn't care if we're friends or not."

"I disagree," Emily said. "I'm sure she feels as bad as—"

The bell above the door jingled, and the girl herself stepped inside.

Instantly, the atmosphere turned tense and uncomfortable. Neither girl acknowledged the other. Swallowing the urge to snap at them both to end the feud right now, Emily directed them to pack up boxes she needed to take to the community center downtown, the space she'd reserved for the event.

Before going to tie up a few loose ends, she left them with one last comment. "The fund-raiser is in two days," she said. "It would make me very happy if you made up before then."

"I stopped at home for lunch today," Seth told Taylor as she buckled herself into the pickup after community service. "A letter came for you."

"Where is it? Give it to me!"

She was way too eager. What was in the thing? Seth frowned. "I left it on the kitchen counter. Who's Kayla?"

"How do you know it's from Kayla?" Paling noticeably, Taylor gave him a stricken look. "You opened it, didn't you?"

"For the millionth time, I don't snoop through your stuff. I saw her name on the return address. Who is she?"

"A friend from home."

"San Diego isn't your home anymore."

"Whatever."

"I thought you texted or went on FaceTime with your friends from San Diego."

"I do. All the time."

"Then why would she send a letter?"

Taylor didn't answer. "Emily says Cat and I should make up," she stated, changing the subject.

Now he knew for sure that she was hiding something. *Teenage girls and their secrets.* For now, he let it go. "Are you going to do it?" he asked.

"Not unless Cat apologizes."

"You could make the first move."

Taylor rolled her eyes. "You sound exactly like Emily."

Emily. She filled Seth's every waking thought. Keeping his distance sucked. He wasn't ready to give up on their relationship, if that was what you called it. Once she'd put the fund-raiser behind her and had more time, she just might change her mind and decide she wanted to see him outside the shelter. Seth was counting on that, and intended to do whatever he could to rekindle her interest.

The thought perked up his flagging spirits. He decided to share what he'd been mulling over since Emily had first suggested it. "I've been thinking," he said.

"Uh-oh." Taylor reached for her earbuds.

"For once, will you just listen?"

With a wary expression, she folded her hands in her lap.

"I think we should get a dog," he said.

Her eyes widened and her jaw dropped almost comically. "You mean it?"

He nodded.

"That'd be epic! How about Paint—the new dog from the shelter? Can we adopt him? Please, Seth?"

He hadn't seen her excited like this since she was a kid, and couldn't stop a smile. "I thought Emily didn't name the dogs at the shelter."

"She doesn't. I named him Paint because of the spot

on his back. It looks like a paint stain. He likes his name, too. He likes *me*, Seth. I'm the only one he trusts. Well, he's *starting* to trust me. I'm sure Emily will approve us to adopt him."

Seth agreed, but he wasn't sure about taking in an abused animal. "There are issues that come with adopting a dog like Paint. He has a lot of emotional problems. That means he can't be left alone for long periods. At first, maybe not at all. He's okay at the shelter with the other dogs and volunteers around, but once he has his own family, he's going to need someone with him all the time. You're in school and I'm starting to work more and more. There are only a few months left to save enough away for that down payment, and I need to work as much as possible."

Taylor looked confused. "I don't understand why buying the house is so important to you."

She'd never shown an interest before, and Seth took heart. "Because I want us to have a place we can stay in, something we own, so that we can set down real roots."

She didn't respond, but at least she didn't roll her eyes or make a snide comment. "What if you took him with you on your calls?" she asked.

"Right now, he's pretty skittish. Big farm animals he doesn't know could upset him, and vice versa."

"At least think about it?"

She was almost begging, making her request difficult to refuse. "I will."

When they arrived home, Taylor was so revved up over the idea of getting a dog that she stuffed the letter in her backpack with barely a glance at it. She even offered to help with dinner, and chattered about Paint and the fund-raiser like a normal kid. Seth couldn't help but feel pleased.

Figuring that whatever was in the envelope couldn't be that important, he enjoyed her upbeat mood while it lasted.

Chapter 20

This is it, Emily told herself as she glanced around the Prosperity Community Center auditorium. The night of the fund-raiser had finally arrived. She was ready with a slide show she'd spent hours putting together. The montage featured many of the dogs that had come and gone, and was sure to elicit tears—and prod people to open their wallets.

Thanks to several adult and community-service volunteers, colorful balloons and streamers spruced up the room, and poster-size photos of adopted dogs and their smiling owners covered two walls. Round, linen-clad tables, and chairs for two hundred people filled part of the large space, with food donated by a local catering service in warmers at several eating stations. In the center of the auditorium, the donation tables with the cards Taylor and Cat had decorated awaited silent bidders.

Now the volunteers who'd set up the room stood

ready to lend a hand wherever needed. The rest would arrive soon, with some staying late to help with cleanup.

Among the first guests to arrive were Emily's mom and Bill. They'd returned from their travels yesterday. Emily had spoken with them, but hadn't had a chance to visit. Though bleary-eyed with jet lag, they looked happy.

"I can't believe you're here," she said, after embracing them both.

"We wouldn't miss your fund-raiser." Bill patted his hip pocket. "There's a nice check in here for the shelter."

"Aw, I appreciate that."

Her mother smiled. "The room looks great, and you look beautiful."

Emily had splurged on a new rose-colored, wool dress and burgundy suede pumps that added nearly three inches to her height. "Thanks," she said. "I feel so tall."

"You look like a runway model. Bill and I can't wait to tell you about our trip."

Emily didn't have a chance to reply before a group streamed inside. "Excuse me," she said. "I'll call you tomorrow."

As more guests came in, she made sure to say hello and introduce herself to those she hadn't met.

Cat and her parents arrived. After greeting Emily, they headed for the donation tables to look over the items.

Less than five minutes later, Taylor and Seth sauntered through the door. In a sports coat, crisply pressed shirt open at the collar, dress pants and polished shoes, he was irresistibly handsome. But then, he was just as attractive in a flannel shirt and jeans.

Lately, things had been so strained between them.

His coming tonight meant a great deal to Emily, and her smile was genuine. To her relief, he offered a smile of his own. That and the appreciative look in his eyes as they darted over her melted parts inside her she hadn't realized were frozen.

"You look beautiful," he said.

"Thank you."

Their gazes caught and held, and her heart almost lifted from her chest. Forget about falling for Seth—she was already there, totally gone, head over heels as she'd never been before. She was in for a lot of heartache, but there was nothing she could do about that but weather through it.

Glancing away, she shifted her attention to Taylor, who for some reason radiated excitement. Which was odd, given that she and Cat were still mad at each other.

"Cool outfit, Emily."

"Thanks, Taylor. I like yours, too. I've never seen you in a dress before."

The girl blushed. "I know, but Seth dressed up, so I did, too. I need to talk to you about that dog I've been sitting with every afternoon."

"I'm a little distracted right now," Emily said. "Can we save the conversation until later?"

"Okay." Taylor glanced across the room, where Cat was standing with a group of adults and teens. "I, um, I need to talk to Cat."

Chin up, she headed toward her friend, who bit her lip and stepped away from the others around her.

"That looks promising," Emily said.

Seth nodded. "I told her she shouldn't run away from her problems. Maybe for once, she listened."

"We'll find out." Resisting the urge to rest a reassuring hand on his biceps, Emily clasped her hands at her waist.

"I should warn you that she has her heart set on adopting that new dog. She already named him."

"You're kidding," Emily said. "Thanks for the heads-up."

Before they could talk further, Bridget, Monica and Bart joined them.

After greeting the two women and meeting Bart, Seth stepped away. "I should go and find Taylor," he said.

"I could watch that man move forever," Bridget murmured as he strode across the room.

Emily's nod elicited a sympathetic look from Monica. "Well, well—I think someone in this room finally took the plunge into the pool of love. When you recover from tonight, call me with details."

Sly, Lana, Dani and Nick showed up next, Dani looking cute in a ponytail and loose wool dress that revealed the tiniest baby bump.

"I'm so glad you're here," Emily told them. "Seth and Taylor are somewhere. Help yourselves to food, and please check out the wonderful donated items and services available for your bid. Sly and Lana, there's a great photo of you and your kids with Brownie over there on the wall."

In what seemed like mere minutes, Mrs. Oakes signaled Emily and pointed at the wall clock. It was time to kick off the evening with a welcome speech. She moved to the front of the room.

"This is Susannah," Emily said, as a slide of the animal filled the screen. "When she first arrived, she was skin and bones, with her left foreleg so damaged it needed amputating. She was also filthy, and crawling with fleas. But she looked at me with those eyes and I was a goner. It's been almost four years since I adopted her, and we've seen each other through some rough times. But no matter what, she's never let me down. That's one reason why I fight for the dogs at the shelter—they love us unconditionally. In return, all they ask for is for us to love them back, give them a safe place to live, and feed and care for them."

Seth couldn't take his eyes off her, and by the silence in the room, others were equally captivated. In elegant heels and a dark pink dress that clung to her slender body and showed off her great legs, she looked spectacular. Her passion for dogs and the shelter was obvious, and her slideshow and accompanying dialogue mesmerizing. A few times he found himself swallowing hard with feeling. Before long Emily's mom and Bill, who were at his table along with Sly, Lana, Dani and Nick, joined everyone else in the room, sniffling and swiping their eyes. Seth knew they'd all give what they could to keep the shelter running.

He was so proud of Emily. He missed her a lot. Tonight looked to be a big success. If only they could celebrate together at the end of the evening...

Taylor and the other high school volunteers had their own table. Seth was relieved to see her and Cat sitting next to each other. From time to time, they bent their heads together, whispering over something. Apparently, they'd made up.

Emily's speech ended. She encouraged her guests to continue enjoying the food, but also to put in their bids.

Seth finished his meal. Between the positive changes in Taylor and the upswing in his patient load, life was looking up. Except for one part of it—the part that in-cluded Emily.

Across the room, sitting at a table with some of her bigger donors, she laughed. He couldn't help smiling. She was something special, and without a doubt, the most beautiful women he'd ever known.

Warmth and tenderness he barely recognized flowed into his chest. For nearly two decades, he'd walled him-self off from deep feelings. Yet now his heart was wide open and filled to the brim. Wonder of all wonders—with love.

He loved Emily.

When had that happened? He sat back hard in his seat.

"You okay, little brother?" Sly asked.

Dumbfounded, he managed a nod. "Thinking about what to bid on."

"You'd better get over to the tables now, before the bidding closes."

Seth was about to do just that when Bill stood. "My wife and I are dead on our feet. We're going home. It was good meeting you all, and good talking with you, Seth."

"Thanks for all you do at the shelter," Emily's mother added. "Maybe we'll see you again sometime." The couple left.

Seth liked them. Deep in thought, he headed for the donation tables. And realized that he'd actually fallen for Emily around the time he'd met her. He just hadn't admitted it to himself until now.

He loved her. Still staggered by the knowledge, he shook his head again.

What was he going to do about it?

While he looked over the silent-auction items and

mulled over the question, a rancher he'd helped a few days earlier asked for advice about a certain blend of cattle feed. Putting his personal feelings aside, Seth discussed the matter with the man.

Then he put in a bid for a weekend for two at the Prosperity Inn, including breakfast in bed.

At the end of the evening, he and Taylor, along with Cat, her parents and several other teens and parents, stayed to help Emily clean up.

"I've never been to a fund-raiser before," Taylor said. "It was so cool. Did you raise enough money, Emily?"

"It looks that way, but I won't know until we tally up the totals. I'll send out an email on Monday. You were all such a big help with this event. I can't thank you enough. And you two—" she smiled at Taylor and Cat "—you finally made up."

The girls smiled at each other. "We did," Taylor said.

Cat nodded. "Taylor's my best friend, and even if I have a boyfriend, she's really important to me."

Taylor beamed.

"Is it okay if she comes to my house tonight, Seth? This time we're going to have the kind of sleepover where just the two of us talk all night."

"Fine with me," Seth said. "As long as you promise to come to our house next time."

"I will."

"You'll need an overnight bag, Taylor," he said. "When we finish here, we'll go home and get it."

"Great." Taylor leaned closer. "What about Paint?" she whispered.

"I haven't had a chance to talk with Emily about that."

"But you're okay with it?"

"If Emily is. She looks a little tired right now, so I'll talk to her about it later." Along with a few other things.

"Thank you!" Taylor did something surprising—threw her arms around him. Right there in front of her peers and Emily.

Emily's smile was heartfelt and joyous. Seth's chest expanded more than he'd ever though possible, and he knew he wanted to see that smile every day for the rest of his life.

Holding nothing back, he grinned at her. But she'd moved away.

On the drive to the house to pack her overnight bag, Taylor was all smiles. "I'm so happy about Paint," she said. Then she got quiet, picking at her fingernail. "I need to tell you something."

Uh-oh. He shot her a wary look. "What's that?"

"I was planning to run away, back to San Diego. That's what was in that letter from Kayla and my other best friend there, Hanna. Money for a bus ticket."

Seth's heart stuttered in his chest. Unable to hold his feelings in check, he blurted them out. "If you left again, it'd kill me."

Miracle of miracles, she neither mocked him nor shut him out. "I know. Prosperity is my home now, and I'm going to send the money back. I have to learn to trust you, just like Paint will learn to trust me."

His eyes grew damp and he had to clear his throat. "That's beautiful, honey. I'm awful glad. Why don't you invite Kayla and Hanna to visit? I'll bet they'd like the snow."

Taylor looked thoughtful. "Maybe they can come over winter break." A moment later she gave him a timid, sideways look, her eyes glittering in the darkness. "Um, Seth? Can I tell you something else?"

Liking this new, talkative teen, he nodded. "Shoot."

"It's kind of hard to say." She almost winced.

God only knew what was coming. Seth steeled himself. "No matter what you tell me, I'll still care about you."

After a lengthy hesitation, she sucked in a loud breath and blew it out. "The day my mom died..." She swallowed audibly. "We had a fight at breakfast, and I—" Tears filled her eyes and flooded her voice. "I said some really mean things to her." Now she was openly bawling. "I wish... I wish I could take them back."

Seth hated when females of any age cried. But Taylor was confiding in him when she was in such pain, and he was more awed than scared. He reached over and squeezed her hand. "She knew you didn't mean it," he said gruffly. "Wherever she is now, I'm sure she's forgiven you."

"You can't know that. I feel so guilty. Do you have any tissues?"

"Not on me, but there are some clean rags in the glove box." While Taylor rifled through the compartment, he went on. "Maybe you should talk to a professional who can help you deal with your feelings."

"You mean a therapist?" Taylor blew her nose. "I guess I could."

They arrived home. During the ten minutes Taylor spent packing, Seth made some weighty decisions. Her eyes once again dry and clear, she stowed her overnight bag in the rear seat of the pickup.

Instead of heading for Cat's after he buckled himself in, he stayed in the carport. "I've been thinking."

"You do that a lot."

He chuckled. "I know. When we buy the house this spring, I want to fix it up nice—starting with your bedroom. If you have ideas about what you want it to look like, I'm all ears."

"Cool. I'll think about it. Can we go now?"

"In a sec. What I want to say is too important to talk about while I'm driving." He waited until he had Taylor's full attention before he started. "I've always thought of you as a daughter. Now that you're with me for good, I'd like your okay to make our relationship permanent. I want to adopt you."

Her jaw dropped. "You mean that?"

He nodded. "I figure that as long as we're adopting Paint, you and I may as well adopt each other."

"Okay," she said softly. Thanks to the carport lights, he saw her smile brighten her whole face.

"Yes!" Seth pumped his fist in the air, and Taylor laughed. "Now I'll drive you to Cat's."

"She's adopted, too."

"I remember."

One hurdle crossed, one to go. Now if he could convince Emily to give him a chance… What if she didn't?

As he turned onto Cat's street some minutes later, Taylor shot him a worried glance. "It feels all tense in here. Have you changed your mind about me?"

He hated that she was so insecure, but one step at a time. "No way," he assured her. It'd probably take a while before she truly believed that he would stand by her, no matter what. He made a mental note to contact a therapist tomorrow and set up an appointment for her. "We're stuck with each other for good."

Taylor let out a relieved sigh. "Then what's wrong?"

It was time to take some of his own advice and face his problems instead of running away from them. He started by leveling with her. "You're right, I do have something on my mind. It's about Emily. I realized tonight just how much I care about her. I want to tell her, but I know how you feel about her and me in a relationship."

"Oh, that." Taylor waved her hand breezily. "I changed my mind. It's pretty obvious you sort of belong together. Go for it."

"Yeah?" He couldn't help grinning. "To quote a girl near and dear to my heart, that's epic."

She rolled her eyes, but a smile hovered around her mouth. "When are you planning to tell her?"

"I'm thinking I'll go over there after I drop you off." He pulled up Cat's driveway. "Have a good time."

"I will. Good luck, Seth."

"Thanks." He figured he'd need it.

Emily stood outside under the shelter's floodlights, shivering in the cold and waiting for Susannah to do her business. It was late and she was tired, but also elated. "We aced the fund-raiser," she told the dog. "If we did as well as I think we did, we'll definitely be around for another year."

If only Seth was here to celebrate the success... But he would never be part of her life, not the way she wanted.

At last Susannah was ready to go inside. With a sigh, Emily turned toward the door. Her feet hurt, but when she'd walked into the apartment tonight, Susannah had begged to go out, and Emily hadn't taken the time to change into comfy shoes.

Someone pulled into the driveway, and the dog began to bark. Emily recognized Seth's truck. Her heart pounding, she froze.

What was he doing here? She'd seen him an hour ago. He wouldn't just drop by, not anymore. Something must have happened. But wouldn't he have called instead? Maybe he had. She'd left her phone upstairs.

Tugging at her leash, Susannah woofed and wagged her tail in a frenzy of excitement.

In what seemed a blink of time, Seth was out of his vehicle and striding toward her. Unable to read his expression, she grew concerned. "Please tell me Taylor's okay."

"Actually, she's fantastic." He greeted Susannah with a pat and a dog biscuit, and then rubbed his hands together. "It's freezing out here. Let's go inside."

Curious what he wanted at this hour, and fearing that he'd decided to resign despite assuring her otherwise and was backing out of his promise like the other men she'd cared about, she nodded somberly. She'd left her apartment door open, and as soon as she unleashed Susannah, the dog hop-limped up the stairs to her doggy bed.

"Going to invite me up?" Seth asked.

Not wanting to hear the bad news in her apartment, Emily shook her head. "Whatever you have to say can be said right here."

"Suit yourself. It's about us."

Emily didn't understand. There was no *us*. "You don't have to worry, Seth," she said, hugging her waist. "First thing tomorrow, I'll start looking for a veterinarian to replace you."

He frowned. "Why would you do that?"

Okay, so maybe he meant to live up to his promise. Deep down, she'd known that, and felt a little guilty for thinking otherwise. Seth wasn't like the other men she'd loved and lost. Once he made a promise, he kept it. Which made him pretty darned special. One of the many reasons she loved him.

On the other hand, if she wanted to get over him, he had to go. "I'm giving you an out," she said.

"I don't want it. Let's sit down."

As bad as Emily's feet hurt, she was too nervous to sit. She remained standing, and so did Seth.

"Watching you work that room tonight…" He shook his head. "You knocked my socks off. If you don't make a ton of money off the fund-raiser, I'll be shocked."

"From your mouth to God's ears." Cocking her eyebrows, she waited for him to say whatever it was that had brought him here.

"You…" Seth broke off, as if searching for the right words. "You're an amazing, beautiful woman, with a heart to match. I'd be a damn fool to let you slip away."

Confused, she stared at him. "I don't understand."

"Let me explain. Years ago, when I lived at my uncle George's, I put a wall around my feelings. I had to. But getting to know you…the wall began to crumble. Stubborn bastard that I am, I fought to keep it intact. I failed." He looked remarkably cheerful about that. "What I'm trying to say is…" He sucked in an audible breath, then exhaled. "I'm, that is, I love you, Emily." His voice cracked with feeling.

Certain she'd misheard, she gaped at him. "No, you don't. You're too busy for love."

"That's what I told myself. Turns out that I was wrong. These past few weeks have been rough, and not just because of the stuff with Taylor. I've missed you, and I want you in my life. Now that the fund-raiser is over and you have more time, is there any chance for us?"

"You're saying that you want a long-term relationship with me?"

"That's exactly what I'm saying."

Could she let her defenses down and take the risk? Trust that he wouldn't leave her? She abruptly sat down. "No way."

His face fell and he joined her on the couch. "I can't accept that. You can turn me down a dozen times and I still won't give up. If it's more comfortable for you, we'll take a step back and move more slowly. Let me take you out to dinner tomorrow night—just dinner. No sex."

That he would do that for her... He was such a good man, and she loved him so much. "Oh, Seth." Her eyes welled up.

"Please don't cry," he said, looking stricken and catching hold of her hands. "All I ask is that you give me another chance."

The warm, caring man searching her eyes was everything she wanted. If he wasn't worth taking a risk for, who was? Smiling through her tears, she silently entrusted him with her heart. "Silly man, I'm crying because I'm happy. I love you, too."

"You mean it?"

She nodded and started to say more, but he stopped her with a kiss. Her thoughts faded away, and for a long time there were no words at all.

Eventually, they broke apart and he rested his forehead against hers. "I've been a real knucklehead."

"I haven't been much better. I was afraid to fall in love. But I'm not scared anymore."

"Now I feel like I just won the lottery."

He kissed the sensitive part of her palm, right at the base of her wrist, and she melted. There was only one problem.

"What about Taylor?" she said. "We both know how she feels about us being together. I don't want her to be upset."

"We talked about that earlier, when I told her I had feelings for you. She said I should go after you."

"She did, huh?"

"Yep." He grinned. "We talked about other things, too. She finally accepted that Prosperity is her home, and she agreed to start therapy. Even better, since we're going to adopt that dog she wants, I suggested that she let me adopt her, as well. She thinks that's epic."

He looked so pleased that Emily laughed. "That's amazing."

He caught hold of her hands again. "Think you can handle a teenage daughter?"

She gaped at him. "Is this a marriage proposal?"

He nodded. "I can't imagine living my life without you."

Emily had to pinch herself to make sure she wasn't dreaming. "Yes, Seth Pettit, I'll marry you."

His entire body relaxed in relief, and his eyes grew suspiciously bright. He swallowed audibly. "I love you, Emily."

"Me, too."

He kissed her again, until she was breathless. Then he pulled back.

"Tonight I bid on that weekend for two at the Prosperity Inn. Even if mine isn't the top bid, we should go in and celebrate. Taylor won't mind—she can stay at Cat's."

"That sounds wonderful. Do you want more kids, Seth? Because at some point, I'd like to have a baby with you."

"Having a little Emily running around, chasing the dogs and bugging Taylor, sounds great to me."

Emily was elated. "Once we're married, do you think Taylor would mind if I adopted her, too?" Emily asked.

Seth thought that was a fine idea.

"There is one more thing," he said. "Once I buy the rental house, it'll take me a year or three to fix it up. Can you live in the midst of a construction project?"

"I could live in a quarantine hut with you and be happy," she teased.

He chuckled, a sound she knew she'd never tire of hearing.

"You never fail to make me laugh." Seconds later, he sobered. "I want to show you just how much I love you, but not on this lumpy couch."

"Then let's go upstairs." Filled with trust and joy for the man she loved, Emily led the way to her apartment.

* * * * *

An avid daydreamer since childhood, **Julie Benson** always loved creating stories. After graduating from the University of Texas at Dallas with a degree in sociology, she worked as a case manager before having her children: three boys. Many years later she started pursuing a writing career to challenge her mind and save her sanity. Now she writes full-time in Dallas, where she lives with her husband, their sons, two lovable black dogs, two guinea pigs, a turtle and a fish. When she finds a little quiet time, which isn't often, she enjoys making jewelry and reading a good book.

Books by Julie Benson

Harlequin American Romance

Big City Cowboy
Bet on a Cowboy
The Rancher and the Vet
Roping the Rancher
Cowboy in the Making

Visit the Author Profile page
at Harlequin.com for more titles.

THE RANCHER AND THE VET

Julie Benson

For Lori Halligan—

Some friends are silver. Some are gold. You're twenty-four karat. Thanks for always being there for me.

And to Lori Goddard—

Just for being you.

Special thanks to the staff and volunteers of the Hinsdale Humane Society for putting up with me being underfoot and for answering all my questions. (Pam and Mary Alex, thanks for the laughs during lunch!) For all of you, it's clear your work isn't a job, it's a calling.

Thanks also to John Milano, one of the wonderful regulars at Starbucks at Custer and Renner in Richardson, for answering my legal questions and helping out when I was at my wit's end.

Chapter 1

"I'm being deployed to Afghanistan. I need you to come to Estes Park and take care of Jess."

Reed Montgomery straightened in his black leather desk chair with the lumbar support, his cell phone clutched in his now sweaty hand as he processed what his older brother had said.

Colt was being deployed to Afghanistan. Soldiers went there and never returned.

Then the remainder of his brother's words sank in. *I need you to come to Estes Park and take care of Jess.*

He loved his niece, but the thought of being responsible for a child left Reed shaking. He didn't want children. The pressure. The fear of screwing up and damaging the kid for life. To top it off, taking care of any kid would be hard enough, but a teenage *girl?* That could send the strongest bachelor screaming into the night.

"Tell me I heard you wrong."

"I need you to watch Jess."

His brother had lost his mind.

Once Reed's brain kicked back into gear and his panic receded, he remembered his niece still had one set of grandparents. "I thought the plan was for Lynn's parents to stay with her."

"That was the idea, but when I called them I learned Joanne broke her hip last month and needed surgery."

"And they're just telling you now?"

"We don't talk much since Lynn died. They blame me for her death."

Almost a year ago, after fifteen years of marriage, Colt's wife had said she was sick of ranch life and had run off with her lover, only to die in a head-on collision a month later. Colt had picked up the pieces of his life, and explained as best he could to Jess that she hadn't been responsible for her mom leaving.

Lynn's death had also meant that Colt had to revise his family-care plan in case he was deployed.

"You weren't driving the car. Her lover was."

"They think if I'd been a better husband, she wouldn't have left. In their opinion I should've spent more time at home and less time with the reserves. Blaming me is easier than accepting the truth."

An only child, Lynn had grown up catered to—spoiled rotten, actually. Colt's wife had been high-maintenance, self-centered and had believed her husband's life should revolve around her.

"Is Joanne doing well enough that Jess could go live with them in Florida?" In addition to being unqualified for the job, Reed thought, his life and business were here in San Francisco. How could he up and leave for Colorado?

"She said she should be eventually, but there's another problem. Their retirement community only lets children stay for a week. Last night Herb brought up the subject at a town hall meeting, and everyone went crazy. The Association of Homeowners thinks if it makes an exception for Jess, within a month they'll be overrun with kids."

"Threaten them with a lawsuit. That'll make them back down. Better yet, give me your in-laws' number. I'll have my lawyer call them."

"You need their phone number, but there's no point in them talking to your lawyer." As Colt rattled off the phone number, Reed added it to his computer address book. "Even if they made an exception, Jess refuses to live in 'an old folks' neighborhood where people drive golf carts because they're scared to drive a car.' That's a direct quote. She said when she stays with her grandparents they never go anywhere. So in her words, she'd be a prisoner."

While he felt bad for his niece, that didn't mean Reed wanted to return to the old homestead and play dad. He'd been happy to see Estes Park in the rearview mirror of his beat-up truck when he left for Stanford. The thought of returning for anything longer than a weekend visit left him queasy.

"You're the parent. Don't ask Jess what she wants. Tell her what she's going to do."

Colt laughed. "That's easy to say for someone who doesn't have kids. I tried the strong-arm approach. She threatened to run away."

"Teenagers say that every time they don't get their way."

"I think she meant it, Reed." Colt's voice broke. "She's been having trouble since Lynn died, but she won't talk about it. Last year she started cutting classes and sneaking out at night to meet friends. Living in a retirement community and going to a new school would only make things worse."

Somehow Reed couldn't connect the sweet niece he'd seen a year and a half ago at Christmas with the teenager his brother described. Jess had been eager to please, had loved school and was an excellent student. He stared at her picture on the corner of his mahogany desk. Her wide smile and twinkling brown eyes spoke of how carefree she'd been. Of course, the photo had been snapped before her mom ran off. He knew how that betrayal had affected Colt, but how could a kid wrap her head around something like that?

And his brother expected him to deal with a teenager who'd lost her mother and was acting out? What did he know about dealing with difficult children? Nothing except the piss poor example his father had given him. His stomach dropped. When Jess pushed him, and she would—hell, all teenagers did, even the good ones—how would he deal with it? Would he react like his old man, with a closed mind and an iron fist?

No, he was better than his father.

He'd worked hard to become the man he was today and, unlike his father, he tried to do something about his anger. When Reed had worried he might repeat the cycle of violence, he'd taken an anger-management class. Of course, going back to Estes Park and dealing with a teenager could test the techniques he'd learned.

The good news was he and Jess got along well. He loved his niece, and to her he was the cool uncle who sent great gifts like the newest iPhone. They'd be okay. "You really think she was serious about running away?"

"I wouldn't ask you to come here otherwise—not

when you could be here up to a year. I know this will make running your business tough."

His cell phone beeped in his ear, alerting him to another call. Reed glanced at the screen. Damn. He'd been trying to get in touch with Phil Connor all morning. Forcing himself to let the call go to voice mail, Reed focused on his brother's problem. "Tricky? Yes. Impossible? No. Could she come here instead?"

"As if dealing with losing her mom wasn't enough, soon after that her best friend moved to Chicago. Now I'm going to a war zone. I'm nervous about uprooting her, too. That's another reason I backed down when she balked about going to Florida. I need you to do this for me. You and Jess are the only family I've got."

The words hit Reed hard. He and Colt had always been close. Even before their parents died, he and Colt had relied on each other, sticking together through all the crap slung at them during childhood. While Reed's life the past few years had been almost perfect, Colt hadn't been as lucky. Life had knocked his brother around pretty well, especially the past year. How could Reed add to Colt's problems? Only a selfish bastard would say no.

"How soon do you need me there?"

"I leave in three days. If you get here tomorrow, that'll give us time to go over things before I leave." Colt's heavy sigh radiated over the phone lines. "If anything happens to me, promise me you'll—"

"Don't say that." While Reed tried to fill his voice with confidence, he knew there was no guarantee Colt would come home in one piece, or come home at all.

"I've got to and, dammit, Reed, you *will* listen. If I don't come back, promise me you'll watch out for Jess. Sure, Lynn's parents would take her, but I'm not sure that's best for her, especially if they won't move to Colorado."

"I give you my word, but you've got to take care. Don't do anything stupid. You don't have to be a superhero."

Colt chuckled, but the sound rang flat in Reed's ears. "Deal."

After ending his conversation with his brother, Reed returned Phil's call and reassured his client that their project was still on schedule. He was proud of his company, of what he'd accomplished. RJ Instruments was small, with only forty employees, but it was *his*. Something he'd created from nothing, and the company was holding its own in the market. They were the up-and-comers in the semiconductor business, making the chips that drove many of today's electronic wonder gadgets.

Of course, all of that could change when he started running things remotely.

Reed turned his attention to his calendar and his upcoming meetings. Some he could handle via Skype. With a laptop and his cell phone, he could run his business long-distance for a couple of months, but more than that? Probably not. His customers would want to see him in person. He'd have to make in-person sales calls to launch SiEtch. He smiled, thinking of their newest product. If he was right, they'd revolutionize the semiconductor industry, but they were approaching some crucial deadlines for release. He definitely couldn't run his business remotely for a whole year until Colt returned.

He hadn't gotten where he was by letting fate toss him around. He'd created a solid business by being proactive. His mind worked the problem, rehashing the immediate issues forcing him to return to Colorado—

the Association of Homeowners' age restriction and Jess's resistance.

No matter what Colt thought, the first step was tackling the association's age restriction. Reed turned to his computer and clicked on his address book to locate Colt's in-laws' number. Then he opened a new email, hit the priority icon and typed a message to his lawyer.

Contact my brother's in-laws to get the contact information for their Association of Homeowners. I need the association to make an exception for my niece to stay with her grandparents indefinitely while Colt's in Afghanistan. Threaten them with an age-discrimination lawsuit. Do whatever you have to, but get the exception. Until I receive the approval, I'll be forced to relocate to Colorado to take care of my niece.

Reed hit Send and leaned back in his chair. Surely when the exemption came through he could convince Jess to see things his way, especially when staying with her grandparents was best for her. There she'd have a woman to talk to and two people who'd actually raised a child, instead of an uncle who couldn't keep goldfish alive.

Next Reed called Ethan, his vice president of engineering, and asked him to come to his office. He'd met Ethan fresh out of college when they'd started working as software engineers at the same company. Eventually Reed had moved to the management track while Ethan pursued the technical route. The guy was a genius in that area, and the first person Reed had hired when he started RJ Instruments.

When Ethan arrived, Reed motioned toward the black leather couch. Then he walked across his office and settled into the wing chair to his friend's right. He glanced up at the print of a hole at Pebble Beach on the wall behind his sofa. Below the photo were the words *The harder the course, the more rewarding the triumph.* He hoped that held true this time.

"I need to update you on something that developed this morning." Reed explained about Colt's deployment and his leaving for Colorado.

"What about the customer calls you're scheduled to make next week?"

When clients had questions or needed hand-holding, Reed picked up the phone or hopped on a plane if necessary and handled the situations. While both he and Ethan understood the technology, over the past few years Ethan had developed issues dealing with some clients, becoming frustrated when they refused to see things his way. Now he'd have to step up and take on more of those responsibilities.

"I hope I can handle most of the issues with conference calls or on Skype. I might be able to pull off a quick day trip." Fly out, meet with the client and rush back to Colorado. Or he and Jess could leave Friday afternoon for a meeting/vacation trip. "But if those options don't work, you'll have to go instead."

"If I have to, I guess I have to."

"I can still run the weekly status meeting as usual via Skype. Between the two of us, we can reassure clients they won't see any difference in our service or attention to detail. We need to make sure everyone understands my being in Colorado won't affect our timelines, either, especially for SiEtch's release."

"I still think we're missing the mark, and we should lower our price point."

No way would he discuss that issue with Ethan

again. They disagreed, and nothing either one said would change the other's mind. "My lawyer's working on getting approval for my niece to move in with her grandparents. Six months at the outside and I'll be back here running things."

Ethan shook his head, and chuckled. "I don't envy you. Six months with a teenage girl? I hope you can manage to stay sane."

"It shouldn't be too bad. School starts a couple of days after I get there. How hard can it be when she's gone eight hours a day?"

Reed's stomach knotted up when Estes Park came into view. The main drag into town was four lanes now instead of two, but even at rush hour, the traffic seemed nonexistent by San Francisco standards and, damn, a turtle moved faster! They passed The Stanley Hotel, a white giant perched on a hill above the town. Farther down W. Elkhorn Avenue, shops catering to the tourists that kept the town of ten thousand alive lined the sidewalks. So many people came to Estes Park to enjoy the scenery, shop and relax. Here, they could get away from their lives and slow down for a while. Recharge their batteries.

Not Reed. How would he face anyone after what he'd done to his father? Sure, he'd changed, but everyone in Estes Park knew who he'd been. That's why when he visited Colt he stayed on the ranch, but that wouldn't be an option now.

As they left the town behind and drove past other bigger ranches, Reed longed to be back in the city where he could blend in with the masses. Where he could walk past people and no one knew him. No one knew what he'd spent a lifetime running from.

When Colt turned down the long gravel driveway to the Rocking M, Reed's chest tightened. Pine and aspen trees stood guard. Others would call the rustic ranch settled among the rugged Rocky Mountains beautiful, maybe even going so far as serene, but not Reed. The mountains loomed over the ranch like silent giants, reminding him of his father—harsh, unyielding and domineering.

Memories bombarded him as the simple ranch house came into view. Colt had painted the place a soft brown instead of the dingy cream Reed remembered and had planted new landscaping, but the alterations couldn't change his memories or the fact that he'd been glad to be free of the place. For Reed, the old man's presence dominated everything on the ranch. Even after all these years and everything he'd done to shake him.

Like staying away from Estes Park while his father had been alive.

"You know where the guest room is," Colt said once they stepped inside the front door. "When you're ready I'll give you the rundown on the place."

While Reed had returned to the Rocking M since Colt owned the place, his visits had so far consisted of a Thanksgiving weekend or a couple of days over Christmas, and he'd avoided going into town. He'd worked so hard to leave his past behind, but that was hard to do when everyone in town knew who he'd been.

Especially Avery.

Ben McAlister, Avery's father, had done him a favor all those years ago, though at the time, Reed had thought it had been the worst thing ever to happen to him.

Your father's an alcoholic who beats the people he claims to love. You've changed this summer, and I hate to say it, but I see glimpses of him in you, son. You need to grow up and deal with your past. Until you do that, all you'll do is drag my daughter down with you.

As Reed trudged up the stairs he told himself he'd be damned if he'd let his memories pull him back.

He walked into the guest bedroom and his throat closed up. While the room looked nothing like it had when he'd lived here—now resembling a hotel room with its nondescript accessories and earth tones—all he saw was the past. He pictured himself as a scared child, huddled in the corner between his bed and the wall as the sounds of his parents arguing shook the house. He remembered how often he curled up on his bed, his chest aching from the blows his father's meaty fists had delivered. He pictured himself as a teenager sprawled on the floor, the world spinning around him from drinking too much beer to numb the pain.

He'd never been able to stand being here for longer than four days. How would he handle staying for possibly a year? One nightmare at a time. And he'd do what he'd always done. He'd focus on work. After dumping his suitcase in the closet, he practically ran out of the room.

When he and Colt toured the ranch, Reed realized almost as many ghosts taunted him outside as in the damned house. They walked past the hay pasture and he remembered how his dad had smacked his head so hard his ears rang for a day after he'd gotten the tractor wheel stuck in a hole and it had taken them over an hour to pull the thing loose.

Don't go there. Remember who you are, not who you were.

He needed to remain focused on tasks and what needed to be done while Colt was gone. If he stayed busy enough he might survive. "I knew Dad sold some land before he died, but I didn't know it was this much."

"Damn near half of the acreage. My guess is once you left he was too lazy to do the work and too cheap to hire hands, so selling off the land and stock was the easiest way to keep a roof over his head and his liquor cabinet full."

"That sounds like our father."

"I've been rebuilding the place, but it's been slow going."

Especially with a wife like Lynn. Reed often thought if she hadn't gotten pregnant in Colt's senior year, she and his brother would've broken up after high school. Instead, his brother had graduated, enlisted in the air force and they got married.

Five years ago when their father died, Colt bought Reed's share of the ranch, and his family returned to Colorado. His brother hoped putting down roots would make his wife happy, since she'd grown weary of military life, something he loved. Something he saw as a calling. Part of the compromise had been that Colt could join the National Guard Reserves. Unfortunately, despite everything Colt did, he didn't get the happy ending.

Reed had gotten the better end of the deal. He'd used the money Colt paid him to start his company.

The dusty smell of hay hit him when they entered the barn, bringing with it reminders of the hours he'd spent toting hay and horse feed to the barn.

"How can you stand living here? Don't the memories get to you?"

"I just remember the bastard's dead and buried. I've had a damned good time changing things around the place. I hope some of them have him turning over in his grave. That gives me a whole helluva lot of pleasure." Colt thumped his brother on the back. "I know this is tough for you."

"I'll be honest. I'm not sure I can stand being here a year." He looked his brother straight in the eyes. "You don't know what it was like after you left."

While they were teenagers, Colt had saved Reed more than once. When their dad went on a tirade, Reed shouted back or argued. He and his father went at it like two bulls stuck in the same pasture. Colt was the one who stepped in to defuse the situation, or he hauled Reed off before his dad could beat him to death. When Colt left for the air force, their father's anger had spiraled out of control.

He'd come home one night to find his dad drunk and spoiling for a fight, hammering on his favorite subject—how Reed was a bastard for leaving him to fend for himself. One thing led to another, and his father had punched him in the face. Something inside Reed had shattered that night, and without Colt there, he exploded.

He whirled, delivering blow after blow until his father collapsed on the floor. His chest heaving, Reed stood over the man who had tormented him for years. Then the reality of what he'd done sank in. He'd stooped to his father's level by taking his anger out on another human being. His father roused enough to scream that he'd make Reed pay. He'd call the police and see that Reed's sorry, ungrateful ass landed in jail.

Panic consuming him, Reed ran out of the house. Hours later, he found himself at the McAlisters' front door. Avery held him while the whole damned mess poured out of him. Then she'd woken up her parents.

Once Reed had explained to Avery's parents what

had happened, Ben McAlister had called his lawyer. When Reed claimed he couldn't afford that, Ben told him not to worry about the money. Without Ben paying for his attorney, Reed could've gone to jail. He never knew the details of how Ben and his attorney got his father to drop the charges. They never said, and he never asked.

That one event had changed him in ways he still didn't understand.

"I've got an idea what it was like. That's why you coming back to stay with Jess was always the backup plan. That's why I didn't want to ask you to do it, and if Joanne hadn't broken her hip, I wouldn't have."

"I'm also worried about dealing with Jess." That and holding his company together, but Reed left out that detail. Colt carried enough weight on his shoulders.

When Reed had first spotted Jess at the airport, dressed in tight, low-cut jeans with a deep V-neck sparkly T-shirt that barely covered her midriff, he'd wanted to turn around and catch the first plane going anywhere.

"If I can't handle being here…if I get your in-laws' Association of Homeowners to make an exception, and I can get Jess to agree, are you okay with her living with her grandparents?"

Colt nodded. "As long as Jess agrees, I'm fine with it."

Reed's fear subsided now that he had a safety net.

"Jess is a good kid. Lynn's leaving really did a number on her. How the hell could she run off on her daughter? She didn't even have the nerve to tell Jess before she left. I had to," Colt said as they walked toward the horse stalls. "Damn, that was hard. You should've seen Jess's face. She looked at me with those big brown eyes of hers, and asked why her mom didn't love her anymore."

Reed stood there stunned. He knew Lynn's leaving had been bad, but Colt hadn't told him what a bitch she'd been. "You sure picked a winner."

"You're right about that. The only good thing I got out of that marriage was Jess. She's worth whatever hell I went through." Colt shoved his hands into his jeans pockets. "School starts the day after tomorrow. It about takes a crowbar to get Jess out of bed, and she takes forever to get ready. Classes start at eight. If she isn't up by seven, she'll be late. You need to leave by seven forty-five."

Reed jotted down information about Jess's routines, the location of important documents and anything else he thought he might need to remember.

"She seems nervous about starting high school this year." Colt shook his head. "I don't remember us worrying about the kind of stuff she does—imagined slights, who's best friends with who, who said what about her outfit. The worst arguments are about boys. Girls are downright mean to each other. And their fights…" Colt whistled through his teeth.

"Worse than ours?"

Colt nodded as they walked past another stall. "We pounded on each other, but then it was over. Not with girls. When they get mad the emails and tweets fly. Girls divide into two camps. Then the tears start. Sometimes for days, and Jess won't talk about it. Then when I think it'll never end, they're all friends again."

Lord help him. He'd rather fight off a hostile takeover than face what Colt had just described. Why didn't society ship all teenage girls off to an island, and allow them to come back only once their sanity returned?

"You're not making me feel better about this. What do you do during all this drama?"

"Drama? That attitude will get you in trouble."

Reed froze as a lilting feminine voice washed over him. How many times had he heard that sultry voice in his dreams? Way too many to count, but never once when he'd come back had he sought her out. He wasn't one to borrow trouble. They were too different. He couldn't live here again, and she wouldn't live anywhere else. More important, though, she wanted children and he didn't.

He glanced over his shoulder at the woman coming out of a horse stall two doors down. She'd been pretty in high school, but the word failed to describe her now. Tall and willowy, even dressed in dirty jeans and a shapeless scrub top, without any makeup, the woman before him could stop traffic when she crossed the street.

Avery McAlister.

Staring at the beautiful blonde in front of him, he knew he'd been right to avoid Avery, because seeing the only woman he'd ever loved hurt worse than any blow he'd taken from his father.

Chapter 2

"Avery, what are you doing here?"

"It's good to see you, too, Reed." Avery laughed nervously as she forced herself to remain outwardly calm despite the blood pounding in her ears.

The last time she'd seen him he'd been tall and lanky, but in the years since, his frame had filled out in all the right ways. His shoulders were broader now, and he might even have grown an inch or two. His chiseled features, strong jaw and short black hair remained the same. Dressed in tailored slacks and a pinstriped shirt, Reed Montgomery, the boy she'd dated and fallen in love with in high school, had grown into a fine-looking man.

And he didn't show the slightest hint of guilt over breaking up with her via email all those years ago.

Avery tried to shut off the memories, but they broke free. She and Reed had met in Mrs. Hutchison's kindergarten class. They'd been seated at the same table and were busy drawing when Bennett Chambers yanked the yellow crayon from her hand. She'd been about to punch him in the arm when Reed whispered something she couldn't hear to Bennett. The boy's eyes widened and he paled, then a second later she had the yellow crayon.

They began dating their sophomore year of high school and fell in love soon after. In their senior year, Reed gave her a promise ring and they started making plans for their future. They both wanted to go to college. He'd received a scholarship from Stanford to study business, and she had one from Colorado State to study veterinary medicine, but he promised to come home as often as he could. Then a month after leaving for California, he sent her a short email. He loved living on the West Coast. He didn't want to come back to Colorado. Ever. He didn't want to get married. He didn't want children. He thought it was best they end things.

Being young, foolish and unable to let the relationship go that easily, Avery had called him. When he didn't answer, she'd left tearful messages on his voice mail, begging him to talk to her, which he never did. Then she wrote long letters that came back unopened.

Staring him down now, she reminded herself she wasn't the naive teenager willing to beg a man not to break up with her anymore, and she was damned if she'd let him see how much his coming back shook her.

"I'm here checking on Charger's injured foreleg. I'm a vet now, and the director of the Estes Park animal shelter." *Take that. I went on with my life and made something of myself.*

"I'm glad you're doing well, though I'm not surprised. You always could do anything you put your mind to."

Except hang on to you.

Their small talk sounded inane considering how intimate they'd once been. "What are you doing here, Reed?"

"I'm staying with Jess while Colt's in Afghanistan."

So that's what had brought him back. She turned to Colt. About the same height as his younger brother and almost as handsome, Colt had inherited their mother's blond hair while Reed resembled their dark-haired father. "I'll keep you and Jess in my prayers while you're gone."

Colt nodded. "I appreciate that."

"You're staying here for what, a year? Eighteen months?" she asked Reed. "You must have a very understanding boss."

"A year. Luckily I own my own small company, and thanks to Skype it shouldn't be too difficult to run things long-distance."

He was still as confident as ever, Avery mused, and yet she wondered if Reed's plan was one that looked great on paper, but wouldn't work well in practice.

"Wow. You own a company."

"It's not as glamorous as people think. I put in more hours than any of my employees, and I get a salary like everyone else. Most of what the company makes goes right back into developing new products."

A cell phone rang. "I'm sorry. I've got to take this call," Reed said.

As he moved away, his phone glued to his ear, Avery turned to Colt. "Are you sure about this? I think running a business long-distance will be harder than he thinks."

"I don't have a choice." Colt explained about his mother-in-law's health issues, the age restrictions in his in-laws' community and Jess's reluctance to live with her grandparents. "Reed will settle in. He'll do right by Jess."

Colt's daughter had gone through so much over the past year. Some women shouldn't have a pet, much less a child, and Lynn Montgomery had been one of those women. Now Jess's dad was being deployed. How much could a teenage girl take?

Avery wondered where she would've been without her mother to talk to during her adolescence. Her dad had been great, but he'd never quite understood things from her perspective. He saw things, well, like a *guy*. Did Jess have any women in her life to talk to now that her father was being deployed and she would be living with her bachelor uncle?

Who had never wanted children.

"Reed hasn't been around Jess very much. Are you sure he can handle this?"

She shook herself mentally. She always did this—got attached to any stray that wandered across her path. Colt was Jess's father. If he thought Reed was the best person to care for his child, who was she to criticize? But neither of them knew what it was like to be a teenage girl, one of the most insecure creatures on the planet.

Reed joined them, irritation marring his classic good looks. "Jess and I have a good relationship. We'll be fine. She's not an infant that needs watching 24/7. Things will be hectic for a while until I've reassured my customers that my physical absence won't affect my business, but then everything will settle into a predictable routine."

Avery laughed. "Predictable routine? With a teenager? Good luck with that."

"She has a point, Reed," Colt added. "Teenagers give

mules stubborn lessons. You'll have to be a little flexible."

"Lucky for me I've got great negotiation skills."

"Good thing, because you'll need them." *Pride cometh before the fall* popped into Avery's mind. With Reed's attitude, one was sure coming. Not that it was her concern. Needing to steer the conversation to a safer topic, Avery said, "Charger's leg is better. I changed the dressing. The redness and swelling have subsided, but keep him away from the other horses a while longer. I don't want the wound getting reopened."

"How much do I owe you?"

Avery waved her hand through the air, dismissing the question. "Nothing. You didn't ask me to come by. I did that on my own. It's the least I can do. By the way, I wanted to remind you Thor is due for his annual shots."

"Thor?" Reed asked, knowing the shots would fall to him to get done.

"That's Jess's dog." Avery reached into her back pocket, pulled out a business card and handed it to Reed. "Call the office and set up an appointment."

"When did Jess get a dog?" Reed asked his brother.

"Must've been a couple of months after the last time you were here."

"The fact that you didn't know Jess has a dog says a lot about your relationship. I bet you're one of those uncles who sends birthday and Christmas gifts, but can't bother with anything else. If that's the case, you're in for a bumpy ride." With that, Avery turned and hurried out of the barn. Reed Montgomery was back, and worse yet, he could still make her heart skip a beat.

When Avery walked into the shelter twenty minutes later to a chorus of barking and meows, she still hadn't regained her emotional balance from seeing Reed. When she'd first spotted him, her palms had grown sweaty. Her heart had raced. All reactions she hadn't experienced with a man in far too long.

She needed to go on a date with someone. Anyone. What had it been? Six months? Longer? That was her problem. She'd been neglecting her social life.

Like that was something new?

When she found time to date, it seemed no one could hold her interest. Invariably she discovered some irritating habit she couldn't overlook, or her boyfriend's future plans conflicted with hers. Whatever the reason, the fun and attraction fizzled out after a few months.

Stop it. Focus on work and quit thinking about Reed and your pathetic love life.

So far the week had been a good one for the shelter. Five dogs, six cats and three horses had been adopted. They'd gotten enough donations to buy animal food to last until the end of the next month. Hopefully the recent events indicated an upward trend.

"Betty Hartman called this morning and said she couldn't come in," Emma Jean Donovan, Avery's volunteer coordinator and right-hand gal, said the minute Avery walked into the front reception area.

"Oh, the joys of working with volunteers." People thought nothing of canceling at the last minute, not realizing how the shelter relied on them to accomplish many of the daily tasks, chores that had to be done, no matter what.

"Because she wasn't here, Shirley didn't have anyone to gossip with, so guess who got an earful?"

"Better you than me, Em."

"All she could talk about was Reed Montgomery being back in town."

"So I discovered when I stopped by the Rocking M this morning."

"You *saw* him? Are you okay?"

While Em had been two years behind Avery and Reed in school, everyone in town knew about their messy breakup. The news had spread through Estes Park High faster than the flu. "I was barely eighteen when we broke up. I got over him ages ago. So what if he's back? I don't care."

"Oka-a-ay." Em drew out the word, and tossed her a sly whatever-you-say-though-I-don't-believe-a-word-of-it grin. "You don't have to convince me. Is he still hot?"

"He looked sort of silly standing there in the barn wearing dress pants and a pinstriped shirt, but I guess he's attractive in a California yuppie sort of way."

Liar. He'd looked better than ever. He'd been a teenager when he left. He was all man now.

"I could get used to California yuppie. If you're not interested, do you mind if I make a play for him?"

"He probably has a yuppie girlfriend, but if he doesn't, go for it." Annoyed with the topic and her internal hell-no reaction to Em's question, Avery steered the conversation back to shelter business. "Has anything happened that I actually *need* to know about?"

"We had an abandoned mama dog and her litter dropped off this morning. The pups are about three weeks old."

So much for the to-do list she'd compiled last night. Avery's top priority now became examining the latest arrivals and getting them ready for foster care. The commotion at the shelter was too much for a mama and her babies, especially for the five weeks until they could be put up for adoption. "Got any ideas of who can foster the little family?"

"It's already taken care of. Jenny will pick them up once you give them the all clear."

"You're amazing."

"And on only four hours' sleep."

"I heard the band was playing at Halligan's. How'd the gig go?"

Music and her country-and-western band were Emma's first loves, with animals a close second. She worked at the shelter to pay her bills, and moonlighted playing at area bars in the hopes that someone would spot her and offer her a record deal.

Emma's face lit up. "The crowd was small but enthusiastic. My new song went over well."

"When your record deal comes through, promise me you'll train someone before you leave me. Not that anyone would do the job as well as you do, but at least then I'll have a chance for survival."

"I am one of a kind." A beaming Emma held out an envelope. "This came by registered mail."

Avery read the return address. Franklin, Parker and Simmons, attorneys at law in Denver. "Let's hope it's good news. Maybe someone left us a bequest in their will."

She tore open the envelope, pulled out the letter and started reading. The missive indeed dealt with a will—Sam Weston's. Twenty-five years ago, when Geraldine Griswald had created an animal shelter, her husband and Sam were hunting buddies. Sam, also an animal lover, rented Geraldine a piece of land with a tiny building along Highway 35 East for one dollar a year. Eventually, the shelter raised money and built a bigger facility.

Avery read further. No. This couldn't be right. The shelter didn't own the land their building stood on? Everyone believed Sam had donated the land to the Estes Park animal shelter over fifteen years ago.

This couldn't be happening.

She read further. Sam's heirs wanted to sell all his land to a developer, including the parcel where the shelter stood. They'd "generously" offered to let the shelter buy their lot if they matched the developer's price of three hundred thousand dollars. Otherwise, they had forty-five days to move.

Three hundred thousand dollars. Just raising a 20-percent down payment of sixty grand would be daunting in the allotted time. Avery swallowed hard and tried to push down her panic.

The Estes Park animal shelter was the only one for miles. If it closed, the other shelters would have trouble dealing with the additional demands on their resources, and the animals would pay the price.

"From the look on your face, I'm guessing it's bad news."

Talk about an understatement, but Avery couldn't tell Emma that. Until she checked into the situation, she'd keep the news to herself. But if she discovered they didn't own the land, everyone would hear about the situation, because they'd need every cent they could get to keep the shelter open.

"Nothing I can't handle." Avery inwardly winced. How could she say that with a straight face, especially to Emma who knew her so well? They'd both pinched every penny thin over the past few months to keep the shelter afloat, but she thought she could come up with sixty grand? Delusional, that's what she was.

"Next thing you'll try to sell me the Rocky Mountains."

So much for keeping the news to herself, because

she refused to lie to Emma. Glancing around the front room, Avery made sure no volunteers or other staff members were around before she told Emma the news.

"What are we going to do? Do I need to update my résumé?"

"Don't you dare. I need your help now more than ever. This is the game plan. While I'm examining the new arrivals, you'll contact the property clerk to find out who they show owns the land."

"What about the board?"

Avery cringed. Harper Stinson, the shelter's board president and a top graduate from the micromanager school of business, had hinted they could solve all their financial problems by cutting staff. If Avery didn't handle the situation carefully, Harper would run amok through the streets of Estes Park with the news of the shelter's impending doom.

"I'll figure out how to tell the board when I have more information." She'd be proactive. Assess the situation and develop a plan before she spoke to them.

"Lucky you."

"The board may be a big help. They've got a wide range of skills and talents, and that's exactly what we need right now."

"When they aren't arguing over who has the best idea and who should be in charge of the project." Emma shuddered. "I still have nightmares about our last dog-washing fund-raiser."

"Thanks for reminding me about that." Three of the board members had taken on organizing key aspects of the fund-raiser. Avery had been forced into the peace-maker role when the lines between the jobs blurred and toes got stepped on. "They'll pull together better this time because it's such a dire situation. You'll see."

"You're such an optimist."

"If I wasn't I'd never survive running a nonprofit agency."

Reed's day started at the bank getting the forms notarized for him to be Jess's guardian while Colt was overseas. Then he and Jess took Colt to the airport. On the drive to Denver, his niece slouched in the backseat texting and ignored her dad's attempts at conversation, while Reed tried to ignore how much Jess's actions hurt Colt.

When Colt hugged Jess, telling her how much he loved her, and how he'd miss her, Reed's eyes teared up. He and his brother shook hands, thumped each other on the back, and Reed reminded Colt not to act like an idiot and get himself hurt. Then he prayed this wasn't the last time he would see his brother.

On the return trip, Jess sat stoically in the passenger seat, texting. After a few feeble efforts at conversation, she snapped that she didn't want to talk. Then she popped in earphones, cranked up her music and shut her eyes.

When they returned to the ranch, she retreated to her bedroom while Reed saw to the stock. A couple of hours later, dripping in sweat, muscles he hadn't used in years sore from hauling hay and water, he crawled into the shower.

After cleaning up, he headed downstairs to work on dinner. He'd learned to cook out of necessity when he and some college buddies lived off campus his senior year. Unable to afford eating out every day and sick of boxed mac and cheese, he'd turned to the internet and the Food Network.

He glanced at his watch. Not even six and he felt as though it was after midnight. As Reed added chopped garlic, onions and ginger to the chicken breasts cooking in the skillet, the aromas engulfed him. Though the sleek stainless-steel-and-earth-toned kitchen looked nothing like the one he remembered growing up, he still could see his mom standing in the same spot as he did now.

Life had been so different before she died of breast cancer.

He often wondered why she had married his father. Talk about opposites. His mom loved to cuddle up with her sons every night before bed and read to them. He could still hear bits and pieces of *Green Eggs and Ham* read in her soothing voice. His mom quickly and generously offered support and encouragement, while his father tossed out criticism and orders. When his temper exploded at his sons, his mom stepped in and smoothed things over or took the blows. She also kept his father's drinking in check. All that changed when she died.

Reed tossed sliced carrots, snap peas, broccoli and soy sauce in the pan. Nothing he'd ever done had been good enough for his father. When he showed an interest in business and computers, his father took that as a personal rejection. Ranching had been good enough for Aaron Montgomery and his father before him—why the hell wasn't that good enough for Reed? His father expected, no *felt,* his sons owed it to him to stay at the ranch and take care of him in his old age.

As if either he or Colt would do that after the hell their father put them through.

After plating the chicken and sautéed vegetables, he walked to Jess's room and knocked on the door. High-pitched barking sounded from inside. "Dinner's ready."

The door opened, and Jess stood there, a brown Chihuahua clutched to her chest. The dog immediately growled at him. "This is Thor?"

"What's wrong with my dog?" Jess asked, her voice laced with distrust and irritation.

Did all teenage girls twist the simplest questions into knots?

"When your dad told me you had a dog named Thor, this wasn't the image that came to mind." He'd envisioned a border collie or a shepherd mix. A dog that would be useful around a ranch, not one that fitted in a girl's purse. "Why'd you name him Thor? Don't girls usually name their dogs Mr. Boots or Prince Charming?"

"And you know that because you're such an expert?" Still clutching the dog, she stalked past him toward the kitchen.

He still couldn't get over the difference in his niece's appearance since he'd seen her last. With her dark brown shoulder-length hair and wearing enough makeup to start her own makeup counter, she was fourteen going on twenty-two.

When he reached the kitchen, Jess was seated at the round oak table, her dog settled on her lap. He was having dinner with his niece and her dog. Dogs belonged under the table begging for scraps, not seated on someone's lap. He opened his mouth to tell her to put Thor down, but paused. A fire burned in her eyes, as if she dared him to say something, as if she was spoiling for a fight. He'd entered labor negotiations where people looked at him with less animosity. A smart businessman picked his battles carefully.

Reed reached for the plate of chicken. The dog peered over the table and snarled.

"Does he growl at everyone, or is it just me he doesn't like?"

"He's very sensitive." Jess picked up a small piece of chicken and fed the morsel to her pet. "In his head, you came and Dad left. It's kind of a cause-and-effect thing."

"You sure it's okay for him to be eating chicken with soy sauce and all those spices?"

Jess rolled her eyes and made a tsking sound with her tongue as though she was the Dog Whisperer and he the idiot who couldn't spell *dog*.

This charged silence couldn't continue between them. Even he could tell she was bottling up her emotions, and anger simmered barely below the surface. Better to bring things out in the open than have them explode later, but how?

"What about you? What are your thoughts?" Reed kept his voice level and unconcerned.

"It's not like I had any choice."

"When I was your age, not having any say about something ticked me off big-time." Not that his father had ever noticed. Or would've cared if he had.

Jess shrugged and handed her dog another bite of chicken.

This was getting him nowhere. Could he use a strategy he applied to employees with Jess? Build a team atmosphere? "I know this is hard for you, and I've got to admit, it's not easy for me, either. Since Mom died when Colt and I were a little younger than you are now, we grew up in an all-male household, but I'm not that bad a guy, am I?"

Jess eyed him cautiously. "I don't know. The last time you were here, you left the toilet seat up. That really ticks a woman off, you know."

The chip Jess carried around on her shoulder had to

be getting heavy. Maybe if he made her laugh, she'd loosen up. "In a show of good faith I'll invest in one of those toilets that have an automatic seat-lowering feature."

His niece smiled, ever so slightly. "Whatever."

"I wouldn't want to have to call your dad and tell him you fell into the toilet."

"Eww! Thanks for putting that image in my head!"

Her bright giggle thrilled him, easing the tightness in his chest. Maybe they could make a go of this. At least long enough for him to change her mind about staying with her grandparents. "I haven't worked on a ranch since I went to college." He'd gone to summer school to avoid coming back. "I'll be relying on you a lot."

Her smile faded, and her chocolate eyes darkened. "If you think I'm going to do all the work around here, forget it."

"I was thinking of you as an expert consultant." Giving someone a title helped an employee feel vested in a project. She nodded, but remained quiet. "Do I have any redeeming qualities, or am I a total pain in the ass?"

As Jess eyed him he could practically see the biting comment forming in her mind. Then her gaze softened. "You're a good cook. Even better than Dad, so at least we won't starve."

It wasn't much, but it was something.

The next morning at five Reed dragged himself out of bed, threw on jeans and a T-shirt and headed for the barn. He went to the hayloft and grabbed a bale, jumping when a rat scurried over his boots. At least it wasn't a snake. He'd never gotten used to them. What was the rule about which ones were poisonous? Something about red, black and yellow being a friend of Jack or killing a fellow, but that's all he recalled. Making a mental note to check Google for poisonous-snake sayings for future reference, he tossed the hay out of the loft.

While his muscles strained against the unfamiliar work, part of him had come to enjoy the physical exertion. The upside was he collapsed into bed at night exhausted enough that being back in his old bedroom didn't prevent him from falling asleep. Of course, he didn't sleep all that well, either, but one out of two wasn't bad.

He filled the hay bins in the stalls, then gave each horse some grain and fresh water. Next he went in search of a saddle, surprised to find his old one in the tack room. He smiled, remembering how he'd saved for a year to buy it. He ran his hand over the suede seat and the basket-weave tooling, then lifted the saddle and carried it into the stall of a calm chestnut. His body went into autopilot, his hands efficiently accomplishing the task of saddling the horse.

He rubbed the horse's neck. "Go easy on me. It's been a while since I've done any riding." Then hauled himself onto the animal. The old leather creaked under his weight. His heels tapped the horse's flanks, and the animal responded. So far so good. He was in the saddle, not on his ass in the hay.

As he made his way across the ranch toward the cow pasture, Reed settled into a rhythm with the horse. The stiffness he'd woken up with from tossing and turning most of the night eased with his movements. Colt had told him to keep a close eye on the cows. For a small herd, Colt said, they caused a surprising amount of trouble. Most of which revolved around finding holes in the fencing and traveling to Sam Logan's land.

The soft summer breeze teased his skin. The house

disappeared from view, and he relaxed. Urging the horse into a gallop, he felt the tension drain from his body. He'd forgotten how freeing it felt to be on top of a magnificent animal riding hell-for-leather to nowhere in particular. Just running.

Recalling how often he and Avery had ventured into the national park to get away and just be together, he smiled. They'd ride and then stop near a mountain stream to talk and make out. There he'd been happy. At least until he returned home.

The herd came into view, thankfully still where they belonged. After a quick check of the fences Reed returned to the house, showered and then headed for Colt's office, where he pulled up an email from his lawyer.

He had a problem. According to his attorney, there was some federal act that let communities set age restrictions as long as they met certain criteria, like 80 percent of the houses having someone over fifty-five in residence. As long as they maintained that, the neighborhood could keep kids from living there.

After firing back instructions for his lawyer to check into the community's compliance, Reed glanced at his watch. Seven in the morning, and he hadn't heard Jess stirring. If she didn't get moving soon, they'd never make it out the door on time, and he'd start his day behind.

When he stepped into the hallway that led to the bedrooms, an alarm clock's irritating beep greeted him. How could she sleep through that?

He knocked on her door. Nothing. He knocked harder. "Jess? Are you awake?"

High-pitched yips masquerading as barking came from behind the door, but nothing from his niece. Now what? He sure as hell wasn't going in her room. Then, between the alarm beeps, he heard snoring. He pounded on the door. "Jessica! Shut off your blasted alarm, and get your butt out of bed!"

More yipping, followed by "All right!"

He glanced at his watch. "I'll expect you downstairs for breakfast in twenty minutes. That will give you ten minutes to eat and brush your teeth, leaving five minutes to gather what you need for school before we head out."

He heard her shuffling around the room before the door flew open and he faced a scowling Jess dressed in boxer shorts and an oversize T-shirt. "You worked out how much time I need to brush my teeth and gather my stuff?"

"What's wrong with a schedule?"

"Nothing if you're the TV Guide Channel." She brushed her bangs out of her face. "Don't get your shorts in a wad. I've got plenty of time. They won't count me late on the first day."

He hadn't given a thought to the school counting her tardy. "We've got to leave by seven forty-five. I have an eight-thirty conference call." Also, he refused to set up bad habits. Managing his staff had taught him it was easier to create good patterns than to break poor ones.

"That's not *my* problem. I'll be down when I'm good and ready." She slammed the door in his face.

At seven-fifty he called his assistant to push back his conference call. He and Jess left at seven fifty-five.

When he returned to the house at eight-thirty, he opened the front door, stepped inside and slipped, nearly ending up on his backside.

Glancing down, he discovered puddles—and they weren't pee—dotting the wooden floor. As he stared at the trail heading upstairs toward the bedrooms, he wondered if he'd shut his door.

"Thor, you better not have gone in my room, or you'll be in trouble." *I'm threatening a dog. Three days with Jess and I'm going crazy.*

He followed the trail right to his open bedroom door. Peering in, he discovered the damned dog sleeping on his pillow, away from the mess he'd created on the rest of the bed. "You're out to get me, aren't you?"

Not wanting to put off his conference call a second time, he made his way through the minefield to Colt's office, shut the door behind him and decided to deal with it all later. He spent the next hour reassuring clients that his being in Colorado wouldn't affect their business, while pretending his life hadn't become an exercise in surviving teenage angst and cleaning up after a vindictive Chihuahua.

After ending his call, he found rubber gloves, paper towels and a bucket to tackle Thor's messes. He'd muck out an entire barn before he'd pull this duty again. Any repeat incidents and he was calling in a hazmat team.

Next he retrieved Avery's business card from his wallet and punched in her number. As he waited for her to answer, he stormed into Jess's room.

Didn't every girl with a Chihuahua have a carrier-purse thing? Clothes covered the floor, making it look like a patchwork quilt made by a color-blind quilter. He scanned the disaster zone. If she had something to put the dog in, he'd spend the better part of the day finding it.

No way was he letting the little monster ride in Colt's truck unconfined. Some things were sacred, and a man's truck was in the top two. He headed for the kitchen to find a substitute carrier as Avery's voice answering the phone floated over him.

"I need your help."

Chapter 3

"Jess's dog has the runs." Reed walked into the kitchen. He glanced around the room. What could he use? "Can I bring him in?"

He flung open cabinet doors, searching. The plastic containers he found were too small, and Thor could get out without a lid. Then he spotted cloth grocery sacks hanging on the pantry door. He smiled and snatched one up.

"Thor's sick? Bring him in. On Thursdays we don't open until noon, but I'm going in early to do paperwork. I'll meet you at the shelter in twenty minutes."

Sack in hand, he thanked Avery, said he was on his way and returned to his bedroom. Maybe he'd get lucky and she'd keep the dog for a couple of days.

When Reed walked into the room, Thor eyed him suspiciously. Reed inched closer to the bed, trying to appear casual. The dog sat up and growled. Reed strolled to the dresser, opened a drawer and dug around inside.

I'm trying to carry off a sneak attack on a dog. I'm not going crazy. I'm there.

He stalked toward the dog, and Thor bolted under the bed.

Damn. No way was he getting on the floor to catch the mutt. Instead he returned to the kitchen. When he looked inside the fridge he found deli ham. He stormed back to the bedroom, tore off a chunk and dropped the treat on the floor beside the bed. Seconds later, a little brown head appeared and gobbled up the meat. Reed tossed down another piece, this one farther away. Two tries later, he snatched up the dog, dumped him in the cloth bag and looped the handles through each other so Thor couldn't hop out, leaving enough of an opening for air to flow.

As he left the house, he realized fate seemed determined to throw him and Avery together. What were the powers that be trying to tell him? He shook his head. He didn't care. All he wanted to know was how to get them to leave him alone.

Avery stopped at the front desk to locate Thor's file, and giggled thinking of Reed dealing with a Chihuahua with the runs. When she opened the door for him five minutes later, irritation darkened his handsome features.

"Where's Thor?" Then she noticed the black cloth grocery bag dangling from his large hands. Hands that knew her body well. No. She couldn't think about that. Focusing on the sack, she saw it move. She bit her lip, trying to hold in her laughter, but failed. "You put him in a grocery sack?"

"Woman, I've been pushed about as far as a man can be. You're taking your life in your hands, laughing." The minute he started speaking the dog growled. Reed glared at the bag. "And you better be nice to me after the bomb you dropped on my bed."

"He didn't."

"He sure as hell did, and all over the wooden floors."

The absolute horror on his face made her laugh harder. "I'm sorry. Really I am." She giggled one last time thinking of his reaction when he'd found his bed. It was amazing the dog was alive.

"It's funny to you because it wasn't your bed."

"Bring him in." She stepped aside for him to enter, and Reed's musky cologne tickled her senses. As he handed her the sack, she remembered how his scent clung to her clothes after they'd been necking, which led to images of the two of them together and a sudden spike in her heart rate.

Stop it. Trips down nostalgia lane led nowhere but back. She was all about moving forward with her life, and hoped she'd find someone who wanted the same things she did—a loving marriage and raising their children in the same town where she'd grown up. Something that Reed never would do.

"After I examine Thor, I'll let you know what's going on." For a minute she stood there, the silence between them shouting volumes.

He shifted his weight from one foot to the other. "This is awkward, isn't it?"

"I don't know what you expect me to say. I wasn't the one who ended things between us."

She'd told herself she'd gotten over him. But until she'd seen Reed in the barn the other day, she hadn't realized how much anger she still carried. They'd made love the first and only time the July after graduation. She'd loved him so much, wanted to spend the rest of her life with him, and then the relationship was over.

"We'd talked about our future so much, and never once did you mention the fact that you didn't want children. How could you have left out that important detail?" Giving voice to her anger and throwing the words in his face felt good. Closure. She finally had what she'd never known she craved.

"I don't know what to say other than I was young. When I got to college, I started thinking about what us having a future meant in practical terms, and it hit me."

"You gave me a promise ring, and then you never came back."

"I couldn't. Once I got away, I felt free. I didn't want to lose that, but you're right. I should've called you."

But it had been worse than that. She'd left messages begging for him to talk to her. Ones that he'd never returned.

Let it go.

"I was an ass, and I'm sorry I hurt you." He stepped toward her, then froze, as if he wasn't sure of what to do next. "Can we start over with a clean slate? Be friends?"

Friends? The word shouldn't have stung her pride, but it did.

Avery nodded. That would make things easier when they ran into each other, and in a town of less than ten thousand people, their paths would cross. "I'll call you when I know what's going on with Thor."

Dismissing Reed, Avery reached into the sack, lifted Thor out and snuggled with him for a minute. She waited for the sound of the door opening and closing as Reed left, but after a moment she glanced over her shoulder, finding him still standing there. "Is there something else you need?"

A familiar look flashed in his cobalt eyes as his gaze locked with hers. Her heart fluttered. Was he thinking the same thing she was? How much they'd once thought they needed each other?

"Jess will be worried when I tell her about Thor. Can I bring her by after school?"

"Absolutely. Chances are it's nothing serious, and he'll probably be ready to go home by then."

Reed nodded and then turned and walked out of the exam room. When she'd said they could start over, she'd thought doing so would make things easier. Then she'd asked him if he needed anything else, and now she wasn't so sure. The look she'd glimpsed in his eyes moments earlier was the same one she'd seen years ago, right before he kissed her.

Later that afternoon, as Reed sat in the pickup lane at Jess's school, his thoughts returned to Avery. He was thankful that they'd cleared the air. In a town the size of Estes Park, they'd run into each other. Now maybe things wouldn't be as awkward.

Who was he kidding? Things would still be awkward. Everything he'd loved about Avery—her giving spirit, her quiet strength, her down-to-earth nature— was still there, but there was something more now. Something more refined. Her appeal had heightened over the years. She was one of the most beautiful women he'd ever seen, and yet she seemed unaware of the fact.

The truck's passenger door opened, a red backpack flew behind the seat. Jess slid in, the leather seat squeaking with her movements. He tossed out the obligatory "How was your day?" and she responded with the typical teenage response of "Fine."

"I took Thor to the vet. He wasn't feeling well. I came home to messes all over the house."

Her eyes widened, and her lip quivered. "What's wrong? Is he okay? What did Dr. McAlister say? Is he home?"

The more questions Jess asked, the higher her voice rose. He rushed to reassure her. "Avery—Dr. McAlister—said it probably wasn't serious, but she was going to run some tests. I said we'd stop by after school to check on him."

Minutes later, at the shelter, Avery walked into the exam room, Thor snuggled in her arms. Jess raced toward them.

"We gave this guy some fluids because he was a little dehydrated, but that's nothing to worry about, Jess," Avery commented in a soothing tone as she placed Thor on the metal table. "I ran some tests, but didn't find anything."

"Then why'd he get sick?"

Avery shrugged. "He might have eaten a plant or something outside that upset his system. Who knows. To help with the diarrhea I want you to give him some medicine once a day. The front desk will give you the dosage information when you check out."

Reed bit his lip to keep from saying he'd told Jess she shouldn't have given her dog the chicken last night, but he did toss a knowing glance in her direction.

"Let me show you both how to give Thor the medicine." Avery reached into her scrub-top pocket and pulled out a plastic syringe filled with the pink liquid. When Reed remained nailed to his seat, both she and Jess turned to him. "I can see fine from here. I'm responsible for Jess. She's responsible for the dog. That's the chain of command."

Jess shook her head and faced Avery. "He doesn't like Thor."

"The dog doesn't like me," Reed countered. As if to prove the point, Thor peered around Jess, glared at Reed and growled. "See."

"That's actually natural. Chihuahuas bond strongly with their owners and tend to distrust people they don't know. Isn't that right, Thor?"

Reed frowned. The danged mutt wagged his tail. But then, what male wouldn't be hypnotized into submission receiving Avery's full attention?

"Thor doesn't understand why Colt is gone and you're here," Avery continued. "That adds to his uncertainty, but Jess can help him accept you."

Acceptance? All he wanted was the dog to stay out of his way, and do his business outside. He could live with distant disdain.

Avery glanced between Reed and his niece. "Jess, would you go to the front desk and get some dog treats so we can work with Thor?"

When the door shut behind the teenager, Avery faced Reed, her hands on her hips. "Did it ever occur to you that Thor is upset with you because he senses the tension between you and Jess?"

"I love my niece."

"Then prove it. You need to get to know her as a person. You need to show an interest in her life."

Reed stiffened. "That's going to take time. I just got here."

"Remember she's your niece, not one of your employees. And FYI, a good start would be making an effort to get along with her dog."

Before he could answer, his cell phone rang. He glanced at the screen and answered the call without so much as an *Excuse me*.

"What's up, Ethan?"

Avery shoved her hands into her lab-coat pockets and took a deep breath. "Get off the phone. My time is valuable. I've got other animals waiting."

Reed ended his call with a terse "I'll call you back."

The exam-room door swung open and Jess returned with the treats. The teenager glanced between the two adults. "Jeez, you two look like you're about to take a swing at each other. What did I miss?"

Was that how they looked? Reed paled and stepped back.

"It's nothing. Just a difference of opinion." Avery cleared her throat. "Jess, if you want to help Thor accept your uncle, he should take over caring for him for a couple of days."

"I don't know." Jess clutched her dog against her chest. "I want them to get along, but he's my dog."

"I understand. We can still do some things that will help." She asked the teenager to sit in a chair by the door while she worked with Reed. "Both of you need to reinforce Thor's good behavior with praise and treats, while you ignore the negative. Let me give you an example. Jess, if you're holding Thor and he growls at your uncle, put him down and turn your back. If he doesn't growl or act aggressively, Reed, you need to give him a treat and praise him in a high-pitched voice." She demonstrated. "We call it a Minnie Mouse voice."

"You've got to be kidding." Reed shook his head. "You're determined to crush my ego today, aren't you?"

"Like yours can't take the hit?" Avery teased.

"I'm willing to try if you are, Uncle Reed. Then you could help me give him his medicine."

For a moment, despite the dark eyeliner, Jess's wide brown eyes filled with innocence and she looked her age. How the hell could he say no to her when she looked at him like that? Had he ever been that innocent or trusting? Even before his mother died? "We'll give it a shot."

Avery spent the next couple of minutes working with him and the dog. At one point he looked at Avery and said, "Thor's not the only one who needs reinforcement for positive behavior. I want some props for my effort here."

"Good job, Reed." Avery tossed the words out in a high, squeaky voice.

"That wasn't what I had in mind."

"Too bad. That's all you're getting." Their light banter reminded him of how comfortable he'd always felt with Avery. He'd been in love with her for dozens of reasons, one being how at ease he felt with her, but that was before he damn near beat his dad to death. Before he'd talked to her father and realized he loved her so much he had to let her go because she deserved better than he could give her.

Being back here still wasn't good for him, and she refused to live anywhere else. His thoughts stopped him cold. "I've got the idea. Jess and I can work on this at home." Before Avery could say anything, his cell phone rang again. "We done here?"

Avery nodded, handed the dog to Jess and headed out of the room. He answered the call and told the client he'd call back in five minutes. Then he joined Avery and Jess at the front desk. Reed scanned the bill, amazed that the charges were bigger than the dog.

"Avery, what's this I hear about the shelter not owning the land our building resides on?" The sparkle disappeared from Avery's gaze, and she stiffened as though someone had tied a broom handle to her back. Reed turned to see a woman with short salt-and-pepper hair dressed in jeans and a T-shirt with an elk on the front stride toward them.

Avery made the introductions. "Reed, Jess, this is Harper Stinson, the shelter's board president."

Years ago, when he'd been on the board of his boss's pet charity, Reed had learned a lot about the people who served on them. Some were crusaders. Others were out to make community business connections. Others still were bored housewives looking to find purpose. But no matter who they were, everyone had an agenda. What was this woman's?

"So, you're the Reed Montgomery that has everyone in town talking. I want you to know I'm keeping your family in my thoughts and prayers," Harper said. "We'll all be glad when your brother's back home safe and sound."

No one more so than him.

Jess tossed him a let's-go look. "Thor and I will wait outside."

As the door swooshed open and thunked close with Jess's exit, Reed glanced at Avery. "I appreciate you working Thor in this morning. I hope you got some paperwork done after I left."

When he turned to leave, Harper partially blocked his exit. "Since you brought up the topic of paperwork, Avery and I are developing a new business plan for the shelter. What do you think—"

"Reed's a busy man. He doesn't have time for shelter business," Avery insisted.

Her stiff posture and the way she nibbled on her lower lip told him Avery had reached her patience limit. Something was going on between these two. Any businessperson worth two cents knew better than to discuss their business in public, especially in front of strangers.

"Avery's right about that. I've got my hands full with Jess and my own company."

"Our main sticking point is staffing issues," Harper continued, completely ignoring his and Avery's comments. "I'm sure you know that while no one likes to cut staff, sometimes it's necessary to lower operating costs."

Now he knew her agenda. Harper wanted him to back her up against Avery. "I've found people often latch on to that solution because it's easier than working to find other ones," he said.

He glanced at Avery and found her eyes shining with gratitude. When she smiled, his insides twisted, and he swore his chest puffed out.

Avery flashed him a tight smile. "Reed needs to go, since Jess is waiting for him. I'm sure she has homework to do. If you have any other problems with Thor, call me."

As he left he almost pitied Harper. He'd seen that look in Avery's eyes today, and unless he missed his guess, Harper was in for a stinging lecture on business etiquette.

As Avery ushered Harper into her office, she struggled to control her temper. How dare she burst into the shelter and take her to task in front of Reed and Jess? Worse yet, she'd tried to pull Reed into their disagreement and use him to get her to knuckle under.

As Avery sank into her worn desk chair, it squeaked

under her movement. Before she could explain her position, Harper said, "Why wasn't I informed the minute you received word from Sam Weston's lawyers?"

"I wanted to research our options before talking to you." Avery placed her folded hands on her desk. When her fingers started tingling, she loosened her grip. "If you need to talk to me about shelter issues, especially our disagreements, I'd prefer we discuss things in private."

Three months ago, Avery had loved her job. Harper's predecessor had valued her opinion and trusted her instincts. He'd allowed her to do her job. All that had evaporated once Harper assumed control of the board and insisted she be consulted on every issue.

The more she delved into the business side of the shelter, the less Avery liked her job. Holding her hand out for donations and managing a staff weren't why she had gone to vet school. While she'd taken a couple of business classes in college in preparation for opening her own office, she hadn't enjoyed them.

When she'd accepted the shelter's offer, the board had hoped to hire an executive director within six months. She'd figured she could hold on until then, but that was over a year ago. The plan was that this year's Pet Walk would allow them to hire a director. Then she could focus on what she loved, taking care of animals and educating owners. So much for that.

"I know it's been hard for you to understand that working for a nonprofit organization in a small community means everyone knows your professional business, but that's a fact you need to adjust to," Harper said, her tone bordering on condescending.

Avery concentrated on her breathing, counted to ten and mentally listed Harper's good qualities. She truly cared about animals. Her heart was in the right place. She possessed valuable business connections and used them to recruit new shelter supporters. A great ambassador and advocate, she donated generously.

Her temper reined in, Avery said, "Our disagreements need to remain between us. You wouldn't want me to discuss problems I had with your shop or your merchandise in front of customers. I expect the same professionalism from you."

Realization dawned in Harper's eyes. "My mistake. I was upset about the news that we don't own the land. However, I do believe Reed could be a valuable resource for us."

The last person Avery wanted invading her professional life was Reed. "While he knows the corporate world, he lacks experience in the nonprofit arena and with fund-raising, and that's our biggest concern right now," Avery said in hopes of channeling the conversation to the task at hand. "The first thing we need to do is move up the date of the Pet Walk. I spoke with the executors. If we take out a loan to buy the land, the papers must be signed by the deadline. Since the land price is three hundred thousand, that means we need sixty thousand dollars for the down payment."

Harper paled. "The most we've ever raised from the Pet Walk is thirty-five thousand, and that was in a better economic climate."

Avery refused to let the shock and worry in Harper's voice rattle her further. They could do this. They had to. "Getting more and bigger sponsors is the key. I hope to tap some of my brothers' contacts."

Avery's oldest brother, Rory, modeled designer jeans for a large New York–based clothing company. Her brother Griffin was the host of the reality show *The*

Next Rodeo Star. "If I can get Devlin Designs and Griffin's network to write us big checks, that'll go a long way to achieving our goal. However, the first thing we need to do is make sure that buying this land is our best option."

Harper tapped her manicured nail against the chair arm, something she did frequently as she thought. The habit grated on Avery's tightly strung nerves. "No matter what we do, we'll have to obtain a loan. To give us one, the bank will require proof we can afford the increase in our monthly operating costs."

Yesterday, Harper's micromanaging had been Avery's biggest problem. Now her shelter needed sixty thousand dollars to remain open, and the only man she'd ever loved was back. What she wouldn't give for a time machine.

Friday afternoon, Reed sat jotting down discussion points for Monday's staff-status meeting as he waited for Jess in the school's pickup lane. Thank goodness for wireless technology to make productive use of otherwise wasted time.

The truck door flew open, Jess's backpack flew behind the seat and then the door slammed shut. He rolled down the passenger window. "Where are you going?"

"Out with friends."

"Get in. I'll drop you off after we talk."

"They're waiting for me."

"If I don't get more details, you don't go." Reed almost winced as similar things his father had said rang in his ears. He inhaled deeply before he continued. "Text them that I'll drop you off in a few minutes."

The door flew open again, and this time Jess crawled

in, mumbling something about the Spanish Inquisition and teenagers having rights, too.

As the line of cars inched forward and Jess texted away, he asked about the specifics of her plans.

"We're going to hang out. We might go to a movie."

"What movie? Who with? What time will it be over?"

"I don't even know if we're going to a movie, so how can I know when it'll be over? Dad doesn't give me the third degree."

Reed wasn't sure if he believed her, but whether he did or not didn't matter. He was here, and Colt was in Afghanistan. Instead of saying that, he reiterated his stance that without enough details, she didn't go.

"We talked about going to the new Robert Pattinson movie, and before you ask, it's PG. I'll be home around eleven."

"Your dad said your curfew was ten-thirty."

"Whatever."

She was testing him and, he suspected, trying his patience on purpose. Did she really think her dad wouldn't tell him about her curfew or that he wouldn't remember? "How are you getting to the movie?"

"Jeez, my teachers ask less questions on quizzes. We were going to walk downtown and shop first, then go to McCabe's for pizza. If we go to a movie we'll walk. Otherwise we'll go back to Lindsey's house."

As he pulled out of the school parking lot onto the street, Reed said, "Text me when you know whether you're going to a movie or to a friend's house. I need to know where you are so I can pick you up."

Jess rolled her eyes. "You want to fit me with a GPS?"

"Don't tempt me," Reed said.

Later that night, as Reed sat on the couch, a beer in his hand, watching the Colorado Rockies game, he thought over his first week. So far there hadn't been any major fires to put out at work. Most of his clients understood his situation. The two customers he'd been scheduled to visit next week had agreed to conference calls instead.

He and Jess had settled into a routine. To deal with the departure-time issue, he'd set all the clocks ahead five minutes, which meant they left for school relatively on time. After two days of him banging on her door at seven, Jess started getting up on her own. A success in his book, especially considering neither of them had done bodily harm to the other.

He stared at the spreadsheet in front of him, but couldn't focus. How pathetic was it to be working on Friday night? Usually he met friends for a couple of drinks. They talked shop, investments and sports. Or he'd go out on a date, although he hadn't done that in a while. After all, what were his chances of having a decent relationship with a woman with his parents' marriage as an example? Colt had tried that, only to end up with a less than pleasant foray into wedded bliss, and Colt wasn't nearly as like their father as Reed was.

He had to get out of the house before he went crazy. Not knowing what else to do, he snatched his cell phone off the coffee table and dialed Avery's number before he could reconsider. "Do you want to go out for pizza? You know, test out this friendship thing."

"I've got plans."

He told himself not to ask, because he wasn't jealous. He didn't want to know if she was seeing someone, but the words refused to stay put. "Hot date, huh?"

"Yup. It's Griffin and his wife Maggie's first night

out since they had their baby, my gorgeous, amazing niece, Michaela. I'm meeting them at Halligan's."

"Griffin's a father? The world's ending, and I didn't have a clue." Her brother getting married and becoming a family man was like saying the Pope had become an atheist.

"He went on the reality show *Finding Mrs. Right*."

"So he married a gorgeous bachelorette?" Now, that made sense and sounded more like Avery's playboy brother.

"No, he didn't. How he and Maggie got together is actually a funny story."

"Tell me about it at Halligan's," Reed said, fishing for a formal invitation.

"You remember what the place is like, right? A down-home country bar. Not like the fancy California clubs you're used to where everyone's dressed to the nines and sits around sipping expensive wine and chatting about their investments."

Was that what she thought of him? How close she came to the truth shouldn't have stung, but it did. "Are you saying I won't fit in?"

"Between the peanut shells on the floor and the spilled beer, your expensive designer duds wouldn't last the night."

He couldn't miss her derisive tone, or the implication. He was a city boy now, wouldn't fit in and he no longer interested her. Now he was going no matter what she said. He had something to prove.

"I'll see you there."

"I'll be with my family."

"I've spent almost as much time with them as my own." And, with the exception of Colt, he had liked hers a whole hell of a lot better. "Are you saying you don't want me to come?"

"I know I said we could be friends, but I'm not sure I'm ready for us at Halligan's."

He knew what she meant. Us *together* at Halligan's. The down-home bar and grill had been everyone's favorite hangout, no matter their age. He and Avery had spent a lot of time together there. Laughing. Talking. Planning.

"It's Friday night. It's been a long week with Jess. Taking care of her and running my business long-distance is tougher than I expected." And the responsibility was weighing him down. "I need to get out, and I haven't spoken to anyone from town other than you since I left. Remember old man Aldridge and how pitiful he looked every Friday night?"

Tom Aldridge sat at the bar alone until he'd had a couple of beers. Then he wandered from table to table, telling the same lame jokes until someone finally took pity on him and asked him to join them.

"That could be me."

Silence met his request.

"What is it, Avery? You afraid you can't keep your hands off me?"

Avery's husky laugh reached deep inside him. "That'll be the day."

Chapter 4

As Avery sat at a table at the edge of the dance floor with Emma and her sisters-in-law, Elizabeth and Maggie, she still couldn't believe Reed had asked her out. Sort of. She'd almost dropped the phone. Though he'd added that they should test out "this friendship thing," warning bells had clanged so loudly in her head that her ears rang.

Part of her wanted to see what their relationship would be like now that they weren't fumbling teenagers. They'd always had great chemistry, and it had been so long since she'd wanted to be with a man.

The problem was she knew they couldn't have anything permanent, and she wasn't sure she could handle a casual relationship. She'd never done well with those.

"I talked with Mick," Emma said, referring to Halligan's owner. "He said we could put pitchers on the bar for donations. I thought I'd call you up onstage to explain what's going on with the shelter before we start our set."

"Sounds good." As Avery glanced again at the front door, she trailed her index finger through the condensation that had formed on her beer bottle. Luckily she faced the entrance, allowing her to keep her door preoccupation under wraps.

"What is it with you tonight?" Emma asked as she leaned closer.

"I keep thinking about work." She hoped her friend would be satisfied with her answer.

She was distracted all right, but not by her job. When she'd said they could start over as friends, she'd never expected Reed would press the issue. She'd imagined their truce would mean if they met on the street they'd smile, nod at each other and go on their way.

But once again she and Reed had different plans. Okay, so he wanted to test their new friendship. What was the big deal? As she'd told him, he wasn't irresistible.

Yummy and tempting, yes. Irresistible, no.

She possessed a decent amount of willpower, and a place with loud music and lots of people provided a great opportunity to test their new relationship. She could handle this.

If that were true, how come her stomach fluttered with butterflies as if she was waiting for her date to arrive?

"Liar." Emma's voice echoed the tiny one inside Avery's head. "Who are you watching for?"

So much for not appearing obvious. "Reed called and said he'd drop by tonight."

"Who's Reed?" asked Maggie, Griffin's wife.

"A high-school boyfriend." Avery tossed out an abbreviated, sanitized version of their past.

Questions flew at her.

"What's he like?" This from Elizabeth.

"How do you feel about him being back in town?" Maggie asked.

"Are you thinking about getting back together?" Again from Elizabeth.

"She said she's not interested," Emma scoffed.

"I can speak for myself, thank you." *Note to self. Never go out with friends when you're the only one not in a relationship. They feel compelled to meddle.* "Reed's different now than when we dated. He's gone all California-yuppie, arrogant CEO."

And they still wanted different things out of life.

"That's what I said about Griffin—that we had nothing in common and he was arrogant." Maggie's green eyes twinkled with amusement.

When Avery's brother had been the bachelor on *Finding Mrs. Right,* Avery had laughed herself silly watching her playboy brother date gorgeous women supposedly to find a wife. Instead of marrying one of the bachelorettes, he'd fallen for the average girl, the show's director, Maggie.

"Just because you could knock some sense into a man as thick-headed as my brother and make things work despite your differences doesn't mean everyone can."

"It's funny you said that, Maggie. I thought the same thing about Rory when we met, especially the arrogant part," said Elizabeth, Avery's other sister-in-law. "I think there's something to the saying opposites attract. Maybe you shouldn't write Reed off so fast, Avery."

Rory had met his wife on a horseback-riding tour on the family ranch. Elizabeth, a New York advertising executive, had offered Rory a modeling job, which he'd eventually accepted to earn the money to pay for their mother's first round of cancer treatments.

"You said Reed called you? Maybe he wants more than friendship," Maggie added.

"I heard he stood up for Avery when Harper got on her case. That doesn't sound like a man with nothing more than friendship on his mind to me," Emma said.

Avery glared at her friend, trying to send her a support-me-don't-pile-on look. "Don't you have to warm up your voice for your set, or test the speakers or something?"

Emma glanced at her watch. "I've got plenty of time."

"You don't think his calling means he wants to pick back up with you?" Elizabeth asked.

"What is it? National Find-Avery-A-Date Day and no one told me? Reed called because he was bored." Or at least that's what Avery told herself. He hadn't meant anything more.

"You said he grew up here. Why didn't he call an old *male* friend?"

Leave it to Maggie to pick up on that detail and have the nerve to ask the question.

"He said he hasn't kept in touch with anyone since he left." Avery thought about that. Granted, working on the ranch and studying to get top grades had left little time for friends, but he hadn't kept in contact with anyone? He really had left town and never looked back.

"But he kept in touch with you?" Maggie asked.

Avery shook her head and explained the reason for Reed's return. Then she told everyone how she'd run into him when she was at the Rocking M checking on a horse, and how she'd seen him again when he brought Jess's dog into the clinic.

"Wow. A single guy, suddenly having to parent a teenage girl, run his business long-distance and all without any friends or family for support. He's got a tough job ahead of him."

Avery knew that, but hearing Elizabeth say the words put things into a different perspective. She'd been so thrown off balance from seeing Reed that she hadn't thought of things from his point of view. He had taken on a huge undertaking and had no one he could count on.

He has you.

No. She refused to listen to the nagging voice that wanted her to save the world. She owed him nothing. Certainly not help. Not after all these years.

"If he doesn't want to get back together, why would he call you?" Emma tossed out.

"Quit making a big deal out of this. It's simple. He said I'm the only one he's talked to since he got back to town, and when he got bored he called me."

"Considering you two used to date, I'm surprised your mom hasn't taken Reed under her wing. She has a tendency to do that," Maggie said. "Not that I'm complaining."

Both Avery's sisters-in-law had firsthand experience with their mother-in-law's matchmaking. When Elizabeth first arrived in Estes Park to shoot a commercial, Avery's mom had insisted she stay at the ranch. When she'd balked, Nannette McAlister had said if Elizabeth didn't stay, there wouldn't be a commercial. That ended the discussion. Maggie had experienced similar subtle coercion when she and Griffin arrived to film the final episodes of *Finding Mrs. Right*.

"Don't give Mom any ideas. That's all I need—her going into matchmaker mode." Especially since her mother had always liked Reed, but only because Avery hadn't told her everything. Avery couldn't bring herself to tell anyone all that had happened. How she'd left messages on Reed's voice mail begging him to talk to her, and how she'd almost given up her desire to have children to keep him.

"That might not be all bad," Maggie countered, pulling Avery back to the conversation at the table.

"She did a pretty good job where Rory and I were concerned."

But her brothers had been different. Deep down inside, they both wanted the same things as their wives—a home and family. Unlike her and Reed. "I can handle my own love life, thank you very much."

Emma burst out laughing. "Not from what I can see. When was the last time you had a date?"

Longer than she wanted to admit or discuss. "That's not important."

Maggie stared at Avery, a curious look on her face. "Why don't you date more?"

Because she'd given up. Too many first dates that left her not wanting a second. She wanted someone who would still make her heart skip a beat when they really knew each other. A man she loved enough to overlook his annoying habits, and every man had a few of those.

When the trio at her table looked as if they'd launch into another inquisition, Avery raised her hand. "Leave it alone, okay? So I haven't been dating a lot. That doesn't mean going out with an old flame is a good idea."

"Doesn't mean it's a bad one, either," Emma said.

Choosing to ignore her friend's comment, Avery glanced at the entrance again to see the door open, and Reed step inside. The rosy glow of sunset framed him as he stood in the doorway dressed in formfitting jeans and a red-and-black-plaid shirt. Then she noticed his feet. Cowboy boots. Gone was the yuppie businessman.

Her pulse skyrocketed. He looked so relaxed, so approachable. As though he belonged here. He looked like the man she'd fallen in love with.

Not good.

She swallowed hard. A hand waved in front of her face. She turned to see Elizabeth grinning at her. "I'm guessing from the look on your face that's Reed?"

Avery nodded.

Maggie, the only one with her back to the door, actually scooted her chair around to get a better view. "He doesn't look very yuppie to me."

No, he didn't. Unfortunately.

Avery knew the minute he spotted her. He nodded, smiled and made his way toward her.

For a brief moment she wondered how big a scene it would cause and how much teasing she'd have to endure if she made a break for it and hid in the bathroom.

"Oh, he's delicious, and you want to just be friends? You either need your eyes checked or your standards are too high," Maggie teased.

No, what he wanted me to give up is too high a price to pay.

"He zeroed in on you the minute he walked in the door," Emma commented.

"And that's not a friendship look," Elizabeth added.

"It doesn't matter what he's thinking. That's all there's going to be between us," Avery responded as she stood. When a chorus of "Where are you going?" chimed out, she said, "If you think I'm letting Reed get anywhere near the three of you, you're crazy."

* * *

What a time warp, Reed thought as he stood inside the bar. Halligan's hadn't changed in the years he'd been gone. Formica-topped tables and industrial-style chairs littered the space. Wood paneling gave the place a warm, homey feel. The intoxicating smell of burgers wafted through the air.

Unlike being at the ranch and the house he'd grown up in, being in Halligan's didn't stir up bad memories. Instead the bar and grill conjured up images of him and Avery spending their nights playing pool and darts after they'd grabbed a burger. Here he'd been able to forget, at least for a while, the hell at home.

He spotted Avery seated at a table near the stage. Most women spent so much time, energy and money on their appearance, but not Avery. Her look was effortless, and always had been. Approachable. No matter what she wore, she possessed a grace, a natural beauty that very few women could compete with. His gaze locked on her as he started weaving his way through the maze of tables.

Would people see him as the successful businessman he'd worked to become or would they still view him as one of the poor Montgomery boys? No mother to care for them and a father who worked them every minute they weren't in school or sleeping. They'd pitied him without even knowing how bad things had been. Not even Avery or her family had known until the night he'd shown up at their door, the proof of his father's abuse discoloring his face. Until then his father had been smart enough to hit his sons where it wouldn't show for fear of losing his free ranch hands.

"Reed Montgomery? Damn, that can't be you?"

"Afraid so." He turned to see a blast from his past,

slightly stockier than he remembered, but there was no mistaking that round face and lopsided grin. Brian Haddock, a friend from high school, strolled toward him, his hand outstretched.

"I was sorry to hear that Colt got deployed, but good thing he has you to come see to the ranch for him. That is, if you can remember which end of a horse to feed."

He shook his old friend's hand. "I think I remember. It's the end with fewer flies, right?"

Brian chuckled. "I never got the chance to thank you for all the help you gave me in physics our senior year. If it hadn't been for you, I'd have lost my football scholarship."

"I heard about your injury. Tough break."

After an amazing college football career as an offensive lineman at Colorado and being named an all-American, Brian had been drafted by the Chicago Bears in a late-round pick. Then in his first regular-season game, a freak accident on a broken play had ended his promising career.

"Luckily I had an education to fall back on. I have my own insurance company. What are you up to these days?"

"I own my own company, too. RJ Instruments. We manufacture computer chips for electronics."

Brian reached into his pocket, pulled out a business card and handed it to Reed. "I'm on the city government board of trustees. Your company's exactly the type we're trying to get to relocate here. Our new slogan is Move to the Mountains. We've got some great incentives."

With the cost of doing business in California rising he'd been mulling over relocating, but Estes Park? Not likely. Too many ghosts drifted around here, and not only at The Stanley Hotel.

"It's Friday night. I don't want to talk business. Call me next week, and we'll set up a time to talk." By then he'd have a polite no-thank-you response formulated.

"I'll do that. We can have lunch, my treat. We'll talk a little business and reminisce."

Reed's gaze locked on Avery, who'd either gotten tired of waiting for him or had realized he needed rescuing, because she'd started walking toward him. "Excuse me, Brian, but I told Avery I'd meet her here, and I've left her waiting too long."

Avery, unaware of the enthralled males she left in her wake, stood out like a thoroughbred among mules. He shook his head. Where had that analogy come from?

Maybe it was true. You could take the boy out of the barn, but you couldn't wash all the manure off his boots.

He met her halfway to her table. "You were right. Halligan's hasn't changed a bit."

"I think the town would riot if anyone tried."

Once seated, Avery introduced Rory's wife, Elizabeth. He'd have put his money on the pretty, petite blonde being married to Griffin. Then Avery introduced him to her other sister-in-law, Maggie. Griffin's wife was the opposite of what he'd expected. She was tall, with shoulder-length dark hair. If it hadn't been for her striking green eyes, he'd have labeled her downright plain.

"So you're the woman who married Griffin."

Maggie shook her head. "I keep hearing how no one expected Griffin to marry. From the way everyone says that, you'd think I was one of the seven natural wonders."

"Even though I was a freshman and Griffin was a senior, I heard some pretty wild stories about him."

When Maggie smiled, the twinkle in her eyes told him she more than likely sent her husband on a merry chase. "We'll definitely have to talk. A woman never knows when she might need a secret weapon."

"Or blackmail material," Avery added.

The jovial banter reminded Reed of dinners in the McAlister home. How many days had he sought refuge there when he couldn't face life in his own house?

"Reed Montgomery? You cost me five dollars. When my husband told me you'd come back to stay with Jess, I told him he'd lost his mind and bet him that he was wrong."

He stared at the slender waitress. Her face held more lines and her hair was now dusted with silver, but he recognized the face. "Hello, Mrs. Hughes. I'm sorry you lost the bet."

"That's all right, I'll win the next one, and call me Cathy." Genuine affection laced the woman's voice. "How are you and Jess getting along?"

The good news is we haven't knocked each other senseless yet. The bad news is that's still a possibility.
"We had a rocky start, but things are getting better."

Mainly because they couldn't get any worse.

"I worry about her. Being a teenage girl is tough enough, but to have to go through those years without a mother around? No girl should have to deal with that."

Which was exactly why she should live with her grandparents. At least Colt's mother-in-law had raised a child. Of course, look how that had turned out, but weren't people supposed to learn from their mistakes? Even if they hadn't, certainly they'd do a better job than he would.

"It's good to see you. Now that your father's dead and buried, don't be such a stranger. I don't like to speak ill of the dead, but I'll make an exception with that man. When I heard what he'd been doing to you two boys all those years, well, being a good Christian woman I couldn't run him out of town on a rail, but I sure thought about it." She placed a delicate hand on his arm and leaned forward. "All the time you were in here, and I never knew what you were going through. If I had, I'd have hauled you out of that house myself, and made sure that man never got near you again. Anyone around here would have if we'd known."

The ache in his heart burned. He'd never suspected that. He'd felt so alone, when he needn't have.

"Now, what'll you have to eat? I see Mick giving me the evil eye from the bar because I'm standing here chatting too long." She nodded toward Halligan's owner. "I'm taking his order right now, so don't get your shorts in a knot." Then she returned her attention to Reed. "Our buffalo burgers are still the best you can find anywhere."

After Cathy took his order and left, Reed sat frozen in his seat, not sure what to say or do. His ghosts had definitely come out, but in a much different way than he'd expected.

"You okay?" Avery leaned toward him. "I'm sorry Cathy mentioned your dad. I know you never liked talking about him."

His phone sounded, alerting him to a text and saving him from having to deal with Avery's comment. He pulled his phone out of his pocket and scanned the text from Jess.

"More business?" Avery said, her tone filled with disapproval.

He shook his head. "It's from Jess. She's at the movies with friends. She was just letting me know what time I need to pick her up at the theatre."

Elizabeth said, "It's got to be hard suddenly being responsible for a teenager while running a company long-distance."

"Things got easier by the end of the week when I didn't have to use dynamite to blast Jess out of bed." She still retreated to her room after school, though, while he worked in her father's office. Then at dinner—that was rough. He'd had better conversations with former girlfriends than he did with Jess. "Teenage girls are an entirely different species. No matter what I say or do, she gets her nose out of joint."

"One time my brothers got so upset with my moods—" Maggie flashed air quotes "—they threatened to lock me in a closet."

"Now, that's a thought."

"I didn't have any problems with her when you two picked up Thor," Avery said. "We got along well."

"You speak the same female language." His niece and Avery's comfortable interaction made his inability to connect with Jess that much more obvious, reinforcing the fact that he wasn't meant to have a family.

The ping of guitars tuning up floated through the room.

"I can't believe it. Our husbands are walking this way," Elizabeth said, pointing toward the poolroom.

"I thought we'd have to hunt them down to dance," Maggie added.

Reed stiffened as Avery's brothers approached. What did they know about what had happened between him and Avery? He searched the men's faces. No sign of anger. They hadn't charged him yet, screaming that they planned to tear him apart. Maybe, since Rory had been in college and Griffin on the rodeo circuit when he and Avery broke up, they didn't know all the gory details.

"Reed here tells me he has some pretty interesting stories about you," Maggie said when her husband stood beside her.

Griffin kissed his wife on the cheek. "That was all before I met you. I'm older and wiser now."

Maggie laughed. "At least half the time."

"I'd say more like twenty-five percent," Rory quipped before he turned to Reed. "If you have any problems around the ranch, let me know. I'll be glad to help out."

The unexpected offer caught Reed off guard. "Thanks, I'll keep that in mind."

Griffin turned to Reed. "Man, Colt threw you into the deep end of the pool, didn't he? I don't know if I could take suddenly being responsible for a teenager. Talk about scary."

"Watch what you say," Rory's wife teased. "Half the people at this table used to be teenage girls."

Rory put his arm around his wife. "You're wonderful now, and I'd be lost without you, but you've got to admit teenage girls can be frightening."

"Like you guys have room to talk," Avery said. "You two were idiots when you were teenagers."

Reed glanced at the smiling faces surrounding him as the good-natured gibes bounced around the table. Cracks had flown around his family's table, but not like these ones. His dad's had been meant to pierce the skin. Everyone left the table bruised one way or another.

"I didn't understand girls when I was in high school. Throw in all the changes in society since I graduated, and I don't know what to do most of the time," Reed said.

"No one does," Rory added.

"My plan is to lock Michaela in her room when she turns thirteen and let her out when she's thirty." A look of horror passed over Griffin's face. "And I don't even want to think about dating."

Maggie patted her husband's hand and smiled. "I can't believe you're worried about that already. She's only six weeks old."

Avery laughed. "Watching you raise a daughter is going to be so much fun."

Reed shuddered. "Thank God Jess isn't dating or talking about boys." That would send him over the edge into complete insanity.

"I bet she's talking about boys, just not to you," Avery added.

"Don't tell me that." Reed clutched his heart, only half in jest. Dealing with boy troubles could give him a heart attack. "You're not helping my stress level."

From up on stage, a female spoke into the microphone, commanding their attention.

"I'm glad we've got a good crowd tonight, because the Estes Park animal shelter needs your help." The speaker turned to their table. "Avery, come up and give everyone the details."

"Excuse me—duty calls," Avery said as she stood. Once on the stage, she continued, "We've found out we don't own the land our building sits on. To keep the shelter open and to obtain a loan, we've got to raise the money for a down payment. We've got pitchers on the bar. Ours are the ones with the dog collars wrapped around them. When you pick up a drink and tip the bartenders, think about all the good work the shelter does, and drop a few bucks in our pitcher, too. Now, let's have some fun!"

As the band started playing, memories of him and Avery listening to country-and-western music and dancing on this same floor stirred within him. How often had he lost himself in her arms? She'd been his refuge.

After her brothers and their wives left to dance, he sat waiting for Avery. They had such a history, but when he tried to talk to her tonight he was about as smooth as a gravel road. You'd think this was a first date. He thought about what she'd said on the stage. The shelter needed money because they didn't own the land their building sat on. Land wasn't cheap. Raising that kind of cash could be tough in this economy. When she returned, he asked, "How much money do you need to raise for the down payment?"

"Sixty thousand."

"Putting a pitcher on a bar and asking for donations won't get you that kind of money."

"I know. That's why I'm moving up the date for our annual Pet Walk."

"What's a Pet Walk? Can it raise the kind of money you need?"

"People pay a registration fee to come with their pet. We have vendors selling things, food and contests. It's like a carnival for people and pets. We have some attendees who raise money by getting pledges for walking at the event. One year we raised thirty-five thousand."

"That's a long way from getting the down payment."

"Earlier you said you didn't want to talk about work. I don't, either." She stood. "Let's dance."

He watched the other couples. Some of the moves looked the same. "I haven't line danced in years."

"Suit yourself." She tossed the words over her shoulder with a sly grin as she headed for the dance floor, leaving him sitting by himself.

She glanced his way, hooked her thumbs in her jeans pockets and glided to the left swaying her hips. She licked her lips and smiled, a tempting, see-what-you're-missing kind of grin. Her step held an extra bounce. Her skin glowed from exertion. He resisted the urge to wipe his moist palms on his jeans and sat glued to his seat, mesmerized. On the outside looking in.

The sexy minx is taunting me.

The woman probably enjoyed poking sleeping bears, too. Damned if he'd let her challenge go unanswered. He held her gaze as he stood and walked toward her. When he reached her, she stared him down. "Finally screwed up your courage, huh?"

"The moves look pretty much the same. I bet line dancing's like riding a bicycle."

It took only a minute for him to realize how wrong he'd been. He invariably went left when he should have gone right. He stomped his foot when he should've tapped his heel and kicked. Making a fool of himself wasn't how he had envisioned the night going.

Halfway through the first dance he huffed and puffed to keep up, something that shouldn't be happening considering how much he worked out. Then he sidestepped when he should've kicked, and came close to running into her. Focusing on his footwork, he prayed he wouldn't stomp on her foot. The thought no sooner zipped through his head then he did exactly that. "Sorry."

Way to impress a beautiful woman. Almost knock her down and then tromp on her foot.

"Luckily I'm wearing boots. Otherwise you'd be in trouble." She sashayed beside him, making him remember how graceful she'd always been. Then he whirled around and bumped into a short fortysomething man who looked vaguely familiar. The slight man swayed on his feet. Reed reached out to steady him and ended up wrapping his arms around him instead. He righted the gentleman and stepped away, embarrassment racing through his veins. "You okay?"

Could this get any worse?

"I'm fine, Reed, son. Good to see you back, and don't you worry. I'd be a mite distracted, too, if I was dancing with a pretty thing like Avery."

"Now we're going to slow things down," said the singer/guitarist who'd called Avery up on stage earlier. "We've had a request from Griffin McAlister for the first song he and his wife, Maggie, danced to here at Halligan's."

Reed smiled. Finally he'd be able to put his arms around Avery the way he'd wanted to all night.

"I don't know about you, but I think it's time for a cold beer." Her chest rose and fell rapidly.

No way was she getting away from him. Not after he'd endured her teasing about his moves. He slipped his arm around her waist as he pulled her closer. "Are you still afraid you can't keep your hands off me?"

Her chin tilted up. Apparently she still couldn't turn down a challenge. He almost grinned, but controlled the urge for fear of scaring her off.

She slipped her right hand into his, while her left slid up his chest. His pulse accelerated. The simple touch was surprisingly electric. Maybe this hadn't been a good idea.

What was wrong with them sharing each other's company? They were both adults. He should just enjoy this, and if it led to more, they could handle it.

"Nice dip with Mr. Hendricks, by the way," Avery

teased, her eyes twinkling with amusement. "You used to be a great dancer."

"Maybe you should give me private lessons."

"Check line dancing on Google and watch a video."

He should stick to them being friends and lay off the innuendos, but he couldn't help himself. Now that he held Avery in his arms, the idea of leaving things at friendship felt unsatisfying.

As they swayed to the music, the lyrics about a cowboy on the road missing his girl floated over him. Avery's familiar earthy scent swirled around him. He remembered how he'd lost himself in her when things got rough at home. She'd been the anchor he clung to, the quiet in his life amid the storm of his father's tirades and abuse. He'd often wondered how different life would've been if he'd grown up in a household like the McAlisters'.

He leaned closer until his lips rested beside her ear. How long had it been since he'd allowed himself to get close to someone?

"Do you wonder what it would be like between us now?" he asked.

He sure as hell did. Ever since she'd walked out of the stall in Colt's barn. The images had kept him awake and throbbing more than one night since he'd returned.

"No." Her expressive eyes and her breathy voice contradicted her statement.

"Right now I'm wondering." His lips pressed against the tender skin behind her ear, and he felt her shiver. Her head rested on his shoulder, and her warmth seeped into him. Need overrode what little common sense he possessed. Hell, common sense was overrated, anyway.

His lips traced a path down her neck, while his hand caressed her lower back, encouraging her to get even closer. Her thighs brushed his groin, and she gasped. Her gaze locked with his, and he couldn't resist her. He lowered his mouth to hers and gently covered her lips, searching and testing. To hell with everything but her and him together.

She nuzzled the sensitive spot behind his ear. Being with her like this felt right.

His phone vibrated in his pocket. His heart hammered so loudly he wondered if she could hear the beat over the band. Dazed and strung tighter than a barbed-wire fence, he stepped away, instantly feeling cut adrift. He dug his phone out of his pocket and glanced at the screen. Estes Park Police Department.

"Avery, I have to take this."

She folded her arms across her chest, anger replacing passion in her gaze. "Are you so worried about staying connected, about your business, that you can't miss a call?" She shook her head. "You're going to miss out on what's really important in life, Reed."

Chapter 5

His pulse rate still revving, Reed watched Avery storm off and then worked his way through the couples on the dance floor, heading for the front door.

"Reed Montgomery? This is Officer Blume."

"Is it Jess? Is she okay?"

"She's fine, but I've got her here at the station. I understand you're her guardian while her father's gone."

As his heart rate slowed and his panic subsided, his anger kicked in. Jess had texted him earlier to say she was going to a movie with friends. He glanced at his watch. He was to pick her up at the theater in half an hour. She'd lied to him. "What happened?"

"She spray-painted graffiti on the animal shelter."

He told the officer he was coming and climbed into his truck. Colt hadn't mentioned things about Jess doing anything that would get her in trouble with the law.

Wait a minute. Jess vandalized the shelter? That

didn't make sense. She and Avery had gotten along well when they'd picked up Thor. A lot of the irritation that filled Jess's voice when she talked to him had been absent with Avery. Something wasn't right. His gut told him Jess wouldn't damage the shelter. Someplace else, maybe, but not where Avery worked.

What the hell was he going to do about this, and how could he tell his brother that Jess had gotten hauled into the police station?

Deal with the police first. Then worry about telling Colt.

And he refused to think about Avery and how good it had felt to hold her. How kissing her had him remembering all their good times and made him wonder if leaving her had been the biggest mistake of his life.

As Avery left the dance floor, she tried to deny that Reed's touch had sent more excitement and electricity bolting through her than she'd felt in years. When he'd kissed her, she'd forgotten everything but him.

How had she let things get this out of control? And how did she set them right again? How dare he think he could stroll into town and pick up with her as if he'd never left?

Agreeing to dance with him. That's where things went wrong. Touching Reed. Big mistake. She'd set out to prove something to herself, and she sure had. She'd proved she had less willpower than she'd thought where he was concerned.

New survival game plan—stay as far from Reed as possible.

Her phone rang. The screen revealed the number of the Estes Park police. Her mom—had something happened? Please, no. She glanced around the bar and saw both her brothers. If something had happened, the authorities would call Rory first, but maybe he hadn't heard his phone. Panic making her heart race, she answered the call and stepped outside.

"Dr. McAlister, this is Officer Blume. I need you to come to the police station. A group of teenagers vandalized the shelter."

Thank God, her mother was fine. Vandalism she could handle. Officer Blume proceeded to tell her that the teenagers had scattered when they arrived, but they'd managed to apprehend one suspect. She told the officer she'd be there in a few minutes, and rushed back into Halligan's to offer a quick explanation to her family.

As she headed for the police station she wondered why teenagers would vandalize the shelter. They'd never had any issues like this before. Were these simply bored kids or was this caused by someone's frustration with the shelter?

When Avery parked at the police station, Reed emerged from the truck beside her. "What are you doing here?" she asked.

"The police picked up Jess for vandalism. That's the call I got at the bar."

Avery joined him on the sidewalk, her head spinning. "Jess? When the police told me teenagers had vandalized the shelter, the last one I would've suspected was Jess. There has to be some mistake. She wouldn't do that. Not when she adopted Thor from us."

"That's exactly what I thought, but the police caught her there with a spray can. They also said she won't tell them anything, especially not who else was there."

"You mean *you* don't know who she was with?"

"She mentioned a friend named Lindsey, but not

her last name." Reed pinched the bridge of his nose. "I asked her so many questions about what she was doing tonight. How could I forget to ask for full names of her friends?"

"This is all new to you, and there's a lot to remember."

He straightened. "You can bet I'll get the whole story out of her now."

The hard set of Reed's mouth and his clenched fists surprised her. She'd never been afraid of him in all the years she'd known him, but she'd seen glimpses of anger when he talked about his father.

And there had been that one night after graduation when he'd shown up at her door, purple and blue discoloring his swollen cheek. He'd collapsed against her and confessed how his father had been beating him for years. He'd told her how things had grown worse since Colt moved away. Without his brother there to defuse matters, Reed nearly beat his father to death.

Once he'd stopped shaking, she'd coaxed him into the chair in her father's study while she woke her parents. After quickly explaining the situation, she begged them to help Reed.

Her father called his lawyer and the two men shut themselves in her father's office with Reed. Then the police arrived. Afterward, Reed wouldn't tell her anything other than that, thanks to her father, he wouldn't go to jail. Her father likewise refused to supply details, claiming it wasn't his place.

"Don't assume the worst and jump on Jess the minute you see her. Give her a chance to explain," Avery said now.

"As long as she tells me exactly what happened we'll be fine."

"And if she won't? Remember, you're dealing with a fourteen-year-old. You promised Colt you'd be flexible."

"And I will be. I don't care who she talks to about what happened, but she *will* talk."

"Adding your current mindset to typical teenager attitude won't be productive or pretty." Avery clasped Reed's arm, halting him. Tense muscles rippled under her palm. "What's going on here? I know Jess is in trouble, but she wasn't picked up for doing drugs or drinking. She hasn't hurt anyone. Why are you so angry?"

"Why aren't you more upset? She vandalized your shelter."

"Don't change the subject." She inched closer and squeezed his arm. "Tell me why you're so upset."

He jerked away, rejecting her comfort. Fine, that was probably best for both of them. She wouldn't make the mistake of offering it again.

"I'm responsible for Jess. She's been testing me. I've got to show her I won't tolerate this. No, it wasn't drugs or something worse. *This* time."

"I know you take your guardian role seriously. That's who you are." She wanted to hold him, ease his fears, and the thought left her shaken. "You're worried Jess's behavior tonight could lead to bigger issues, and it's your job to ensure that doesn't happen."

"Damn right it is."

"Jess has always been a good kid. I think there's something else going on here. Is she acting out because her dad's gone? Is she hanging around with the wrong crowd? Guys focus on getting the facts and finding a solution, but you're dealing with a teenage girl. You need to find out *why* she did this. You can't just get angry with her."

The shelter was her problem, not why Jess was acting out. Helping Reed and getting attached to him and his niece would complicate her life, but more important, it would take time and energy away from her job. And she could so easily get emotionally involved—but she couldn't forget what had driven them apart.

Still, she thought of Jess, and how Reed's current mood could react with hers to make things worse. Avery stepped closer and reached out to him, but pulled back at the last moment. Instead, she peered up at him. "Reed, lighten up. She hasn't joined the Mafia. She spray-painted the shelter. This is very fixable."

His stance softened as he reached for her hand. He clasped her fingers so tightly she almost winced. "I'm glad you're here. You always helped me keep things in perspective. I'm so scared of messing up. What do I know about kids? Look at the example I had for a father."

Her heart ached for the pain his father had caused, both emotionally and physically. Staring into his worried gaze, she wished he hadn't said anything. How could she leave him alone to deal with the situation after what he'd just said?

"We'll handle this together."

"Thanks." He released her hand, took a deep breath and smiled faintly. "I'm going to hold you to that."

When they walked into the police station, Officer Blume met them at the front desk. "Someone driving by on the highway saw a group of teenagers spray-painting the shelter." The officer faced Reed. "Your niece was the only one caught at the scene. She won't tell us anything. We checked her phone and have an idea of who was with her, but unless she corroborates that, all the blame falls on her." Officer Blume turned to Avery. "Does the shelter want to press charges?"

"If it were up to me, I'd let things go with restitution, but it's shelter policy that we prosecute in cases like this," Avery said to both men.

"Would you give us a minute alone?" Reed asked the officer.

The other man nodded. "I'll finish the paperwork for your niece's release and be back in a minute."

Once he and Avery were alone, Reed said, "There isn't any way you can avoid pressing charges?"

"I'm afraid not. Since it's a shelter policy, there's nothing I can do. I'm sorry. If I could let things go at restitution, I really would."

He nodded. "Thanks for that. How am I going to tell Colt Jess got arrested?"

The weariness in his voice tugged at her heart. He really was in over his head. "Colt will understand. She's a teenager. They do stupid stuff like this." She placed her hand on his arm, and he placed his hand over hers. "Now you know more, and you'll watch her closer for other signs of problems."

"I don't know if I can do this. It's so much responsibility. That's why I never—"

Though he cut himself off, she knew what he'd been about to say.

That's why I never want to have kids.

She pulled away and walked across the waiting room to sit in one of the wooden chairs against the wall.

She wouldn't get involved with Reed again. Some risks were worth taking and some were just plain foolish because the odds of succeeding sucked. Having a relationship with Reed fell into the latter category. She'd help him with Jess, but that was as far as things would go. She hadn't been willing to compromise all those years ago and give up having children, and she couldn't now.

When Officer Blume returned with Jess's release papers, Avery reiterated that the shelter would be pressing charges. As the officer went to get Jess, Avery and Reed stood awkwardly beside each other.

"You lied to me," Reed said the minute the teenager arrived. His low voice rippled with restraint.

"No, I didn't. When I talked to you, I was at the movie, but it was lame, and we left."

"Then you should've called me to pick you up. What the hell were you thinking? You committed a crime."

Jess stood there, her body rigid, her arms crossed, looking at the floor.

Reed shoved his hands into his front pockets. "I want to know who you were with and why you did this."

"I don't want to talk about it."

Why couldn't Reed see his heavy-handed attitude was only making Jess more adamant to best him? Avery stepped forward and placed her hand on the teenager's arm, but Jess refused to meet her gaze. "Why would you do this to the shelter?"

"It wasn't me," Jess insisted.

"The police caught you there with spray-paint cans," Reed said.

"I was there, but I didn't do anything."

"Then who the hell did?" Reed fired back.

Jess fidgeted with the hem of her black skull-print T-shirt. "I tried to talk them out of it, but no one would listen. Really I did." Jess finally met Avery's gaze. Guilt shone in her eyes.

"I believe you, sweetheart." Avery wrapped her hands around the girl's icy ones. Her mind raced trying to recall who Jess's friends were and why they would damage the shelter, but nothing came to mind. But then, who could figure out how teenagers' brains worked, or rather, didn't work? "You've got to tell us who was with you."

"I can't."

Reed held out his hand, practically shoving it under his niece's nose. "Give me your cell phone. I bet you've got texts that'll shed light on what happened."

Jess stepped back. "You're not my father. You've got no right to look at my phone because you don't pay for it, and there's nothing on it that implicates anyone."

"That's all right. I'll get the information another way." Reed's strong voice rang with unflinching authority. "The police checked your phone. I'll get Lindsey's last name from them. Then I'll call her parents."

Jess squeezed Avery's hands so tightly her knuckles cracked. "I'll say she wasn't there, and then there's nothing the police can do."

"A crime was committed and your friends need to be held accountable for their actions."

"I can't tell the police. You don't know what it's like in high school." Jess's panicked gaze locked on Avery. "Tell him he can't do this. I'm already a freak—the girl whose mom ran off with the computer-repair guy and got herself killed. There are people who don't want anything to do with me because of that. If I squeal on my friends, I'll be a complete outcast."

Avery tried to catch Reed's eye, but his stare remained focused on Jess. Things had always been black-and-white to him.

"Then that's the price you'll have to pay," Reed said.

"That's easy for you to say. You won't be the one sitting alone at lunch while all your former friends sit at another table whispering about you."

"What kind of friends are they if they ran off and left you to take the blame?" Avery asked, hoping to make Jess see how she'd misplaced her loyalty.

"I'll find out who Lindsey is, so you might as well tell me." Reed ground out the words.

"How can you do this to me?" Jess's voice broke and her eyes filled with tears. She turned to Avery. "Can't you make him understand?"

Avery glanced between the stubborn pair. Neither one showed any signs of backing down. Someone had to play peacemaker. "Reed, can I talk to you in private?"

"There's nothing to talk about."

"Please?"

Avery's soft plea and the worried look in her eyes when she placed her hand on his arm pulled him back to reality. The anger stirring inside him startled him. Worse yet, it reminded him of his father.

A vision of the man, his eyes bulging, nostrils flaring as he railed at him, flashed in his mind. Was that how he looked to Jess and Avery?

He turned and walked across the room, his knees growing weak, Avery beside him.

"Being a hard-ass isn't working. All it's doing is making her more adamant about protecting her friends. You have to back down. Colt told me about Jess threatening to run away. She can only take so much."

"I know. I don't think she would really do it, but just because she's threatened to run away doesn't mean I can overlook what she's done or the fact that she won't tell the police who was with her. She has to tell them everything."

"Can't you see she's not going to? All you're doing is alienating her."

"She vandalized your shelter. You should be backing

me up and helping me get the names out of her. Instead, you're coddling her and encouraging her to defy me." Reed shoved his hands into his pockets. "She's being overly dramatic about her friends' reaction."

"No, she's not. You don't know what girls can be like, or how fragile their psyches are. She could be right that her friends would ostracize her."

"We're talking a legal issue here, Avery."

"I know, but I'm more concerned about her emotional state. If she's willing to take the fall for her friends, let her. My mom and dad used to talk about natural consequences. They said those were often worse than any punishment they could give us. Lay things out for her, that if she won't tell on her friends, the natural consequence is she'll end up in juvenile court to take all the blame. It might teach Jess a good lesson about friendship."

What Avery said made sense, though he balked at the idea of letting Jess's friends get away with a crime. But those kids weren't his problem. Jess was. "Maybe you're right, and I should let her face the consequences."

"Trust me."

The words hung heavy between them and had nothing to do with the situation surrounding Jess. "I always have."

Avery nibbled on her lower lip. "I think letting the court deal with Jess is the wisest thing to do."

He nodded, whatever might have passed between them now gone. When they rejoined Jess, he said, "I'll ask you one more time to tell me who was with you, and before you answer, be aware that the shelter's policy is always to press charges in cases like these. Dr. McAlister has no say in the matter. That means when the shelter presses charges you'll end up in juvenile court, and there won't be anyone else to take the blame."

"I understand," Jess said, though he doubted she truly grasped the implications of her decision. "I'd rather go to court than betray my friends."

"I admire your loyalty, Jess, but I think your uncle's right," Avery added. "Your friends don't deserve you." Then she turned to him. "Will you two be okay if I head home? I have an early surgery scheduled for tomorrow."

Reed nodded, the anger he'd felt gone, thanks to Avery. What would he have done if she hadn't been here to help him, to smooth things over when he'd been on the brink of letting his frustration consume him?

He couldn't even think about what might have happened.

The next morning Reed stared at his brother's image on the computer screen as he updated Colt on his daughter's antics. "I'm out of my league here. You've got to talk to Jess about what happened. Make her tell you who she was with."

"I'll talk to her, but my guess is she won't tell me any more than she told you. When Jess makes up her mind, there's no changing it."

Reed chuckled. "Sounds like someone else I know."

"Yeah, you." His brother laughed. "For what it's worth, I would've handled things the same way you did. As a parent, I've learned sometimes I have to let my kid fall flat on her face."

"Her friends shouldn't be getting away with this."

"They're not my problem. I'm more worried that Jess got pulled into this stunt. I thought she had more sense than to go along with the crowd."

"I'm screwing up with her. I can handle running my

own company, but dealing with Jess is bringing me to my knees." His voice broke and he paused to collect himself. "I'm saying things that sound so damned much like our father."

"You're nothing like that bastard, if that's what you're worried about." His brother's confident reassurance offered Reed little comfort. "Have you had any luck with getting the association to make an exception for Jess?"

"Not so far, but my lawyer's working on it." He explained about the federal act. "Have you talked to your in-laws? Do they have an idea when they can come stay with Jess?"

"I got an email from them the other day. Joanne's doing better. She started physical therapy, but she's not up to traveling yet."

"What do you think about me threatening to go to the media if the association won't change its position?"

"I guess I don't have a problem with that, but I'm still not sure Jess is better off with them." Colt turned to the voices escalating in the background. "I gotta go. I'll talk to Jess as soon as I can and I'll back you up. Don't worry. You're doing better than you think."

"Stay safe."

After his brother responded with a quick "Will do," they were disconnected. Reed shook his head. He was doing better than he thought? In what universe?

He couldn't risk losing control with Jess, or making bigger mistakes. He picked up his phone, called his lawyer and asked what he'd found out.

"I checked on the occupancy issue, and they're in compliance."

With the way his luck had been running of late, why did that not surprise him? "Threaten to contact the local media, and if the association doesn't concede, do it."

"Are you sure that's what you want to do? There's an outside chance it could backfire and be bad publicity for the company."

"It won't backfire. We're talking about a widowed soldier and his teenage daughter. The public support will be overwhelming."

He was done being nice. Time to play hardball before he messed up even worse with Jess.

Two days later, Reed and Jess stood before Juvenile Court Judge Hoffman.

After Reed had taken away her cell phone and grounded her per Colt's instructions, Jess had adopted a two-pronged approach to dealing with him—avoiding him and pretending he was invisible. He figured the justice system would take care of punishing her further, but their strained relationship had started wearing on him.

"You're not doing a very good job as a guardian, Mr. Montgomery." The judge stared down at Reed from his seat behind the massive oak bench, the American and Colorado flags standing watch behind him.

No kidding. Thanks for letting me in on that secret.

"Taking care of a teenager is new to me, Your Honor." Weariness seeped into him. He felt as if he'd aged ten years since he'd met Jess at the airport. At this rate, he'd die of old age in three weeks.

"If you don't have the skills to do the job, then you'd better find a way to get them. You've been given a huge responsibility. Your brother's in Afghanistan serving our country. He shouldn't have to worry about his daughter. It's time to cowboy up."

When Judge Hoffman looked as if he expected a response, Reed replied, "Yes, sir."

"Young lady, I hear you refuse to tell the police who

was with you Friday night," Judge Hoffman continued, his stern voice booming through the courtroom.

"I was alone." Jess crossed her arms over her chest. What could be seen of her coffee-colored eyes through the long bangs hanging in her face blazed with teenage defiance.

His teenage-girl-remote-island idea looked better all the time.

"The witness said she saw four teenagers," Judge Hoffman countered.

"I won't betray my friends."

"That concerns me. Protecting your friends when they commit crimes is not using good judgment." Judge Hoffman's gaze scanned the gallery. "What do you have to say about all this, Dr. McAlister?"

Avery, dressed in a black skirt and white blouse, stood and moved forward. Reed couldn't help staring. He remembered her having great legs, but not ones that belonged on a pin-up poster.

"While I can't overlook what Jess did, I understand her reluctance to be more forthcoming. Teenage girls can be very cruel, especially if they feel betrayed, and that's likely to be how her peers will see her talking to the authorities." Avery glanced toward Reed and Jess. "From what Jess told me, there has been unkind talk about her mother. She fears if she names names things will get worse."

The judge nodded. "I'm well aware of how insensitive teenagers can be. I also understand how difficult losing her mother must have been and now having her father in Afghanistan, but it can't excuse her behavior."

"I agree, but what Jess needs right now is guidance and stability," Avery responded. "My mom was such a big source of advice and support for me as a teenager.

I can't imagine what I would've done without her at Jess's age."

"Thank you for your input, Dr. McAlister." Judge Hoffman shuffled through the papers in front of him. "I don't have a repair estimate. Do you have that information?"

She handed the bailiff a packet of paper. "Max at Jenson's Paint has given me an estimate. Now, the labor to have the building painted would be—"

"The labor's not going to cost anything because Miss Montgomery's going to paint over her artwork." Judge Hoffman jotted down something before his gaze returned to Jess. "You're at a crossroads, young lady. I'm hoping my actions will make you think about choosing a better path than the one you're on right now. I also suggest you take a good hard look at your friendships, and the fact that those you were with left you to take the blame. That says a lot about their character."

"Yes, sir," Jess replied.

"I want to make it clear that I won't tolerate further shenanigans," the judge continued. "Jessica Montgomery, I sentence you to thirty hours of community service to be served at the Estes Park animal shelter. That's in addition to however long it takes you to paint over your little art project." He turned his focus to Reed. "Mr. Montgomery, you need to keep a closer eye on your niece and work on your relationship."

Reed nodded. Wanting to work on his relationship with Jess wasn't the problem. How to do it was his stumbling block.

"Now, Dr. McAlister, I'm glad to hear you say you feel Miss Montgomery needs guidance, particularly from a wiser, older female. While I can't require it of you, I'd like to see you personally supervise her at the shelter. You're a respected member of our community, and Miss Montgomery would greatly benefit from interaction with you. I'd also like you to keep in touch with me as to her progress."

Avery's first reaction was to blurt out that with the shelter in such financial trouble she didn't have time to work with a teenager who had issues, but she couldn't. She couldn't risk offending Judge Hoffman, not when he was one of the people she'd hit up to write a nice fat check. Instead of giving in to her frustration, she plastered a smile on her face. "Your Honor, I'll be happy to work with Miss Montgomery at the shelter. Our next volunteer orientation is at the end of September. I'll get the information to her."

"I want her volunteering as soon as possible." The judge's narrow gaze locked on Jess. "You obviously have too much free time on your hands, young lady, and I intend to fill some of it immediately."

"I'll be happy to put Jess to work as soon as possible."

"See that you do, Dr. McAlister. I trust you and Mr. Montgomery to work out those details as well as the ones associated with getting the shelter painted." The judge banged his gavel, and the bailiff called for the next case.

If only she could dismiss this case as easily. What she wouldn't give for one of those little gizmos from *Men in Black* right now. She'd pop on her shades and zap Reed's memory about the other night at Halligan's clean so he'd forget how she'd practically crawled inside his skin when he kissed her. That would make dealing with him now much easier.

Unfortunately, she'd have to tough it out the old-fashioned way—by pretending the incident had never happened.

Chapter 6

When Reed and Jess joined her outside the court-room, Avery focused on the teenager rather than Reed. "There's something I need to know, and I expect an answer. I think I deserve one, since you adopted Thor from us." After Jess nodded, Avery continued, "Do you think your friends will do further damage to the shelter?"

"I don't think so. They were pretty freaked out and upset by me getting caught."

"Not enough that they owned up to what they did," Reed said.

"They did say they were sorry," Jess added.

Avery could see Reed preparing to launch into another pointless lecture. Before he could, she said, "As far as I'm concerned, we're starting over. As long as you do a good job at the shelter, we won't have any problems. Everyone deserves a second chance. But if you hear anyone talking about vandalizing the shelter again, please let me know so I can take precautions."

Jess nodded.

Avery turned her attention to Reed. He looked so handsome dressed in rancher chic, meaning he'd added a sport coat to his black jeans and T-shirt. Her heart fluttered, and she ignored her budding emotions. "We need to get something straight. Our policy is that volunteers Jess's age must be accompanied by an adult. The shelter isn't a drop-off center."

"I wasn't sentenced to community service."

Like she was any happier about this than he was? If she had her way, she'd avoid him like a friend with the flu. "It's our policy, and I can't make an exception. If you don't volunteer with Jess, she won't be able to fulfill her community service."

She could almost see past his steely blue gaze to the gears churning in his head as he searched for a loophole to wiggle through.

"Lucky you, to get two volunteers for the price of one."

Lucky wasn't the word she'd have chosen. "I'll expect you both at the shelter tomorrow after school with whatever Max says you need to paint the shelter."

Reed and Jess stood outside the shelter, paint supplies spread out at their feet. Reed stared at the words *Animals shouldn't be in jail* sprayed across the shelter wall in brightened paint. "What do you think of your friends now that you're here and they're out there having fun?"

Jess shrugged. "Since I'm grounded, the teachers don't let us talk in class, and my phone's locked up, so I haven't seen or talked to my friends much."

"I'm not sure that's a bad thing, since they hung you

out to dry. They should be here helping you." He pulled a roll of blue painter's tape out of the bag of supplies they'd purchased and twirled the roll between his fingers. "What do you know about painting a building?"

"You mean there's more to it than dunking the roller in the paint and moving it over the wall?"

He explained how she needed to tape around the windows and trim, then pointed to a place where the paint had flaked off. "You need to use the scraper we bought to make sure the surface is smooth before you paint. Otherwise it'll just peel again."

"How do you know so much about painting?"

He thought about the judge's comment that he work on his relationship with Jess. Now was as good a time as any. "What's your dad told you about when he was a kid?"

"Not much. One time I asked him how he learned to be such a good dad, and he told me that he just remembered what his father did and did the opposite."

"That sounds just like your dad." Colt could learn from the roughest experiences and come out better for having survived. "I learned how to paint a house when your dad was sixteen and I was your age. Our dad made us paint the house. I wanted to just jump in and get the job done. Your dad talked with the guy at the paint store to make sure we knew what we were doing."

"Didn't your dad show you what needed to be done?"

"He wasn't big on doing much work or explaining what needed to be done. He preferred criticizing afterward."

Despite Colt's careful planning and them taking care while they painted, he'd screwed up. Not Colt. Just him. He couldn't even remember how, but his dad had found something he wasn't happy with and knocked Reed around. His ribs ached for days. Closing his eyes, he tried to focus on something positive. Avery's smiling face as they danced at Halligan's materialized before him. Once he was in control again, he opened his eyes and reached into the sack at his feet. The plastic rustled as he searched for the scraper. He held the item out to Jess. "Tell you what—I'll tape around the windows and the trim while you go over the rough spots with the scraper."

As she accepted the tool, her huge grin tugged at his heart. "Thanks. That would be great."

"What's your favorite subject in school?" Reed asked as he tore off a strip of blue painter's tape and started taping around the window.

"I'm taking a creative-writing class and I like that a lot. I think that and computer programming are my favorites. Though I don't like them as much as I liked the website design class I took this summer."

"That's a really growing field, and it pays well. The guy I hired a couple of months ago to redo my company's site charged a fortune."

"Maybe I'll be good enough to help the next time your site needs updating," she added cheekily. "I'll even give you a family discount."

"It's a deal."

Reed's cell phone rang. When he answered the call, Ethan launched into a monologue on his difficulties with a product demonstration and how unreasonable the customer's demands were. From experience, Reed knew that until Ethan had vented, he wouldn't listen to anything else.

When the connection grew fuzzy, he walked around the yard searching for better reception. A minute later, Jess touched him on the arm. "Is everything okay? It's not about Dad, is it?"

He put his hand over his phone. "Don't worry. It's nothing serious, and it's not about your dad. It's work stuff."

The worry left her eyes, and her posture relaxed as she returned to scraping, while he returned his call. When it broke up again and the connection failed, he received a text from Ethan. "Urgent I speak to you on a decent phone line. Having problems. Can't fix. Need to send them to you so we can discuss."

He replied asking his vice president to check the shelter's website for a fax number and to send the information there, and said he'd call him from a landline.

"I need to go inside and get a fax. I'll only be a minute."

Jess smiled. "I'll be here."

Avery spotted Reed's truck in the shelter parking lot when she returned from her meeting with Harper to discuss the information she'd compiled on other available properties. As Avery suspected, when she factored in remodeling an existing structure or building a new one, the cheaper properties turned out to be more costly, making purchasing their current property the best option. Now all they had to do was raise the sixty grand for the down payment. She shuddered. No matter how many times she heard the amount and told herself the goal was obtainable she still felt an initial flutter of panic.

Once inside, she checked in with the front-desk volunteer, Mrs. Russell, a former life-skills teacher who answered the shelter phones one afternoon a week. She and her black toy-poodle mix, Chandra, were practically Pet Walk legends when it came to the Best-Dressed Pet category.

"Anything I need to know about?"

"We've got everything under control."

"That doesn't surprise me in the least. I can't wait to see what you come up with for Chandra to wear at the Pet Walk this year."

The older woman smiled. "I've pulled out all the stops but that's all I'm going to say. I don't want to ruin the surprise."

Avery told Mrs. Russell she'd be in her office working on the last details for the Pet Walk if anyone needed her. When she reached her door, she froze.

There sat Reed, all six foot two of him, looking enormous and even more masculine seated behind her ancient metal industrial desk. The hum of the fax machine on the stand by the door brought her back to earth.

"I thought you and Jess were painting outside this afternoon."

"We are. I just had something to take care of." He shifted in her chair, and it squeaked in protest. "How do you get any work done sitting in this rickety thing? It's damned uncomfortable, too. You need a chair that fits your position in the organization."

Was he serious? That's what he had to say when she found him making himself at home in *her* office? "I make do because the shelter can't afford new office furniture. The only way I'll get a new chair is if Santa puts one under the tree this Christmas."

What was she going to do with him here? An image of them rolling around on her desk appeared in her mind. As the heat raced up her neck into her face, she told herself she couldn't do that. At least not here.

When the fax machine quieted, he said, "Would you check to see if that's for me?"

She grabbed the paper, scanned the cover sheet and walked across the room. As she handed him the papers, she asked, "Why is someone sending you a fax here?"

"My VP's doing a customer demo, and he's having trouble. I texted him to fax the details to me so I can help him."

Wait a minute. If Reed was in here, where was Jess? "Did you leave Jess alone outside? You're supposed to be supervising her."

"She'll be okay. She's not five."

"You don't get it. We have the policy regarding children under sixteen volunteering with a parent or guardian because of liability issues. I could get in trouble with the board."

"Help me out here. You know what it's like being in charge. Sometimes things go to hell."

How could she say no when he put it that way? She'd sound like an unreasonable tyrant. Why did Reed asking for favors as other volunteers often did get under her skin? Because something about him made her feel out of control.

"I need to make a quick call on a landline. My cell keeps dropping my calls. Would you mind if I used your phone?"

She gave him a tight-lipped smile. "By all means, my office is at your disposal."

He smiled openly as his gaze searched hers. "You always were a sport. Everyone can always count on you."

She grimaced. Yup, people could count on her and Old Faithful. That was just what a girl wanted to hear from a guy, especially a handsome ex. "Since you obviously missed it, I was being sarcastic."

"I didn't miss it. I ignored it."

That silly comment, said with the engaging smile she was so familiar with, made her grin. The man could charm his way out of the stickiest situation if he put his mind to the task.

"Go ahead. Read your fax. Make your call. I'll supervise Jess until you're done."

"Thanks, you're a pal."

Ouch. That comment hurt as much as *You always were a sport* had. But wasn't that what she wanted? For Reed to see her as nothing more than a friend?

The words *Be careful what you wish for* taunted her as she stopped to get a bottle of water before she headed outside in search of Jess.

Why did Reed have to come back now when she was finally content with her life? The past few years had been tumultuous. Her father's death had shattered her world, leaving a huge void. Then her mother's cancer diagnosis had shaken her further. Now all she wanted to do was establish her career, settle into a routine and, she hoped, some time in the not-too-distant future find a man she could share her life with. Then Reed had swooped back into town, sending her flying around like a dry leaf in a strong autumn breeze.

She rounded the corner, spotted Jess and smiled. The teenager had almost as much paint on her clothes as she'd gotten on the wall. "You're doing a great job, but it looks like you'll have to do a second coat. I can still see the lettering."

She joined Jess and handed her the bottle of water. Why would someone paint *Animals shouldn't be in jail* on the shelter? "I know I asked before, but I'd really like to know. Do you know why whoever vandalized the shelter did it?"

"If I tell you, will you promise not to do anything about it?" Jess nervously fingered the water bottle's label. The plastic crackled in her hand.

Avery nodded. "I promise. The only reason I want to know is to make sure we don't have future problems."

"One of my friends let her dog out in the yard and forgot about him when she went out. The dog dug a hole under the fence and got loose. Animal control picked him up and brought him here. Her parents were pissed and made her pay them the money it cost to get him back."

"Thank you, I appreciate your honesty. I know your friend thinks it was terrible that she had to pay to get her dog back, but she was really lucky. A lot of times when a dog runs around loose we don't get a happy ending. Her dog could've gotten hit by a car because she was irresponsible."

"I really did tell her spray-painting the shelter wasn't a good idea," Jess added. "Can I ask you a question and you won't get mad?"

Avery considered stipulating as long as it didn't concern Reed, but decided the less she mentioned him the better. "Seems only fair."

"What's up with you and Uncle Reed?"

Such a simple question, but one so complicated to answer.

Avery considered tossing out a flippant comment or diverting Jess with another question, but that didn't seem right. Jess knew something was going on between her and Reed, or she wouldn't have asked.

"Your uncle and I have known each other since kindergarten. That makes it easy for us to push each other's buttons."

"My mom used to say that when a guy teases you or gives you a hard time it's because he likes you."

The mom who couldn't stick around had actually given Jess a worthwhile piece of advice? "I think that's true at your age, but it's different with adults."

"I don't know if I believe that."

That's my story and I'm sticking to it. "Reed and I really don't know each other anymore. He's changed a lot since he moved to California."

"You mean he wasn't always such a jerk?"

"He was always—" Avery paused, searching for the right word. Obviously things were still difficult between Jess and her uncle. She refused to make things worse by bad-mouthing him. "He's always been focused. In school he wasn't happy getting an A. He had to get the highest score in the class. He's trying with you. I know he loves you a lot. It's just that he's clueless about what to do."

"My dad was kinda that way when Mom died."

"But he got better, right?" After Jess nodded, Avery added, "Reed will, too."

Jess dunked the roller in paint and moved farther down the wall. "Did you two ever date?"

Avery froze, trying to decide how to respond to the awkward question. *Dated* hardly described their past relationship. He was her first love. The first man she'd imagined spending her life with.

"Yes, we did, but we broke up when we went to college."

"I think he still likes you."

No, Jess, don't say that. Anything but that.

Avery almost asked, *Really, you think so?*

Lord, I've been transported back to junior high. She remembered how she and her friends speculated about what guys liked what girls. Next thing she'd be asking Jess if Reed talked about her and what he said.

"Surely he's got a girlfriend in California."

The roller stopped. Paint dripped onto the grass at Jess's feet as she stared at Avery.

Now I've done it. She thinks I like him, too.

"If he's got a girlfriend, they don't talk very much." Jess resumed painting. "He's on the phone all the time, but it doesn't ever sound like he's talking about anything but business."

That answer left Avery far happier than it should have. She had to end this conversation before that gleam in Jess's eyes got any brighter.

"Hey, what are you two talking about?"

Avery glanced over her shoulder and spotted Reed walking toward them. "We're talking about how attached you are to your phone."

Jess laughed. "You're on the phone more than anyone I know."

As he strode toward them, looking so sexy and confident, Avery realized how easy it would be to care for him again. She had to get out of here while she still possessed a sliver of willpower. "I'll leave you to finish up here. I'm off to see who I can tap for a donation."

Coward, the little voice inside her taunted as she walked away.

That night as Reed and Jess cleaned up after dinner he said, "Were you and Avery really talking about how much I'm on the phone?"

"And other stuff. She said we'll need to put another coat of paint on the wall." Jess picked up a plate and placed it in the dishwasher.

"We can take care of that tomorrow afternoon. Did she say anything else? Anything about me?" Right after the words left his mouth, he cringed. Living with a teenager was rotting his brain. He sounded like a lovestruck tenth grader.

Before Jess could answer the oven timer went off.

He went to shut it off, and noticed the oven wasn't on. "What's the timer for?"

"Dad said I could Skype him at six o'clock tonight."

He waved toward the door. "Go. I'll finish cleaning up. Tell your dad I said hello."

"I will." Jess tossed the words over her shoulder as she darted out of the room.

The kitchen back in order, Reed returned to his room and booted up his laptop. There was a message from his lawyer waiting in his inbox. Surprisingly, threatening to go public with Colt's story had failed to change the association's stance, forcing his lawyer to contact the media. Apparently a reporter, Sylvia Parsons from WTLV, First Coast News in Jacksonville, was waiting for his call. Reed glanced at his watch, adjusted for the time difference and figured since it was only eight in Florida, he might as well call now.

"I heard about your niece's situation, but I wanted to talk with you to see if the story is something we'd be interested in featuring," Sylvia said in a smooth, made-for-TV voice. "I have to admit I'm a little confused. Since you're able to stay with her in Colorado, why do you need the association to make an exception for your niece to live with her grandparents?"

She needs to stay with them because I'm incompetent. I'll mess things up so bad she'll spend the rest of her life on a therapist's couch processing the nightmare.

"My brother's original plan was that his in-laws would come to Colorado if he were deployed. Unfortunately, his mother in-law recently broke her hip and needs to stay close to her doctors. Because I'm a bachelor, I was the backup plan. What do I know about raising children?" He paused and tried to loosen up. He sounded as dry as a corporate annual report. He needed to get Sylvia to step into Jess's shoes. "Think back to when you were fourteen. Can you imagine living with your bachelor uncle?"

The reporter laughed. "Are you saying dealing with a teenager is tough?"

"Don't get me wrong. My niece is wonderful, but Jess would be much better off living with her grandparents. They've raised a child. They're better equipped to nurture and guide her. Jess needs the stability they can provide."

A moment passed and then Sylvia said, "This is exactly the kind of human-interest story our viewers want to hear about. I'll contact your niece's grandparents and the association for their take on the issue. May I call you if I have further questions after I speak with them?"

"Please do."

Sylvia ended the call by thanking him for his time and said she'd let him know when they planned to air the story.

Reed guessed it would never make it to air because the association would buckle after talking to the reporter. No one wanted to look as if they weren't supporting the country's servicemen and women and their families.

Maybe the day hadn't been a total loss after all. Jess would be better off with her grandparents, and he could return to his life and his business. That was good news. Wasn't it?

Chapter 7

Since Reed and Jess had finished painting the exterior wall the day before, today would be their first day as official volunteers, and Avery was out to set Reed straight. Again, yesterday, he'd strolled into her office to make business calls, send faxes and use her computer. Each time he assured her he'd be only a couple of minutes, and somehow he'd left her feeling that she couldn't tell him no.

Today would be different. She'd be firm but polite. The shelter's fund-raiser was only weeks away and she couldn't concentrate on her work with him popping in and out of her office like a Whac-A-Mole. She'd also make it clear that now that he was an actual volunteer, she expected him to give the shelter his full attention, unless a genuine, bona fide emergency came up at his company.

When the pair arrived, she greeted them as she would

any other volunteers on their first day, ignoring how great Reed looked in his worn jeans, tight Stanford T-shirt and his cowboy boots. She ran through the shelter rules and then paused and looked at Reed. "When you're here, I expect your full attention to be on what you're doing. That means, unless it's something that absolutely can't wait, we prefer you not make any personal calls. Are we clear on that?"

"Got it," Reed replied, though she could see in his gaze that he was already distracted.

"So what do you want us doing today?" Jess asked.

"I'll give you a choice. You can either clean the kennels or the cat boxes or bathe the dogs. What'll it be?" She bit her lip to keep from smiling as she waited for Reed's reaction.

She felt a twinge of guilt at asking him and Jess to do some of the less pleasant jobs, but the shelter was like any other business: those with seniority got the plum assignments.

"That's your idea of a choice? Haven't you heard of assessing volunteer strengths and assigning them tasks that best utilize their skills?" While his expression remained calm, a note of distaste crept into his voice. "Don't you have anything more managerial that needs to be done? Or maybe we could walk the dogs?"

She knew his type. He thought volunteering at the shelter would be a sweet gig that consisted of playing with kittens and walking dogs. He was one of those volunteers who turned squeamish or arrogant when it came to the less desirable tasks that needed to be done.

"You haven't even been volunteering five minutes, and you're questioning me." Avery paused, shoved her hands into her pockets, and struggled to control her rising frustration. She dealt with opinionated volunteers all the time and had developed a great repertoire of phrases to gently get her point across without offending anyone. She could manage him—and she could build a rocket ship in her spare time and fly to the moon for her next vacation, too.

"I'm sure you have some great ideas on how you could help the shelter, but the new manager at the Pet Palace is stopping by tomorrow morning. If he likes what he sees, the company could become a generous sponsor for the Pet Walk. That means today everyone's working on getting the animals and the shelter looking their best. *Everyone's* cleaning."

Reed turned to his niece, his arms crossed over his broad chest. "No way am I cleaning cat boxes."

"What do we have to do to clean the kennels?" Jess asked.

"You scoop up the poop and hose them down." Avery sneaked a peek at Reed.

His eyes widened and his jaw tightened for a minute before he regained his control. Avery bit the inside of her lip to keep from laughing. Turning the tables on him and issuing orders could become her favorite pastime.

"That doesn't sound great, either," Reed snapped. "How about we sweep and dust the place?"

Avery opened her mouth to give Reed a lecture on who was in charge at the shelter but stopped. You'd think she and Reed were the two teenagers the way they jockeyed for control.

"What is it with you two?" Jess waved her hand between the adults, and her irritation slammed into Avery. "In the interest of world peace, I'm choosing. We're bathing dogs today. I bathe Thor all the time." The teenager faced her uncle, shaking her index finger at him.

"If you say one word about it, Uncle Reed, we'll clean cat boxes, and I'll make you scoop the poop."

"I guess she told us." Avery laughed, relieved that the teenager had broken the tension. How did Reed so easily get on her nerves?

"Bathing dogs it is," Reed said.

Avery motioned for Reed and Jess to follow her. "Let me show you the grooming room."

She gave them a quick tour of the rest of the offices, as well as the dog kennels and cat area, and then she took them inside a small room that housed plenty of cupboards, a refrigerator and a large metal tub. "One of our dog-walker volunteers will bring in a dog."

Avery explained the process, how to work the sprayer and where towels were located. Then she asked if they had any questions.

"Jess and I can handle it. How hard can it be?" Reed flashed her a confident smile.

Avery bit her lip. She couldn't wait to hear what he had to say in twenty minutes when he was drenched and covered in fur. Avery pointed to the plastic aprons hanging on pegs along the wall. "You'll want to put one of those on. It'll keep you from getting completely soaked. I'll check back in a while. Wish me luck. I'm talking to the head of Griffin's network to ask for a donation."

"What's your strategy?" Reed asked.

"I'm going to tell him about the shelter, our current problem and ask for a donation." What did he think she was going to do? Call up a network executive, chat with him for a minute and then ask him to make cookies for the bake sale they planned to have next month?

He shook his head, as if she'd committed some ridiculous mistake like going into Starbucks and ordering soda. "That's not a plan for success."

Avery noticed Jess's fist clenched around the apron she held. Her gaze darted back and forth between the adults. *She's waiting for round two to start.* Jess's life didn't need any more turmoil. "Jess, will you go see Emma, my volunteer coordinator? Her office is next to mine. Tell her I said she's to take you to meet Mrs. Hartman. She'll be bringing dogs to you to bathe."

After glancing between the two adults again, probably to make sure they wouldn't come to blows while she was gone, Jess left.

"We have to find a way to get along," Avery said once the door closed.

"I thought we got along pretty well the other night at Halligan's."

Reed's harsh expression left no doubt about what he meant. Heat raced through her. She crossed her arms over her chest, trying to channel the energy darting through her body into confidence.

The other night was a mistake. She couldn't force the words past the lump in her throat. Despite knowing better, she couldn't think of what had happened between them that way. Not when she'd felt alive in a way she hadn't in years. "That was a social setting. This is my business. I can't have volunteers questioning every decision I make."

"I asked a couple of questions. What's the big deal?"

She wanted to prove she was in charge. Reed should've realized that the moment he walked in the door today. The challenging gleam in her eye when she'd offered him the unappetizing choice of tasks had been the first tip-off. Then she'd stood there and explained how to wash a dog, as if it was rocket science and he was a grade-school kid.

Anyone could handle washing a dog. Get the dog wet. Throw on the shampoo. Scrub. Rinse. Simple.

"I'm used to being in charge. Taking orders has never sat well with me." Part of the baggage his father had left him with.

"Can't you see how much it bothers Jess when you do that? Did her parents fight a lot before her mom left?"

Had Colt's marriage been like their parents', where the fights rattled the rafters and occurred more often than the weather changed? He remembered how those fights had left him with knots in his stomach and scared to leave his room for fear of what he'd find.

He hadn't considered how his and Avery's disagreements would affect Jess. He hadn't seen them as any big deal. He should've realized his niece would see them differently, but he hadn't. How did Avery always see what he missed? Again, he'd been clueless, while Avery understood. Just another example of what a lousy father he'd be.

"I don't know much about Colt's marriage. He never talked about it, but things can't have been too good. She was having an affair and ran off."

"I'm worried that us not getting along reminds her of what happened between her parents."

Reed remembered how he and his brother had felt as they hid in their room trying to block out the angry words that their parents hurled at each other. But his situation with Avery wasn't the same. They weren't married. Still, there was definitely something between them. Something strong that they both fought against, and damned if he knew what to do about it. But he could keep Jess from getting caught in the crossfire.

"What's going on with us? We never used to argue

like this." He shoved his hands into his pockets, uncertain of how to continue.

"We're different people than we were in high school." Avery resisted the urge to pick at her fingernail. "I care about Jess, and I don't want our disagreements to hurt her. I'll make an effort to go easier on you, if you'll work on questioning my decisions less."

He nodded. "It may not have seemed like it, but I want to help. I just went about it the wrong way. I thought I could give you a new perspective on approaching executives for donations. Charities ask me for money all the time. To convince a major corporate player to write you a big check you have to tell him what it'll do for his business."

"This isn't the first time I've done this."

"Small-business owners are more tied to the community than major national corporate types. Why should a global company care about a little animal shelter in Estes Park?"

"Because the host of one of their most popular reality shows cares about it."

He stepped toward her, not sure of what he intended to do, but needing to erase the censure on her face. "Why won't you let me help you where I can do the most good?"

He wasn't sure what he'd done, but he'd made another mistake. Just as he'd done with Jess. What was the deal? He'd never had this much trouble with women before.

"What makes you think you can breeze in here after all these years and give me advice? Worry about your own life. Mine's off-limits." Though her voice remained level and calm, her irritation came through loud and clear.

Her words cut through him. His own life? What did

his consist of? He had his business. Nothing else, except for a brother and a niece he saw briefly on major holidays. Other than Colt and Jess, who would care if he stepped into the street tomorrow and got hit by a bus?

That was the way he'd chosen since he left Estes Park. Why did the fact sour his stomach now?

Because Avery saw him and his life as lacking, and pitied him for it.

Instead of addressing her comment, he turned the conversation back to fund-raising. "When you call these executives, don't ask them if they want to donate. Give them a number and ask if you can count on them for that amount."

Before Avery could respond, the door opened and Jess returned with a scraggly, wire-haired dog of an indeterminate color. "Mrs. Hartman said to keep a close eye on Baxter because he's an escape artist."

Avery strolled over to the dog and scratched him behind the ear. "He's been known to wiggle out of his collar."

"She also told me the people who adopted him returned him," Jess said, her face filled with concern. "She said he was here for months before."

"He kept getting out of the backyard. The couple who adopted him wanted an outside dog. Baxter wasn't a good fit for them." Avery scratched the mutt under his chin. "We just have to find the right family."

"With that face? Good luck."

"That's mean, Uncle Reed," Jess said as she patted the dog. "Looks aren't everything."

He nodded toward the animal. "He'd better hope someone else thinks that, too."

"He'll be a loyal companion to whoever earns his trust." Avery glared at Reed as if he'd said her baby was ugly. Then she glanced at her watch. "I've got to go. I have to make that call."

After Avery left, Reed turned to Jess. "Since you're the one with experience, you're in charge."

Reed crossed the room and looked down at the mutt standing beside his niece. Instead of growling like Thor, Baxter looked up, wagged his rat tail and then yawned. "You're not fooling me with the tame routine, buddy. I've been warned about you."

"I agree with Avery." Jess scratched the dog behind his floppy big ears. "There's something about him. How could they give up on him after only a week?"

Reed slipped his arm under the dog's belly and lifted him into the metal tub. "He's got a street-smart look to him. He'll be fine."

"What if no one else wants him?"

Reed didn't have to be a trained therapist to realize there was more going on here than Jess worrying about this stray. But that didn't mean he knew what to do about it. "You've got more than this mutt on your mind. Want to talk about it?"

Jess reached for the leash attached to the tub, hooked it to the dog's collar and then turned on the water. "I heard on the news that some soldiers were killed in Afghanistan." When her voice cracked, she bit her lip and paused.

"I'm worried about him, too. That's why every time I talk to him I remind him to be careful."

Jess's lip quivered. "Sometimes that's not enough. People get hurt over there every day."

He put his arm around her shoulder. "We'll just have to pray that he stays safe."

"What if Dad doesn't come home? I won't have anyone."

Her pain reached inside him and squeezed the heart he hadn't been sure he still possessed. He and Jess were so alike. Both alone and determined to hide the fact. "You'll have me."

Jess eyed him as if she wasn't sure if she believed him but couldn't bring herself to voice the words. Not that he blamed her. What had he done to earn her trust?

"I mean it. You can count on me. You and your dad are the only family I have. Being the older brother, he saw me through some tough times when I was a kid." How many times had Colt hauled him away when things got too heated between him and his father? If it hadn't been for his brother, Reed probably would've beaten the hell out of his father much sooner, or his father would've killed him for trying. "There's nothing I wouldn't do for him, and the same is true for you."

The rush of water on metal and the chug as it swirled down the drain filled the awkward silence between them. As what he'd said hung between them, Reed realized he meant every word. Then the dog nudged Jess.

"Okay, boss, what do we need to do first?" Reed asked.

Jess waved her hand under the water and used the sprayer to douse the animal. The unmistakable smell of wet dog wafted through the air. "Quick, hand me the shampoo."

After Reed handed her the squirt bottle with *shampoo* written on it in purple marker. Jess poured a generous amount of liquid into her palm and scrubbed the dog.

Reed's phone dinged, indicating a text, but remembering what Avery had said about remaining focused on shelter business, he ignored the message. Two more pings came in quick succession, followed by his phone ringing. "Since you've got things under control, do you mind if I check my phone?"

"I don't know." Jess dumped more shampoo into her palm. "Avery said we shouldn't take any calls unless it's an emergency."

"I won't know if it's important until I check my messages."

"Okay, but if we get in trouble, you're on your own."

Reed pulled up the message. The dog shifted, and Reed guessed the mutt was about to shower them by shaking. Not wanting to get sprayed, he stepped a few feet away.

"Uncle Reed, I need your help."

He glanced at Jess as he shoved his phone into his pocket. The dog twisted and turned, trying to squirm out of his collar. Jess reached for the dog, trying to yank the collar back down and get the dog under control. Before Reed reached them, Baxter wiggled free. Jess lunged for the dog, but he ducked under her arms and jumped out of the tub. "Catch him, Uncle Reed!"

Reed raced forward, putting himself between the door and the dog. Baxter stopped. As he reached for the dog, the animal shook itself, spraying shampoo-laced water everywhere, including in Reed's face. Eyes stinging from the soap, he managed to wrap his arms around the dog.

The mutt licked his face and squirmed against him. "Great. This dog likes me." As Jess rushed toward him, he called out, "Slow down. The floor's wet."

Before he finished his warning, she started slipping and sliding. He reached for her, and the dog bolted out the door

After regaining their balance, he and Jess raced out after the escapee, but all Reed could think about was how Avery would think he was a complete ass. That was, if she didn't kill him.

Though Avery wouldn't admit the truth under any form of torture, what Reed had said about soliciting donations made sense, and she decided to implement his suggestion with the network executive Griffin had told her to contact. After a minute of small talk, mostly centered on Griffin and Maggie's daughter, Michaela, Avery asked the man to commit to a five-thousand-dollar donation.

His response--that he'd be happy to—combined with her excitement almost knocked her out of her chair. "That's wonderful. I can't tell you how much I appreciate your generous donation."

Five thousand dollars was beyond generous, and more than doubled the amount any one sponsor had donated last year.

Frenzied voices bounced through the shelter. Something was wrong. Avery knew the sound of chaos when she heard it. She wrapped up her call before whatever mess had developed descended on her. That was the last thing she wanted a man who'd agreed to donate five thousand dollars to hear.

She'd no sooner ended her call when a soaking-wet Baxter charged past her office, a trail of bubbles floating behind him. As she headed for her door, she shouted, "Keep all the doors closed. Baxter's loose."

Not good. What had gone wrong? She barreled out of her office and ran into something solid. Strong arms wrapped around her as she fell. Glancing upward, she recognized Reed a second before they hit the unyielding tile floor with him under her.

"Guess bathing dogs was harder than you thought."

Instead of her voice sounding critical, the words came out in a husky rush. All she could think about was his hard body under hers. Her body tingled with excitement as she rolled off him.

"That dog's a menace." Reed stood beside her, his shirt damp and clinging to his muscled frame.

As she worked to keep her breathing even and regain control, she straightened her top, refusing to look at him. When he held her all she could think about was how right it felt to be in them.

"Baxter's like you. He wants things his way, doesn't take direction well and is hard to teach."

"Touché. You can't teach an old dog new tricks."

"Yes, you can. It's all a matter of giving him the right incentive and encouragement."

"That applies to males in general."

No way was she going there with him. Flipping a switch inside her head, Avery slipped back into director mode, hoping that would calm her raging hormones. "What happened? How did bathing a dog turn into a prison break?"

"Avery, he's headed your way," Emma shouted from somewhere. Seconds later, Baxter bounded down the hallway.

"Stop," Reed commanded.

Avery stared openmouthed as the dog skidded to a halt at Reed's feet.

"I'm sorry, Avery." A breathless Jess materialized beside them, a leash and collar dangling from her fingertips, which she immediately slipped on the dog. "I thought I had Baxter under control, but by the time I realized I needed help and called out to Uncle Reed and he got off the phone—"

"Jess, take Baxter back to the bathing room," Avery said, her voice and her entire body tight.

Her temper had reached its limit. She couldn't take this. She couldn't handle Reed being here at the shelter. So much weighed on her. She needed order at work right now, and Reed had thrown her entire life into a state of chaos.

Once Jess and the dog were out of sight, Avery whirled around to face Reed. "I asked you to give your work here at the shelter your full attention. I told you how important it was that we get the animals and the shelter cleaned up for the visit tomorrow. What was it this time? What was so important that you were on the phone instead of concentrating on what you were doing here?"

When he started to answer, she waved her hand in the air to halt him. "Never mind. I don't want to hear it. I'm done. Jess can still volunteer here, but I don't want you to come back. You may not take what we do here seriously, but we do. I can't have someone screwing things up for us, especially now." She knew she was overreacting, but she couldn't help it. "Do you know what this would've looked like to the Pet Palace manager? It would look like I don't have control of the situation."

Which she didn't whenever Reed was within twenty feet of her.

"You can't tell me things always go according to plan," he countered.

The arrogance in his gaze only fueled her anger. "No, they don't, but if you can't put the shelter first, I don't want you here."

Screw the shelter's policy regarding student volunteers. She'd figure something out to help Jess continue volunteering and complete her community service, but she couldn't take Reed invading her work environment any longer. She started to walk away.

"Wait a minute, Avery. Let me explain."

She glanced over her shoulder at Reed. He stood there, his hands shoved into his jeans pockets, his gaze pleading, but she didn't care. It was too little, too late. "Nothing you can say will change my mind. I'll drop Jess off on my way home. Now leave. After all, that's what you're good at."

Chapter 8

After driving Jess home, Avery returned to the shelter and headed straight for Emma's office. Thankful to find her friend still there, she sank into the corner armchair, but then jumped up again and started pacing. "Can you believe what Reed did today? He's driving me crazy. How can everything he does push my buttons? And how dare he come in here and give me advice about soliciting donations, like he knows anything about working for a nonprofit agency?"

"Calm down, because if you don't, I'm going to make you hold a puppy in order to lower your blood pressure before you stroke out."

Avery laughed as she collapsed into the chair across from her friend. "Is that your way of saying I've gone off the deep end?"

"I've never seen you like this before."

"I've never had an ex-boyfriend invade my work life before."

"You sure things are over with Reed? When you two were dancing at Halligan's the other night, I almost ran for a fire extinguisher things got so hot. When was the last time you felt that kind of heat with a guy?"

A couple of her past relationships had come close, at least in the beginning, but the chemistry never lasted with anyone. Except Reed.

"Somewhere along the way you forgot about having a life."

"I have one." She had her family. A challenging job. Okay, right now it was too challenging, but it was a good job. She had friends. So she didn't have a love life right now. A woman couldn't have it all, all the time.

But that didn't keep her from wanting it all. She dreamed of finding a relationship like her parents had had. One where they were best friends and lovers. One where he made her laugh and stood by her during the tough times. With someone who would give her children. Something Reed would never do.

"Let me amend that. You forgot about having a love life," Emma shot back. "You need to find a guy you're attracted to and sleep with him."

If only the problem could be solved that easily.

"That's not my style." Avery picked a long white dog hair off her jeans. "I want more than that."

Her friend shook her head. "I know. You're a soulmate kind of gal. Personally, I don't see what's wrong with being happy with someone just for right now."

Avery refused to settle. If she did, she knew eventually she'd resent her decision, and that emotion would sour the relationship. Realizing those two things had been what had finally helped her move on after Reed. "You're right. I should be happy right now."

Avery stared at her friend and took a deep breath. "I threw Reed out and told him not to come back. The question is how we keep people from finding out Jess is volunteering here without a parent or guardian supervising her."

Panic flared in Emma's eyes. "We can't. It's impossible to keep a secret in this town, and we've got two of the biggest gossips for volunteers. You have to let Reed come back. If you don't, I'll be inundated with requests from other parents for us to make an exception for their kids." Emma laughed. "I can see the headlines now. Volunteer Director of the Estes Park Animal Shelter Admitted to Psych Ward After Being Driven Insane by Unruly Preteen Volunteers."

"I can't have him here." Avery's body ached from the pain having Reed back in town dredged up. While her family knew Reed had broken up with her via email, no one knew the whole story. She started telling Emma about her past with Reed, and soon everything tumbled out. Every agonizing detail she'd held on to for too long.

Her hands clutched together in her lap, Avery peered at her friend. "I can't see my life without someday having children."

"He's been gone a long time. Maybe he's changed his mind about kids."

"I can't take the risk. I hurt so bad the last time. I can't go through that again." Tears stung Avery's eyes.

"Well, then, he's out." Emma's matter-of-fact attitude eased Avery's fears. "All we have to do is find someone other than a staff person to supervise Jess. If my mom wasn't so allergic to animal dander, I'd ask her to help us out."

Avery smiled, latching on to the answer. "I've got the perfect solution. I'll ask my mom."

The only problem was how to get her mother to agree without letting her know why she really didn't want Reed around.

The next day, as Reed sat at the desk in Colt's office trying to focus on the spreadsheet in front of him, he still couldn't believe he'd gotten fired from a volunteer job. He'd never been fired from anything before.

Leave. After all, that's what you're good at.

Maybe Avery throwing him out was for the best. Common sense insisted that was the case, but he'd still picked up his phone more than once to call her. Damn, he'd created more than a little chaos yesterday. He considered sending her flowers, but she wasn't big on stuff like that. She valued actions. She'd tell him unless he changed his behavior, he'd wasted his money. He needed to make things up to her, wanted to prove she was wrong, that business wasn't all that mattered to him.

Making things right. That's what counted with Avery, but how could he do that?

The shelter. He could make a donation.

He did a Google search and located the Estes Park animal shelter's website. The first thing he noticed was that the site took too long to load and looked amateurish. The colors were hard on the eyes. The pictures looked like stock photos. It was poorly organized and not very user friendly.

He had trouble locating information on the Pet Walk, and when he did click on the link, there was no mention of the shelter's precarious financial situation, but he did locate a donation link. However, once he got there, he had to navigate past numerous screens. With his finger resting on the mouse about to click Submit, he stopped. Making a donation wasn't any different than sending flowers. It took no effort, no work. Lip service. That's what Avery would say.

Curious about how Avery's site compared to others, he searched more animal-shelter sites. As he went, he bookmarked the ones he liked, and jotted down notes.

He really had wanted to help yesterday, but he'd ended up doing the opposite. She'd been right. All he'd thought about was his business, feeling his problems trumped hers in importance. Looking back now, he recognized the strain that clouded her usually bright blue eyes. The shelter's financial situation had to be wearing on her.

The shelter was a business. Avery's business. Logically he'd known that, but somewhere in practice, he'd forgotten the fact. He was a volunteer expected to do a job—whatever Avery, or any other staff member, decided needed to be done.

He'd been an arrogant bastard, and as a result he'd caused problems for Avery.

She'd been right to throw his sorry ass out.

The alarm on his phone went off, reminding him to leave to pick up Jess from the shelter. As he drove through town and waited in the parking lot for his niece, a plan on how he could make amends with Avery started forming.

"How did volunteering go today? Is Avery still mad at me?" he asked when Jess climbed into the truck.

"I don't know because we didn't talk about you. You were really a jerk. How would you like it if someone came into your company and questioned everything you told them to do?"

"I know. I want to do something for Avery, but I need your help."

Jess tilted her head and stared at him skeptically. "Why should I help you? What's in it for me?"

"If you do, I'll give you your phone back."

"What about computer privileges?"

"You're pushing it."

"Then you're on your own. Avery's not mad at me."

Damn. Jess had him over a barrel, and they both knew it. "Deal. I want to put together a marketing proposal for the shelter and develop an updated website to show Avery. Maybe create a plan for Twitter, Facebook and Pinterest to increase visibility there, too."

As they made their way back to the ranch, he smiled as they passed Swanson's Ice Cream Shop where he and Avery had shared more hot fudge sundaes than he could count, and McCabe's Pizza, another favorite hangout. Not all his memories were bad.

He and Jess talked about options for the website. When they arrived home they headed into Colt's office. Reed moved the leather armchair closer to the desk for Jess and then settled into the desk chair. They spent the next half hour checking out other shelter websites.

Avery had been right about Jess, too. He needed to make an effort to find out who his niece was. Instead, he'd shown up, been preoccupied with his own problems and expected her to fall in line. Working together on the website could be a good start to fixing that problem.

An image of him decades from now taunted him. His business days behind him, he sat alone in a retirement home staring at a picture of his niece and her family that he'd gotten in her last Christmas card. One he cherished as his only connection with family.

Was that what he really wanted?

"I don't know if I'm good enough to design a website for a real business," Jess said, pulling Reed away from his thoughts.

"We can give it a shot. I picked up a lot from the consultant who updated my company website a few months ago."

"If we have problems, I could contact my summer-school instructor."

"That's a great idea." He pulled up the Estes Park animal shelter website. "Look at this."

Jess shuddered. "That's scary bad. That red is awful, and the rest of the site is too dark. It needs happy colors. Soft ones that make people feel all warm and fuzzy inside."

"You have a good eye." He pulled up another shelter's website. "The most important thing for the shelter right now is raising money, but there's nothing on their site about how bad the situation is. This one has a graph showing how close they are to their fund-raising goal."

"That's cool. We should add something like that."

He jotted down her suggestion on the paper to his right before he returned to the site. "The information on the Pet Walk's buried way down here." Reed scrolled down the page. "We also need to simplify the online donation process."

Jess nodded. Then she tilted her head and smiled. "I know why you're doing this. Avery told me you two used to date. You've got the hots for her. You're hoping if you do all this stuff she won't be mad, and she'll go out with you."

Reed told himself he didn't have ulterior motives, and even if he did, Avery wouldn't be easily swayed.

Every day, Avery crept into his thoughts more. Seeing her, being with her made being back bearable. Life in Estes Park was a lot more fun when he was with Avery.

"That's not it. I'm doing this because I messed up. Part of being responsible is making up for what I did. Since Avery won't let me back in the building, this is one way I can do that. Plus, the shelter provides a valuable community service. I want to help them raise the money they need."

"That's so lame, and you're such a liar."

That might be true, but he'd never admit it.

That night as Avery and her mom stood in the kitchen making spaghetti and meatballs, Avery chatted about her day, intent on working up to the subject of her mom supervising Jess. "I spoke to the bigwig at Griffin's network today. He agreed to donate five thousand dollars. I'm starting to believe we can raise the money for the down payment."

"I have every faith in you."

Still not ready to broach the real issue, Avery told her mom about the Pet Palace manager's visit. "I'm hoping they'll agree to be one of our sponsors for the Pet Walk. It's really been a hassle moving up the event, but if we didn't, we'd never raise the money in time."

Her mom stopped stirring the sauce and glanced at Avery, her brow furrowed. "How about you get to the point?"

"And here I thought I was being subtle. I should've known I couldn't put anything over on you." Avery grabbed a deep breath and chose her words carefully. "Jess Montgomery's supposed to be volunteering at the shelter to fulfill her court-ordered community service, but Reed's too busy managing the ranch and seeing to his own business. He doesn't have time to supervise her, but I can't overlook our rule about kids under sixteen needing an adult chaperone."

Avery bit her lip. She sounded as if she was twelve and trying to divert her mom from the real issue by laying the situation out in one long recitation. "I was hoping you'd be willing to volunteer with Jess and supervise her."

Her mom turned and slowly crossed her arms over her chest. The look she leveled on Avery clearly stated Nannette McAlister knew good and well her daughter was trying to put a hat on a pig. "You said you can't put anything over on me, so why did you try spinning that tale when you knew I'd see right through it?" Her gaze softened. "What really happened between you and Reed? And keep in mind, I heard how cozy you were at Halligan's."

"Who told you, and what did you hear?"

"Griffin said you two were dancing so close *he* was embarrassed."

Avery winced. With her brother's past, her mom probably imagined she and Reed had been seconds away from tearing off each other's clothes and doing the deed in the middle of the dance floor. With no option left but the truth, Avery said, "Reed's driving me crazy at the shelter, Mom." At the shelter? Reed was driving her just plain crazy. "Every time I tell him what to do, he suggests what he should do instead, and he's on the phone constantly with his work." Avery explained about the Baxter incident. "I can't have that kind of disorder at the shelter right now. I have so much to worry about already."

"You should work this out with him."

No way. Every time she saw Reed she lost her common sense, her temper or her self-control. No matter what happened, things didn't go well. Being around Reed was like being the only person at work without a cold. Even with constant hand washing, sooner or later, the bug worked its way past her immune system.

"I know, but now isn't the time. Not when I've got all I can handle keeping the shelter open. Once the Pet Walk's over, and we've got the loan, then I can cope with Reed." She prayed she'd slide this little white lie past her mom. If she did, she'd never tell another one.

Her mom reached out and brushed her cheek. "Of course I'll help you."

"Despite what Griffin said, Reed and I aren't getting back together. It's too late for that. Promise me you won't play matchmaker."

"The thought never crossed my mind, and even if it had, doing that would be as productive as planting my garden in January. I learned early on that you kids have minds of your own."

"Thanks, Mom," she said, praying that her mother stuck to her word.

"That boy had a rough life growing up. He didn't have the advantage of having wonderful parents like you did."

Avery kissed her mother on the cheek. "You're right about that." She paused and then asked a question she'd often wondered about. "Why didn't anyone ever call child welfare on Reed's dad?"

"Your dad and I never knew Aaron Montgomery was physically abusing his sons until that night Reed showed up at our door with that awful bruise on his face. As far as I know, no one knew how bad things were for those boys. They never told anyone, and no one ever saw marks on them. Their father saw to that."

"I don't understand why Reed never told me."

Nannette turned off the stove, and walked to the kitchen table with Avery following her. Once settled, she clasped her daughter's hand. "Reed and his brother always were proud. When their mother died, their father refused everyone's offers of help. Those boys worked so hard to take care of themselves. How would you have acted if he had told you?"

"I'd have supported him. I'd have helped him however I could have."

"How would he have seen your reaction?"

As pity.

"That boy has been running for years. It can't be easy for Reed being back in that house with the memories he has of the place," her mother continued.

"This isn't the first time he's been back."

But now that Avery thought about it, when he'd visited Colt and Jess over the past years, no one had mentioned seeing him in town. The only way anyone knew Reed had been there was because Colt told them.

"No, but this time he's staying longer than a weekend, and now everyone knows what his life was like growing up. I said I wouldn't play matchmaker, and I won't, but I will say you could do a lot worse than Reed Montgomery."

Before Avery could respond, the back door opened and in walked Griffin and Maggie. Griffen cradled Michaela in his arms. Avery's heart ached. Her mother wouldn't say she could do a lot worse than Reed if she knew what Avery would have to give up to be with him.

The next few days went by in a blur for Avery. She lined up vendors for the Pet Walk. She met with the local media about the shelter's predicament and the date change for the Pet Walk. Volunteers updated the signs and posters around the town. They'd called and emailed every registered participant. She'd spayed or neutered the latest batch of adoptable animals and attended to an injured horse they'd received when his owner abandoned him.

Her life was running smoothly again. Each night she fell into bed exhausted but satisfied with what she'd accomplished, and she'd started to believe the shelter would reach its sixty-thousand-dollar goal.

And she hadn't seen Reed since she'd thrown him out of the shelter.

When he arrived to pick up Jess, he waited in the parking lot. What had she expected? That he'd pick Jess up one day, wander into her office and fall at her feet to apologize?

Nannette's laughter floated through the air a second before she and Jess entered the office. "Avery, did you know Jess is a budding author? She let me read a piece for school she wrote about the shelter. I told her she needed to show it to you."

"I know you're busy. You don't have to read it, but I got an A on the assignment." Pride shone on Jess's face as she clutched the paper in her hand.

Avery's heart melted. This young girl was eager to please and desperate for attention, while so afraid she'd disappoint. The woman hadn't deserved this wonderful child. "I'd love to read what you wrote."

As Jess walked across the room and handed Avery the paper, she marveled at the changes in the teenager since she'd started volunteering at the shelter, and especially since she'd been with Nannette. Jess had blossomed. The sullen, angry teen was gone and she'd started making new friends. Apparently she'd finally realized friends who threw her under the bus weren't the best kind to have.

Once Avery had read Jess's paper on the value animal shelters provided for society, she said, "This is amazing. You've really captured the heart of what we do here."

"Tell her your idea," Nannette coaxed.

"I noticed no one's written a blog entry for the shelter in a while," Jess said.

Avery winced. Blogging was yet another aspect of the director's position she loathed. The board had brought up the subject in their last meeting, emphasizing the growing importance of social media and how they were woefully behind the times. From their expectations and her expanding job description, they must think she had twenty-eight hours in her day. "So I've been told recently by the board. It's on my to-do list, but I'll admit it's at the bottom."

"I could write one about the animals who need to be adopted, and what we do here at the shelter. It's important work, but people don't realize we do more than find homes for strays."

"I think that's a great idea. I'll have to approve your blog before they go online."

Jess nodded, her brown hair falling in her face. "I thought we could link it with our Facebook page, which needs work, too, by the way."

That was the story of Avery's life lately and everything she did—needs work, under reconstruction. "Let's see how the blog goes first. We can use your paper as the first one. I appreciate your help. You've got great ideas and tons of enthusiasm, but I don't want your schoolwork to suffer."

The teenager rushed forward and enveloped Avery

in a tight hug. "Thanks for taking a chance on me. I won't let you down."

As she held Jess, Avery reminded herself she wasn't to become attached to Reed or Jess. Unfortunately it was too late for both.

Chapter 9

That night after dinner as Jess and Reed sat side by side at her father's desk working on the shelter website, she said, "I brought up your idea of me doing a blog with Avery today after she read my paper, which she loved. She's putting it online tomorrow as my first entry."

"I told you that paper was great." Reed had been pleased when she asked him to proofread her assignment. "With your writing skills and the way you talked about the shelter, I could see you having a future in marketing. That is, if you don't choose a career in the computer field."

Since they'd started working on the shelter's website and the social-media plan, Jess had talked more than the entire time he'd been in Colorado before that. She'd started asking his opinion about issues with friends and her schoolwork. They'd talked about colleges and things that would help on her applications. When he told her what he thought, he saw glimpses of respect in her eyes. Hell, even the damned dog had softened toward him, growling at him only every other time he came near the mutt.

"Avery said my volunteering at the shelter and doing stuff like the blog will look good on college applications. I'm thinking about volunteering there even after I'm done with the community-service gig."

While he looked forward to working with Jess on shelter business after dinner each night, he wasn't keen on how many of her sentences started with the words *Avery said*.

"You've been a big help with the website, Jess. You've got a real talent for web design."

"Another compliment? From you? I can't believe it."

He stared at his niece. Had he been that quick to criticize, but slow to praise? Yet another legacy from his father that he needed to overcome.

Still beaming from his praise, Jess said, "When are we going to show Avery what we've come up with?"

"If we get these last tweaks done tonight, you can show her tomorrow."

"You'll come with me to present it, right?"

"We'll do a dry run of the presentation to prepare you, but it's probably best you leave my name out of it. If Avery knows I helped with the design she'll probably hate it on principle."

"If a guy went to all this work for me, I'd think it was sweet. I bet Avery would, too. You should tell her. I know you like her."

That hardly described what he felt for Avery. Obsessed about. Craved. Needed, almost to the point that he couldn't sleep at night. Those sentiments came much closer.

"Giving her suggestions about her job and running the shelter was what got me into trouble. Promise you won't mention my name when you talk to Avery."

"I think you're wrong, but I promise."

Avery glanced up from the paperwork spread across her desk and smiled at Jess standing in the doorway.

"Can I talk to you for a minute, if you're not too busy?" the teenager asked, a nervous smile quivering on her lips.

"I've always got time for you."

As Avery said the words, she realized they weren't simply a nicety she tossed out. She truly meant them. Since Jess had started volunteering at the shelter, they'd come to know each other, and she caught glimpses of herself in the teenager.

Jess possessed a good heart and a gentle soul under all the harsh makeup. She took the world's problems, or at least the shelter's, to heart. *Just like I did at her age.*

"I was looking at the shelter's website and it got me thinking. I took a class on web design last summer." After she sank into the chair opposite Avery, Jess reached into her backpack, pulled out her computer and placed it on her lap. Her gaze remained riveted on her hands resting on the laptop. "I've been thinking about the shelter's website a lot lately. I started playing with some ideas, and I put together a new website for you to look at."

"I'd love to see it." Avery moved a stack of papers from her desk to the one open spot on the credenza behind her. "Scoot your chair over here, and show me."

A big smile on her face, Jess placed her computer on the desk in front of Avery and turned it on. While the machine booted up, the teenager moved her chair beside Avery's.

"I can't believe you created a website in your free time. Designing one is a lot of work."

"That's what people think, but it's not that big a deal when you know what you're doing."

When the website appeared on the screen, Avery leaned forward in her chair. "Wow. I don't know what to say. This is incredible! It's so professional."

The soft peach tones were a vast improvement over the dark colors they currently had. Below the shelter's logo were the page buttons. Beneath that, a banner contained an idyllic picture of a family gazing lovingly at the family dog. The animal snuggled up against the young son and daughter. Beside the photo on the left was the phrase "Celebrating pets and the people who love them." To the right were adoption and donation icons.

Jess scrolled down the site. "Stuff like the Pennies for Paws and the Pet Walk were scattered all over the page before. Putting them all here makes it easier for users to find what they need." She pointed to the left side of the screen. "All they have to do is scroll down."

"I agree. I can't wait to show this to the board. And you did this all on your own? You've got some skills, girl."

Beside her, Jess tensed ever so slightly. "I'm glad you like it."

The words were right, but Jess's tone was wrong. What had happened? Avery thought about what she'd said. "Are you worried about me taking this to the board for approval?"

"Not too much."

If it wasn't the board, then what had caused the change? *And you did this all on your own?*

Reed had been a computer whiz. In high school he and his dad had fought over him wanting to computerize the ranch's finances and breeding records. His father had insisted he didn't need a "damned machine" to do the brain work for him. Now Reed owned a large computer semiconductor company. Avery pegged him as the kind of owner who kept a close eye on every aspect of his business, including the company's website.

Jess is worried I'll be mad if I find out Reed helped her.

But that didn't make sense. Mr. Workaholic wouldn't take time away from his business to revamp the shelter website. She was imagining things.

"Do you want to present this to the board?"

Jess shook her head. "Ms. Stinson will have a cow if she finds out I was the one who created this."

"Come on. Seeing that would be worth it right there."

Jess giggled. "Definitely, but it's more important that the shelter gets a good website. Hopefully the new site will help with the fund-raising."

The tightness in Avery's chest loosened. She'd been right with her first instincts. Jess was worried the board would reject the design if they knew a teenager had created it. Reed had had nothing to do with this.

Good thing, because if he had, she might have to re-think the whole he-was-a-complete-ass thing.

When Jess told Reed she needed a dress for the Fall Social, his first instinct was to give her his credit card. Then common sense kicked in. Giving a teenage girl his credit card, even with a strict spending limit, sounded as smart as asking a coyote to watch Thor. But that wasn't his biggest worry. After seeing Jess's fashion choices, his worst nightmare was that she'd come back with a skintight dress made out of cellophane wrap.

While he hadn't wanted the guardian role, he'd taken it on and he wasn't about to slough it off. He could handle shopping with Jess now that their relationship had improved. He was a man who knew what looked good on a woman. That didn't mean he'd enjoy the task. In fact, sitting in the dad/husband chair in a small women's boutique waiting while Jess tried on dresses felt as if he'd died and gone to hell.

After ten minutes, she strolled out of the dressing room, a scrap of red fabric tossed over her arm. "This one's perfect."

"What? I sat here all this time, and I don't get to see it on you?"

"I told you it's great. Don't you trust me?"

He bit his tongue to keep from blurting out hell no, she was a teenager. "My footing the bill entitles me to see the dress on you."

"Like you know what's fashionable."

"I live in California, and I date a lot."

He thought about his previous relationships. Whenever a woman hinted about getting serious, he moved on. He stopped calling, ignored her texts and let her calls go to voice mail. If she failed to get the hint, he tossed out his standard excuse that work had gotten demanding. Then he'd suggest they take a break, and that ended things.

Remembering his anger-management class, he focused on his breathing, counted to ten and then replied in a calm voice, "If I don't see the dress on you, I don't buy it. That's the deal."

She stood there glaring at him. "Are you serious?"

"Absolutely."

She whirled around and stormed back into the dressing room, only to emerge a minute later.

His jaw dropped, and for a moment he had no idea what to say other than she looked as if she belonged in a singles bar or on an episode of *Jersey Shore*.

How did she get the skintight red thing on? Nonstick cooking spray had to be involved. He bit his tongue and counted to ten. While he might not know what was suitable for a fourteen-year-old girl, he sure knew what wasn't when he saw it. "Keep looking. That one's a no. It's not appropriate."

So much for their improved relationship. The teenage defiance he'd become so familiar with returned to her gaze full force. This was not going the way he imagined. Okay, maybe his idea that she'd try on a couple of dresses and buy something modest and longer hadn't been realistic, but this was insane.

"There's nothing wrong with it. *Everyone's* wearing dresses like this."

Right. Every twentysomething *woman* who was out trolling for a man. He doubted any parent of a teenage girl would let her out of the house in the dress. "Maybe so, but I know when a woman looks desperate for attention, and that dress screams it."

Pain filled Jess's eyes. Reed cringed. How could he be such an ass? He was his father's son. That was how. The man had never cared who he crushed as long as he won the argument.

Why the hell do you want to study business? You think you can be one of those big-shot CEOs? Not hardly. You were raised on a ranch. You might leave, but you'll never get the smell of manure out of your nose.

His mind raced, trying to figure out a way to salvage

the situation. His confidence faded. He was out of his league. When he encountered resistance in business he stated the facts, relied on research and pointed out past trends. But this? He had nothing. No experience. No facts, and he knew squat about teenage fashion trends.

"I don't need you to pay for it. Dad gave me a credit card to use for emergencies."

"Good try, but no."

"I knew I should've asked Avery to go shopping with me. I never should've told you about the dance." Jess stormed back into the dressing room.

Reed sat there, his fingers digging into the uphol-stered arms of the chair, clueless as to what to do. He needed help. Avery would've done a much better job.

That's what he needed. An expert. At least Avery had once been a fourteen-year-old girl. She couldn't be as clueless as he was. He grabbed his cell phone and dialed. When Avery answered he blurted out, "Don't hang up. I need to talk to you about Jess."

"Is she okay?" Concern laced Avery's voice.

He explained the situation, and how things had dis-integrated. "The dress Jess wants to buy looks like it belongs on a twenty-five-year-old who's out to hook a husband the old-fashioned way. Come convince her that I'm right and she needs to pick out a more appro-priate dress."

"I can't. I'm on my way to John Sampson's to exam-ine his new foal."

"That's perfect. Stop by the store on your way to his place. It'll take five minutes, tops. You'll come in, tell Jess the dress is awful and then you're done." When Avery didn't jump at his suggestion, he added, "All I've done so far is make her mad. Help me out here. Please?"

Her sigh radiated over the phone lines. "I'm not doing

this for you. I'm doing it for Jess, so she doesn't get made fun of at the dance."

He didn't care why Avery agreed, as long as she did.

As Avery drove across town she imagined Reed's response if he thought Jess's choice inappropriate. Reed, always strong-minded and sure of himself. He'd probably made things worse with some stupid comment like the one he'd made to her on the phone about the dress being one a woman would wear to "hook a husband the old-fashioned way." Everything Jess did lately screamed of her need for attention, but he couldn't seem to understand that. Instead his responses fueled the teenager's natural inclination to prove she knew better.

They were two stubborn mules who'd die of starvation rather than share the feed trough.

When Avery walked into the small boutique she found Reed sulking in a chair, Jess's red backpack at his feet. He nodded toward the dressing rooms. "She's in there."

Avery grabbed a shirt off the closest rack and headed inside. "Jess?"

The teenager poked her head out from behind a red curtain in the middle room. "What are you doing here?"

"I stopped in to do a little shopping. When I went to try on this top, I saw your uncle outside the dressing room. I hear you're looking for a dress for the dance. Have you found one?"

"I did, but Uncle Stick-in-the-Mud says he won't pay for it." Jess reached behind her, grabbed the garment and showed the dress to Avery. Then she bit her lip and her eyes teared up. "He said it makes me look like I'm desperate for attention."

Yup. The situation had played out pretty much as she'd expected. "Like he knows about women's fashion.

Try the dress on and let me see. Maybe we can work on him together and change his mind."

"You'd do that?"

"We women have to stick together against the chauvinistic, arrogant men of the world." Avery pulled back the curtain on the dressing room next to Jess's and placed the shirt on the hook inside while Jess smiled and ducked back into her room. A minute later she waltzed out. On top of being bright red and skintight, the thing was short enough that Avery wouldn't have had the nerve to wear it. After plastering a smile on her face, she motioned for Jess to follow her.

When they met Reed, Avery knew immediately what he wanted—for her to blast Jess with how tacky she looked and tell her to find something else. Didn't he realize that tactic wouldn't work any better for her than it had for him?

As Jess preened in front of the three-way mirror, Avery pretended to critically study the dress from all angles. "That dress is so cute." She forced out the words, thankful when she didn't choke on them.

Then she caught Reed's expression in the mirror. His eyes bulged at her words and he looked as if he'd jump out of his chair any minute. The man had the patience of a four-month-old puppy. She was willing to back him up, mainly because he was right about the dress, but not in the approach he expected. Her way would get the job done while smoothing Jess's ruffled feathers, but it would take time. Her gaze locked with his and she smiled, hoping to calm his rising temper.

"I'm not sure about the color, though." Avery paused. Finesse. That's what the situation required. "Have I ever told you how much I learned about fashion, especially what colors look good on people, when my sister-in-law shot Rory's commercial at the ranch?"

"That's right. Your brother's a model," Jess said, her gaze softening.

"Elizabeth spent a lot of time picking out the shirt he wore for the commercial. She had to make sure the color was right for him."

The teenager smoothed her hand over the red dress, uncertainty flashing in her eyes. "What's wrong with the color?"

"You've got such a great complexion, perfect really, but the color of the dress has an orange cast. It makes your skin look a little yellow."

The teenager stared at her reflection. "Really?"

Avery turned to Reed. "You see what I mean, don't you, Reed? This dress does nothing for her beautiful coloring."

He nodded obediently. "You're right. I don't know how I missed it."

"Guys never notice subtleties. They just know a dress isn't right, but they don't know why." Avery glanced at Reed and shook her head. "We can find something that has the good features of this dress, but in a color that suits you better."

As she and Jess walked through the shop, Avery steered Jess to more appropriate dresses. She picked up a couple of garments, mumbling comments about them being too young for such a mature teenager and then replaced them. Biting her lip, she selected a pink dress with a high round neck and a blousy fit, and pointed to Reed. "I bet this is something he'd think you should wear."

"What's wrong with it? I think it's cute," Reed responded, a glare darkening his features.

She and Jess giggled. Over the teenager's head, she noticed Reed smiling. Maybe he'd caught on to the game after all.

Next Avery selected a dress with a simple black tank-style top and a flowing skirt with a bold tie-dyed print. "This would be fantastic on you. It would highlight your great skin and make your eyes sparkle."

"It looks awfully long," Jess commented.

"We can hem it. That's no big deal if the rest of the dress works." She held the dress up to the teenager. "I have the perfect necklace to go with this. One with Swarovski crystals that I could lend you."

Five minutes later, Jess returned to the dressing room to try on four completely appropriate dresses.

"How about that? The big bad businessman had to call in reinforcements to deal with a teenage girl," Avery taunted as she stood beside Reed. "You can't always lay down the law with her. It only makes her dig in her heels and want to get the best of you. She's strong-willed and knows her own mind. Kind of like someone else I know." That was a big part of Reed and Jess's problem. They were too alike. "Sometimes all banging your head against a brick wall gets you is a major headache."

"I'm smart enough to know when to call in an expert in the field to avoid a bloody battle."

"For a moment when we first came out of the dressing room, I thought you were going to blow everything."

"When I heard you say that damned dress was cute, I almost did, but then I realized what you were up to."

Before he could respond, Jess returned, looking like a beautiful young woman. Avery smiled. "Jess, you look gorgeous. Doesn't she look amazing, Reed?"

"She looks beautiful." Jess beamed at her uncle's genuine praise.

"Do you have some heels that would go with this dress?" Jess shook her head, and Avery asked what size shoe she wore. "I wear a half size bigger, but I might have something you could borrow."

"And you'll loan me that great jewelry you told me about?" Avery nodded, and Jess stared into the mirror. "You're sure we can get this hemmed in time?"

"Absolutely. Have your uncle drop you off at my house tonight. We'll pin up your dress and you can raid my closet for shoes." She'd also drop some subtle hints about makeup.

"What time? If you like pizza we could bring dinner."

"That's the least I can do," Reed added. "Is pizza with spinach and fresh tomatoes from McCabe's still your favorite?"

He remembered what kind of pizza she liked? So what if he did? He'd been an ass at the shelter the other day. Bringing her pizza wouldn't fix that.

Snarky words about what he could do with that idea sat perched on her tongue. Then she caught the look of excitement and anticipation shining in Jess's eyes. Eating pizza and hemming her dress were the kind of things she'd done with her mother before big high-school dances. "I'll see you at Twin Creeks around six."

"You're still living at home with your mom?" Reed asked.

"For now."

After Jess skipped off to the dressing room, Reed said, "The way you managed her was pretty damned amazing."

"Since my work here is done, I'm off to the Sampson place."

When she turned to leave, he reached out and placed a hand on her arm. "I know I'm bringing pizza tonight, but let me buy you a nice dinner Friday to thank you for saving my ass. I'll pick you up after I take Jess to the dance. She was about to deck me when I called you."

Her regret kicked in as she pulled away from him. "I agreed to you bringing pizza for Jess's sake and to keep from making a scene, but as far as I'm concerned you're just somebody that I used to know."

"Let me make it up to you Friday."

"You aren't getting this. I don't like who you are now, but even if I did, I'm busy Friday night. My friend's the guidance counselor at the high school, and when they were coming up short on chaperones, she called in a favor. I'll be at the dance Friday night playing chaperone."

"Mrs. Palmer said we still need volunteers, Uncle Reed," Jess said as she strolled out of the dressing room, her selection clutched in her hand. "I told her I'd ask you to help out."

"I'd be happy to."

Avery flinched as he flashed her an I've-got-you-now grin.

If that's what he thought, he was so wrong. "We've already done the high-school dance thing. Remember? I don't know about you, but I have no desire to relive those years."

Chapter 10

"Call me when I need to pick you up," Reed said to Jess as he pulled up in front of the sprawling ranch house at Twin Creeks.

"You're not coming in?"

Avery had made it quite clear this afternoon that he wasn't welcome. A disturbing sense of loss filled him. When he and Avery had dated, they'd studied at her house after he finished his chores, which often turned into him staying for dinner. Twin Creeks had given him a glimpse into what normal family life could be. "I've got work to do."

"Sure you do. It doesn't have anything to do with the fact that Avery's still mad. If you'd tell her about the website, she wouldn't be, you know."

The McAlister house had been the closest thing to a home he'd ever really had, and now he was unwelcome because of the person who'd once gained him entrance.

Avery. She made him laugh. She kept him on his toes and made him think about the world outside his office. And she lit a fire in him, a need so deep that it left him wanting to be the kind of man she respected.

But what could he offer her? Sure, he could offer her financial stability, but what else? Certainly not children. Dealing with Jess was one thing. Children of his own? He refused to tempt fate.

He turned to Jess. "I don't want Avery knowing about the website."

She jerked the truck door open and stomped up the walkway to the front door, carrying the pizza box to Nannette McAlister, who greeted her on the porch.

As the pair exchanged words, he waved. Mrs. McAlister didn't wave back, but instead strode toward the truck, her brow furrowed. He rolled down the passenger window and braced himself for a lecture.

"It's bad enough that I heard about you coming home from Mabel Withers. With as many meals as you had at this house I deserved better than that, and now I hear you're not staying tonight."

Instead of making him feel guilty, her concern pleased him. He knew the more she picked at him, the more she cared. "Mrs. McAlister, you're looking as pretty as ever."

While heavier than she'd been years ago, she still looked very much like the woman he remembered. Her short spiky hair, now flecked with silver, added to her saucy look.

"Flattery won't get you out of hot water with me, Reed Montgomery, but you just keep on trying."

"I'd have to be a fool to think a compliment would do that, Mrs. McAlister. I'd love to stay for dinner, but I have work to do."

"What are you going to do? Go home and make dinner for yourself? Or skip eating?" Hands on her hips, she continued, "The work will still be there later, and don't you think it's about time you started calling me Nannette?"

Knowing the futility of arguing with her when she had her mind set, he turned off the ignition and climbed out of the truck.

When he joined her on the walkway, she enveloped him in a hug like the ones he'd once received from his mother. "It's good to see you, son. You've been gone too long."

"You may not say that after tonight. When we saw Avery today, she was still pretty mad at me."

Jess stared at him as if he had the intelligence of a two-year-old when they joined her on the porch. "If you'd tell her about—"

"The longer we stand here, the colder the pizza gets." He tossed his niece a keep-quiet glare.

Nannette glanced between him and Jess, her confused stare lingering on him, indicating she figured something was up, but instead of saying anything, she opened the front door and stepped aside for them to enter.

As Avery's mother led them through the house to the kitchen, she said, "Avery told me all about the dance and your dress, Jess. I can't wait to see it on you."

The ease he'd felt when he walked into the McAlister house disappeared when he walked past the room that had been Ben McAlister's study. Reed's stomach twisted.

Nannette's and Jess's voices created a buzz around him. He forced himself to keep walking as the memories clawed at him, threatening to pull him under.

He still remembered sitting in that office, scared to death about going to jail and disgusted with how he'd lost control and beaten his father until the man begged for mercy. He still remembered what Avery's father had said that night.

All you'll do is drag my daughter down with you.

A hand touched his arm. Nannette was staring at him, worry etched on her face. "Are you all right, dear?"

Words refused to form in his head.

Nannette squeezed his arm. "Let it go. It's time."

"I don't know how."

"Reed, I'll give you a bit of wisdom like I would my own children." Nannette's eyes filled with the same loving look he remembered from his own mother, and his heart ached over what he'd lost. "We can choose to remember the past, or we can put it in its place and look to the future."

Jess glanced over her shoulder. "What's going on? Is something wrong?"

Shoving his memories back into the dark cavern of his mind, he smiled at his niece and walked toward her. "Nothing's wrong. Let's eat."

When they walked into the kitchen Avery frowned. "I didn't expect you to come tonight." Then she turned her back and opened the kitchen cupboard.

Message received. He should've dropped Jess and the pizza off.

"I should leave."

Nannette glanced between him and her daughter. "Absolutely not. I invited you to dinner and you accepted. Whatever's going on between the two of you is just that, between you two. Now, let's all sit down at the table."

Awkward silence enveloped the McAlister kitchen,

periodically broken by the clunk of glasses on the wooden table.

"Has Jess told you what a great help she's been at the shelter?" Nannette finally said.

"Baxter almost escaped today on his walk with Mrs. Hartman." Jess opened the pizza box and grabbed another slice, having devoured her first one with unladylike speed. "I think he's tired of being at the shelter."

"So I'm not the only one who can't control him?" Reed froze. The minute he'd spoken the words, he regretted them. Avery's eyes darkened. Her lips pressed into a thin colorless line.

Why the hell hadn't he kept his mouth shut? Why did he bait her?

Because even her irritation was better than indifference. Love and hate. Two sides of the same coin. As long as she got angry, she still cared.

"I bet Mrs. Hartman wasn't distracted because she was on the phone." Avery stared at him, challenging him to deny her statement.

"The nasty looks flying between the two of you are bad enough. Poor Jess and I feel like we're in a combat zone. I won't tolerate snide comments. If you don't start being nice to each other, I may just lock you in a room together and refuse to let you out until you solve your problems."

Reed laughed, but noticed Avery didn't share his humor.

"She means it." Avery shuddered. "She did that once to Rory and Griffin. They were in there for an hour."

"That's a great idea, Mrs. McAlister," Jess said. "I say we do it."

"Truce?" Reed asked.

Avery nodded.

"How's the fund-raising going?" Reed asked, hoping to steer the conversation to a safer topic.

"I asked the exec Griffin put me in touch with to donate five thousand dollars, thinking I'd be happy if they donated half that, and he agreed."

Reed smiled. "I see you took my advice."

"For your information, I was already doing what you suggested."

"Both of you know my rules about the dinner table." Nannette's calm, flat voice echoed through the room.

"Yes, ma'am," she and Reed replied in unison.

Those who fought at the table went away hungry. "Either get along or leave."

"I've got a better idea," Avery said as she stood. "Jess, if you're done eating, we should get to work on your dress." Then she scooted out of the kitchen before he could object.

The next night Avery stood with her friend Rachel, the school's counselor, in their old high-school gym, decorated with purple, white and silver streamers. "Remind me again what this chaperone gig entails," she said, taking a sip of watery fruit punch from the plastic glass she clutched in her hand.

"It's pretty simple. We make sure none of the kids sneak off, spike the punch or do anything else inappropriate," Rachel said. "With you here, I can keep my eye on the troublemakers."

Since her statement opened the door, Avery figured she might as well walk through it and see what she could learn about Jess. "Is Jess Montgomery part of that group?"

"No. I couldn't believe it when I heard about what happened with the shelter. She's going through a tough

time, but I suspect she got pulled into something. She's
so afraid of losing her friends. That's her biggest problem."

"That's what I thought, too."

She scanned the gym as a dutiful chaperone should,
and spotted Reed and Jess as they entered. While Jess
headed for a group of girls clustered under one of the
basketball hoops, Reed stood inside the door, looking
as sexy as ever in black jeans and T-shirt paired with
a black blazer. A tan Stetson and boots completed his
look.

"Is that Jess's uncle? Mr. Tall, Dark and Dreamy
who just walked in?"

Avery nodded.

"That man looks fine." Rachel practically drooled as
she watched Reed walk toward them. "I've heard you
two were once an item. Have you picked back up where
you left off, or is he fair game?"

What was it with her friends? Emma had asked if
Avery minded if she made a play for Reed, and now
Rachel. *You'd think he was the only eligible bachelor
in town.*

"I don't care who Reed dates."

*Better duck for cover before God sends a lightning
bolt to strike you down for that monster lie.*

When Reed joined them, Rachel morphed into someone else before Avery's eyes. Her confident friend who
possessed a master's degree in counseling and had graduated magna cum laude from Duke twirled a strand of
auburn hair around her finger, smiled and peered up
at Reed.

"Thank you for agreeing to chaperone the dance. We
don't get many fathers volunteering, much less uncles."

"No problem." Reed turned to Avery, his gaze unreadable. "Thanks again for your help with Jess. She looks great *and* appropriate."

"I was happy to help her." Avery's throat tightened. This stilted conversation was worse than arguing with him.

Rachel flirted with Reed, tossing her hair and giggling at his jokes. Her friend had been working with teenagers too long, Avery thought, because tonight she was acting like one. After five minutes, Avery excused herself, claiming she needed to go to the restroom.

It was going to be a long night.

Once in the bathroom, she splashed cold water on her face. She needed to get a grip. She kept telling herself she wasn't interested in Reed, and yet whenever another woman showed interest, her nose got out of joint.

Figure out what you want, and either fish or cut bait.

Resisting the urge to hide in the bathroom to avoid the issue altogether, she squared her shoulders and headed back to the gym.

Untwist your big-girl panties and deal with it.

When she returned, she spotted Jess at the punch bowl and joined her to say hello. "You look amazing, Jess."

"Thanks." The teenager fingered the crystal-and-rose-quartz necklace that Avery had loaned her. "I just saw a couple sneak off to the janitor's closet."

Avery searched for Rachel, but couldn't locate her. The she noticed Reed was nowhere to be found, either. Surely they couldn't have gone somewhere together. She almost laughed. Rachel was the school's counselor. No way would she go off with one of the chaperones. But then where were they? "I'll find Ms. Palmer. She'll know how to deal with this."

Jess shrugged. "Okay. It's not my problem if Haley

and Brad have half their clothes off by the time she gets there. You two can explain it to their parents, the principal and the—"

"Where's the closet?"

Avery followed Jess through the halls. The last thing she needed was to be blamed for two teenagers going at it like rabbits while she was chaperoning the dance. Harper would rake her over the coals for that. She could hear her board president now. *How can we trust you to manage the shelter and its funds properly when you can't supervise a group of teenagers at a dance?*

When they reached the closet, Avery knocked on the door. "You're busted. Come out now."

"I'd love to, but the door's locked."

"Reed?" Avery turned to Jess. "What's going on?"

The teenager revealed a key ring, unlocked the door and shoved Avery inside with a surprising amount of force, sending her careening into Reed. Her momentum threw him off balance as he wrapped his strong arms around her.

Before they could regain their footing, the door slammed shut and the deafening sound of the lock clicking echoed in the small closet.

"Jess, unlock the damned door," Reed yelled as he banged on the door.

"Let us out," Avery pleaded.

"Not until you talk about why you're mad at each other."

"I promise we will. Just let us out." Avery's mind spun, trying to think of how to convince the teenager. "You can trust me, Jess, really. We'll work this out."

"I don't know. Mrs. McAlister told you to work things out last night, but you didn't."

"We will now. Won't we, Reed?" Avery turned toward the man fuming beside her. "Tell her!"

"What's important here is you're asking for trouble doing this." Reed's voice rippled with frustration.

Avery poked him in the ribs and whispered, "Don't say that."

"I don't know where you got the keys to this closet, but that alone could get you into trouble," Reed continued.

"Now's not the time for a lecture." Avery ground out the words, trying to fill her voice with force, while remaining quiet enough that Jess couldn't hear. "Remember the dress-shop incident."

"It doesn't matter how I got the keys. What's important is I have them and I didn't steal them."

"If you don't let us out right now, you're grounded. I'm taking away your phone, your computer, the TV and anything else I can think of." Reed's voice rattled with the force of his anger.

"Then I might as well get my money's worth." The *tap, tap* of high heels on industrial tile faded.

"Why couldn't you keep your mouth shut? I almost had us out of here." Avery banged on the door. "You just *had* to play the hard-ass in charge."

Yup, he'd screwed up again. Despite the way he acted with Avery and Jess, he was a logical, rational, good guy. Why couldn't he do something right when Avery was around? Because all his blood got diverted from his brain the moment he saw her and his testosterone overrode his common sense.

He upended a crate of rags, sat it in front of Avery and patted it. "We might as well get comfortable, since it looks like we'll be here for a while." He turned over a second one and settled his long frame awkwardly on the makeshift chair. "We can't go on like this. We didn't always see things the same way, but we respected each other. Didn't we?"

"So what happened? What's going on between us now?"

"Beats the hell out of me." He stood, needing to pace, but realized that he couldn't take more than a step or two.

"You asked me the other night if I wondered what things could be like between us now."

He nodded and held his breath, not sure where she was headed with the conversation and not liking the tightness in his chest.

"Since you asked me that, I've been wondering about it. A lot."

He'd sure as hell been thinking about the same thing, almost nonstop, but where had her thoughts led her? Probably not the same place as his—that they'd burn each other up from the heat they generated if they ever got together again.

How did a man respond to a comment like that? Certainly not with what he was thinking. Glancing at Avery, he tried to think of what to say, but decided his best bet was to keep his mouth shut.

In the dim light from the overhead bulb, he saw Avery swallow. Then she licked her lips. "What do you think of us becoming friends with benefits?"

Avery's words stopped Reed in his tracks. He collapsed onto the crate. He was dreaming. He'd fallen, hit his head and was suffering from a brain injury. He was hearing things. Any of those were more likely than that he'd actually heard Avery say they should start having casual sex.

"Excuse me?"

"We're both wondering about it. If we become—" She paused, shifting her weight. The plastic crate under her squeaked. "If we did get more involved, we'd know, and then we can both move on."

He frowned. Obviously she wasn't as excited by the thought as he was. Why would she think he'd settle for that? He wanted more from her. The revelation left him weak. "What do you mean 'move on'?"

"It's like when I tried to give up chocolate for Lent one time. Once I decided to do that, I saw chocolate everywhere I went. Someone brought brownies to work. Emma wanted a chocolate cake for her birthday. The more I tried to resist the cravings, the stronger they got." She folded her hands on her lap in an uncharacteristically demure pose. "After Lent was over and I could have all the chocolate I wanted, I found it wasn't a big deal."

What the hell was going on? Casual sex didn't fit with the Avery he knew. Then he really looked at her and noticed her picking at her nails. She did that only when she was nervous.

He stood, stumbled the two steps to close the distance between them and knelt in front of her. His hands covered hers. Then words he never thought he'd say if a gorgeous woman asked him to have no-strings-attached sex with her tumbled out of him. "Could we start with going on a date?"

Her crystal-blue eyes darkened like a stormy sea. She pulled her hands out from under his and crossed her arms over her chest. "You don't want me? You're telling me no?"

He'd have laughed at her ridiculous assumption, but he knew it would piss her off more. "That's not what I meant."

She scoffed. "Then explain it to me."

"If you and I make love again, it will be a very big deal, and it won't be just a casual fling." He linked his hands with hers and drew her to her feet. Then he lowered his lips to hers. Her body instantly relaxed and molded to his. Fire raced through him as if he were made of drought-stricken grass. Avery clung to him, her hands running over him, exploring, teasing, fueling his need.

He ran his hands through her hair, marveling at the silken texture. Her lips nibbled at the sensitive spot where his neck joined his shoulder as she ground her pelvis against his hard flesh. Blood pounded in his ears, blotting out every thought but the feel of her in his arms.

Her heated breath fanned his neck. He'd been missing out on so much by shutting himself off emotionally for years. "Avery, I've missed you. More than I ever realized."

"I'm right here. Where I've always been."

His mouth captured hers, all the longing he'd felt for years flowing out of him into her.

A click sounded somewhere around him, but he ignored the sound. A door creaked and giggles echoed in the small room. He and Avery jumped apart. He ran a hand through his disheveled hair, while Avery straightened her blouse. A few minutes longer and who knows what Jess would've walked in on.

"I knew you two liked each other, but, jeez, you're setting a bad example."

Jess had returned to release them. There was no denying the truth now.

The next morning as Avery examined the shelter's newest feline arrival she realized she and Reed had never actually decided how to proceed with their relationship. They'd talked about dating, but then they got distracted. She smiled at the memory of Reed's kisses.

After Jess discovered them in the closet, they'd spent the remainder of the night talking, dancing and being proper chaperones. When the dance ended he walked her to her car and kissed her good-night.

But where did they go from here?

"Emma said I'd find you here." Reed's strong voice sent excitement coursing through her system.

She looked up to find him leaning against the doorjamb of the exam room, none of the uncertainty or awkwardness that she felt over what happened last night evident on his classic features.

"Want to go out for dinner and a movie tonight?"

"Sure." She scratched the tabby behind his ears in effort to keep her hands from fidgeting. She hadn't been this nervous the first time he asked her out when they were both sixteen.

He smiled, and butterflies set up residence in her stomach, their wings beating at a frantic pace. "I'll pick you up at seven."

Then he said he knew she was busy and was gone before she could protest, leaving her just as unsure about where things stood between them. Guess she'd find out tonight.

She finished the cat's exam and turned him over to Carly—a part-time vet tech and a prime example of why never to judge a book by its cover. The tech might look tough with all her arm tattoos, piercings and short spiky ebony hair, but there wasn't a softer heart around.

She returned to her office to check her emails. One week. That's all they had left until the Pet Walk. They'd registered a record number of people for the event. At fifteen dollars each, they'd already exceeded last year's total in that regard. Many of the attendees had said they'd stepped up their pledging efforts, which would help, too. Smaller sponsors had kicked in twice as much money as last year, while Devlin Designs and Griffin's network had each donated five thousand dollars. Those amounts still floored her. In previous years, the shelter's largest sponsors gave, at most, two thousand dollars. Any other year she'd be thrilled with what they'd achieved, but would all her work be enough to reach their goal?

The first thing she noticed when she reached her office was the big black leather desk chair with a giant bow wrapped around it.

Even before she opened the card placed on the seat, she knew it had come from Reed. She lifted the envelope and sank onto the chair. Air whooshed out from under her. She leaned back and sighed. Now, *this* was a chair.

Inside the envelope she discovered a sheet of folded computer paper. Reed's bold handwriting was scrawled across the page. "Consider this an early Christmas gift. I didn't want you to have to wait for Santa. Enjoy. Reed."

That was so like the man she'd fallen in love with years ago. She'd wondered if the sensitive Reed was still there, buried deep within the workaholic. Now she knew.

But what should she do about her feelings? The things that drove them apart, his living in California, her life being in Colorado and their different expectations about children, still existed.

But things were different, too. Reed would be here for a year until Colt returned from Afghanistan. They had time to figure things out. Maybe his views on children would change after spending time with Jess. He probably didn't realize it, but his relationship with Jess had changed a lot already.

Nothing ventured, nothing gained. If she didn't explore a relationship with Reed now, she'd always wonder what might have been. Better knowing than forever wondering.

She wanted to see Reed to tell him how much she wanted to be with him.

History had repeated itself. She was in love with Reed. Again.

Chapter 11

Ten minutes later, Avery parked her truck by the Rocking M's barn, walked to Reed's front door and knocked. What could she say? *Hey, thanks for the desk chair. I don't think you're a complete ass anymore. In fact, I think I might be in love with you?*

Maybe not.

When he didn't answer, she walked to the barn. Once inside, she inhaled deeply, trying to control her racing thoughts. The familiar earthy smells washed over her. A horse nickered, and then she heard Reed's low voice.

"Hey, pretty lady. Let me take a look at that leg." The horse whinnied. "I'll be gentle."

His voice rippled through her, leaving her warmer than a man had in—well, she couldn't remember how long.

"That a girl. I need to figure out why you're favoring this leg." Mesmerized, she followed the sound of his voice.

Avery's heart fluttered. This was the Reed she used to know. The gentle cowboy who spent hours in the saddle with her exploring the world around them, who teased her and whom she loved to distraction.

She entered the stall and found him kneeling beside a chestnut mare, his large hands cradling the animal's hoof.

"Do you want me to take a look at her, since I'm here?"

"It's just a stone. I can handle it." He released the animal, reached into his back pocket and pulled out a pocketknife. "What are you doing here? You aren't going to cancel our date for tonight, are you?"

"I wanted to thank you in person for the chair."

"I thought I'd help Santa out this year." His boyish grin made her insides as gooey as caramel inside chocolate.

"It was very sweet of you. I'm sure it'll greatly increase my productivity."

"I'm glad you like it."

She thought about the website. Jess hadn't done the work by herself—Avery would bet on it. "You helped Jess with the website, didn't you?"

"Did she tell you? She promised me she wouldn't."

No matter what Jess said about designing a website being easy, doing one took time. Time that Reed had taken away from his own business to help hers. "She didn't say anything. I guessed. Why didn't you tell me?"

"You were pretty mad at me—not that I blame you." He worked to dislodge the stone. "I was an ass at the shelter, and you had every right to throw me out. I went on the shelter's website to make a donation, and then I realized you'd say I was taking the easy way out. I wanted to do something that would help you and the shelter, but Jess did all the hard work. I was just the idea man."

"I've known the website needed work, and the board's been on my case about it, but I didn't have the money or the time to deal with it." Avery stopped. This conversation wasn't going at all as she'd imagined, but then she wasn't sure what she'd expected.

You expected by now you'd be in his arms.

She'd made the move at the dance, and she wasn't about to do the same thing here. She possessed *some* pride. "I see the ranch work is coming back to you, city slicker."

"It's been like riding a horse, except for the sore muscles part."

"That's what you get for letting yourself go."

How had she gotten those words out, even as a joke?

He straightened, a mischievous glint in his eye. Then he leaned back on his heels. "Take a good long look, sweetheart. Then tell me you think I'm out of shape."

Her heart rate spiked. His jeans and tight T-shirt revealed a physique most men would sell their soul for. She could keep the shelter running for a year if she sold posters with a picture of him in this pose with the fire raging in his eyes like it was now. She'd seen that smoldering gaze countless of times before, but this was different. Reed was different. Stronger. Even more sure of himself and, she guessed, more sure of what he could make her feel.

As he advanced, the small confines of the horse stall became more intimate. The air crackled from the passion firing between them. His gaze raked over her. "Want me to prove what kind of shape I'm in and how much stamina I've got?"

"Yes, please."

Reed smiled, and her heart did cartwheels. "I'll do my best."

"I said that out loud? I didn't mean to."

"I'm so glad you did, darling."

As he closed the distance between them, she realized how much she wanted this. How much she needed *him,* and not just physically. He'd changed, but deep inside, he was the same man she'd loved since kindergarten. Strong. Decisive. Sensual. He was part of so many of the memories she held dear: birthdays, prom, graduation, being accepted to college.

Their lives were intertwined.

As his lips covered hers, she melted against him. Desperate to touch him, she pulled his shirt from his jeans and slid her hand under the material, finding warm, firm skin. Strong muscles flexed under her palms, and his groan rippled through her. It wasn't enough. She tugged at his shirt, but her hands tangled in the garment. He gently swept her hands aside and finished the task.

She stepped back to admire him. His broad chest rose and fell with his rapid breathing. "I take it back. Every last word I said about you being out of shape."

Then she was in his arms again, and his lips found hers. She deepened their kiss, growing bolder. Her hands moved over him, exploring and teasing as she reacquainted herself with his body. She refused to worry about the future. Nothing mattered right now but Reed and being with him.

* * *

Avery filled his senses as her hands roamed over his heated body. Over in her stall, the horse nickered. What was he thinking? "We're too old to make love in the barn."

"I can't wait."

He cupped her face in his hands and kissed her. All the passion he felt, all the emotions he kept so tightly reined in poured out of him. He hadn't realized it, but he'd been dreaming of this moment for years. "I've made so many mistakes with you. I want to do this right."

"Trust me. You are."

She caressed him through his jeans. He moaned, and for a moment he gave in to the pleasure of her touch. Pleasure built, threatening to consume him. His control fading, he scooped her into his arms and headed for the barn door.

As he walked outside, she alternated between kissing his neck and nibbling on it. Her hands caressed his chest, finding his sensitive nipples, sending his motor revving into a new gear. "Keep that up and I might drop you."

"I'm capable of walking."

He set her on her feet, and pulled her against him. He ground his erection against her pelvis as his hands covered her breasts, kneading the tender flesh. Her steamy breath fanned his heated skin. When she moaned, he almost exploded. He lifted her again, and this time practically ran to the house.

Once in his room, he placed Avery on the bed. Despite vowing to go slowly, to savor every minute with her, he couldn't. They frantically worked to undress each other. Urgency and need churned inside him, growing with her every touch as they tumbled back onto the bed.

Her hands and mouth everywhere on his body tested his control, making him feel like an untried youth. As he caressed her heated flesh, she writhed beneath him, and her nails dug into his shoulder.

"Now. Please," she urged.

He rolled away from her and searched in the nightstand for a small foil packet. Seconds later, he pulled her under him. As he eased into her, he bit his lip to keep from crying out. How could he ever have left her?

They moved together. Tension escalated inside him, building and straining. His hand slipped between them and he stroked her. Her gaze locked with his. The naked emotion in her eyes stunned him. He'd never connected with anyone the way he had with Avery. She always could see into his soul.

He drove deeper and her body tightened around him as she climaxed, sending him to his own fulfillment.

Afterward, as he cradled Avery in his arms, Reed found a sense of peace he hadn't known he craved. What he'd found with her—the completeness, the fulfillment—left him stunned and more than a bit shaken. He remembered how much he loved her. How she'd kept him grounded and made him feel that he could do anything.

She awakened a part of him he'd thought no longer existed. The part that longed to be connected to someone. The part that knew life would be better if he came home every night to someone who loved and understood him. If he came home to Avery.

What had he done?

"Why'd you break up with me in an email? Why wouldn't you return my calls?"

He closed his eyes as her soft questions evaporated his joy. Memories crowded in on him.

"Mom said you've been running for years. Was I one of the things you were running from?"

He stiffened beside her, reluctant to spoil the perfection they'd shared, but she had the right to know. She deserved the truth. He owed her that. He should've told her before they made love, because knowing who he really was and the stock he came from could have changed her opinion of him.

"I told you things were bad at home, and I hated being there, but I never told you how bad things were. My dad used to beat my mother, and when she died, he started in on me and Colt." The story poured out of him. The helplessness he'd felt at first over his father's constant criticism and unrealistic demands, and how he'd resented his mother for staying. Instead of taking her sons and leaving the first time her husband beat her, she rationalized his behavior. If she were a better wife he wouldn't hit her. If the boys would do what their father said, everything would be fine.

The words his father hurled at him one night hammered away at him. *What makes you think you've got what it takes to make it anywhere but here? You think you're smart, but all that book-learning can't change who you are. You think you're better than me? You aren't. Mark my words, you'll be back here someday with your tail tucked between your legs.*

"That night I nearly beat my father to death made me take a hard look at my life. Your dad said he saw glimpses of my father in me. Like I didn't realize that every time I looked in the mirror. But he was right. My anger was getting out of control."

Her hands cupped his face, forcing him to meet her unwavering gaze. "I never once worried you'd hurt me."

"I did. I was worried enough that I took anger-management classes while I was at Stanford, and things got better. But when I'm here, I'm scared I'll get pulled back under. Your mom was right. I have been running. From my past. From my fear. From you.

"When I got to Stanford I could start over. No one knew me. I left my past behind. I couldn't come back. Then I thought about you, and how I couldn't see you living in California. I couldn't ask you to leave your family. And you wanted kids. You'll be a wonderful mother someday. I see it every time you're with Jess. You always know how to handle things, how to make her feel better."

"You're doing better with her than you think."

He twined his fingers with hers, needing her strength, her comfort. "I've screwed up so many times with her it scares me."

"But you admit your mistakes and you work to fix them. That's what a good parent does."

"I couldn't deal with the stress." Avery, forever the optimist who saw the good in everyone, no matter how hard she had to look. "I wrote you an email and didn't return your calls because I couldn't bear anything more personal. I couldn't tell you how worried I was about dragging you down with me."

Her hand, the one not clutching his, rested on his chest above his heart. He wondered if she noticed how fast it was beating. "You should have told me. I'd have understood. I would've helped you."

Of course she would have. That was part of the problem, back then and now. She always knew what to do. She always cared. She was always too good for him.

Knowing he wasn't good enough for her, that he never would be, he gathered her into his arms. While the first time they made love had been unbelievable, they'd both been almost frantic. Now he wanted to take his time. He wanted to forget about everything else and lose himself in Avery.

The day of the Pet Walk, Avery arrived at Stanley Park at the unholy hour of six-thirty to begin setting up. Sun glistened off the mountains surrounding the park. She still couldn't believe how wonderful the past week had been. After she and Reed had made love that afternoon, she'd returned to the office and worked on details for the Pet Walk. Then she met Reed for dinner and a movie. Their first date. No doubt about it, she was madly in love with him. Since then, they had spent every spare hour in each other's company. And now she finally understood what had driven him away.

Her mom had been right. He'd been running from his father and his past. No wonder he hadn't wanted to return to Estes Park. Why couldn't he see what strength it took for him to be here?

But what about her? When she thought of her childhood, Reed was there in almost every memory. She suspected the same was true for him. Did that mean being with her dredged up things he'd rather keep buried? And if it did, could they ever move past that?

She refused to think about that.

Just enjoy being with him, and worry about the future later. You've got time. At least a year.

"You look like you could use some caffeine."

She turned to find Reed beside her, a white Starbucks cup in his hands and an endearing grin on his face.

"Tell me that's a nonfat vanilla latte."

He nodded, handed her the cup and kissed her cheek. "Some things about you never change."

She sipped her drink and felt the warmth seep into her. Heat from the coffee and from Reed's fervent gaze.

"I needed that." She glanced around. "Where's Jess?"

"I dropped her and Thor at the shelter. She's helping Carly with the animals she's bringing. What can I do? Consider me your executive assistant."

"Cool." She grinned wickedly at him. "My own personal assistant."

"Not that personal. At least, not here."

"Later?"

"Absolutely." He kissed her lightly, and electricity dashed through her from his tender touch. "What happens at one of these things?"

Avery pointed to the trail near the dog park. "Our vendors and sponsors set up tables along here. It's kind of like a mini pet mall. We've got pet products, rescue groups and local businesses. We've even got an airbrush artist this year who will paint a picture of someone's pet on a T-shirt or a hat. The best part is, he's donating a portion of his sales today." She pointed to the large shelter. "We'll have brats, chips and drinks for sale there. We've got a lot of people who are walking for pledges today, and they'll follow the trail."

"This is quite a production. I had no idea the event was this big. I'm impressed."

His genuine praise flowed over her.

"Avery?" Emma's voice came over the walkie-talkie in her pocket. "Grant Timmons wants to know if you picked up the podium from the church."

"It's in the back of my truck." She turned to Reed. "Since you have so wonderfully demonstrated what great shape you're in this week, would you mind providing a little extra muscle?" When he nodded, she spoke into the walkie-talkie. "I'm sending Reed to the parking lot. He'll help Grant unload the podium and get it in place."

While Reed saw to that task, Avery checked in with Carly to see what adoptable animals she'd brought to the event. She found her and a group of volunteers clustered around the shelter van unloading dogs. Hopefully a few of these souls would find forever homes today.

"How many dogs did you bring?"

"I've got seven. I'll go back for the cats. I thought I'd bring ten for the cat corner we'll set up in the small shelter."

Feeling Carly had things under control, Avery had turned to leave when she heard a particular bark. No. It couldn't be. Carly wouldn't. But as Avery stood there watching, Carly opened a crate and out jumped Baxter.

"Carly, can I speak with you for a second?" She pointed to a spot ten feet away under a group of trees.

"You brought Baxter? Carly, what were you thinking?"

"I was thinking this is his best shot to find a home." The dog strained against the leash the vet tech held. "Baxter, sit."

The dog barked and tugged harder.

"Baxter, sit," Avery said in her authoritative veterinarian voice. Instead of obeying, the dog jumped up on her. "Down." This time when he failed to listen, she stepped away, out of leash range. "We've never had a dog fight or an animal running loose before. I don't want to start today. Not when we've got so much at stake, and somehow Baxter always brings chaos with him."

Kind of like someone else she knew, though Reed appeared to be on his best behavior today.

"We've got to give Baxter this chance. I'll put a harness on him and have Nikki take him. She can handle him," Carly said, referring to one of their most experienced volunteers. Then she scratched Baxter's head. "How can you say no to this face? He deserves a shot to find his forever home."

How could she refuse that pitch? "I'll trust your judgment, but at the first sign of trouble, he's gone." Avery glared at the dog. "Got that, buddy? You don't get three strikes today. One and you're out. Don't blow this chance."

For the next hour Avery spoke with various vendors and sponsors as they set up their displays along the walkway. As she stood chatting with one of their biggest donors, the owner of the area pet cemetery, her phone rang. After mumbling a quick apology, she tugged it out of her pocket and glanced at the screen. Principal Jacobson. The high-school principal was scheduled to be one of the contest judges. When she answered, she discovered he'd eaten some bad sushi and wasn't going to be able to make it. She assured him it was fine and told him she hoped he felt better soon.

"One of your judges can't come?" Reed asked as she shoved her phone into her pocket.

"We'll be fine. I still have two judges." Harper and her teenage niece. Great. That meant Harper would be running the show. Avery chided herself for being so negative. Harper would be fine. She just didn't seem to get that these contests weren't really about who was "best," but about who showed the most heart. Last year's pet-lookalike winner had been a six-year-old girl with long curly brown hair and her white miniature poodle.

When she was asked how she and her dog looked alike, she responded, "We're both beautiful inside and out," winning over the audience and the judges.

"I can fill in."

Reed's offer caught her off guard, but she was happy to take any help she could get.

"That would be great," she said, and proceeded to fill him in on his duties, emphasizing that the events were meant to be fun and lighthearted.

With Reed at her side, she touched base with the remaining business people and sponsors. An important part of her duties included making sure everyone felt appreciated for their support and participation in the event, no matter how small.

"I get it now," Reed said after they spoke with an insurance agent. "You're really like a CEO."

She nodded. "Just on a smaller, more personal scale. But that's not why I went to vet school. When the shelter's doing well enough, I'll be glad to hire someone to take over my director duties."

"You don't enjoy that part of your job?"

She explained that when she'd taken the position, the plan had been that the shelter would hire a part-time director within six months. "I love being associated with the shelter and helping animals that don't have anyone. I love working with people, but I want to do more education, more working with pet owners. A lot of what I do now is management-related, writing grants and budgeting. Not exactly my thing."

A few feet in front of her, Avery spotted a familiar face and smiled. "Mrs. Russell, how are you today?"

"I'm still here, so I must be doing fairly well." Then the woman turned to Reed. "Do you remember me, young man?"

Avery stiffened. Reed had taken a class with Mrs. Russell in junior high, but would he remember the woman after all these years? "Reed's been gone a long time, Mrs. Russell, but I'm sure—"

"How could I forget you? I think of you every time I make pizza. I still use the recipe I got in your class."

The eighty-year-old blushed like a schoolgirl and patted Reed's hand. "I can admit it now that I'm retired—you were one of my favorite students. You didn't think cooking was beneath you, and you were always willing to help other students who were culinarily challenged."

"That's kind of you to say, ma'am."

"I'm proud of you both," Mrs. Russell continued. "Avery, you're doing wonderful work at the shelter, and, Reed, I hear you've made quite a name for yourself in the business world."

Not wanting that part of his life to intrude today, Avery asked, "Are you entering Chandra in the best-dressed pet contest?"

"Of course, dear. She's got to defend her title."

Reed grinned and raised his hand. "I've got to stop you right there. As one of the judges, I shouldn't be hearing this. I take my responsibilities very seriously."

"We wouldn't want anyone saying Chandra had an unfair advantage because a judge heard that she's won the contest the last three years in a row," Mrs. Russell stated, her tone and expression serious.

"Exactly," Reed responded.

Avery checked her watch. "It's later than I thought. We need to head toward the contest area." When they arrived at the designated spot, Avery took the podium, thanked everyone for attending and asked all contest participants to head toward the open area near the baseball field.

At eleven o'clock, on the dot, she called forward the first contestants in the best-dressed category, a girl named Eva and her shih tzu, dressed in a pink tutu. "Are you a dancer?"

"Tiffany and I both like to dance." Then she and her pet demonstrated. The dog stood on her hind legs, bounced a little and then twirled, while her owner pirouetted beside her.

The crowd clapped, and Avery asked the pair to parade before the judges' table.

When they reached Reed, he smiled, scribbled notes on the sheet in front of him, and said, "You two are great dancers."

Next, Avery called forward Mrs. Russell and Chandra. The toy poodle wore a white wedding dress complete with a veil and tiara. "Now, this is a dress any bride would envy," Avery said into the microphone.

"I had so much fun making this for Chandra. My neighbor Eleanor was going to bring her poodle, Max. I made him a tux and top hat, but she had another engagement."

The crowd laughed at Mrs. Russell's choice of words.

"That's too bad. I'm sure Chandra and Max make a beautiful couple. Now, if you'll walk over to the judges—"

"We know the routine, dear."

Avery smiled as the elderly woman sauntered to the judges' table, Chandra following, her silk train trailing behind her.

"Mrs. Russell, the dress is amazing. Chandra looks radiant," Reed said when the pair reached him.

As Avery called forward the last contestant, Jacob, a young boy dressed in a Broncos jersey, and his dog, Harry, a Lab mix wearing a similar shirt, she smiled at how Reed was throwing himself into the spirit of the contests. Who would've figured? After chatting with the boy, she sent him to parade in front of the judges.

"I'm a big Broncos fan, too. Who's your favorite player?" Reed asked.

"Von Miller," Jacob said. Then he frowned. "I don't stand a chance of winning against that wedding dress."

"Chandra's a tough act to beat for best-dressed." Reed tilted his head toward Harper and the other judge, a high-school cheerleader. "Especially with two female judges."

The boy nodded in male understanding.

Avery drifted closer to better hear the conversation.

"There's still the pet-lookalike contest. I think you'd stand a good chance in that one."

When the young boy beamed, Avery's heart swelled. She'd always known Reed had a soft heart. He didn't see it, but actions like this told Avery that he'd be a good father.

Minutes later, after she'd announced that Chandra was the winner of the best-dressed contest, she saw Jacob talking to Emma—she hoped about entering the lookalike contest. Mrs. Russell gushed over her prize, a gift certificate for a portrait of Chandra in her winning costume, provided by the airbrush artist at the event.

When Emma brought her the contestant list for the lookalike contest, Avery saw Jacob's name. Despite some tough competition from a bald man and his bulldog, Jacob and Harry ended up walking away with the win and a basket full of dog treats and toys donated by the Pet Palace.

When the contests were over, Avery reminded the crowd about the Frisbee-catching exhibition and K-9 police dog demonstrations. The day couldn't have been going any better.

"Baxter! Come back!" Carly shouted.

Avery closed her eyes. She'd jinxed it.

She glanced toward the vendor area. People scrambled on the pathway to catch Baxter or get out of his way, she didn't know which. The sound of raised voices and dogs barking, punctuated with periodic screams, grew deafening as she raced toward the bedlam.

"The escape artist is here?" Reed asked as he raced beside her.

"We've got to catch him before anyone gets hurt or we have a dog fight on our hands."

Visions of lawsuits danced in her head.

"We'll get him." Reed assured her.

"Look for his bright orange Adopt Me vest."

"I see him," Reed said. "Go right, toward the Pet Palace booth."

She ran, calling Baxter's name.

"Baxter, come!" Reed's booming voice, ringing with authority, cut through the turmoil.

Avery stared in disbelief as the blasted dog froze, turned their way and calmly trotted toward them. When Baxter reached them, he lunged for Reed.

"Sit," Reed commanded as he grabbed the dog's leash.

The dog plopped down beside Reed and shoved his black nose into Reed's hand, his tail creating a decent breeze as it wagged.

"Wow, how'd you do that?" a breathless Carly asked when she joined them. "He won't listen to anyone, especially when he's on the lam."

Reed shrugged. "Beats me. Dogs don't usually like me."

But Avery knew. There was something in Baxter that

connected with Reed. They didn't know much about the dog's past. The police had brought him in as a stray. His shaggy coat had been so matted they'd had to completely shave him. He'd been a good ten pounds underweight and somewhat standoffish, but something about Baxter had tugged at the staff's hearts. She thought about what her mother had said: *that boy's been running for years.* That was it. Both Reed and Baxter had survived tough pasts. Avery bit her lip as tears filled her eyes. What would it take for Reed to stop running?

"I'm sorry, Avery. You were right. I never should've brought Baxter." Carly reached for the leash.

Baxter whined and pressed himself against Reed's thigh.

"I'll take him back to the shelter." This time when Carly reached for the leash, Baxter barked.

"Stop it," Reed snapped, and the dog quieted. "I'll get him to the van."

"I don't know, Reed," Avery said.

"Trust me."

His low voice ricocheted through her. This was more about them than it was about Baxter. Reed's gaze, open and yet beseeching, tugged at her heart.

Trust him? If she loved him, how could she not trust him? She nodded. "I do."

As Reed walked beside Avery, Baxter trotting alongside them, he realized he'd seen a different side of her today. They actually had more in common workwise than he'd thought.

Through watching her, he remembered what life could be like as part of a close-knit community. He'd actually enjoyed talking with the townspeople there, and they'd seemed genuinely interested in his life since leaving Estes Park. The pity he'd seen in people's eyes growing up had been absent today. He'd felt almost as if he belonged.

Because of Avery.

"I don't know how we're ever going to get this guy adopted now." She glared at the dog, who appeared oblivious to her irritation. "You'll be forever known as the holy terror who ran amok at the Pet Walk."

"You really think he won't find a home?"

"I've always said there's a person for every dog. It just takes a while sometimes, but he's been here so long already. He's been returned once and now this."

"How long do you give him before you—" He couldn't bring himself to say the words.

"We're a no-kill shelter, so he won't be euthanized, but staying so long isn't good for an animal. Volunteers interact with them, but after a while they can become depressed."

He stared at the mutt, who responded by wagging his tail. Jess had been right. There was something about this dog.

Don't look to me for help, buddy. Hit up some other guy. I've got enough problems.

"How about I take you out to dinner tonight?" Reed said, needing to change the subject.

Avery frowned. "I'd love to, but after we're done cleaning up here, we have to count the money, do some preliminary accounting and prepare the bank deposit."

He leaned down and kissed her lightly. "I'll be waiting when you're done."

Later that afternoon, Avery sat at her desk with the shelter's bookkeeper, Mary Beth, reconciling pledges and preparing the bank deposit. Piles of checks, cash and Pet Walk paperwork were spread out in front of them.

"Do you have the numbers yet? How did we do?" Emma poked her head inside the office door.

"Once Mary Beth gets the donation jar money tallied, we'll have the totals."

"Look who I found knocking at the back door." Emma stepped aside and Reed materialized in the doorway, a take-out food bag in his hands.

"I know Avery didn't eat much at the event, so I brought dinner for everyone." He walked across her office and placed the sack on her credenza. The spicy tang of barbecue filled the room. "I'll even play waiter. We've got barbecue-beef sandwiches, coleslaw, potato salad and baked beans."

He asked what each one of them wanted, dished up their orders and brought the food to their desks. Avery smiled as she thanked Reed. She could get used to this kind of pampering.

After they'd finished eating, Mary Beth reached down by her feet and picked up a plastic container that had once held dog treats but was now covered with paper emblazoned with the shelter logo and the word *Donations* in big letters. She unscrewed the lid and dumped the contents out in front of her. Coins plinked as they spilled out onto the wooden desktop. Bills rustled against checks. While the bookkeeper separated that money, Avery returned to tallying the pledge amounts and Emma went to call the raffle winners.

"What else can I do?" Reed asked after he'd cleared away the remnants of their meal.

"You don't have to stick around," Avery said.

"I want to see how you guys did today." Then he

tossed her a steamy look that said, *And the more I help, the sooner I can get you alone.*

Avery felt the heat rise to her cheeks as she grabbed the stack of checks to her left. "You could photocopy these for us."

He nodded and took the checks from her. "If you give me your bank stamp, I'll take care of that while I'm at it."

She reached into her desk, found the deposit stamp and handed that to him, as well.

"How's the chair working out?" he asked.

"It's amazing. Not only is it comfortable, but I feel so important sitting in it."

"You *are* important."

Her heart caught at his words. But how important was she? Important enough for him to stick around once his brother returned? Important enough to give her a child?

"Hey, you two. I'm still here, you know," Mary Beth teased.

Avery felt herself blush more. How could she have forgotten that she and Reed weren't alone? The man sure messed with her focus.

Reed mumbled a quick apology and shot out of the office, his cheeks a little red as well, while Avery returned to reconciling pledges. A few minutes later, Mary Beth said, "I've got the donation-jar total for you, Avery—$832.75."

Avery added the amount to her spreadsheet, clicked, and the total amount popped onto the screen. She patted her hands on her desk. "Drum roll—$60,213.45! We did it! We raised enough for the down payment."

Emma ran into the office shouting and hugged Mary

Beth. Reed rushed in, too, and swept Avery up in his arms. "I knew you'd do it. I'm so proud of you."

They'd saved the shelter. She was in love with a wonderful man. Life couldn't get much better.

Chapter 12

Reed and Jess settled into a pattern. A couple of nights a week they ate dinner with Avery and Nannette at the McAlister ranch. He'd started volunteering at the shelter again with Jess, but this time he did so unquestioningly, with a smile.

Since today hadn't been their day to volunteer, after he picked up Jess from school they'd come straight home. Now she was holed up in her room working on homework, while he got a little more work done before starting dinner.

Even work was leveling out. Customers had grown accustomed to working with him via Skype, and Ethan had settled in to his new duties. A week had gone by since Reed had received a panicked, the-sky's-falling phone call from him.

Then it hit him. He'd been happier the past few weeks

than he'd ever been. Not just content, but downright silly and filled-with-hope happy. And he was in love.

But what about the future? Could he give Avery what she needed in life, what she deserved? His cell phone rang, interrupting his thoughts. Vowing he wouldn't worry about that now when he had months to figure things out, he answered the call.

"Ethan approached me about a job," Blake Dunston, Reed's key software engineer on the SiEtch project, said. "He insists you're on the wrong track with this product, and you've misjudged the market. He's starting a new company to make a cheaper version of SiEtch. He claims he's got copies of the software and the hardware specs on his home computer. He plans on starting there and modifying what we've done to create his product."

Reed's breathing accelerated. His hands started sweating as he tried to process what had happened. His best friend, the man he'd built his business with, had betrayed him.

As if that wasn't bad enough, if word about his actions got out, and Reed had indeed been wrong about the market, this could ruin his business. And here he was in Colorado, thousands of miles away from it all. Rage boiled inside him. If he ever got his hands on Ethan…

He'd what? Beat the hell out of him like he had his dad?

A headache bloomed between Reed's eyes. He and Ethan had gone around the issue like dogs chasing their tails. Unfortunately, nothing he said changed Ethan's shortsighted opinion that product cost was the key factor, while Reed emphasized the need for 3-D transistor capacity. That's what would set their product apart from others in the market. The discussion had ended when he said RJ Instruments was his company, as was the decision on how to proceed.

He realized their relationship had changed once he became Ethan's boss. The more his company grew, the more distant they became. But to betray him like this? After all the years they'd worked together?

"Has he approached anyone else?"

"Word is he offered Tom Merrick a job, too," Blake replied.

It figured Ethan would want the project's key hardware developer on board.

"What did you tell him when he offered you the job?"

"I said I needed to talk to my wife tonight before I gave him an answer. Then I called you."

Good. That gave him a day before Ethan got wind something was up. "I won't forget this, Blake, and I'll make my thanks more tangible after I've dealt with it."

Reed's hands shook as he speed-dialed his lawyer's number. He quickly detailed his conversation with Blake. "What can I do to stop him?"

"I'll file for a temporary injunction in civil court. You need to contact the San Francisco district attorney and file a criminal complaint because he's stealing company assets."

Reed grabbed a pen and paper from the desk and started taking notes. "Do you think we can get the injunction?"

"We'll need affidavits from Blake and Tom for the civil hearing. Those, plus the fact that we've got a patent pending on the product and Ethan signed a no-competition clause, all strengthen our case."

Immediately after ending his call with his lawyer, Reed contacted the district attorney, who told him they'd be happy to file charges. The catch? He had to appear in person and the appointment was tomorrow morning.

What was he going to do about Jess? Today was Tuesday. He hated to pull her out of school, especially since she had a math test tomorrow. But what other option did he have? Avery.

He punched in her cell number, but had to leave a message. "A major problem's come up at work. I've got to fly to California. I should only be gone a day or two. Can Jess stay with you until I get back? Call me when you get this."

Avery heard her phone ring, but as she was in the barn examining Twin Creeks' new foal under the watchful, nervous eye of his mother, she let the call go to voice mail. After she finished the animal's exam and cleaned up, she settled onto the couch with a glass of iced tea to check her messages, but before she could, the doorbell sounded.

When she answered the front door, Jess, her eyes red and swollen, burst into tears.

"What's wrong?" Avery rushed forward and enveloped the girl in a hug. For a minute Jess clung to Avery and sobbed. Her wrenching cries tore at Avery's heart as she rubbed the girl's back. "Is it your dad? Did you get bad news?"

Please, don't let it be that. This dear child won't survive losing him, too.

"Dad's fine. It's Uncle Reed," Jess croaked out.

Avery's heart rocked. Had something happened to him? She forced the words out. "Is he okay?"

A new wave of sobs gushed forth. Avery held Jess tighter. "You've got to calm down enough to tell me what's wrong. I can't help unless I know what happened."

"Can I stay here?"

"Of course."

All teenage bravado stripped from her gaze, Jess's eyes screamed of her anguish. Whatever had happened was bad. Very bad.

Avery forced herself to remain calm as she ushered Jess into the living room. Despite her urge to bombard the teenager with questions, she patted the couch beside her and grabbed a calming breath before saying, "Tell me what happened."

Jess melted onto the couch, dropping her backpack at her feet. "I just talked to my grandparents. They got approval for me to live with them in Florida until Dad gets back."

Reed was okay. The fist squeezing Avery's heart loosened. This she could deal with. "I know they love you very much, but just because they have the okay and want you to live with them doesn't mean you have to."

Tears welled up in Jess's soft brown eyes. "They said to thank Uncle Reed. He contacted a reporter. He said if they didn't let me stay with my grandparents while Dad was gone, the whole world would find out they weren't supporting a serviceman fighting for his country."

Avery's heart rebelled against the thought. Reed wouldn't do that. He'd promised Colt he'd take care of Jess. He knew she'd threatened to run away if she was forced to move in with her grandparents.

Taking care of her and running my business long-distance is tougher than I expected.

No. He'd changed since he made that comment at Halligan's weeks ago. Jess mattered to him. They both mattered to him.

"He doesn't want me." Jess's pain emanated from her in waves, mirroring Avery's.

Avery's mind spun as she processed everything. Nothing made sense. She'd seen the difference between Reed and Jess. Genuine love existed between them. He couldn't fake a relationship that well.

But how well do you really know him? He was gone for years, and hasn't been back that long. Don't go there now. What's important is helping Jess.

Avery shut off her own emotions. "I know he loves you very much."

"Then why would he want to get rid of me?"

"Have you talked to him about this?"

Jess shook her head. "I left and came here."

Hope, tiny and fragile, sprouted inside her. Avery wouldn't assume the worst. She'd give Reed the benefit of the doubt until she spoke with him.

"Things aren't always what they seem. Talk to him. Maybe there's been a misunderstanding. Reporters often have an agenda. Maybe your grandparents heard what they wanted to hear. Give your uncle a chance to explain."

Please let it be that he contacted the reporter weeks ago and forgot to stop what he'd put in motion once his circumstances and feelings changed.

"What's the point?" Jess scooped up a decorative pillow off the couch, hugging it close to her chest. "He'll either tell me he doesn't want me or he'll lie about it. No matter what he has to say, I don't want to hear it." Her lip quivered. "What's wrong with me? First my mom ran off. She never even told me she was leaving."

"Don't *ever* think your mother leaving was your fault. I didn't know her well, but my guess is she had—" Avery paused. *Your mother had severe problems and was a selfish, unfeeling bitch.* She swallowed her anger. "Your mom and dad had problems. Plus she was dealing with other issues that had nothing to do with you. That's why she left."

And if she'd given a rat's ass about anyone but herself she'd have told you it wasn't your fault before she skipped town with her lover.

"Then Dad left for Afghanistan, and now Uncle Reed wants to get rid of me."

"Your dad didn't have a choice. That's his job."

"If he really loved me, he'd get a different one so he could stick around."

Jess had a valid point, but admitting the fact wouldn't help the teenager now.

"When your dad gets home you need to tell him how you feel. I bet once he knows how much you need him around, he'll resign from the National Guard."

"That's months away. What can I do now? I can't live with my grandparents. I love them, but I'll die if I have to live with all those old people. I won't know anyone at school. I won't have any friends. They don't even have internet access, so I can't Skype or talk to anyone on Facebook." The longer Jess talked, the more frantic her speech became. "I'll run away. That's what I'll do."

"Whoa. Slow down." Avery placed her hand over Jess's and squeezed. "Breathe. I want you to—"

"I won't live with my grandparents in an old folks' neighborhood."

"The first step is to talk to your uncle."

"Can't I live here with you and your mom? I won't be any trouble, I promise. I can do all the cooking and cleaning. I'll earn my keep."

Avery bit her lip. She wouldn't cry. Jess needed a calm and in-control adult. "You know we'd love for you stay with us, but it's not that simple. Your uncle Reed is your legal guardian. We'd need his approval and your dad's, but I think we're getting ahead of ourselves. The first thing you need to do is talk to your uncle. Be honest with him. Tell him what your grandparents said and that you don't want to live with them. See what he says."

"What if he doesn't care what I want?"

Then I'll pound some sense into him.

"I care, and so does my mom. We'll do whatever we can." Her cell phone rang, and she glanced at the screen. "It's the shelter. I need to make sure it's nothing important."

When she answered the call, Emma said animal control had picked up a stray that had been hit by a car. She was fairly certain its leg was broken, but added it might need to be amputated. Though Emma wasn't a vet, she'd seen enough similar cases to offer a reliable assessment. "Have Carly take X-rays. I'm on my way." She ended the call and explained the situation to Jess. "I need to go into the shelter. Why don't you come with me?"

"Can I stay here instead? I don't want to see anyone now."

"You shouldn't be alone."

"Isn't your mom around?"

Avery glanced at her watch. "She's at book club. She'll be home in an hour or so."

"I'll be fine. Go."

Avery sat there, torn. "I could call Doc Brown to see if he could fill in for me."

"I don't need a babysitter."

Now she'd insulted Jess. It was only for an hour. She could text her mom, explain things and ask her to come home sooner. "When I'm done at the shelter, we'll talk to your uncle together. Everything will be all right. I promise you won't have to live with your grandparents if you don't want to."

She'd make sure. No matter what she had to do.

An hour later, Avery returned to the ranch. While the dog's leg was broken, it wasn't a bad enough break to require amputation. She'd splinted the leg, left Carly with instructions to watch the animal and call if anything changed, and made a quick exit before anyone else sidetracked her.

As she climbed out of her truck, her mom pulled up beside her. She was just getting home now? "You didn't get my text about what happened with Reed?"

"I shut my phone off at book club. I guess I forgot to turn it back on."

Avery explained about the call Jess had received from her grandparents and how she'd left her at the ranch alone. Then she raced up the walkway, unlocked the front door and burst inside, yelling Jess's name.

Silence. What had she done? Panic jolted through Avery, making her heart slam against her ribs. "She's not answering me, Mom. What if she did something silly? I never should've left her alone."

Worry lined her mother's face. "I'll check in the barn. You search the house."

Five minutes later, they met in the kitchen, neither one having found any trace of Jess. "I've got a bad feeling about this. She took her backpack."

"That doesn't mean anything. She takes that thing everywhere, even to the shelter," Nannette said. "She's probably at a friend's house, or maybe she went home to talk to Reed."

"You didn't see the hurt in her eyes. What if she ran away like she threatened to do when her dad talked to her about living with her grandparents? I should've made her come to the shelter with me."

Nannette gave Avery a quick hug. "You can't undo

the past, so quit stewing over it. You go to the Rocking M. See if she's there with Reed. Since she's mentioned her friends a few times, I'll start making calls."

As Avery drove through Estes Park, she alternated between saying prayers that they'd find Jess and reminding herself that she couldn't deck Reed the minute he opened the door for setting this mess in motion.

"Did you get my message?" he asked when he opened the door. Dressed in black slacks, a white button-down shirt and his expensive loafers, he looked the way he had when he'd first returned to Estes Park.

"What message?"

"I found out that my vice president of engineering, the guy I left in charge, stole my company's latest product and is planning to start his own company. I need to fly to California to file charges with the San Francisco district attorney. Then I've got to obtain affidavits from the employees he offered jobs to for the temporary injunction hearing. Can Jess stay with you for a few days?"

"Then she's here?"

He nodded. "She's in her room. I was about to tell her dinner's ready."

"Thank God. I was so worried when I came home and she wasn't there. Have you two talked? She was so upset when I saw her."

"What? Why's Jess upset? She was fine when I picked her up from school." Worry and confusion filled Reed's gaze.

Jess was here, but they hadn't talked? The hairs on the back of Avery's neck stood up. Something wasn't right. She tore through the hallway shouting Jess's name. "Which room is hers?"

"First door on the left," Reed said from behind her. "What's wrong?"

Not bothering to knock, she burst into the room, finding it empty. She faced Reed. "You didn't even know she was gone? When was the last time you saw her?"

"After we got home I went into the office to work, and she went to her room."

"School ended at three-twenty. She showed up at my house at four in tears." Avery glanced at her watch. "That was almost two hours ago. How could you do this to Jess? How could you hurt her like this when she loves you so much?"

"What do you think I did?"

"Her grandparents called. They said to thank you for getting the homeowners' association to make an exception for Jess to live with them. Tell me it's not true. Tell me you didn't want to dump her on her grandparents."

Tell me you weren't leaving me, too.

"Wait a minute. I put that in motion weeks ago. I'd forgotten about it."

"How could you even think about doing that when you knew how she felt about living in a retirement community?" Avery's voice rose with her anger. "You knew she'd threatened to run away, and you didn't care. How could you be so callous?"

"I'm not. Colt and I talked about this. He knew how nervous I was about making mistakes with Jess. He said if Jess agreed, he was okay with her staying with her grandparents. I didn't even know the approval came through, and if I had, I'd have talked to her. I never would've made her go to Florida if she didn't want to."

What he said sounded so reasonable, so logical, but

could she believe him? Would Jess? "We've got to find her. I really think she's run away."

Reed massaged the knot that had formed in his neck. Damn. How could everything hit the fan at once? He needed to leave for Denver soon or he wouldn't make his flight. The longer it took him to reach California, the more time elapsed before legal measures went into place. His business, his livelihood, all he had was on the line right now. His employees' livelihoods hung in the balance, as well.

"Slow down. You could be jumping to conclusions." His heart raced as he worked to logically assess the situation. He scanned Jess's room searching for any noticeable changes. Clothes lay scattered across the floor and on various pieces of furniture. The place looked like the same disaster zone. "Jess can't have run away. Look. All of her stuff's still here."

The rattle of dog tags sounded behind them in the hallway, and his heart rate slowed. He turned and, for the first time since he'd arrived, was genuinely glad to see Thor. Thank God the mutt was still here. "Jess wouldn't leave Thor if she ran away. She's probably at a friend's house."

"We've got to call the police," Avery insisted.

"They'll ask if we've contacted all her friends and where we've searched." He pulled out his cell phone and called his niece. After four rings, her voice mail kicked in. "Jess, I heard your grandparents called. Let me explain what happened. Call me as soon as you get this message. It's not what you think."

He turned to Avery. "Colt has a couple of PTA directories in his desk. We can use those to call people to find out if anyone's seen her."

Once back in the office, he dug around in the top drawer and pulled out two small purple booklets. "I'll take last year's. She's talked to you more about her friends than she has me." He handed the other booklet to Avery. "It'll take me an hour and a half to get to the airport. When I get there I'll call to see what you've discovered, and I'll make more calls. That is, if we haven't heard from Jess by then."

"You're still going?" Avery shook her head as disappointment hardened her gaze.

"I have to. The D.A. said I have to file charges in person. I've got an appointment first thing in the morning. Having criminal charges in the works will strengthen my case for the injunction. My company's invested a lot of money and time in the SiEtch project. Losing it could bankrupt me, and put all my employees out of work. I've got some money saved, so I'd be fine, but not everyone does."

"I'll find Jess. I've come to love that girl, you know. I defended you to her. I told her that she was wrong, that you loved her—"

"I do."

"If you did, you'd have been out the door to search before I finished telling you what had happened. I thought you'd changed. I was a fool to fall in love with you again."

"You love me?" Joy burst through him, white-hot and blinding.

"The man I love would never do this to Jess. She feels you abandoned her just like her mother did. You're not the man I thought you were." Avery stormed to the front door.

"Avery, that's not fair." He reached out to her, but she stepped away.

"Go to California. I hope everything works out with your business. I hope it fills the hole deep inside you."

"I don't have a choice. If I don't go, I could lose everything."

"You don't get it, do you? You've already lost everything that matters."

Chapter 13

Thirty minutes outside town, the words Avery had hurled at him pounded in his head, leaving Reed with a massive headache. He kept telling himself that Jess hadn't run away. She couldn't have gone far without her clothes and Thor. He had time to make things right with her once he ensured his business wouldn't go belly-up. Then he could fix things with Avery.

He had to save his business. People counted on him to protect their jobs. It was all he had.

It was all he had?

If he died tomorrow, who'd show up at his funeral? Colt and Jess, if her father tied her up and hauled her to the service. Some of his employees would come, but how well did he know any of them? What a damned sorry commentary on his life.

Was that what he wanted at the end of his life? To

look back and have nothing to show for himself but a company?

He thought about his mom, how much he'd loved her and how she'd always encouraged him. When she'd died, he'd been angry at her for leaving him and Colt alone to cope with their father. He'd raged against her, wondering if she'd left his father things would've been different. She'd been the only one who had thought he could take on the world. The only one other than Colt who believed in him.

Until Avery.

What the hell had he done? He'd been running for years. He realized now, trying to prove something to a man who, even when he'd been alive, hadn't possessed the ability to love or approve of anyone.

His father was long cold in the grave, but he still controlled Reed's life and his choices.

How could he throw away what he had with Avery and Jess?

If his business failed, he could start over. He could get a job. Hell, he could move in with Colt and put his energy into making the Rocking M the best damned horse ranch in the country. He had options, and he'd pull any and every string he could to see that his employees found jobs, too. His business wasn't everything.

Avery and Jess were his life. Family. That's what mattered. What lasted. Avery had helped him, even when he'd been a complete ass. She'd been there for him…smoothing things over with Jess.

All those years ago when he'd desperately wanted and needed a family, he'd never seen that he had one. With Avery. Her family took him in. Her parents treated him the way they did their own children. They'd encouraged him, supported him and helped him through the worst time in his life. He'd had everything he'd ever wanted with Avery, and he'd thrown it all away because he'd been afraid he'd turn into his father.

His mother had let fear rule her life. Fear of his father. Fear of living on her own and having to provide for her sons had kept her with an abusive man. Reed refused to live that way any longer.

He turned into a gas-station parking lot. He had to get back home. The word rattled around in his head. Estes Park, home? The thought ricocheted through him. It *was* home, and he was in love with Avery. Hell, he'd probably never stopped loving her.

He knew that he wanted her in his life—forever.

As he pulled back onto the highway to head home, he prayed it wasn't too late to undo the damage he'd done with both her and Jess.

Avery and her mother called everyone they could think of, and no one had seen Jess since school ended. They'd enlisted the rest of the McAlisters to search. Even Maggie with little Michaela in her stroller went around town asking businesses if they'd seen Jess. The longer they went without finding a trace of the teenager, the more certain Avery became that she'd run away.

Her panic and her anger multiplied. How could Reed have left for California? Couldn't he see that the trouble with his company was nothing compared to the situation with Jess?

He insisted they weren't sure Jess had run away. They might not have been then, but Avery was positive now. When she talked with him later, if he wouldn't call the police, then she would, and she'd contact Colt.

She'd do whatever she had to in order to find Jess before something happened to her.

Oh, Lord. A devastated fourteen-year-old girl on the run. A predator or pimp's prime dream.

Her cell phone rang.

"Any news?" Reed asked.

"Nothing. My family's been searching since you left. No one's seen Jess since school got out."

"What about Lindsey?" Reed's voice broke. "Have you talked to her?"

Tears pooled in her eyes and she bit her lip to keep from crying. "They haven't spoken much since Jess started volunteering at the shelter, but I tried her, too."

"I'm on my way back. I'll be there in half an hour, tops. It's going to be tough reaching Colt. Contact the National Guard for help with that. After I talk to my brother, I'll call the police and ask them to issue an Amber Alert."

Reed was coming back. Maybe he wasn't a lost cause.

When she met him at the door twenty minutes later, she found his face drawn, features tight.

"You came back for Jess."

"Not just for her. I couldn't leave things like they were between us, either. Nothing matters if I don't have you in my life." He stepped inside and wrapped his arms around her, and her anger disappeared as the need to comfort him washed over her. Whatever was or wasn't between them, they'd deal with it later when Jess was safe.

"Reed, I'm so worried."

He stepped away. "Me, too. She's such a wonderful kid, and I hurt her so badly."

She recognized the pain in his eyes. He *had* changed. Looking into his anguish-filled eyes, she knew he finally saw things from Jess's viewpoint.

"A chaplain's waiting for your call. He'll put you in touch with Colt via Skype."

Reed nodded as she led him into the ranch office. Looking at him seated behind the massive oak desk that had once belonged to her father, she remembered what he'd said about the last time he'd been in this room. Now here he was, his life in turmoil again. She scooted an armchair closer to the desk as he waited to connect with his brother.

"Colt, I've screwed things up with Jess." Reed told his brother about his conversation with the reporter. "I don't know what happened, but the association changed their minds, and I never got word. Your in-laws called Jess before I had a chance to explain things to her. It looks like she ran away."

Weariness and guilt lined Reed's face. His shoulders hunched. Avery placed her hand over his and squeezed, wishing she could do more.

"Don't beat yourself up," Colt said. "It's as much my fault as yours. I told you I was okay with what you were doing. Just find her."

"Do you know anywhere she might have gone?"

"You've checked with all her friends?" Colt asked, fear similar to his brother's evident on his face.

"Avery's called everyone she can think of, and her family's searched the town. No one's seen Jess since school. Is there anyone she'd confide in?"

Avery leaned closer to the screen. "Colt, there has to be something we're missing. Something we haven't thought of. Does Jess have any friends we might not know about? A friend she met at camp or somewhere like that?"

"That's it." Reed beamed at her. His hand covered hers, and squeezed. "Colt, when we talked on the phone that first time, you said Jess's best friend moved soon after Lynn died. Where does she live?"

"Hannah's in Chicago."

Adrenaline coursed through Reed, shoving aside his panic. He knew where Jess was. Knew it in his gut. "And Jess has the credit card you gave her in case of emergency."

While he asked his brother where he kept the account information, Avery opened the drawer in front of her and retrieved paper and pen. Then she jotted down the information Colt gave them.

"I'm at Avery's right now. When I get the company's phone number, I'll call to see if Jess booked a flight. That'll be quicker than trying to find her computer and tracing it that way."

"And the airport wouldn't think twice about a teenager flying alone, especially because only ticketed passengers can go to the gate," Avery added.

"I pray you're right," Colt said, his voice shaking with emotion.

"I'll let you know what we find out."

Five minutes later, they were in Colt's office and Reed was on the phone with the credit-card company. He learned Jess had purchased a one-way ticket to Chicago.

"Jess booked a nine-forty flight to Chicago." Reed called information and asked for the Denver police department's number. His heart drummed painfully in his chest as he prayed Jess had arrived at the airport in one piece. A lot of things could happen to a young girl alone between Estes Park and Denver. While she acted all tough and self-sufficient, working with Jess at the shelter and watching her with Avery had shown him her kind heart. She could be so trusting. What if someone preyed on that?

His hand shook as he laced his fingers with Avery's. She peered up at him, when she asked, "What if something's happened to her? What if some nutcase found her?"

"Jess is a smart girl. The situation with her friends and the court taught her a lot about blindly trusting people. She'd be cautious."

He prayed he was right. When the police answered, he explained the situation and gave the officer Jess's flight information. He turned to Avery. "I'm on hold. They're calling airport security to see if she's there."

He squeezed Avery's hand as elevator music filled his ears. What if they didn't find her? He placed his phone on the smooth mahogany desk and put it on Speaker. Whatever they learned, he wanted Avery to hear it firsthand.

"The airline shows she boarded the plane," said the voice over the phone. "Security is on the way to remove her from the flight. They'll hold her until you get there. We're sending an officer, as well."

Reed started shaking and tears filled his eyes as the stranglehold on his heart loosened. After he ended the call, he grabbed Avery. He held her for a minute as relief flowed through his veins. Jess hadn't paid the price for his stupidity. "Right after I hug the daylights out of her, I'm going to blister her ears. How could she put herself in such danger by going to Denver alone?"

Avery's tears soaked his shirt. He kissed her temple and released her. "Call your family and the chaplain so he can contact Colt. Tell them we've found Jess. I'm heading to the Denver airport to get her."

"I'm coming, too."

He swiped a hand across his eyes. Things could have turned out so differently. Apparently God did, indeed, as his mother used to say, protect fools and children. At least, He had this time.

Once on the road to Denver, Avery called her mother and the chaplain with the news that they'd located Jess. When she finished those tasks, Reed said, "I meant what I said. Nothing matters—success, money, my company, none of it—if I don't have you in my life. I love you. I want to spend the rest of my life with you, marry you, but—"

"Yes." Joy burst within her as tears spilled down her cheeks. She thought she'd gotten over him, that she'd stopped loving him, but she hadn't. She'd merely buried her emotions and quit feeling much of anything. She'd given up on men and on love.

"Are you sure? I'm a mirror image of my father. What if we're alike in more ways than just our looks?" His hands tightened on the steering wheel and a vein throbbed wildly in his neck. "I nearly beat him to death. What if I lose control like that again? You're so wonderful. Your family's great. The kind that accepts everyone who walks in the door. I don't deserve you."

"That's what this is all about? You're worried you're not good enough for me?"

Reed nodded.

"May I get down from the pedestal please?" Avery asked.

"What are you talking about?"

"You've put me on a pedestal, and that's not where I want to be. I'd rather walk along beside you."

"I spent so much of my life being angry. At my mother for not leaving my father, for dying. At my father for being such a bastard. Since being back here, what I've been feeling scares me."

"Have I ever made you angry?"

He smiled for the first time since Jess had gone missing. "Is that a rhetorical question?"

She chucked. "Exactly. In all those times, I never once worried you'd hurt me. Then there was the night at the police station. You were so mad at Jess, but you never lifted a hand toward her."

"I thought about it."

"The important thing is you *didn't*. Why can't you see that? Why can't you see what I do? A good, caring man desperate to do right by his niece and everyone else around him."

"Because I don't know what I would've done if you hadn't been there."

"You wouldn't have hurt Jess." Her voice rang with her certainty. She longed to hold him, to reassure him, but all she could do was rub his arm. The man wasn't capable of violence. "If you think about it, deep down you know that. Your father attacked you. Did you fear for your life?"

"I don't know. Maybe. All I remember is that I couldn't take the beatings anymore."

"You were defending yourself. If my father did to me what your dad did to you, I'd react the same way.

I might not have the physical strength to beat him, but I'd hit him with whatever I could get my hands on, and I wouldn't stop until he didn't get up. Does that make you scared that I'll hurt you?"

"It's not the same."

"Your father isn't the only one who makes up who you are. Did you get your business sense from him? Is that where you got your negotiating skills?"

He paused. His gaze focused on the road stretched out in front of them. "I remember one day before Mom died. While she was cooking dinner, Colt and I were sitting at the kitchen table working on homework. When Colt had trouble with his math, she came over to help him. She said he had to keep trying because getting a good education was important. She told us she wished she'd finished college, and that she'd dreamed of owning a clothing boutique, but she quit school to support her parents when her father became sick and lost his job."

He'd lost his mother so long ago. He carried childhood memories that probably had been overwhelmed by his dominant, unyielding father. Avery remembered his mother. Always smiling, she'd been genuine, affectionate and giving. All things Reed had to shut off to survive once she died.

"Your business skills came from your mother. She's in you, too, though you don't realize it. You have her kind heart. You've done so much for me and for the shelter. You've worked hard to get to know Jess. You've learned from your mistakes."

"How can you say that after today?"

"You screwed up. We all do."

"I still don't know about children. The chances of me continuing the cycle of violence—"

"Did Colt beat his wife or Jess?"

"I'm not my brother."

"And you're not your father. I can't believe you're afraid of a baby. You've been thrown into the deep end of the pool parenting-wise with a teenager, and you're scared of a baby? Plus, you'll have Griffin to turn to for advice. We can babysit Michaela to practice. By the time we have children you'll be a pro."

He could either live his life in fear or he could take a risk, and end up having it all. "If you're willing to take a risk on me—"

"Isn't that what I've been saying?" Avery rolled her eyes. "Now, is your proposal still on the table?"

"If you'll have me, yes."

Two hours later, when the police ushered Reed and Avery into a small security office in the airport, he still had no idea what he'd say to Jess.

For a minute, he stood in the doorway staring at her, looking tiny sitting in the industrial metal chair.

She refused to look at him. He deserved that.

He walked forward, settled in the chair beside her and glanced at Avery for a shot of courage. He took a deep breath and faced his niece. "Jess, I don't know what to say except I screwed up."

"You wanted to get rid of me."

"When your dad asked me to stay with you, I was so scared I'd mess up, or worse." He clutched his knees to keep his hands from shaking. "My father used to beat the hell out of me."

"And Dad?"

Reed nodded. "Your father was the best big brother. He protected me when he could, and I can't tell you how many times he pulled me away before my dad and I could really go at it. One night after your dad moved away, my dad hit me. I nearly beat him to death. I was scared I might flip out one day and hurt you, too."

The ache in his chest eased. Letting go of the secrets he'd carried for so long felt freeing. "I had my lawyer working on getting your grandparents' Association of Homeowners to make an exception for you to live there before I left California. I really believed that was best for you, but I never would've forced you to go live with them if you didn't want to."

He wouldn't mention that Colt knew what he'd been doing. Jess didn't need to feel as if her father had been conspiring against her, too.

She still hadn't looked at him.

"I've made more mistakes dealing with you than I have in my entire life. Talking to the reporter before I'd spoken with you was the biggest, but I'm willing to learn." He placed his hands over Jess's, and she finally glanced up at him.

Her soft brown eyes glistened with tears. *She's so young, and I hurt her so much.* "I love you, Jess. I always have. It took me a while to adjust to this stand-in-dad stuff, but now that I'm getting the hang of it, I like it."

She pulled her hands away from him and folded them in her lap. "Remember that day at the shelter when we were bathing Baxter?"

He nodded.

"I said if Dad died, I wouldn't have anyone. You told me I'd have you. You lied to me."

Her justifiable pain cut through him. "I said that after I talked with the reporter, and I meant it. I was so happy with you and Avery that I forgot I'd even spoken to her. I should've called her back and told her to forget about doing the story, but I didn't."

"What if you change your mind again?" Jess asked.

"You have no reason to trust me, but I won't change my mind. While I don't deserve a second chance, if you give me one, I'll do right by you. I'm willing to grovel if that'll help."

Jess smiled ever so slightly and then bit her lip. "It might."

"I was an ass."

"And I'll be happy to remind him of this if he ever starts acting like one again," Avery added from the other side of the room.

"What about my grandparents?"

"Now, listen up. I'm not going anywhere," Reed announced. "I'll explain things to them. Even if they eventually come to stay with you here, I'm not leaving. And if you want to keep living with me when that happens, I'll tell them that. You're stuck with me. Got it?"

Jess turned to Avery. "You're my witness."

"Count on it."

He knew he had a long way to go to regain Jess's trust, but at least she was giving him the opportunity. That was more than he deserved. "Now let's get out of here." Jess stood and he put one arm around her. Together they walked toward Avery. "Let's go home."

Avery clasped his hand. "Since we're at the airport, you should take the next flight to California. Save your business."

He shook his head. He had work to do at home with his family. "I'll contact the district attorney in the morning to see if he'll make an exception and start the paperwork without me being there."

"What have I missed?" Jess asked.

After he gave her a brief explanation of his business situation, she said, "Could we go with you? I've always wanted to see San Francisco."

"Don't you have a math test tomorrow?"

She nodded, disappointment filling her gaze. Then she pouted. "Maybe we can go some other time. I just wanted to spend some time with you."

He laughed, seeing through her ploy, but thrilled by her actions. "Just because I was a jerk before and have a lot to make up for doesn't mean you can pout and I'll be a pushover."

"You can't blame a girl for trying."

He glanced at the two females who filled his life with love. So what if she had a test? "I'll write school a note saying you were sick. After what's happened today, I'm not sure I want to let either one of you out of my sight."

Later that week when they returned from San Francisco, Avery couldn't help but smile as Jess regaled Nannette with the details of their trip. Reed stood on the patio grilling more burgers for the rest of her family, who were due to arrive any minute.

Her family.

She, Jess and Reed were just that. While he'd met with the district attorney to file charges, obtained the necessary affidavits and worked with his lawyer on a temporary injunction against Ethan, she and Jess had played tourists. They'd driven down Lombard Street, famous for its eight hairpin turns in one block. They'd visited Alcatraz, ridden the cable cars and seen the Golden Gate Bridge.

"Reed says we'll go back to San Francisco when we can stay longer, because he wants to show us all the stuff we didn't have time to see." Jess's face glowed with enthusiasm as she explained how she and Reed had picked out Avery's engagement ring.

Staring at the simple, but way too large, emerald-cut ring, Avery realized that the fact that selecting it had been a family affair made the ring even more special. She and Reed hadn't set a date yet. They both wanted Colt at their wedding. He'd be the best man, and she'd asked Jess to be her maid of honor.

Plus, Avery wanted Reed to take time to settle things with his business before they dived into wedding plans. His lawyer indicated that, with the testimony from his employees and the no-competition clause Ethan had signed, Reed wouldn't have any problem preventing his former friend from releasing a similar product. While in San Francisco he'd assembled his employees to discuss relocating to Estes Park. He said the company would pay relocation costs and give raises to those who wanted to move. For those who chose not to, he'd pay a year's severance and offer assistance in finding other work.

Reed materialized beside her and kissed Avery lightly on the lips. "A penny for your thoughts."

"That's all they're worth?"

"I gave you a ring, but you want me to ante up for your thoughts?"

She laughed.

"Baxter, no!" Jess yelled. "Uncle Reed, your dog ate my hamburger and now he's chasing Thor."

Reed shook his head and turned to Avery. "Those obedience classes can't start soon enough."

"The good news is he hasn't run away once since we brought him home from the shelter."

"The mutt knows a good thing when he's got one."

He bent and kissed her long and deeply. Her heart overflowed with love. Life couldn't be any better.

His hands framing her face, his gaze open and loving, he said, "Looks like Baxter and I are both done running."

* * * * *

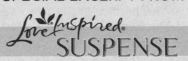
Abigail Jones stared at the blackening eastern sky and
shivered. She was more afraid of the strangers lingering
in the shadows along the Coney Island boardwalk than
she was of the summer storm brewing over the Atlantic.

Early September humidity made the salty oceanic
atmosphere feel sticky while the wind whipped loose
tendrils of Abigail's long red hair. If sixteen-year-old
Kiera Underhill hadn't insisted where and when their
secret meeting must take place, Abigail would have
stopped to speak with some of the other teens she was
passing. Instead, she made a beeline for the spot where
their favorite little hot dog wagon spent its days.

Besides the groups of partying youth, she skirted
dog walkers, couples strolling hand in hand and an old
woman leaning on a cane. Then there was a tall man and

enormous dog ambling toward her. As they passed beneath an overhead vapor light, she recognized his police uniform and breathed a sigh of relief. Most K-9 patrols in her nearby neighborhood used German shepherds, so seeing the long floppy ears and droopy jowls of a bloodhound brought a smile despite her uneasiness.

Pausing, Abigail rested her back against the fence surrounding a currently closed amusement park, faced into the wind and waited for the K-9 cop to go by. His unexpected presence could be what was delaying Kiera.

"Come on, Kiera. I came alone, just like you wanted," Abigail muttered.

Kiera had sounded panicky when she'd phoned.

"Here. Over here" drifted on the wind. Abigail strained to listen.

The summons seemed to be coming from inside the Luna Park perimeter fence. That was not good since the amusement facility was currently closed. Nevertheless, she cupped her hands around her eyes and peered through the chain-link fence. It was several seconds before she realized the gate was ajar. *Uh-oh. Bad sign.* "Kiera? Is that you?"

A disembodied voice answered faintly. "Help me! Hurry."

Don't miss
Trail of Danger *by Valerie Hansen,*
available September 2019 wherever
Love Inspired® Suspense books and ebooks are sold.

www.LoveInspired.com

LISEXP0819

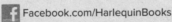

SPECIAL EXCERPT FROM

H HARLEQUIN®

SPECIAL EDITION
™

*After escaping her abusive ex, Cassie Zetticci is
thankful for a job and a safe place to stay at the
Gallant Lake Resort. Nick West makes her nervous
with his restless energy, but when he starts teaching her
self-defense, Cassie begins to see a future that involves
roots and community. But can Nick let go of his own
difficult past to give Cassie the freedom she needs?*

Read on for a sneak preview of
A Man You Can Trust,
*the first book—and Harlequin Special Edition debut!—
in Jo McNally's new miniseries, Gallant Lake Stories.*

"Why are you armed with pepper spray? Did something
happen to you?"

She didn't look up.

"Yes. Something happened."

"Here?"

She shook her head, her body trembling so badly
she didn't trust her voice. The only sound was Nick's
wheezing breath. He finally cleared his throat.

"Okay. Something happened." His voice was gravelly
from the pepper spray, but it was calmer than it had been
a few minutes ago. "And you wanted to protect yourself.
That's smart. But you need to do it right. I'll teach you."

Her head snapped up. He was doing his best to look at her, even though his left eye was still closed.

"What are you talking about?"

"I'll teach you self-defense, Cassie. The kind that actually works."

"Are you talking karate or something? I thought the pepper spray…"

"It's a tool, but you need more than that. If some guy's amped up on drugs, he'll just be temporarily blinded and really ticked off." He picked up the pepper spray canister from the grass at her side. "This stuff will spray up to ten feet away. You never should have let me get so close before using it."

"I didn't know that."

"Exactly." He grimaced and swore again. "I need to get home and dunk my face in a bowl full of ice water." He stood and reached a hand down to help her up. She hesitated, then took it.

Don't miss
A Man You Can Trust *by Jo McNally,*
available September 2019 wherever
Harlequin® Special Edition books and ebooks are sold.

www.Harlequin.com

Need an adrenaline rush from nail-biting tales
(and irresistible males)?

Check out **Harlequin Intrigue**®,
Harlequin® **Romantic Suspense** and
Love Inspired® **Suspense** books!

New books available every month!

CONNECT WITH US AT:

Facebook.com/groups/HarlequinConnection

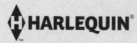 Facebook.com/HarlequinBooks

Twitter.com/HarlequinBooks

Instagram.com/HarlequinBooks

Pinterest.com/HarlequinBooks

ReaderService.com

H HARLEQUIN®

**ROMANCE WHEN
YOU NEED IT**

SGENRE2018R

Love Harlequin romance?

DISCOVER.

Be the first to find out about promotions,
news and exclusive content!

 Facebook.com/HarlequinBooks

 Twitter.com/HarlequinBooks

 Instagram.com/HarlequinBooks

 Pinterest.com/HarlequinBooks

ReaderService.com

EXPLORE.

Sign up for the Harlequin e-newsletter and
download a free book from any series at
TryHarlequin.com.

CONNECT.

Join our Harlequin community to share
your thoughts and connect with other
romance readers!
Facebook.com/groups/HarlequinConnection

HARLEQUIN®

**ROMANCE WHEN
YOU NEED IT**